# THE YOUNG CLEMENTINA

Charlotte Dean's disappointments in love and life have piled up over the years, until she finds herself living in a dour London flat and deriving a semblance of contentment from her job at a small private library — even though it means shutting her heart away. But when circumstances compel her to return home to the countryside to care for her niece, she is fearful of the tasks required of her, and what it will mean to open her heart once more. Can she meet the challenges ahead, and heal her loneliness, as she builds a life for herself and young Clementina?

*Books by D. E. Stevenson*
*Published in Ulverscroft Collections:*

VITTORIA COTTAGE
MUSIC IN THE HILLS
WINTER AND ROUGH WEATHER
LISTENING VALLEY

## SPECIAL MESSAGE TO READERS

## THE ULVERSCROFT FOUNDATION

**(registered UK charity number 264873)**

was established in 1972 to provide funds for research, diagnosis and treatment of eye diseases. Examples of major projects funded by the Ulverscroft Foundation are:-

- The Children's Eye Unit at Moorfields Eye Hospital, London
- The Ulverscroft Children's Eye Unit at Great Ormond Street Hospital for Sick Children
- Funding research into eye diseases and treatment at the Department of Ophthalmology, University of Leicester
- The Ulverscroft Vision Research Group, Institute of Child Health
- Twin operating theatres at the Western Ophthalmic Hospital, London
- The Chair of Ophthalmology at the Royal Australian College of Ophthalmologists

You can help further the work of the Foundation by making a donation or leaving a legacy. Every contribution is gratefully received. If you would like to help support the Foundation or require further information, please contact:

**THE ULVERSCROFT FOUNDATION**
**The Green, Bradgate Road, Anstey**
**Leicester LE7 7FU, England**
**Tel: (0116) 236 4325**

**website: www.foundation.ulverscroft.com**

D. E. STEVENSON

# THE YOUNG CLEMENTINA

*Complete and Unabridged*

ULVERSCROFT
*Leicester*

First published in Great Britain in 1935
under the titles *Divorced From Reality*
and *Miss Dean's Dilemma*

Republished in 1966 as *The Young Clementina*

This Ulverscroft Edition
published 2020



*A catalogue record for this book is available
from the British Library.*

ISBN 978–1–4448–4414–6



Published by
F. A. Thorpe (Publishing)
Anstey, Leicestershire

Set by Words & Graphics Ltd.
Anstey, Leicestershire
Printed and bound in Great Britain by
T. J. International Ltd., Padstow, Cornwall

This book is printed on acid-free paper

# Contents

# Part One

# *Charlotte's Friend*

# 1

## *A Bunch of Country Flowers*

I wonder how a hermit would feel if he had spent twelve years in his cell and were called back to the world to take up the burden of life with its griefs and worries and fears; if he had passed through the fire of rebellion and achieved resignation; if his flesh had been purged by sleepless nights and his mind had found the anodyne of regular daily work. Would he feel afraid of the world, afraid of the pain awaiting him, afraid of his own inadequacy to deal with his fellow men after his long, long years of solitude? Would he refuse to listen when the world called, when his conscience whispered that his duty lay outside his cell, or would he gird up his loins and go forth, somewhat reluctantly, into the world which had turned its back upon him for twelve years?

My mythical hermit is standing at the parting of the ways, and so am I. Two roads are open to me, one lonely but well known, peaceful and uneventful; the other full of dangers and difficulties which I cannot foresee. Do what I like I cannot determine which road to take. There is a fog in my brain which clogs its working and prevents me from weighing the points at issue. I have tried to think out my problem for days

— and nights — without getting any nearer a solution of my difficulties. Let me try to write it out for a change.

The idea of writing down one's difficulties and perplexities is not a new one. Great men have found it valuable in clearing their minds and helping them to wise and deliberate judgment — why shouldn't I, in my smaller way, find a solution to my difficulties in the same manner? My mind needs clearing, God knows, and if pen and paper will help me to clear it, I shall not grudge the time or the labor involved.

* * *

Having got thus far I sat down at my bureau and reached for my pen. Where should I begin? The roots of the matter lay buried thirty years deep — or very nearly so. Should I start in the present and go backward, digging up pieces of the past as I required them, or should I start in the time-honored manner with my birth in Hinkleton Parsonage on a cold, wet, windy night in the autumn of 1895? The first method seemed full of pitfalls, and the second a weariness of the flesh. My soul turned from the labor of writing with sick disgust.

And then, quite suddenly, I saw the way to do it — an idea came to me which simplified everything and made the labor of writing a pleasure; and, just as a duster, with a dash of methylated spirit, clears a dusty window, so my view was clarified. One moment the window was obscured and I could not see through it, and the next moment it was crystal clear and I was looking out at the winding paths of my life.

The idea which came to me was this, that I should write my whole story for *you*, and then, since you will never read it, I should read it with your eyes, and give myself your advice. I knew that it would be a pleasure to write for you. I have often wanted to pour my troubles into your sympathetic ear, and here was the opportunity, here was the excuse. The words would flow out of my pen easily, confidently, I need not hesitate to wonder whether you would understand, nor to change a sentence lest you should read it amiss, for you are one of the understanding ones, my dear, and the milk of human kindness is in your heart.

You do not remember me, of course — how could you remember — since the only time I ever saw you was three years ago, riding down Piccadilly on the top of a bus. What was there for you to remember — a tall, gawky woman, a woman with long limbs and a lean, tired face? A woman neither young nor old, with gray eyes and crinkly brown hair. She was dressed in a shabby black coat and skirt and a dark red hat of the coal-heaver type, which happened to have just gone out of fashion at the time. Did you see this woman? You looked at her, of course, you smiled at her, you even spoke to her in a curiously deep voice. You thanked the shabby stranger for rescuing a bunch of wild flowers which had fallen under the seat and you said, somewhat apologetically, 'I am taking them to a country woman who lives in a basement. She likes country flowers best, you see.'

There was meadow-sweet in the bunch, and dog-roses, and ox-eye daisies, and a host of other flowers which country children pick in the meadows and the hedges about their homes — country children with rosy faces and tangled hair.

I realized at once that you understand things; you were of the understanding kind. You were prosperous, that was obvious from the clothes you wore. (Your coat and skirt of navy blue flannel was plain but well cut, your black hat was perfect in its crisp line, your shoes and stockings, your gloves, your bag, the orange silk scarf twisted carelessly round your neck were all good, carefully chosen, the best of their kind. I noticed the soft wave of your dark hair and the smooth, well-tended texture of your slightly tanned skin). You were prosperous and comfortable, your life was a life of ease, but you still understood the feelings of those less fortunate than yourself, you still cared to understand.

How much easier it would have been for you to buy flowers in London for that woman you were going to see — how much easier than picking them yourself in the fields and meadows which lay about your pleasant country home and carrying them up to town in the train and the bus! You didn't do the easier thing; you did the thing that would give the more pleasure. All this flashed through my mind in a moment. Almost before you had finished speaking I saw you in the fields, picking those flowers to take to town for the country woman who lived in a basement. I had settled you in the country in a beautiful house, I had given you a park full of old trees casting grateful shadows on the thick grass, I had given you a rose garden with a sundial, I had given you a husband, horses, cars, dogs.

I buried my face in the sweetness of the country flowers before I handed them back to you.

'She will love them,' I said.

'You don't think they will make her homesick?' you asked, raising your dark eyebrows a trifle, and looking at me anxiously out of your night-blue eyes.

'They may,' I told you. 'They have made me homesick, you see. But it was worth it.'

'Pain is worthwhile sometimes,' you said.

We looked at each other gravely (I wonder if you remember), I knew that we could become friends — we were friends already, I knew that we could talk to each other about things that mattered, not always agreeing perhaps, but always understanding and appreciating each other's views. I knew that we could be silent together without discomfort, sitting over the fire and dreaming, letting a few words fall and then lapsing into more dreams. I knew — from that little quiver at the corner of your mouth — that we would see the same jokes, the tiny droll incidents which defy you to put them into words so delicate and evanescent they are.

Could I ask you your name, or tell you mine? Would you think me mad, a woman you had met for a few moments on the top of a bus, with whom you had exchanged a dozen words? I couldn't do it, of course. I was too shy, too bound by the conventions of the civilized world (were you too shy, or didn't you care?). I was too shy to ask you your name, and so I let you go. You smiled at me as you went. I never saw you again.

I never saw you again — what made me write those words? False words they are, false and misleading. You have been with me every day, you have shared all my jokes, you have read with me in the evenings and exchanged thoughts and criticisms. You have walked with me in the park, and had tea with me in my tiny sitting room. We have sat over the fire together talking of the past and surmising about the future. You are my only real friend, you see, the only woman friend I have ever had. I had always longed for a friend, a woman friend of my own generation, wise and witty and tender.

Of course I know that you have forgotten me long ago, you are not lonely like I am. You have a husband to share your life, a house to care for, a garden to enjoy, perhaps you have children. You would think it crazy that a woman you met three years ago for ten minutes should think of you as her greatest friend, but you would not grudge me the consolation of your shadowy presence if you knew what it meant to me.

Just one thing more before I begin my story — I have always called you Clare. I never knew anybody called Clare, but I love the name and it seemed to suit you. I had to have a name to call you when I needed you. 'Clare!' and there you are, sitting in my shabby old chair, smiling at me and waiting for me to begin.

# 2

## *The Hermit in the City*

It is easy, now that I am doing it for you, to get on with this business of writing. I can tell you anything and everything. But everything is too big an order, so I must try to pick and choose, telling you a little here and a little there so that the woman who is me will emerge clearly from the pages — the real me, with all my faults, and all my mistakes. I must choose carefully, for I have not much time and my leisure for writing is stolen from my sleep.

From nine-thirty in the morning until six o'clock at night I work in a library, docketing the books, reading them through and recommending them to those people I think they will suit. The library is not one of those bright modern places where books, waiting to be bought, smile at you from tastefully arranged tables in gay paper jackets, but a musty dusty room on the ground floor of an ancient building, visited principally by old gentlemen with gold-rimmed spectacles and elderly ladies with woolen stockings — sometimes a little wrinkled about the ankles. You know the type, Clare. We have often laughed at them together, laughed at them quite kindly, even a little tenderly; they are so anxious and serious and polite, polite even to the library assistant at Wentworth's. Occasionally an author drifts into the library and peers round at the dusty shelves in dismay. 'Oh — er — I was told that this was a geographical library,' he says. 'Have you — er — up-to-date travel books here?' 'Any book that adds to the geographical knowledge of the world,' he is informed. 'A book about Borneo,' he says deprecatingly (or Canada or the Antarctic perhaps). 'A book about Borneo — something not too — er — heavy. Just to give one an idea of the — er — country and its inhabitants. A little local color — perhaps you can advise — '

Perhaps I can, because I make a point of reading all the books that come into the library — or at least glancing through them — and because this is my job and I have been at it for twelve years. Twelve years is a long time to spend among books about Borneo and Canada and the Antarctic. 'Ah, thank you,' he says, flipping over the leaves and examining the illustrations with studied carelessness. 'This *does* seem the kind of thing — this seems exactly — '

Authors often leave their sentences unfinished like that — at least the kind who come to Wentworth's do — and they are always men. Women authors seem to bother less about local color, or perhaps they bother more. Perhaps they actually pack a couple of suitcases and trek off to Borneo or Canada or wherever it may be, before they send their hero there to hob-nob with head-hunters or to track moose.

Twelve years I have been there, with kind little Mr. Wentworth and his books. I was twenty-three when I went, and now I am thirty-five. The twelve best years of my womanhood have been given to Wentworth's. At first I rebelled against the imprisonment, and the monotony of my days. I watched the shafts of sunlight struggle through the dim windows and move slowly from shelf to shelf and across the wooden floor. The same golden sun was shining in the meadows at Hinkleton, glancing with dazzling sparkles upon the river; the flowers were growing under its warm touch, turning their faces, their small bright faces, toward their God; the trees were busy too, opening fat buds and spreading their tender green leaves to catch its rays. Birds were singing in the woods and the small woodland animals were throwing off their winter languor and hurrying about their summer ploys. Often and often the slow difficult tears formed upon my lids and were brushed hastily aside lest they should fall upon my ledger and leave immortal trace of my weakness and misery. But that has passed, and now I am resigned to the life; I even find pleasure in it. The books — I have always loved books and I love them better now — are my greatest solace. I can take a travel book in my hands and voyage across the world. China, Burma, Jamaica — the very sound of the words is an enchantment bringing me sights and sounds, and odors that my senses have never savored.

So the day passes, and it is six o'clock. Mr. Wentworth comes out from his dark, poky little office and closes the door.

'Time, Miss Dean,' he says, smiling at me

pleasantly. 'No more voyages tonight, except in dreams.'

I smile, too, because I like the little man, he is kind and considerate, he does not interfere with me, he lets me alone to do things in my own way — an admirable employer.

I take my coat down from the nail behind the office door and fare forth on the last voyage of the day, the voyage through London's streets with London's multitudes jostling at my elbows.

We will walk home together, Clare, for you are coming to tea with me today. We will take a bus to Hyde Park Corner — a crowded bus I'm afraid, for this is one of London's busiest hours — and walk across the park. It is autumn now, the leaves upon the trees are beginning to change color. Jack Frost has been here in the night and touched them lightly, so that here and there a patch of flame glows among the green. It is my birthday today, Clare, and I have bought a tiny cake. Perhaps you will think it rather a foolish thing for a woman of thirty-five to do — to buy a birthday cake and eat it all by herself with a dream companion, for her birthday tea; but I have missed so much in life that other women take as their due that you must forgive me my foolishness.

And now we have turned up France Street and reached the main door of No. 71. There is no lift here to take us up to the top floor which has been my home for twelve years. A tiny flat it is, high up among the chimney pots, two rooms and a tiny kitchen and a bathroom all my very own. I have tried to make it bright with distempered walls, and gaily colored chintz, but the smuts of London wage a continual war upon cleanliness and brightness, and I have neither the time nor the money to fight them with success. Mrs. Cope, my 'daily woman,' comes in and does battle while I am at my work, but although she uses an incredible quantity of cleaning material — the sinews of her war — the result is indecisive, to say the least of it. There are some good pieces of furniture here, the grandfather's clock which blocks my tiny hall came from my old home at Hinkleton. Its large pale face is one of my earliest recollections, so too the melodious chime of its hours. It stood in the hall at the Parsonage, and served us faithfully for many years, the whole timetable of that large rambling understaffed old house depended upon its slowly moving hands. My father gave it to me when he died because he knew I loved it, because I had wound it for him when he became too frail to climb upon a chair and attend to it himself, and because I understood its idiosyncrasies. He always called it Jeremiah, for its chime was melancholy, set in a minor key. Everybody knew it as Jeremiah; even Mother, who thought the joke was unbecoming in a parson, had been heard to refer to it as Jeremiah in times of stress. 'It's a quarter to one by Jeremiah, and Martha has not got the potatoes on!'

So Jeremiah came to me, in spite of the fact that Kitty wanted him, and that he would have looked well in Kitty's spacious mansion, and blocked the hall of my tiny flat. Kitty had so much, she had taken so much from me, that I felt I was justified in refusing her Jeremiah — she did not want Jeremiah as much as I did.

I took a few other things when the old home was broken up; things that Kitty didn't want; shabby things that had been in my life ever since I could remember — the old schoolroom chair, with its creaking basketwork frame and knobby cushions, the old schoolroom bureau, scored with the thoughtless kicks of childish feet — these were the things I wanted. They were familiar things, kind and friendly, I took them with me to cheer my loneliness and lighten my exile. It is curious, isn't it, that things you know well never look dirty and dilapidated — other people's old furniture looks shabby and moth-eaten. 'I would never have that horrible old couch in my room,' you say. But your own old couch is every bit as bad and you are not disgusted with its appearance; it is your friend, you see, and you remember it when it was new and smart. Friends that you have known for a long time and love very dearly never seem to grow old.

I'm afraid my flat must look very shabby in your eyes, Clare, but I hope it looks comfortable and cozy. Mrs. Cope lighted the fire before she left, there is a nice red glow in its heart and the yellow flames shoot up cheerfully. Pull in your chair, my dear, and let us be comfortable. It is cozy, isn't it, Clare? Tonight, it seems to me more comfortable and cozy than it has ever done, because I may be leaving it. I may be leaving all these things which have been in my life for twelve years — I've got to decide whether I am leaving it or not and I haven't very long.

If this had happened ten years ago — even five years ago — I should not have needed anybody's help to decide what to do. I was a rebel then; I pined for freedom. I would have shaken the dust of Wentworth's from my feet at anybody's bidding and fared forth to any job which promised luxury and leisure and the right to walk out of doors when the sun shone. But now I am deeply sunk in a groove and I shrink from any change. I have led the life of a hermit in the heart of a city — you can, you know — and I find, somewhat to my surprise, that I don't want to leave my cell.

# 3

## *Days of Friendship*

We must go back — right back to my childhood at Hinkleton Parsonage — I must try to make you see those days because the seeds which were sown then have grown into trees and are now bearing fruit. The seeds were sown, and the trees grew up, there was blossom, and then fruit — bitter fruit some of it.

I was born in the Parsonage at Hinkleton, a big old-fashioned rambling parsonage, with a huge garden — untended for the most part since father's stipend would not stretch itself to cover the wages of a competent gardener. It was a paradise for children, a paradise of old trees with low branches inviting the most timid climber to the perils of ascent; of wild flowers growing like weeds through feathery grasses; of moss-covered paths winding among dense shrubberies where one could play at brigands or big game hunting without fear of interruption. I was the eldest child, and, four years after, came Kitty. Mother nearly died when Kitty was born, she was warned that there must be no more babies, so the little son that Mother wanted so desperately could never be hers. She withdrew into herself after that — so father told me during those last four years that he and I spent alone together

— she withdrew into herself, and, although she was a good wife and a kind mother, there was no life in her, no zest for enjoyment.

I remember the night when Kitty was born. My father had told me that God was going to send me a companion for my play — a little brother, or a little sister, whichever He thought best. I was pleased and excited at the idea and immeasurably disappointed at my first sight of the 'companion.' Was this the best that God could do? I asked father. 'She'll grow, my dear, she'll grow,' father replied smiling at me kindly. 'In a year or two she'll be quite human. Have patience, Charlotte.'

She was christened Clementina after Mother, but we all called her Kitty. She was so like a kitten, soft and warm, with pleasing ways and tiny velvety hands that could scratch if she did not get what she wanted. Quite soon, just as father had predicted, she became human and lovable — if not a companion, at least an amusing and enchanting toy.

A child's world widens like rings made by a stone dropped into a pool. First the house became familiar to me, and then the garden. The church came next, its tall gray walls and slender columns springing upward to support its arching roof were a source of never-ending wonder to my mind. The music awoke in my body a strange excitement, especially when the organ played alone, and the vibration of harmony filled the church with invisible angels. I thought it a pity that the church garden was full of stones; it was not nearly such a pretty garden as ours. Did God like stones in His garden better than flowers, I wondered? The village was the next place to swim into my ken. I trotted round after Mother when she did her shopping or took soup to the sick and consolation to the sorrowing. I liked the village; it was a friendly place, full of smiling faces and pleasant words. Later still I added Hinkleton Manor to my world. It lay about a mile off across the park — an old gray house with polished floors and shining furniture which smelt agreeably of beeswax and turpentine. The Wisdons had dwelt at Hinkleton Manor for generations; they were Lords of the Manor in the old-fashioned way. The villagers regarded them with awe and affection, the County with respect.

I can't remember the first time I saw Garth Wisdon. However far back I peer into the past Garth is always there. He was a small, thin boy, nearly three years older than myself. He was quiet and gentle — much more so than I was. Mother said he was too quiet, healthy boys ought to be rough and noisy, but I don't think she would have been so fond of Garth if he had been wild and rough like an ordinary boy. Her own boy — the little son of her dreams — was a quiet, ghostly presence in her life. It is difficult to tell whether it was Garth's nature to be quiet, or whether the circumstances of his life made him so. Hinkleton Manor was a quiet house — spacious and leisurely. The only sounds that broke its stillness were the ticking of clocks, and the murmur of voices in the kitchen premises where the well-trained servants went about their business. Garth's mother died when he was born. He and his father lived together. He was, quite naturally, the apple of his father's eye, and the heir to the Manor and to all the traditions of the Wisdons. Over the carved oak fireplace in the hall, in old English lettering, was the coat-of-arms of the Wisdon family — 'Valorous Men, Virtuous Women' — and above were the Lion and the Lily of the Wisdon crest, emblems of courage and purity. Pictures of Wisdon ancestors hung in the hall, and in the dining room, and on the walls of the wide staircase, Wisdons who had fought in England's battles or striven for her welfare in times of peace. The line was old and honored; it had always stood for truth and justice, for upright dealing, and for devotion to England's best interests. Garth did not talk much about the traditions of his family, but his pride in them was a living force.

There were very few houses of the better type within reasonable driving distance of Hinkleton, and those few were childless. Garth and I became inseparable companions. We played together in the Parsonage garden and in the woods surrounding the Manor; we sailed down the River Hinkle (which meandered lazily through the Manor grounds) in a little tub of a boat which had belonged to Garth's father when he was a boy. Marvelous adventures we had — some real and some imaginary. The woods were filled with the creatures of our play — lions and tigers, Red Indians and crocodiles, King Arthur's Knights and Robin Hood's Merry Men, brigands and pirates all had their turn. The woods of Hinkleton provided suitable backgrounds for every play that caught our fancy;

we knew every path; we had discovered the best trees to climb. The whole place was a happy hunting ground for Garth and me.

Scarcely a day passed when we did not meet. The path linking the Parsonage and the Manor was well worn. It started from a small wooden gate in the hedge beyond the lawn and wound through fields and a wood of mixed trees, it climbed a wooded hill, where the local gray rock peeped out through the soil and descended into the grounds of the Manor on the other side. On the top of the hill there was a pile of rocks — big gray igneous boulders they were — and this was our favorite meeting place. How often I have sat there on the topmost boulder looking out over the treetops at the glorious spread of fields and woods and pasture land that lay below waiting for Garth to come! How often have I hurried up the hill to find Garth sitting in the same spot, waiting for me!

I suppose the hill must have had some local name — if so I never knew it — we called it 'Prospect Hill' from the hill so named in *Swiss Family Robinson*, a book we both adored. We read and reread this amazing work until we almost knew it by heart and the characters became our friends.

Prospect Hill and the *Swiss Family Robinson*, how the names bring back the past! I can see Garth now — a small, thin figure in a Norfolk suit, with thick, black hair — sitting in a niche of rock on Prospect Hill bent double over our worn and dog-eared copy of the *Swiss Family Robinson*. He would sit like that for hours, reading solidly, while I — less sedentary by nature — climbed about the rocks or dabbled happily in the little spring which oozed out beneath a boulder. I did not mind his absorption, for he was always conscious of my presence however deeply buried he might be; sometimes he would lift his head and call out 'Char, Char, where are you? Listen to this,' and would read out, in his shrill, boyish voice, some passage in the great work which especially appealed to him or which he thought might 'do for a game.' The only time that Garth and I fell out was when Tommy Hatchett came to spend a month at the Parsonage. He was the son of an old college friend of father's and his parents were abroad, so father offered to have him and give him a little coaching in the holidays. Tommy was a complete contrast to Garth — a round-faced, snub-nosed schoolboy, very frank and jolly and full of mischief. He was the same age as Garth, but bigger and stronger. Tommy was quite ready to be friendly and to join in all our games, but Garth resented his advent. It was a clear case of two being company and three none. I was too young to realize that Garth was jealous of Tommy; I could not understand why Garth went off by himself and refused to join in the games. All I could see was that Garth had been a splendid playmate, and now he was not.

We had it out one morning when Tommy had been caught by father and incarcerated in the study to do some Latin prose.

'Why won't you play properly now?' I asked Garth, with the uncompromising directness of eight years old.

'You've got Tommy,' Garth said. 'You don't want me now.'

'I want you too,' I replied. 'It's not nearly so much fun without you.'

Garth's face lightened. 'Come on then, Char,' he said. 'We'll go and hide from Tommy — just you and me.'

'But, Garth, I can't,' I cried. 'I promised to wait for Tommy — he won't be long — and then we can all go up to Prospect Hill and play at shooting bears in the Rocky Mountains.'

Garth swung round at me with blazing eyes. 'All right, all right,' he said savagely, 'you can go and play bears with Tommy, but you needn't think I'm coming. You can play with him all day and all night, I don't care.'

'Oh, Garth, let's all go together.'

'No,' he shouted. 'No, you can play with me or Tommy — choose which of us you want.' He shook my arm. 'Choose,' he cried, 'choose which you want.'

I chose Garth, of course, he was my other self and I could not do without him, but my morning was ruined by the vision of a lonely Tommy wandering round the Parsonage garden looking for somebody to play with, and, more likely than not, being seized by Martha and deputed to pick the raspberries for jam.

The little incident impressed me very deeply because of Garth's unprecedented behavior. Garth was always so quiet and thoughtful, so gentle and considerate, and today he had been wild and rough, he had frightened me and hurt my arm.

Tommy went away quite soon after that, and Garth and I settled down into our old ways, and played contentedly at the old games. We had both forgotten Tommy in a week. I never saw him again, never thought of him until I saw his name among the killed in a casualty list in the war; and then, quite suddenly, his face appeared before my eyes, his frank, cheery, snub-nosed face, and the memory of his short visit to Hinkleton Parsonage came back to me as clearly as if it had happened last year.

I would not have mentioned his name, Clare, for he played such a tiny part in my life, but I felt I must tell you about the only quarrel that Garth and I ever had — as children — and Tommy was its cause. Except for that one month, there were no clouds between Garth and me. No, not even one the size of a man's hand.

Garth was in and out of the Parsonage every day, and sometimes we were bidden to tea at the Manor. Tea in the nursery with hot-buttered toast and iced cakes, with Nanny presiding over the big brown teapot, calm and serene in her blue linen dress and starched apron. She had taken Garth from his dying mother's arms and she is with him still.

As we grew older we were promoted to tea in the library with Garth's father; it was very grand and grown up, but not nearly so comfortable. Mr. Wisdon was old — a tall old man with thick, wavy, white hair — he had been a man of fashion in his day and he had the fine, courtly manners of an older generation. Even toward us he was ceremonious and polite, cold, austere, slightly withdrawn. I never saw Mr. Wisdon laugh, and rarely smile. It was said in the village that he had not laughed since his wife's death.

His manner was chilling and somewhat alarming. It was an ordeal to walk out of the room through a door held open for you by Mr. Wisdon. One would have needed silk petticoats and a sweeping train to accomplish the feat with equanimity, and I, a schoolgirl, with a blue serge skirt which always seemed to sag at the back, and black cashmere stockings which always seemed to have lumpy darns up the leg, could never accomplish the feat without feeling incredibly foolish. I was so conscious of the sagging skirt and the darns, not to speak of my long, gawky legs and red hands. Kitty was different, of course, she smiled at Mr. Wisdon, and went out with a hop, skip and a jump — but then Kitty's skirt never sagged.

A string of governesses and tutors came and went at the Manor during Garth's childhood. We children took it as a matter of course that they should come and go — father taught *us*, of course, but Garth was different. Looking back I wonder why none of them managed to stay, they can't all have been fools — fools or knaves was Mr. Wisdon's verdict upon them. They came and went — tall and short, fat and thin, hearty and lugubrious — we got quite a lot of fun out of them one way and another. The housekeepers changed too, and the servants, only Nanny stayed on through the changing years. The last time I was at Hinkleton Manor (I went down for a night about six years ago for old Mr. Wisdon's funeral) she was just the same. The same comfortable kindly creature, her plump bosom covered by the square white bib of her spotless apron, her black hair, innocent of a thread of gray, scraped back into a little knob at the back of her head. I flung myself into her arms and hugged her, for she brought back the past so vividly. It seemed to me that all had changed, only Nanny remained the same; she hugged me back, and said, with that astonishing lack of tact which had always characterized her, 'Oh, Miss Char, my poor lamb, how old you look!'

* * *

Father was worried about Garth's education. He used to say that it took a man six months to learn his pupil and that then, and only then, could he get the best work from him. (It is an old-fashioned idea, but, like all father's ideas, there is something in it.) Father would shake his head sadly when he heard of another change of tutor at the Manor, shake his head and frown and purse his lips. He was very fond of Garth, and he thought that Garth's future was being jeopardized by the lack of continuity in discipline and study. I see now, looking back, that father tried to keep his hand on Garth's pulse. He would ask him into his study and talk to him, drawing him out and imparting useful advice as he knew so well how to do.

One summer holidays he provided Garth and me with shiny black copy-books and advised us to keep a record of our days. 'It is a valuable exercise,' hc said with his kind smile, 'and you will find it useful as you grow older.' Garth looked at his book with some surprise. 'But you can buy diaries, sir,' he said. 'All ready with dates and a space for every day.' 'I know you can,' replied father, 'but a bought diary is anathema to the true diariest — take Pepys as your model, his diary was not divided into equal parts — a bought diary starts with the erroneous assumption that all days are alike, or at least equal in length. We all know the assumption to be false. For Monday I may require three pages, for Wednesday three lines. If my diary is divided into equal parts I have the same space for both days. On Monday I am tempted to be telegraphic, or even to miss out some essential portion of my theme, on Wednesday I am tempted to be verbose.'

Garth and I began our diaries together — everybody knows the lure of a virgin copy-book — Garth lapsed a little when he was at Eton, but in the holidays his diary ran to pages daily. I often wondered, when I lacked material for mine, what he found to say (in speech I was the more facile) but I never knew, for our diaries were strictly private. It was the Unwritten Law that we should not 'crib' each other's diaries, and we never broke it. We left our diaries lying about in the schoolroom or the summer-house secure in the conviction that they were sacred from alien eyes. It was only later, when Kitty was promoted to the ranks of the literate that we learned to secrete our diaries — Kitty did not observe the sanctity of the Unwritten Law. The habit, begun in childhood, continued with me throughout the years. If I had nothing else to write about I still had books, and I often found that a few lines of criticism, written months ago and forgotten, saved me from a second reading of the same dull tome. There is a pile of copy-books in the drawers of the battered old bureau which I had rescued from the school-room at the Parsonage. I scarcely ever look at them but I know that they are there and the knowledge is, somehow, comforting. They mirror my life from a contemporary standpoint, they are a material evidence of the troubles that I have borne, of the storms that have failed to wreck me, of the calms that have failed to discourage me.

I missed Garth dreadfully when he went to Eton. Kitty could not share in the make-believe games which had so delighted Garth and me. Her imagination could not people the woods with redskins and outlaws. She liked playing with dolls; she liked playing at houses, or shops. I used to play at her games because she could not play at mine, but I found them dull and monotonous after the wild freedom of the woods. The mornings were occupied with lessons. Father taught me himself and he made everything interesting. He was a born teacher, with ideas upon education greatly in advance of his time. I enjoyed my hours with him, they passed quickly — he led my mind from one point to another, so that I learned almost without knowing it. In the afternoon I took the path over the hill to the Manor stables to exercise Garth's pony and his dog. It was a routine life, busy and useful. The days passed quickly.

The holidays were too short for all the things that Garth wanted to do. Old haunts to be revisited, old pleasures to resume.

I lost Garth for a little while during his schooldays at Eton; he slipped away from me in spirit. That was bound to happen, of course, and I should have known it if I had not been so ignorant of the world. He was unhappy at Eton I think — although he never said so — the lack of privacy irked him (he had always had as much privacy as he liked). He was homesick for Hinkleton and the freedom of the woods. When he went on to Oxford he was happier and more settled. He became once more the companion of my childhood's days. At Oxford his time was at his own disposal, he could be solitary if he wanted. He could shut his door upon the world and take leisure for thoughts and dreams. And, because he was not always in a crowd, he was able to make friends with people who appealed to him, and to pick and choose a few congenial spirits. Garth was more *normal* during those years at Oxford than he ever was before — or since. I see that now, when I look back. At the time, of course, I saw nothing beyond the day. I sorrowed when Garth went from me and rejoiced when he returned.

It was while he was at Oxford that he grew so amazingly. As a child he was small for his age, and then he suddenly shot up into a very tall, thin young man. Later he filled out and became broad-shouldered and deep-chested, but he always retained the narrow hips and long lean legs of the born runner. I have only to shut my eyes to see Garth as he was in those far-off days. His long spare frame, his dark hair that fitted his small well-shaped head like a cap. His blue eyes, dreamy or eager as occasion demanded, were rather deeply sunk in his sun-tanned face. He had a short straight nose, and his mouth was large and mobile, the mouth of an actor, full of expression. His feet and his hands were long and thin, he had long sensitive fingers.

What else can I tell you about that Oxford Garth? (I want you to see him clearly, Clare. It is so important that you should see Garth clearly in his early days, before he was embittered and disillusioned by the world.) He did not care for games — perhaps that was one of the reasons why his time at Eton was unhappy — he ran well, and swam, but the passion of his life was, and still is, riding. Garth rode magnificently, he was absolutely fearless, and yet he was not reckless, nor inconsiderate of his horse as fearless riders often are. When he was on a horse, he and his horse were one in body and spirit. He could rouse a shirker, or quiet a nervous animal with a touch of his hand.

* * *

My thoughts go back to the last peaceful summer at Hinkleton — how happy we were. Childhood was over, for I was seventeen and Garth twenty, but the storms of life had not yet broken upon us. Garth came down from Oxford for the long vacation. He arranged to read Latin with father, for Latin was a weak subject of Garth's and it was holding him back. None of the many tutors had succeeded in making Latin come alive for Garth, and Eton and Oxford had failed to remedy the lack of grounding. The days were full of bright sunlight and father loved the sun, so Latin was read in the garden under the big old tree which cast its long shadows over the tennis lawn. I could see them sitting there if I glanced out of the windows in the intervals between bed-making and dusting which were my daily lot. Garth's dark head was bent studiously over the book from which he read. Father listened and commented and watched the birds. Sometimes father was called away in the middle of the lesson — his time was never his own — and then I went down to talk to Garth and the beds were left to look after themselves. We talked a great deal that summer. Talking took the place of games. Garth told me about his life at Oxford, about the long quiet afternoons on the river, and about the old beautiful buildings which had housed learning for so many generations. He told me, too, of his ambitions — to travel in unvisited places and to write books which should add to the knowledge of the world we live in. He would be Lord of the Manor when his father died and would find enough to do looking after the property, and traveling. The passion for traveling had always been with him, it had found expression in our childhood games of make-believe, but now these were left behind and Garth was looking forward to the reality. I envied him his secure manhood and the future which seemed so bright. To voyage to distant countries and strange lands, to meet in the flesh the people and animals of our imaginings seemed to me the apotheosis of desire.

'What a pity you are a girl, Char!' Garth exclaimed when we had been discussing the matter for hours. 'If only you had been a boy we could have gone off together and explored the world.' How fervently I echoed his wish!

We were friends, old tried friends. We understood each other in that far-off summer of 1913.

Kitty was rather left out of it when Garth came home. I see that now, though I did not see it at the time. She was a child then — just thirteen, and she liked attention and petting. Garth and I found her something of a nuisance, she had no qualms about forcing her company upon us, and her company was a check upon our talk. We escaped from Kitty whenever we could.

Kitty loved Hinkleton Manor, not for the beauty of it and the old historical associations with the Wisdon family, but for the comfort and luxury of its well-appointed rooms and trained servants. Even then, young as she was, Kitty loved luxury as a cat loves warmth.

'Wouldn't it be lovely to have a house like this?' she whispered to me one day when we had been bidden to tea at the Manor, and were waiting in the drawing room for our hosts to appear. 'When I'm grown up I shall marry a rich man and have a house exactly like Hinkleton Manor.'

I laughed at the childish ambition.

'You can laugh if you like, Char,' Kitty said, 'but you'll see I shall. I would be absolutely happy if I had a house like this for my very own.'

'You will have to find a husband first,' I said lightly.

'Yes,' she said thoughtfully.

'And the richest men are not always the nicest husbands.'

'I wouldn't mind,' she said, 'not if I had a house like this. Wouldn't it be lovely not to have to make your own bed, and to have a fire in your bedroom every night, and lovely things to eat every day? I shall ask you to stay with me, Char.'

'That will be very kind of you,' I told her. 'But perhaps I may have a husband of my own by then — and a house too.'

She looked at me curiously, and said no more. I wonder, now, what she was thinking. In some ways Kitty was older than I was, in other ways she was incredibly babyish for her years. It was a strange mixture and rather intriguing — you never knew which side of her nature was going to appear. I wonder, now, whether she was thinking that someday I might marry Garth and be mistress of Hinkleton Manor.

# 4

## *The Birthday Dance*

Garth's twenty-first birthday was the following May. He came down from Oxford with some friends and the old Manor woke to life. There was a cricket match on the village green and a garden party for the tenants and the villagers. It was a glorious day, warm and sunny and bright. I remember it as if it were yesterday, the marquee with the long tables of cakes and jellies, the crowd of excited children playing games in the big meadow.

* * *

After dinner there was a dance at the Manor for us. It was my first dance, I was eighteen. I had a new dress to wear for the occasion. The village dressmaker had made it for me. We had put our heads together over pictures and patterns and had evolved a masterpiece — or so we thought. It was a pale yellow net, full in the skirt, and reaching to my ankles. The bodice was of the cross-over pattern, like a fichu, and was softly draped to give fullness to my thin breast. An orange-colored rose nestled in the corsage. I thought it was beautiful, and indeed it was not a bad result for inexperience to achieve.

Mother came to my room when I was nearly ready, to help me, and give the finishing touches to my appearance. I saw surprise in her face as she stood in the doorway, leaning upon her stick which her rheumatism had made essential. 'My dear,' she said softly, 'you are quite beautiful!'

I was so touched at the unaccustomed praise that I took her in my arms. We kissed each other gravely. I shall always be glad to remember that.

I saw the same look of surprise and pleasure in Garth's face as I came down the wide stairs of the Manor into the hall, where the introductions and gay chatter which precede a dance were in full swing. He sprang up the stairs to meet me, and took my hand, whispering urgently that I was to keep all the waltzes for him — 'All of them, Char.'

'All of them,' I agreed gravely.

The evening was full of excitement and pleasure — it is like a dream of happiness when I look back — I danced with Garth's Oxford friends and found an unexpected fount of conversation for them; I danced with Garth again and again. Mr. Wisdon took me in to supper, and I swept through the door like a ship in full sail.

It was the night of my life, Clare. I was so happy, so carefree. Nothing went wrong. My hair behaved beautifully, my dress was perfect, I was a success.

Garth walked home with me. I chose to walk, for the night was mild and dry, and I was too excited to feel tired or sleepy. There was no moon, but the path was familiar to our feet, we needed no light to find our way over that path. We strolled along together, and the red tip of Garth's cigarette glowed like a little beacon in the dark. We did not speak; speech would have broken the spell of enchantment which had fallen upon us. We understood each other so well that there was no need for words.

He took my hand as we climbed the steep slope, where the little path went zigzag among the gray rocks, and I felt the pulse racing madly in the firm clasp of his fingers. I was quite sure that Garth loved me, and I knew that I loved Garth — this was the perfect flowering of our perfect friendship. It did not need his kiss to tell me what I had become to him — I had known it all the evening and the knowledge had lifted me up and glorified me — but the kiss was very sweet.

We lingered for a few moments on the top of the hill — our own beloved Prospect Hill — even then we did not speak. We were very innocent, very young, and this strange new feeling for each other had frightened us a little. It was the end of a beautiful chapter in our lives — a new chapter had begun, just as beautiful, more so perhaps, but the chapter of our childhood's friendship was finished forever.

We went down the hill together hand in hand.

As we neared the Parsonage I saw the windows were lighted — the house, which should have been asleep at this hour, was wide awake — something must have happened. My heart leaped like a mad thing. While I had been enjoying myself at the Manor, something

— something dreadful — had happened at home. Garth saw the lights too, he shared my fear. He drew my hand through his arm and we hastened down the slope and across the lawn. Martha must have been watching for my return, for the french window of the drawing room was flung open and her broad figure appeared at the top of the steps.

'What is it?' I cried, seizing her hand and gazing anxiously into her face, raddled with weeping. 'What has happened? Oh, Martha, what has happened?'

She told me that my mother was dead.

Later, when Garth had gone, and I was alone with my father in the shabby old library I learned the few details of her death. We sat hand in hand watching the dawn come over the hill. 'Her heart failed quite suddenly,' father said. 'She was going up the stairs to bed. Martha and I carried her into her room and laid her on the bed. There was no time to fetch Dr. Gray. She lay for a few moments, breathing quickly, and then she whispered, 'Don't send for Charlotte. Let her enjoy — tonight. She doesn't have much pleasure, poor child.' '

These were her last words; her last thoughts had been for me. I wished I had done more for her. I wished I had understood her better. I wept in father's arms.

# 5

## *Years of Waiting*

Three things happened to change me from a child. Three things, one after another. The birthday dance, Mother's death, and, a few weeks after that, the war. After the long peaceful years of childhood the three things happened so quickly that there was no time to think. I was eighteen when the war came — it was a bad age to be. I was too old to take it — as Kitty took it — with the excitement of a child over a new experience. Too young to remember another war, to have achieved philosophy and to realize that it would pass. To eighteen things do not pass quickly — neither grief nor pleasures — a trouble seems to be for all time. Eighteen cannot see through present darkness to future light.

The war was incredible to me, a nightmare of pain. I could not believe that a few miles away across the sea men were killing each other — civilized men killing each other like savages — I could not believe it at first. Nothing that had gone before in my life had prepared my mind for such a thing. I had read of wars in history but I had never visualized them. They had happened long ago, and the people who fought in them were not real to me, not real, everyday people like ourselves. I can't explain the horror and perplexity of my feelings; it is no use to try. Nobody could understand what I felt unless they had felt it, and if they have felt it they can understand without any explanation at all.

At first I could not believe it was true. And then gradually I came to believe it, and the war settled upon my spirit like a dark cloud. It was always there, that dark cloud, it never lifted for a moment. I knew, as I went about my work that men were dying every moment, dying in agony, and the guns were roaring day and night.

Garth went at the very beginning (war was in the Wisdon blood), and men from the village whom I had known all my life, men who had never been out of Hinkleton in their lives, who had spent their time in peaceful pastoral pursuits, went off to fight for England. The postman, the jobbing gardener, the boy from the farm, they all went. Some of these men returned, wounded, maimed, sick in mind and body, and some of them would never return. So the war came to be a reality, a grim dark burden that pressed upon my mind night and day, shutting out the sunshine, poisoning the wells of life.

What did you do in the war, Clare? I did nothing. There was father, you see. I had to stay with him and take care of him. All of a sudden he became old, old and helpless. It was the war, even more than Mother's death, that aged him and broke his heart. Mother's death was a natural thing to him, we all die sooner or later, and he was not rebellious. God had taken her from him and he could say, 'Thy Will be done'; but the war was unnatural, he felt that the war was an Evil Thing, he felt that God was hiding His face.

Nowadays quite a lot of people think about the war as father thought, but, at the time, the idea was unpopular. The clergy waved banners like the rest, and declared that God was on our side. Father thought that God was on nobody's side. Father thought that the world had gone mad, and God was angry. His sermons caused some trouble; it was only because he was so well beloved in the parish that they did not cause more.

He was so aged and broken that he could not undertake Kitty's education; we arranged for her to go to a boarding-school at Bournemouth. She was very happy there, the life suited her, and the companionship of the other girls went to her head like wine. She made innumerable friends — different ones each term — and stayed with them in the holidays. It was much more fun than coming home to Hinkleton.

Father and I lived a very lonely life during those four years of war. Garth was in Flanders; Mr. Wisdon shut up the Manor and took a flat in London. He said he could not stand the quiet of Hinkleton; he must be near the center of things. Garth led a charmed life, first in the line and afterward on the lines of communication. He came down to Hinkleton once to see father, he had heard disquieting accounts of father from a man who came from Hinkleton village, and whom he had met abroad. We walked together in the garden and talked about the flowers, he told me that the flowers in Flanders were very pretty.

I had to warn him not to talk to father about the war, I warned everybody that came. It worried father so, it upset him, he got angry and muddled when he tried to argue about it.

'I shan't talk about it,' he said. 'It's the last thing I want to talk about.'

There was a queer, strained look in his face as he said the words; I had seen it in the faces of other men. It made the horror and agony of war more real to me than any amount of talk. Garth talked to me about the flowers in Flanders, and the look in his face told me that he had been living in hell.

Garth went into the study after that, to see father, and I left them alone, for I knew that they could talk more openly in my absence. I busied myself about the house until I heard the door open and Garth came out. I saw that he was grieved over father's condition, terribly grieved. Garth realized — far more clearly than I who was with father constantly — how changed he was, how broken and aged. There were tears in Garth's eyes when he said good-bye.

'I think he will be better when it is over,' I said, trying to comfort him.

'If it is *ever* over,' Garth said. 'I feel as if the war had been going on forever, and will never stop. If it ever does stop, Char, and I'm alive, I shall come back to you.'

'Come back safely, my dear,' I told him.

When the war ended Mr. Wisdon came down to Hinkleton and opened the Manor. He hoped that Garth would be demobilized soon after the Armistice, and he bought a couple of hunters for the winter. But the time dragged on and no news came. It took a long time before Garth's demobilization papers went through. He was on the staff, and there was more work to do than ever.

That winter of 1918 was a difficult time — the awful nightmare of killing was over, but everybody was very weary, and food was scarce. Influenza ravaged the village, carrying off the strong and weak with nice impartiality.

The only bright spot for me in that long winter was the coming of a curious old man to Hinkleton. He stayed at the Hinkleton Arms for weeks while he studied father's church and made drawings of the nave. Hinkleton Church is very old and beautiful. I should have told you more about it for it played a big part in my life — especially during the war years when I was so lonely and unhappy. I don't think I could have survived those years if it had not been for the church. When everything seemed dark and dreadful I would go there and sit for hours, letting the peace which passeth all understanding sink into my soul. Sometimes it failed, but usually it was successful and I came out into the sunshine or the rain, feeling that God was somewhere, and that things must come right.

The church is of gray stone, beautifully simple and bare, and the windows are of that clear, transparent glass which transmutes the sunbeams to shafts of jeweled light. I can never see a ruby without thinking of the windows of Hinkleton Church and of one window in particular — the subject is Ruth, gleaning in the fields, her dress is the color of the purest ruby in the world.

The strange man who appeared in Hinkleton that winter of 1918 knew all about churches, and stained glass windows — he was writing a book upon the subject. He taught me many things about the church and revealed beauties which I had not appreciated. He found a leper window in the south wall, and obtained permission to open it up and glaze it with plain glass. He raved about the leper window for hours to anybody who would listen. I was quite willing to listen to Mr. Senture, for I was weary of my own company. It mattered little to me whether he talked about the window, or the stained glass or the beauty of the arching roof. Sometimes he would tire of these subjects and talk about his invalid wife (she was the passion of his life, he wrote to her every day). He talked about what he would be able to do for her when his book was published, and the money came rolling in. I grew very much interested in Mr. Senture's book, it pleased me that our own lovely old church was to be made the subject of a book, that there would be pictures of it for all the world to see. The book was eventually published — Mr. Senture sent me a copy of it — and I have often wondered whether he made any money for his invalid wife. I loved the book, of course, but it would not appeal to a wide public, I am afraid.

We went over to Canterbury one day — Mr. Senture and I — he wanted to make some notes about the cathedral and to see an old friend who was a keen archaeologist, and he offered to take me with him. I think he thought I had rather a dull life and was sorry for me; he was a kind old man. I enjoyed the day. It took us hours to get to Canterbury and hours to get home, for the trains did not fit in well, but even the long, tiresome journey was a pleasure to me. I had been for so long a prisoner in Hinkleton that I felt like a child on a Sunday school excursion. We had lunch at a tea shop, explored the cathedral and came home. It may not sound very thrilling to you, Clare, to spend a day with an old gentleman — most of it in the train — but I was delighted with my outing. We did not get home till long after midnight and that seemed the most amusing thing of all — I was very young.

Kitty came to us at Christmas for a few days. She was going to spend most of the holidays in London with the Eltons — it would be more amusing than Hinkleton, she thought. She brought an invitation to me to go up and spend a weekend with the Eltons while she was there. They were going to have a dance and they thought I might like to come. It was kind of them to ask me, but I never felt at home with the Eltons and their friends — I was too old for them, too old at twenty-three. They were a bright, merry family, too bright to be natural, I thought. Their conversation was too 'modern,' their jokes too personal. I decided to stay at home with father, and I think Kitty was relieved at my decision. I was no credit to Kitty in the Eltons' society.

My friendship with Mr. Senture amused Kitty. She could not understand how I liked to sit for hours in the cold church, taking rubbings of the brasses for him while he talked and made little sketches of the columns and windows for his book. I suppose it was rather a strange taste for a girl of my age, but life at Hinkleton was so dull and uneventful that anything out of the ordinary was an excitement to me.

The winter passed — all things pass if you can only be patient enough, even the longest winter — and in the spring Kitty came home from school, finished. It seemed right that Kitty should come in spring, for she was spring personified, she was laughter and flowers and the singing of birds. She made my twenty-three years look like senility.

Father brightened a little when Kitty came home, he chaffed her quite in the old manner, chaffed her about her new, pretty clothes and her grown-up hair. He made her sing to him in the evenings and she was always glad to sing. She had a pretty voice and had been well-trained by good masters. I was glad to see father so happy for now it would not be so hard to leave him. I was sure that when Garth came home he would want me to leave father and go to the Manor as his wife. Everything seemed to be waiting for Garth, there was a kind of breathless suspense in the soft spring air and the flowers seemed to bloom brighter — it was all because Garth was coming home soon now, coming back to me as he had promised — I had kept my part of the unspoken pact, I was waiting for him.

# 6

## *'It Is Odd How One's Tastes Change'*

It was the end of April before Garth was at last demobilized and returned to Hinkleton. I saw at once that he was changed; changed in himself and changed to me. It was not only that he was older and more assured, grown from the immature boy into the man, used to command, used to make decisions and assume responsibilities. (That would have been a natural change, the logical outcome of his experiences.) Garth was changed fundamentally. He looked at life with different eyes, he was bitter, cynical, disillusioned. He was much more talkative than he had been in thc old days, much more amusing; but his jokes had a cutting edge, they were unkind, and intentionally so — Garth was too clever, too sensitive to the reactions of others to be cruel by mistake.

The boy that I had known so well was a gentle-natured creature, considerate to others and somewhat self-effacing. This man who had come back in his place was ruthless, almost brutal at times. I told myself that the war had changed Garth's nature. The dreadful sights, the agony of suspense, the long years of strain had warped him temporarily. He would get over it, I told myself, and the old Garth would return. I was very patient with Garth, very long-suffering, for I had learned much in those four years — nearly five now — since the beginning of the war. I was no longer a child; I was a woman, used to self-discipline. I tried to be very gentle with Garth, I tried to remember all he had been through but it was no use. Again and again he hurt me, as he knew so well how, again and again he repelled my friendship and trampled on my feelings. I grew afraid of him, for I still loved him, and those we love can hurt us so desperately.

Father invited him to dinner one evening soon after he came home. Father had always been fond of Garth, and he did not see, as I saw, how much Garth had changed. Garth was more gentle to father than he was to other people, more considerate, less cynical. He had always been devoted to father. I decided that evening to wear my yellow frock — the one I had worn at the dance — it had lain in my drawer for five years, wrapped in tissue paper. I took it out that evening when Garth was coming and looked at it — there were tears in my throat — I had been so happy, wearing that frock. It was all gone now, that happiness, the war had killed it. Garth had loved me in that frock. Could it bring back the past? I thought perhaps it might. I thought perhaps the years would fall away and vanish as though they had not been.

Garth arrived before I was ready, I heard him talking to father in the drawing room, and I went in to greet him. He turned toward me as I came in and for a moment his face brightened, the cynical expression faded and he was the old Garth.

And then he bowed in a mocking manner. 'You never told me it was a party.'

'Just you, Garth,' I told him, with my heart fluttering in my breast like a trapped bird.

'I am honored indeed,' he mocked. 'You put me to shame with your grandeur. Why was I not told it was a full dress occasion so that I could have taken my dress suit out of moth-cake and had it pressed?'

Father looked up at me. 'A pretty dress,' he said in his frail, threadlike voice. 'A pretty dress, Charlotte.'

'You think so, sir,' Garth said, looking at me gravely. 'I might have thought it pretty at one time perhaps; it is odd how one's tastes change.'

I could say nothing to him, and he could thrust the knife into my heart and twist it with savage joy. I could only stand there and bear it as best I might.

Kitty ran into the room like a spring breeze. She had chosen to wear a simple white frock — a little girl frock with a high neck and long sleeves — she swept me a curtsy and cried gaily.

'La la — how grand we are tonight!'

They gave me no peace all the evening. It was good-natured chaff on the surface, but beneath it, in Garth's case, there was a strange bitterness that I could not understand. Kitty did not know the significance of the yellow frock, she did not know that every word went through my heart, but Garth knew. Garth was being deliberately cruel, he was torturing me. How I wished that I had not been prompted to wear that dress — I longed to run upstairs to my room and tear it off, but I couldn't do that, I had to brave it out, I had to sit and smile and pretend that I didn't mind. I pretended I had put on the yellow frock for a joke. It was a funny old-fashioned rag, I said; the fashions were more sensible now. I had put it on to let them see what frights we looked in the days before the war.

I realized that night that all was over between me and Garth — it could never come right now. Garth had gone from me forever. But I had not bargained that he would turn from me to Kitty — when I heard of their engagement something died in my heart. I loved Kitty, and I loved Garth — yes, in spite of all that had happened, I still loved him — and now they were both lost to me — both lost.

They were married very quietly in Hinkleton Church. We need not linger here. I shall not tell you about the wedding, Clare, I can't. It was a blur of pain. I moved through the days of preparation like a ghost. You can imagine the wedding as you please — the presents, the flowers, the music, the eager crowd of tenants and villagers waiting to see the bride. Father married them and they went away. It was the last service that father took; the last time he was in his beloved church. He became very ill after Kitty had gone and only stayed with me a few days. I am sure he was glad to go. The world had changed so much; he was uncomfortable in it, lost and unhappy like a ghost from a previous era. His brain had failed, he was muddled sometimes and that worried him. Yes, I am sure he was glad to go.

There was very little money left when father had gone and his affairs were settled. Garth got me the post of assistant librarian at Wentworth's. Garth knew Mr. Wentworth; the dusty old library was a favorite haunt of his. Mr. Wentworth took me on Garth's recommendation, I went there for a month, on trial, and I have been there for twelve years. Mr. Wentworth was old when I went and he seems no older now; there are times in life when age seems to forget you, it busies itself with others, drawing lines upon their faces and painting silver in their hair. Age has forgotten Mr. Wentworth; he is still the same dried-up slip of a man, with kind blue eyes, magnified strangely by his strong spectacles. He can still run up the wooden steps as nimbly as a boy when he wants a book off the top shelf, he can still add up rows of figures in the big heavy ledgers with thc rapidity and precision of an adding machine.

The first day I went to the library he showed me round with grave pride, showed me the different shelves where books about different parts of the world were kept. China to the right of the window and Australia to the left, and books about India above the old-fashioned fireplace. The whole room was shelved from the floor to the ceiling and it seemed to me that I should never learn where to find the book I wanted.

From the first Mr. Wentworth was kind and easy to please, allowing me a free hand in many of the small details of my work.

'You may dust them if you wish,' he said, smiling a little in answer to my inquiry. 'Personally I find it easier to dust the books as I require them.'

It *was* easier, and more satisfactory too. I soon gave up the unequal struggle of keeping the shelves dusted. It was an old, old house, you see, and dust came from every crevice in the walls. It rose from between the uneven boards, as you walked across the room, and hung suspended in the still air, waiting for the strong beams of sunshine to turn its floating particles to gold.

I found my little flat and settled down. Garth and Kitty dropped out of my life. It was better so. Better for me to try to find content in my new life than to hanker after the old. I tried very hard to be content, tried to fix my mind upon the present and forget the past. Sometimes I succeeded and sometimes I failed. The nights were the worst. I could not sleep, and my mind, free from the preoccupations of my work, tortured me with visions of what might have been. I tossed and turned upon my bed, I thought of Garth and our beautiful friendship — now in ruins — I tried to find some clue to the change in him. If I could have found an explanation of the change I could have borne it so much easier, but I could find none. I still loved Garth, and this distressed me because I felt it was wrong — to love a man who had shown me so unmistakably that he did not want my love, to love a man who was the husband of another woman, my own sister, there was something horrible in that. I tried so hard to change my heart, I called in my pride, I turned my mind away from Garth. Night after night my pillow was wet with tears.

The first gleam of comfort came to me in a poem. I had tossed for hours upon my bed and could bear it no longer. I rose and turned on the light and opened a book of poems which I had brought with me from the Parsonage — it was one of father's books, he had always been fond of poetry. I read one or two poems without taking in the sense of what I read, and then suddenly my eye was caught and my attention held. It was quite a small poem called 'Separation,' by Walter Savage Landor.

*'There is a mountain and a wood between us*
*Where the lone shepherd and late bird have*
*seen us*
*Morning and noon and eventide repass.*
*Between us, now, the mountain and the wood*
*Seem standing darker than last year they stood,*
*And say we must not cross — alas! alas!'*

I read it again and again until the words were clear in my brain and I had no more need of the book. Then I put out the light and got back into bed. It was strange how comforted I felt. This man knew — he knew about me and Garth — he knew what it was like to be separated from the one person on earth by a dark, mysterious wood and a high, stony mountain. I was not alone in my experience — not alone anymore. The mere fact that another had walked where I was walking made the path easier for my feet. The mere fact of finding a simile for the mystery which separated me from my love made it easier to bear.

I can't explain why it should have been so; I only know that it was so. I could think of Garth and myself separated by the dark wood and the high mountain and accept it as inevitable. I was still sad — even miserable at times — but the awful agony of longing and searching was stilled. I ceased to rebel. I accepted my fate.

Day succeeded day. My work filled my life. I did not return to Hinkleton for nearly a year, and I would not have gone then if Kitty had not made such a point of it. She asked me to be god-mother to her child, and to go down to Hinkleton for the christening. I did not want to go, and yet I did. London was so hot and stuffy and I knew how beautiful Hinkleton could be in July. A weekend at Hinkleton sounded to me like a weekend in heaven. It would be painful to see Garth and Kitty together, I knew that, but I thought I could bear it, and I told myself that it would look queer to refuse, and I did not want them to think that I grudged them their happiness.

It was a strange visit. I thought Kitty changed, she was very silent when Garth was present, she almost seemed — was it my imagination — *frightened* of Garth. When we were alone together she was fretful and complaining, she complained of the servants, she complained of the nurse, Garth was inconsiderate and the garden needed rain. I put it down to her physical condition, she was still weak and apt to be tearful on the slightest provocation, I thought she would be happier when her strength returned — how could she fail to be happy when she had so much? Garth, on the other hand, was much more talkative than usual; he had developed an entirely new manner, a dry, sarcastic tone that jarred upon my nerves. That first night at dinner he was very gay — I thought his gaiety hollow, but I may have been mistaken. It is difficult to judge the merriment of others when one carries a sad heart in one's breast, and my heart was very sad that night. I had not realized how painful it would be to return to Hinkleton after a year's absence; everything hurt me, even the sunshine as it fell in golden rays upon the broad green lawns. Hinkleton Manor was so beautiful, more beautiful than ever, more spacious and leisurely than I remembered it. The whole place was like a glimpse of paradise after my mean flat in London and the baking streets.

Surely these people, living in such glorious surroundings, *must* be happy; it was my imagination that they were not. It was I who had changed, not they. The pain of seeing my beloved Hinkleton after all these months had warped my outlook and made my judgment faulty. What *could* be wrong with Garth and Kitty? They had everything that they desired, and, now, a little daughter to crown their love.

Garth and Kitty had decided that their son should be christened 'Charles Dean' after his two grandfathers but, as neither he nor Kitty had expected — nor wanted — a daughter, no girls' names had been discussed.

'Rose Marie' was Kitty's choice.

'Nonsense!' said Garth. 'You had better call the infant 'Plain Jane.' She's plain enough in all conscience.'

'Oh Garth!' murmured Kitty. 'Nanny says she's a beautiful little baby.'

'What about Clementina?' asked Mr. Wisdon in quiet tones. 'It was your mother's name, Kitty, and you were christened Clementina — if I remember rightly — so this little creature would be the third member of your family to bear the name. If you want to please me you can give her the name of her other grandmother as well and call her Clementina Mary.'

'Yes, of course, Father,' agreed Garth. (I was glad to see that he looked a little ashamed of himself.)

The christening took place on Sunday afternoon. The old church was full of light; it streamed through the colored windows in jeweled shafts. Dear old church, how I loved it! God's peace seemed to dwell here, and nowhere else in all the world. My heart turned over in my breast as I took the light bundle in my arms and made the old promises for Clementina. She was so tiny and helpless, and I knew that the promises on my part were empty and false. I could have no part nor lot in the upbringing of Garth's child. She stared up at me with big gray eyes, serious wondering eyes — could such a frail creature ever grow up and become a woman?

The day passed. I saw no more of Garth until suppertime. We sat round the table eating, and talking like strangers talk — Mr. Wisdon, Garth, Kitty, and myself. I felt again that a shadow lay upon the house; I saw the shadow in Garth's eyes as he looked at Kitty across the table. I saw it in Kitty's face as she glanced nervously at Garth. Mr. Wisdon looked from one to the other and was silent, crumbling his bread. Garth's laugh rang false, he laughed too often and too loudly. What trouble could it be? What shadow lay upon them all? It must be my imagination, the shadow must be in my own heart, it was my heart that saw ghosts in its own darkness.

My own heart — how it ached over Garth! How it ached over the change in him, over the lines upon his face, the cynicism of his tongue! It was dreadful to me to see the boy I loved in the man he had become, dreadful. When I looked at him I saw the same dark sweep of hair from brow to nape, the same fine features, the same mobile mouth, but a different spirit now occupied the body I had loved — a bitter spirit, a disillusioned spirit that believed good of nobody, that seized upon innocent words and twisted them out of shape and threw them in your face.

I came back to town early on the Monday morning to be in time for my work; I came back from the beautiful spacious rooms and found my flat poky and dark and inconvenient; I came back from the trained servants and well-cooked meals and struggled with Mrs. Cope and was revolted by her hopeless efforts in the culinary line; I came back from broad lawns and shady trees to glaring streets and chimney pots. It took me weeks to regain the small modicum of resignation with my lot which I had previously achieved. I resolved not to go to Hinkleton again if I could help it — what use was it? I only made myself miserable. Hinkleton Manor was not for me.

It was five years before I went to Hinkleton again, and again it was an invitation which I could not refuse. I went down for old Mr. Wisdon's funeral. He had been failing for some time, but, at the last, his death was sudden. On this occasion I only stayed one night and had little chance of speaking to Kitty or Garth. They were busy with their sad tasks, and the house was full of people coming and going all the time. My god-daughter was brought down to the drawing room to see me — or rather for me to see her. She was five years old, a strange, silent child with old-fashioned manners and large, sad eyes. Her hair was pale brown and very straight and soft, it hung down on either side of her face like a curtain. We could find nothing to say to each other (for I had no experience of children) and very soon Kitty sent her back to the nursery.

I still felt a shadow on the house, but it was natural — wasn't it — that the house should be shadowed when the body of its master lay upstairs. Sadness is a shadow; it was the shadow of sadness that lay upon Hinkleton Manor. Soon it would pass — for Mr. Wisdon was old, and it is natural for the old to die — and Garth and Kitty would be happy again. This is what I told myself and what I wanted to believe. I wanted them to be happy.

I did not go to Hinkleton again, but I saw

Kitty occasionally in town. Sometimes she made use of me to find her a maid. I liked that. It was pleasant to feel that I was of some use in the world. We met once or twice and had tea together. She told me what my god-daughter had been saying and complained that Garth spoiled her. She told me her servant troubles; they seemed to bulk largely in her life. Garth began to travel, as he had always intended, and wrote a book about his adventures. When I spoke to Kitty about the book she tossed her head: 'He's always writing,' she said, 'or else hunting, or else he's away from home traveling in some God-forsaken country. I don't see what use it is being married at all,' and then she would change the subject and talk about the latest play. These were the things Kitty talked about when I met her — and I listened. She never wanted to know about my life — and why should she? My life was so monotonous that I would have found it difficult to discuss it with her if she had ever shown any desire to know what I did with myself. There was nothing to interest Kitty in my life. We were miles apart when we met and there was no bridge to throw across the gully. Kitty was a gay, vivacious creature, her golden hair was bright and wavy, her complexion was smooth and creamy, she was dressed, always, in the height of the fashion. I felt the difference between us acutely, I could never be like Kitty even if I had the money to spend upon myself that she had. We were different in every way. No wonder that Garth had chosen Kitty to be the mistress of Hinkleton Manor; she was a credit to it as I could never have been.

'Oh dear!' Kitty would say, picking up her bag and preparing to depart. 'How I wish I lived in town!'

'How I wish I lived in the country!' I would reply.

'You wouldn't if you were in my shoes,' she would cry, tossing her pretty head. 'Not if you had to live with Garth.'

Garth's first book was published in 1929. It was the account of a big game expedition in Central Africa. It had found its way to Wentworth's and I had read it there, and enjoyed it. The old Garth and the new Garth were both in the book, curiously distinct I thought. The imagination of the old Garth was there, and that wonderful power of seeing vividly and recording the vision in a few unusual words. The cynicism of the new Garth was there, that strange contrary twist, that ruthlessness, that tearing of beautiful things in pieces. I found the book moving, disquieting, but I saw that there was life in it; I saw that it was a book which would be read when contemporary books had long passed into oblivion.

So the years passed. I became a hermit in the city and found content.

# Part Two

## *Kitty's Husband*

# 1

## *An Unexpected Visitor*

One blustery evening last March I heard the doorbell ring. I was sitting over my fire reading a book about Japan which had just been published. It was part of my job, and an interesting part, to read the books as they came to Wentworth's. Many of the books in Wentworth's were old and dry, mere treatises upon the lands with which they dealt; but some were new and interesting, some had atmosphere, caught you up out of the grayness of London, warmed you, fed your hunger for beauty and strangeness and adventure.

The book about Japan had carried me to the land of cherry blossom; I came back to the land of wind and rain with a sigh of regret. I heard the wind howling round the chimney pots, the rain clattering on the window. The doorbell rang again, clamorously, urgently, and I got up to answer it.

I found Kitty standing on the mat, she was wearing a beautiful soft coat of caracal, and a small brown hat was perched coquettishly upon her fair wavy hair. Her eyes were shining, and she was breathing quickly as though she had run up the stairs.

'Kitty!' I said in amazement.

'I was afraid you had gone to bed.'

'I was reading,' I told her, opening the door wider.

Kitty came in; I smelt the strong scent she used as she squeezed past me in the narrow hall.

'Jeremiah takes up too much room,' she said laughing. 'You should let me have him you know, I would pay you for him — '

'I like Jeremiah,' I said quickly. It was so like Kitty to offer to pay for something she wanted. (Silly of me to be annoyed, of course.)

Kitty went over to the window and pulled the blind aside. She peered out. 'What a dreadful night!' she said, shivering a little.

'Are you staying in town?' I asked her.

'Needs must,' she replied. 'I've lost the last train. The service to Hinkleton is absolutely rotten. I wondered if you could put me up, Charlotte. I've had a ghastly day chasing after an under-housemaid. You would think, with all this unemployment that they talk about, that it would be easy to find one.'

'Surely there must be plenty!' I exclaimed.

'I can't find one,' she said. 'And my head aches.'

I was surprised that she had come to me. She had not been inside the flat for years, I knew she thought it poky, and shabby, and inconvenient. Why hadn't she gone to a hotel, she would have been much more comfortable in a hotel, and Kitty liked comfort. But, since she had come to me, I could not refuse to put her up. I did not really want to refuse. It was a break in the monotony of my life and I welcomed it. I told her that I would give her my bed and sleep on the couch in the sitting room. She demurred at this but only halfheartedly, and I saw that it was what she had expected.

I busied myself looking out clean sheets and pillow cases. The old Parsonage linen had come to me. It was getting thin now but it was beautifully fine and soft. Mother had prided herself upon her linen.

'May I telephone to Garth?' Kitty asked, taking up the receiver without waiting for an answer.

'Of course,' I said.

She got the connection quickly and I heard her speaking to him as I made the bed and found my best nightdress for her to wear.

'A dreadful day . . . Yes, of course, I have lost it . . . I couldn't help it; I was chasing a wretched housemaid . . . No good at all . . . Well, I wish you would take on the job yourself . . . I'm here with Charlotte . . . Yes, in Charlotte's flat. I'm spending the night here . . . Yes . . . No, she doesn't mind the trouble. Charlotte will speak to you herself . . . Charlotte!'

She called me over to the telephone and put the receiver into my hand. I had no wish to speak to Garth, but there was something compelling about Kitty. She was determined that I should speak to him — I could see that. It was not till long afterward that I saw why she had wanted me to speak to him.

I stood there, feeling rather foolish, with the receiver in my hand. I had nothing to say to Garth, nothing. He was not Garth to me anymore; he had not been for years: he was Kitty's husband.

'This is Charlotte,' I told him, 'Kitty missed her train.'

'That was a pity,' the voice sounded a trifle dry.

'I shall like having her.'

'Good of you,' Kitty's husband said. 'I'm afraid it will be a trouble.'

'No trouble,' I assured him.

Kitty was peering out of the window again; she dropped the blind as I finished speaking and came back to the fire. I looked at her and saw that her cheeks were very pink, and her hand, which she had laid upon the edge of the mantelpiece, was trembling.

'Are you — is anything the matter?' I asked her anxiously.

'I have such a wretched headache,' she said. 'Garth is so inconsiderate, he makes me mad. As if I *wanted* to miss the ghastly train.'

I filled a hot-water bottle and slipped it into the bed. It was all ready now, smooth, and white, and tempting. I prided myself on the smooth perfection of my bed-making.

'It looks nice,' Kitty said. 'And what a pretty nightie! Don't wake me early, Char.'

I told her that I breakfasted at eight and must be out of the flat by nine.

'That's all right,' she said. 'Just leave me to sleep and I can get up later when you've gone. I don't know how on earth you can get up at that unearthly hour — I should be a wreck.'

'I have to,' I replied shortly.

'Rather you than me. It upsets me for the whole day if I have to get up early. Anyhow there is no need for you to wake me tomorrow.'

'I'll bring you your breakfast in bed,' I suggested.

'No, no — just let me sleep.' She laughed. 'I was always a sleepy-head, wasn't I, Char?'

'You won't know where anything is.'

'I'll find out. It will be rather fun. I'll get up later — perhaps about eleven — and make myself a cup of tea.' She yawned. 'Gracious, how tired I am! I could sleep for a week.'

'You don't look tired,' I told her.

'Well, I am,' she said. 'Dead dog tired.'

We kissed each other good night, and I left her to go to bed.

I was tired myself, and the couch was more comfortable than I had expected. I slept well. The time had passed when I could not sleep, when I had turned and twisted, suffering in mind and body, and longing for the dawn. I had passed through all that and had attained resignation and peace within.

The morning came all too soon; I rose at my usual hour and prepared my breakfast on the little table by the fire. I was very quiet as I went about my task, careful not to clatter the plates, nor to rattle the kettle when I put it on the stove. The walls of the flat were thin and Kitty must not be disturbed. I finished my breakfast and left it as usual for Mrs. Cope to clear. I put aside some milk for Kitty's tea, and I managed to unearth a lemon from the recesses of my modest larder — Kitty always used to take lemon in her morning cup of tea, I remembered. Anyhow it was there and she could have whichever she liked. It was lucky about the lemon. I saw that there was enough butter in the dish and I put out the loaf with the knife beside it, and a pot of marmalade. Mrs. Cope would be finished by ten — she had another flat to 'do' at 10:30 — so she would probably have left before Kitty was ready for her breakfast. Kitty would manage now with everything put out conveniently; there would be no need for her to poke in my cupboard for what she wanted.

Mrs. Cope was coming up the stairs as I went down. We were so regular in our hours, she and I, that we usually met on the stairs or in the street. I told her about Kitty and warned her to be quiet. 'Mrs. Wisdon had a bad headache,' I said.

'Pore soul!' said Mrs. Cope easily. 'I'll maike 'er a cup o' tea laiter, shall I, Miss?'

The idea seemed good. I had not told Kitty of Mrs. Cope's daily advent, but that didn't matter. I would save Kitty the trouble of making tea for herself. Mrs. Cope could easily stay a little longer and make Kitty some tea — say about eleven. We arranged the matter like that, and I ran on to catch my bus.'

# 2

## *'Garth Is Mad'*

The days passed. I heard no word from Kitty — I had not expected to hear — sometimes months passed without my hearing from Hinkleton. It was easier, really, to forget that such a place as Hinkleton existed, and to fill my days with the little incidents of Wentworth's, the chatter of Mrs. Cope, and the companionship of books.

And then, quite suddenly, Kitty came back into my life. I looked up from my desk at Wentworth's, where I was engaged in listing books, and there was Kitty standing in the doorway. Her eyes were blinded by the sudden transition from the glare of the summer streets to the dimness of the shop. There was always that pause in the doorway when a stranger came to Wentworth's, the sort of pause a diver makes before he takes the plunge.

Mr. Wentworth hastened forward, he had an eye for a pretty woman and Kitty was indubitably that.

'Miss Dean,' Kitty said with a little catch of her breath. 'She — she works here, doesn't she?'

He bowed and motioned me forward. The shop was empty of customers at the time. I could see that Mr. Wentworth was intrigued by Kitty's arrival, nobody had ever before come to Wentworth's and asked for Miss Dean.

'Kitty, what is it?' I said.

'Oh, Charlotte, I'm in trouble!'

'In trouble?'

'Dreadful trouble. Where can I speak to you?'

'I shall be free in another hour,' I told her.

'I can't wait,' she said. 'I can't wait — couldn't you ask — couldn't you come now?'

She was trembling in every limb. I didn't know what to do with her. Mr. Wentworth was hovering in the background; he sensed that something was wrong.

'Miss Dean,' he said at last, 'if you would care to take your friend into the office — I can see she is upset — a trifle faint, perhaps. The heat, the glare of the streets, I find it trying myself sometimes — or if you would rather go home — '

He was fussing about solicitously.

'Oh, thank you!' Kitty cried. 'If you would let her come — that would be the best way — it is important, very important.'

I fetched my coat and hat; Kitty had a taxi waiting outside; I gave the man the address of my flat and we got in. It was years since I had driven in a taxi through the London streets, I would have enjoyed it if I had not been so anxious about Kitty. She sat forward on the seat twisting her gloves.

'How slowly he is going!' she exclaimed. 'We shall never get there at this rate. They go slowly on purpose, these taxi-drivers, so as to get more money for their fare.'

'What has happened, Kitty?' I asked her.
'Oh God! How can I bear it?'
'What on earth has happened?'
'Wait,' she said. 'I can't tell you here.'

The taxi drew up at the block of flats and we climbed out. Kitty searched in her bag for money to pay the man, it rolled into the gutter out of her nerveless hand. I took her by the elbow and helped her up the stairs.

Mrs. Cope was still in the flat. She always came back in the afternoon to prepare my supper and leave it for me.

'Lor', what a fright you give me!' she exclaimed, gazing at us as though we were apparitions from another world. Mrs. Cope was the type of woman who, at every deviation from the normal routine, is afflicted with 'palpitations.' I was home early today, of course, more than an hour earlier than usual; I saw that the 'palpitations' were imminent.

Kitty sank into the basket chair. 'Send her away, Charlotte, for God's sake!' she exclaimed irritably.

Mrs. Cope had followed us into the sitting room, she heard the careless words, was intended to hear them. Kitty never considered the feelings of servants; they existed only for the purpose of ministering to her needs. When she did not require them they ceased to exist. I saw that Mrs. Cope was hurt and offended — and I was sorry. I liked Mrs. Cope, she was a kindly woman and her chatter was amusing. She was a human being to me.

'Mrs. Wisdon is tired,' I said gently. 'Don't

bother about tea, Mrs. Cope. I will get it myself.'

'Ho!' said Mrs. Cope. 'So Mrs. Wisdon is tired, is she?' She looked at Kitty with a curious expression upon her small determined face.

'Yes,' I told her. 'Mrs. Wisdon has had a tiring day.'

'Ho! She's 'ad a tiring d'y, 'as she? Fancy that now!'

'You will be glad to get home a little earlier,' I insinuated.

She took off her apron and folded it up and fetched her battered old straw hat which hung on a peg behind the kitchen door.

'I knows when I'm not wanted,' she said in surly tones.

'What a frightful woman!' exclaimed Kitty, before the door had shut behind Mrs. Cope's retreating figure. 'How on earth do you bear her, Charlotte? It would kill me to have a woman like that in my house.'

I asked her if she would like some tea.

'Haven't you got anything else?' she inquired. 'Brandy or something — anything — I'm all in, Charlotte. Absolutely dead to the world.'

I gave her some brandy that I kept for medicinal purposes — it was all I had — and made some tea for myself. Kitty sipped the brandy slowly and with some distaste.

'I suppose it *is* brandy,' she said. 'It isn't the least like the brandy Garth has.'

'I never thought it was like Garth's brandy,' I replied a trifle bitterly. 'Garth can afford to pay for the best — I can't.'

'Don't be cross, Char,' she said. 'You're all I've

got now. Garth has gone mad — stark staring mad.'

I paused and looked at her with the teapot in my hand.

'I should never have married Garth,' she continued. 'He changed — you know — changed utterly. He wasn't like the same man. We never got on, never from the first. He was always sneering at me, sneering at my friends. Oh, Charlotte, it's been ghastly! What a life I've had! What a life! Never any fun, never any amusement with him.'

'But you went about — to theaters,' I said in a dazed way. Kitty had never spoken like this before. I had realized vaguely that she and Garth did not get on well together, but not that things were serious.

'Theaters!' cried Kitty. '*Garth* never took me. I went with — with other people. Why shouldn't I? If he chose to live like a hermit, writing all day when he was at home, or starting off at a moment's notice for some outlandish place that nobody ever heard of, was I to sacrifice everything to him? Was I to sit at home waiting for him to come back to me when he chose? I knew he hated my friends and despised them, but I didn't care. They amused me. *He* never bothered to amuse me. I had to find my own amusement. And now — now this.'

'Now what?' I asked her. 'What has happened?'

She took a long envelope from her bag and showed it to me — there were papers in it, typewritten papers, I drew them out of the envelope and gazed at them incredulously. The words upon them swam before my eyes — 'In the High Court of Justice . . . Probate, Divorce and Admiralty Division . . . In the Matter of the Petition of Mr. Garth Wisdon . . . '

'Kitty, what does it mean?'

'They're Divorce Papers. Garth is trying to get a divorce from me,' she cried wildly. 'That's what it means. It has come to that . . . Do you hear, Char? He's trying to divorce me — *me*.'

'But why?' I asked, stupidly.

'Why? Because I've been out to lunch with other men, and to a play occasionally. He's so dull. He wants me to be dull too. He wants to spoil my whole life and make me old and dull like himself. He must be mad . . . you see that, don't you? He must be mad.'

'But he can't divorce you for that — for going out to lunch — '

'No, he can't, he can't do a thing. He's got no proof . . . I shall fight it . . . he'll see . . . he shan't drag me through the mud . . . he'll find I have something to say about it. He can't prove anything wrong — not a thing — he's mad. Garth is mad . . . I shall tell everyone he is mad . . . don't look at me like that, Charlotte. What are you thinking about?'

'I'm just thinking how glad I am that father is dead.'

'Char! Oh, Char, don't be a brute! It isn't my fault; how could I help Garth going mad? There never was anything wrong, it's all made up. He's got to prove it and he can't. You'll see, Char, Garth will be the laughingstock of the — Char, speak to me, tell me it will be all right.'

'How can I, when I know nothing about it?' I asked her in a dazed way. 'I don't understand — anything.'

'Say it will be all right,' she cried, seizing my hand. 'Comfort me, Char. You must comfort me and say everything will be all right. I've had a ghastly day — simply ghastly. I didn't know what to do — my head is bursting — you might be nice to me, Char.'

'Tell me more about it,' I said helplessly.

'I've *told* you all about it,' she replied. 'I've told you the whole thing is made up — a tissue of lies — what more is there to tell you? Char, you must go and see Garth and tell him to withdraw it — or whatever it is they do — tell him he can't divorce me. I can't stand it; I shall go mad — tell him that. You *must*, Charlotte, I've got nobody else, you *must* help me.'

'Where is Garth?' I asked her.

'In Wales. He has been away for weeks, climbing mountains or something. He goes off and enjoys himself, he never thinks of me; he's utterly selfish, utterly selfish. My God, he shall pay for this — this insult.'

She talked on wildly for a long time, wringing her hands and walking about the room. I could make no sense of what she said and I scarcely knew what questions to ask her to clarify matters, the whole thing was so unexpected, so bewildering, so absolutely incredible to me. The only coherent idea in Kitty's head was that I should see Garth, that I should start off at once, for the outlandishly named Welsh village where he was staying, and persuade him to withdraw the petition.

'He'd do it if you asked him to,' she said confidently.

'I'm quite sure he wouldn't.'

'He would, I know he would.'

'Why on earth should he?' I asked.

'Oh, you have always been friends,' she said, looking at me strangely. 'That's why I came to you. If you ask Garth to withdraw it, he will. It's not much to ask — I think you might do that much for me — for your only sister.'

'My dear Kitty, you are quite mistaken. Garth and I . . . haven't been friends for years. He doesn't even like me now. Besides, we don't know, it might be a foolish move. We ought to consult a solicitor first.'

'A solicitor,' cried Kitty. 'Of course, I must go to a solicitor. I've been half mad with the worry of it or I would have thought of it before. Ring up and order a taxi at once.'

She took out a comb and began to tidy her hair in front of the little mirror in my sitting room, and to rouge her lips.

My idea was to take Kitty to father's solicitors — an old-established firm — but Kitty declared they would be no use at all. She knew of somebody else, somebody I had never heard of.

'He's clever,' she said. 'I must have somebody with his head screwed on properly. These old-fashioned firms are no use at all. Mr. Corrieston is the very man. We met him out at a dinner at the Eltons' — Garth couldn't bear him — Garth doesn't like people who are clever and amusing. Mr. Corrieston's the very man — you needn't come, Charlotte.'

'Wouldn't you like me to come?' I inquired in surprise.

'No,' she said. 'It will be better for me to see him alone first. I know him, you see, so it will be quite all right. And I can explain better — there's absolutely no need for you to come. I'll go and see Mr. Corrieston now, this very minute — I can't rest till I've seen him.'

She went.

I didn't know the man's name then, but I came to know it only too well in the weeks that followed. Kitty came up from Hinkleton constantly and had interminable interviews with him. She quoted what he said. 'Mr. Corrieston said so,' was the last word in any discussion. Mr. Corrieston said I was not to go and see Garth; it would be a confession of weakness. Mr. Corrieston said that Garth's neglect of Kitty must on no account be mentioned in court, it would create a wrong impression. Mr. Corrieston said it would be all right if Kitty said this, and that, and forbore to say the other.

I confess the whole affair was beyond my comprehension. I never felt that I understood it. I never got to the bottom of the matter. It was hopeless to question Kitty; she contradicted herself flatly again and again. I tried to find out what her feelings were. Deep down beneath the rage against Garth, which bubbled continually upon the surface, she must surely have some feelings about him. I tried to question her — did she still love him?

'Love him!' she cried. 'How could I possibly love him? He was unbearable. He was always sneering at me in that horrid way — you know that sneering way he looks at you as if you were the greatest fool God ever made. (I *was*, of course, when I married him.) George was sorry for me; he used to take me to shows. I met him sometimes in town for lunch. I knew Garth was jealous of George Hamilton but I didn't care. And then I found that I was being followed.'

'Followed?'

'Yes, followed by a detective — *Garth had me followed.* Did you ever hear of such a beastly thing? He was a horrible little man in a bowler, he followed me when I went to town and met George. He followed me to your flat the night I stayed with you — that's why I was so upset. It was so dreadful for George — the whole thing is dreadful for George. I wish you could meet him, Charlotte, but Mr. Corrieston says it will be better if you don't meet him, better if you don't know him at all. George is so quiet and — and good-natured, he wouldn't hurt a fly. He's amusing too; he's not a dull, dreary creature like Garth.'

'Then why not let the divorce go through?' I asked her, bewildered by the whole thing. 'If you like Mr. Hamilton, and your life with Garth is unbearable.'

'Good God!' she cried. 'You must be mad to suggest such a thing, Charlotte. Do you think I should let Garth drag me through the mud? Do you think I should let him do what he likes without raising a finger to defend myself? And as for George, he would bore me in a month. He bores me already.'

'There's Clementina, of course,' I said, thinking perhaps I had found the solution of Kitty's attitude in her love for her child.

'Oh, Clem!' said Kitty, listless after her outburst. 'Clem is a funny sort of creature — a dull, plain child. I don't know how on earth I could ever have had a child like Clem. George says the same. She's frightfully unattractive.'

I could make no sense of it, no sense at all.

Garth had returned from Wales and was staying at his flat in town. I met him one day in the park and he raised his hat to me with a grave smile and passed on. I thought he looked worn and unhappy. I thought he had aged. His new book had just come out and was causing quite a stir among a certain set of critical people. Garth's books were not for everybody: his first had been the account of a hunting expedition in Africa; his second, a novel. They were alike in being well and carefully written, thoughtful, cynical and amusing. I did not care for the novel, the characters were unpleasing — there was not a pleasant character in the book — but I could see that it was clever, I could see that it had something vital in it, something that promised better things to come.

One day, Kitty took me to see Mr. Corrieston. I had heard so much about Mr. Corrieston by this time that I was sick of the man already, before I had seen him. I went to his office feeling sure that I should dislike him intensely and I found my foreboding correct. Mr. Corrieston was short and thick-set with sandy hair. I thought him like a fox — like a fat fox, if you can imagine such a loathsome animal. I had hoped that Mr. Corrieston would clear my mind for me, would make the whole thing plain and understandable, but he did no such thing. He talked a lot, and he answered my questions, but he never made anything clear. I see now, looking back, that he did not intend me to understand. He could have enlightened me if he had wanted, but he preferred to bewilder me with legal terms and vague contradictory allusions. He and Kitty understood each other perfectly. His manner to her was offensively familiar. He patted her arm with his pudgy hand and called her 'my dear little lady.' He was the pawing type of man, a type I have always detested. Kitty seemed to like it; she smiled at him and laughed at his jokes which were not always in good taste.

'Oh, by the by,' he said, stretching out his hand for a file of papers, clipped together with a stud, 'I've asked Frame to put his best man on to Mr. Wisdon — I told you I intended to have him shadowed, didn't I?'

Kitty nodded.

'You are having Garth shadowed?' I exclaimed incredulously.

'Quite a usual procedure, my dear lady,' Mr. Corrieston assured me. 'Quite a usual procedure under the circumstances. If we could find the woman — there must be a woman, of course.'

'But why?' I inquired.

'There always is,' Mr. Corrieston replied airily. 'The sudden determination of Mr. Wisdon to launch a petition for divorce points to a woman.'

It appeared hazily, through the fog which was clouding my brain, that if this woman could be found and produced, the proceedings would fall through. I could not see why this should be the case, but it was no use asking Mr. Corrieston to explain. The more he explained things the more muddled I became. I thought at the time that he was a stupid man, a man incapable of putting things clearly; I learned afterward that he was diabolically clever.

'There is nothing to worry about,' Mr. Corrieston said to me, smiling his fat foxy smile. 'We shall have to call you, of course, but it is a mere formality.'

'Call me? Do you mean as a witness?' I asked, appalled at the idea.

'Yes, as a witness.'

'But why me? What do I know?'

Mr. Corrieston laughed. 'It is merely a formality, Miss Dean. You remember the night that Mrs. Wisdon spent with you? We shall want your evidence that she spent it in your flat. You remember the occasion.'

'Of course I remember the occasion. She slept in my bed,' I said stupidly.

'That's all we want,' said Mr. Corrieston, smiling more foxily than ever.

'It all hangs on you, Char,' Kitty put in eagerly.

'Not at all,' Mr. Corrieston interrupted her. 'Very little hangs on Miss Dean. We must not make Miss Dean nervous by telling her that she is an important witness when she is nothing of the kind. Her evidence will be very simple, a mere formality.'

'Yes, of course,' Kitty agreed.

'Couldn't you leave me out, if my evidence isn't important?' I asked, grasping at any straw that could save me from an ordeal that I dreaded.

Mr. Corrieston appeared to consider. 'I think not,' he said. 'I think your evidence might strengthen our case. You remember the date of the night in question?'

'No,' I said, 'but I shall have it in my diary.'

Mr. Corrieston rubbed his hands. 'Admirable!' he exclaimed. 'How truly admirable to keep a diary! Let me congratulate you upon your perseverance, Miss Dean. How often have I started upon January first with the best intentions, only to fall away in a lamentable manner before the end of the month was reached!'

'I don't know how you can be bothered,' Kitty said.

'It's just a habit,' I told them.

It was an easy matter, when I went home that night, to turn back the pages of my diary and find that the night Kitty had spent with me was the night of the eighteenth of March.

'Admirable, my dear lady,' said Mr. Corrieston, and even Kitty agreed quite pleasantly that diaries had their uses.

The time of waiting passed unbearably slowly. The Wisdon case was a defended one and therefore had to wait until the undefended petitions had been heard. I realized very clearly during those weeks that Kitty was a woman who lived entirely for herself. Nobody else mattered; nothing mattered except that she should have what she wanted, that she should be comforted when she needed comfort and sympathized with when she needed sympathy. After twelve years, during which I had scarcely seen her for more than a few minutes at a time, she returned to me almost as a stranger; but, unlike a stranger, she leaned upon me to the point of exhaustion. She brought every mood to me, every transitory mood of anger or fear. She had no reticences — except those imposed upon her by her solicitor — she discussed the most intimate details of her life with a frankness that I found embarrassing; she burdened me with her troubles and perplexities and purposely misled me as to the essential facts of the case.

Kitty had become an undisciplined woman. She had been an undisciplined child, for her charm had carried her through trouble and saved her again and again from just punishment for her childish faults; but an undisciplined child can be lovable, can easily be forgiven, whereas an undisciplined woman is a weariness of the flesh. I realized, too, that Kitty had coarsened, not physically — for her body had been cared for with unremitting skill and attention — but coarsened mentally, or perhaps spiritually would be nearer the truth. This new Kitty was so different from the child I had loved that I could scarcely recognize her, and this feeling of strangeness made it all the more difficult for me to give her the sympathy she demanded so urgently. The coarsening of her mental fibers dismayed me. It was more grief to realize her degeneration, than to contemplate the mess she had made of her life, for the one was an inner and the fundamental thing and the other merely fortuitous.

So Kitty came back to me — a stranger in the deepest sense of the word — and leaned upon me with all her weight, and, because she was my sister and had been dear to me in days gone by, I did what I could for her and gave her what strength I had. I bore her no grudge for her long years of neglect, but I could not help feeling that I should have been more help to her in her hour of need if she had not shut me out of her life so completely for twelve years.

# 3

## *Fog in Court*

The strain of waiting for the case to be heard was so great that I was almost glad when the day came. By tomorrow or next day at the latest — for Mr. Corrieston had warned us that it might take two days — the whole thing would be over for good or ill and I would be free to settle down again in my old rut. I was so tired by this time that all I wanted was to be left alone, and I knew that, once the case was over, Kitty would leave me alone; she would have no further use for me. I did not feel the least bitter about this, I simply accepted it as a foregone conclusion, and was glad to think that I should be free. Once her fate was decided she would not require me to lean upon and she would drift out of my life again.

I awoke in the morning with a dull pain in my head, and a strange lassitude in every limb. It was raining hard and the air felt thick and difficult to breathe. I had got a holiday from Wentworth's for the occasion so I rose a little later than my usual hour. This made the day seem like Sunday and my brain was so dazed and befuddled that I found myself thinking what a strange thing it was that the Divorce Courts should be open on a Sunday. I only tell you this,

Clare, so that you may understand what a queer state I was in. I tried to remember all the things that Mr. Corrieston had told me to say, but I could remember nothing except the milk — I was to be sure and say that the milk I had left for Kitty's morning tea had been finished and that half my loaf of bread had gone. It was true, of course, I remembered about the milk distinctly, because I had been a little surprised at the time; Kitty always used to take her morning cup of tea with lemon in it (she was never very fond of milk) but twelve years is a long time and Kitty had changed so much in other ways that it was ridiculous to expect her tastes to remain unaltered. Except for the milk, which I remembered perfectly, there were queer gaps in my brain — and the more I struggled to fill them the more bewildered I became — and there are queer gaps in my memory of what happened on that day. When I look back now the whole day is like a nightmare, fantastic and illusive. I can see myself having breakfast in the flat, and washing up the dishes, and putting on my hat in front of the tiny mirror in my bedroom, and the next thing I remember is sitting next to Kitty in court listening to Garth's counsel's opening speech.

(I suppose I was really ill, worn out with the strain of preceding weeks — an emotional strain and a physical strain combined. The whole affair had upset me terribly and I had no leisure to recover from the blow. Not only had I Kitty to soothe and sustain but I had my work at Wentworth's to carry out as usual — work which demanded its usual quota of time and energy.

When Kitty usurped my usual reading hours I had to read far into the night to keep abreast of the new books which came out almost daily — it was no wonder that I was near breaking-point with the strain. In addition to all this I had contracted a germ and was sickening for 'flu. I did not realize this at the time; I only felt that I was wrapped in a kind of fog through which I had to grope my way. Faces appeared and disappeared confusedly, voices were startlingly loud at one moment, and, at the next, so faint and far away that I had to strain my ears to hear them.)

I looked about me in a dazed way; the court was crowded with all sorts and conditions of people — it was strange that so many people should be interested in Garth's and Kitty's unfortunate affairs. The courtroom was high and slightly Gothic in appearance, red curtains hung behind the Judge's chair. I looked at the Judge with interest. I thought he had a fine face, strong and kind, but he looked weary and disillusioned. It must be a tiring and disillusioning job to listen every day to tales of unhappy marriages and shipwrecked hopes. The jury, on the other hand, looked fresh and eager, this was an event in their lives, not an everyday duty, and I could see that they were feeling pleased and important, all except one man who sat at the end of the front row leaning his head on his hand in an attitude of intense dejection. There were three women in the jury; one of them was quite old with untidy white hair straggling from beneath a black felt hat, the other two were younger, somewhat about my own age I thought.

Garth's counsel was a tall, aristocratic-looking man with a slow, resonant voice and an air of dignity enhanced by his wig and gown. I tried to follow what he was saying, but there was an intermittent booming in my ears which prevented me from hearing his words distinctly. I heard a phrase here and there.

' . . . on the eighteenth of March the respondent went to her sister's flat in France Street . . . She telephoned to the petitioner saying she intended to stay the night with her sister . . . the petitioner's suspicions were aroused . . . '

I lost the next part, wondering why. Why should the petitioner's suspicions have been aroused? The petitioner was Garth of course. Garth was suspicious because Kitty was spending the night with me — strange! And yet after all was it so strange? Kitty had never done such a thing before, never shown any desire to do such a thing before. I had thought it queer myself. My brain could not reason any further nor follow out the implications or possible implications of Garth's suspicions, the thoughts slipped through it like water out of a sieve.

' . . . and so, my lord, I propose to show that the respondent did not spend the night with her sister . . . ' But that was nonsense of course. Kitty had slept in my bed and I had slept on the couch in the sitting room. What on earth did the man mean by saying she 'had not spent the night with her sister?' I looked at Kitty and saw that she was leaning forward watching the speaker with breathless interest, her face looked pinched and drawn, and there was a patch of red in the middle of her cheek. I looked up at the witness-box and saw that Garth had appeared there, he was standing up very straight and his face was in shadow, his eyes were like black holes in the pallor of his face. When he spoke in answer to counsel's questions his voice seemed very loud — much too loud to be clear — he did not seem able to modulate his voice to the acoustics of the court. Garth was nervous; he was hating it all, hating the publicity of the whole thing, hating the questions which were probing into his life and laying it bare for all the world to see. Oh, Garth, why did you do it; why did you take this dreadful step?

The jury was hanging on Garth's words. One of the younger women had her mouth open — but she was rather a nice-looking woman in spite of her unbecoming expression — I wondered if she were married, and, if so, whether it was very inconvenient for her to leave her home for a whole day. Perhaps she was happily married — she had a happy face — and thought the whole affair unnecessary and rather disgusting; or perhaps she was unhappily married — but I did not think so — and her sympathies were roused by the matrimonial troubles of Garth and Kitty.

Garth's counsel was finished. He folded himself in his black gown like a huge black bird closing its wings, and sat down. Kitty's counsel rose with a rustle of silk and papers to cross-examine Garth. I had heard a great deal about this man from Kitty and I looked at him with interest. Mr. Corrieston had told us that he was very clever and that we were lucky to get him. I wondered if we were. He had a flat pale face and prominent teeth, even his wig could not dignify him. Mr. Amber seemed to me a very mediocre sort of person — an entirely different and inferior class of person from Garth's counsel.

Garth was leaning forward now; he looked stern and somewhat defiant. Question and answer followed each other rapidly.

'You were suspicious when you heard that the respondent intended to stay the night with her sister?'

'I was.'

'Why?'

'Because, for one thing, she rarely troubled to inform me of her intentions.'

'*For one thing* — what other reason gave you cause for suspicion?'

'She had never stayed with her sister before.'

'Why had she never done so before?'

'How do I know?'

'Was the respondent on good terms with her sister?'

'That is irrelevant.'

Mr. Amber made a gesture of impatience and turned to the Judge: 'My lord, the witness refuses to answer my questions.'

The Judge bent forward. 'You must answer counsel's questions,' he said quietly. His voice was calm and clear.

'Even if they are irrelevant, my lord?' asked Garth.

'Even if you consider them irrelevant. Your

counsel will protect you from irrelevancy if he considers it necessary.'

Garth bowed and the questions continued.

The court grew unbearably hot and stuffy; there was a dull pain at the back of my neck and behind my eyes. The legal phraseology wrapped everything in fog; the petitioner, the respondent, the co-respondent — these terms obscured the identity of Garth and Kitty and Mr. Hamilton. I had to make an effort to remember which was which and who was who, and the effort exhausted me.

Various witnesses appeared in the witness-box and were examined and cross-examined by Garth's counsel and Mr. Amber. There was a third counsel who sprang up like a jack-in-the-box and cross-examined some of the witnesses — a strange little man with a thin, sallow face and a wig perched crookedly over one eye — I couldn't think who he was nor imagine what he had to do with it, and then I suddenly realized that he must be Mr. Hamilton's counsel, and *that* must be Mr. Hamilton sitting near him. I looked at Mr. Hamilton with interest, and saw a smooth, boyish face, the face of a schoolboy, with round cheeks and round eyes and smooth brown hair parted at the side. He looked bewildered and distressed, as if he were surprised to find himself in such a strange and embarrassing predicament.

I forced myself to listen to the evidence — there was now a small rat-faced man in the box who called himself a Private Inquiry Agent. He was obviously used to giving evidence in court and he gave it well, consulting a well-thumbed notebook from time to time in a professional manner.

'On the night of eighteenth of March I followed the respondent to a house in France Street . . . She disappeared up the stairs. I waited and saw the respondent at the window of the top-floor flat.'

'What did she do?'

'Pulled aside the blind and looked out. I waited a long time . . . I was just thinking it was no good when the co-respondent's car drove up to a house the other end of the street. I engaged a taxi in Well Street and returned to France Street. The respondent came out of the house and entered the co-respondent's car. They drove off rapidly. I followed in the taxi. They went to The Fellsborough Arms, at Maidenhead. It was half past one by that time. I took a room in the hotel. The next morning I saw the respondent and the co-respondent having breakfast in the dining room. I turned up the visitors' book and saw that their names had been entered as Mr. and Mrs. Warner . . . '

I heard it all with amazement — the night of the eighteenth of March was the night Kitty had spent with me. I grasped Kitty's arm and she turned to me with a white face and blazing eyes. 'All lies,' she whispered. 'Bribed by Garth.'

I relapsed onto the hard bench — *bribed by Garth*. Was it possible? No, it wasn't possible. Even my fuzzy brain rejected that explanation. They must have made a mistake; it must have been some other woman that had come out of the house in France Street and driven to Maidenhead — some other woman, not Kitty.

More witnesses appeared; the proprietor of the Fellsborough Arms who had been aroused from his bed to admit 'Mr. and Mrs. Warner' at one thirty-five a.m. on the nineteenth of March; the chambermaid who had taken them their morning tea; the boots who had cleaned the two pairs of shoes which he found outside the door. They appeared in the box, were examined, cross-examined, turned inside out and held up to ridicule, made to look incredibly foolish, and dismissed. My heart sank lower. Soon it would be my turn; I should stand up there with every eye fixed upon me. They would wrangle over me as they had wrangled over Garth. 'My lord, I object . . . ' 'My lord I submit that my friend has no right to put that question . . . ' Would I be able to answer at all when they spoke to me? My voice would never come at the right moment — I felt sure of that — I should stand there dumb, quite unable to explain that it was all a mistake, that Kitty had slept in my bed and the rat-faced man had followed the wrong woman to Maidenhead. I should be struck dumb with sheer terror before the virulence of cross-examination. I had never imagined that it would be so virulent, so searching. When Mr. Amber jumped up to cross-examine he seemed to start with the conviction that his victim was a congenital liar. He wove nets for the witnesses and they fell into the nets and were entangled in their own words. I realized, of course, that, when my turn came, Mr. Amber would be on my side, and Garth's counsel — that quiet aristocrat with the slow resonant voice — would be against me. Would he browbeat me as these witnesses were being browbeaten? Would he turn me inside out and dismiss me with a tired smile and a wave of his hand as if I were unworthy of his time and trouble?

'Oh God,' I prayed, 'make something happen before my turn comes.'

# 4

## *Mrs. Lily Cope*

We adjourned for a hurried lunch in the court refreshment rooms. I could not eat anything, but I drank a cup of coffee and found it cleared my brain a little. Kitty nibbled a sandwich and discussed the case with Mr. Corrieston in anxious whispers. I tried to ask them some of the questions which were torturing me, but I could get no satisfaction from either of them.

'It's all lies,' Kitty said. 'You know it's all lies, Char. The whole thing is made up from beginning to end.'

'Leave it to Mr. Amber,' said Mr. Corrieston smiling foxily. 'Don't worry at all, Miss Dean. Mr. Amber knows exactly what he's doing, just leave it all in his hands and answer his questions clearly and distinctly.'

'But I've got to answer the other counsel too,' I said anxiously.

'It will be all right, just leave it to Mr. Amber,' replied Mr. Corrieston. 'Just leave it all to him.'

We returned to the court and took our seats as before. My terror, which had been slightly dispelled by the coffee and Mr. Corrieston's assurances, returned in full force. I longed to get up and run away. If only I could run away and hide from it all, from the shame, and the disgrace, and the sordid misery — if only I could hide. The court swam before my eyes, I could scarcely breathe.

I was aroused by a voice shouting 'Mrs. Cope,' and to my amazement it was my own Mrs. Cope who appeared in the witness-box; my own Mrs. Cope in her Sunday clothes, wearing a hat which had been given her by me — a red hat I had worn for years 'brightened up' for the occasion with a vivid green wing.

Kitty sat up suddenly and looked at me with hard, suspicious eyes.

'What does *she* know?' she whispered.

'She knows you spent the night with me,' I replied. I remembered now that Mrs. Cope had promised to take a cup of tea to Kitty. We had discussed the matter when we met on the stairs. This fact had slipped my memory until the sight of Mrs. Cope in the witness-box had stirred my sluggish brain and brought it back. It was a good thing they had brought Mrs. Cope, I thought; she would tell them that she had seen Kitty and taken her some tea, and the mistake would be cleared up. Mr. Amber was leaning over, whispering into Mr. Corrieston's ear. He wrote hurriedly on a slip of paper and passed it to Kitty who shook her head and frowned. They seemed worried about Mrs. Cope; it was strange that they should be worried, but there were so many things I did not understand that one thing more or less made very little difference. I left them to their whisperings and frownings, and bent my attention upon Mrs. Cope — her evidence is the only part of the case which remains clearly in my mind. She took with her, into the witness-box, her own aura of personality — her sensible, foolish, honest character shone in her face for all the world to see — she faced the crowded court with equanimity; she brought with her, into that sleepy, frowsty place, a breath of air from the London streets; she dispersed the legal fog like a London breeze. It was no use talking to Mrs. Cope in legal phraseology because she did not understand it (did not pretend to understand it), and it seemed to me that everything would have been much simpler if we had all been like Mrs. Cope.

Mrs. Cope looked round the court and preened herself; she was not in the least frightened, nor dismayed. Is there another country in the world where a woman of Mrs. Cope's class and upbringing could face a judge and jury in a crowded court with confidence in their integrity and in her own rectitude? Is there another country in the world that could produce a Mrs. Cope?

I awaited Mrs. Cope's evidence with eagerness. She would clear up the whole affair and perhaps — I was very ignorant in these matters — there would be no need for my evidence at all. Surely they would not waste their time in questioning me, when they had already got a full account of Kitty's tenancy of my room from Mrs. Cope! It was not until halfway through Mrs. Cope's evidence that I began to realize where it was tending, that far from exculpating Kitty, Mrs. Cope was ruining her irretrievably.

'Mrs. Lily Cope?' inquired Garth's counsel.

'That's me,' nodded Mrs. Cope brightly.

How strange that although I had known Mrs. Cope for twelve years I had never had occasion to learn that her Christian name was Lily! Did anybody on earth look less like a lily than Mrs. Cope — so compact, she was, so red and tough and capable?

'You work for Miss Dean, I believe.'

'That's right. I been daily 'elp to Miss Dean twelve years.'

'A long time, Mrs. Cope' — in a friendly encouraging voice.

'So it is, sir. But Miss Dean and me gets on all right. I likes gentlemen as a rule, to do for, but Miss Dean's no more trouble than a gentleman.'

There was a ripple of laughter in court which quickly subsided.

'On the morning of the nineteenth of March, did you go as usual to Miss Dean's flat?'

'That's right, sir.'

'Will you tell the court what happened that morning?'

Mrs. Cope took a long breath. 'Well, it was loike this. I met Miss Dean on the stairs — just on the stroke of nine it was — ' 'ullo, Mrs. Cope,' she ses ter me. 'Laite as usual,' she ses. That's just our little joke, ye see, sir.'

'You were not late?'

'No, sir. Miss Dean an' me always meets on the stairs. So then she ses ter me that 'er sister's spending the night an' I'm not to waike 'er. She ses ter me, ' 'Er pore 'ead's somethin' awful,' she ses. 'Don't you go maikin' a noise,' she ses. 'Pore soul,' I ses, 'I'll maike 'er a nice cup o' tea an' taike it in.' Miss Dean thinks to 'erself a minute an' then she ses, 'Could you stay laiter today, Mrs. Cope?' she ses. 'Mrs. Wisdon doesn't want to be disturbed before eleven.' Well, I said I would. I 'ad another job, but it didn't matter bein' a bit laite so long as I got it done sometimes. So we settled it all right. 'That's okay,' she ses, an' off she goes. Well I does the 'all an' the sittin' room, goin' about quiet-like, an' then I maikes a noice cup o' tea an' a few bits of toast an' takes it in ter the bedroom, an' bless my soul you could 'ave knocked me dahn wif a feather — there's nobody there.'

'The respondent had gone?'

'Wot's that?' inquired Mrs. Cope with a puzzled frown.

'Mrs. Wisdon was not in the room?'

'Nobody wasn't,' agreed Mrs. Cope.

'Would it have been possible for Mrs. Wisdon to have left the room and gone out while you were in the flat?'

'No, it wouldn't then. She'd 'ave 'ad ter step over me when I was washing the floor in the 'all.'

Another ripple of laughter.

'Then the — er — Mrs. Wisdon must have left the flat before you arrived?'

'That's right.'

'What did you do next?'

'I went an' 'ad a look at the bed an' I sees it 'adn't bin slep' in.'

There was a rustle in the court.

'The bed was — er — made?'

'No, it wasn't made neither. It 'ad bin rumpled about a bit to maike it look untidy, but the bottom sheet was smooth, *an*' the piller. I knows the way Miss Dean maikes beds — as smooth as cream, 'er beds are — An' I knows Miss Dean's linen an' I knows that bed 'adn't bin slep' in.'

Mr. Amber leaped to his feet. 'My lord, my lord, I protest,' he said vehemently. 'The witness's opinion is not evidence.'

They wrangled for a few moments and Mrs. Cope waited patiently while they did so. The Judge instructed the jury to make a note of the fact that it was the witness's opinion, and therefore not evidence, that the bed had not been slept in.

'What did you do next, Mrs. Cope?' inquired counsel sweetly.

'I picks up the nightie — on the floor it wos, an' all of a 'eap, crumpled up — an' the nex' thing is a pin runs straight into me 'and.'

'A pin?'

'That's right. It was Miss Dean's best nightie — cripe der sheen — she'd got it out for 'er sister ter wear. But nobody 'adn't worn that nightie, an' why? Becos nobody couldn't wear a nightie wifout takin' out the pins.'

'But why pins?' inquired counsel. 'To a mere man it sounds rather strange.'

'Ter keep the pleats right,' explained Mrs. Cope. 'I done up that nightie 'arf a dozen times for Miss Dean, an' don't I know the job I've 'ad ironing the pleats down the front. They're crule to iron, pleats are.'

'What did you do next?'

'Well, sir, it seemed a shaime ter waiste the tea

so I ’ad it myself — I was feelin’ a bit queer, yer see. I’m subject to palpitations an’ I was a bit upset loike. So I ’ad the tea myself an’ felt all the better. An’ then I washed up and went on ter Mr. Smith’s. I was about a hour laite, yer see, what wif one thing an’ another.’

Garth’s counsel sat down with a satisfied smile, and Mr. Amber rose to cross-examine Mrs. Cope. He did not make much of her. Her evidence was too firm to shake, and it was to her advantage that she did not understand his more subtle questions, so that the traps he laid for her unwary feet failed to catch her. When she did not understand the question, she did not answer, and the questions put in plainer language lost a great deal of their sting.

‘On the morning of the nineteenth of March you met Miss Dean on her way to work.’

‘That’s right,’ said Mrs. Cope.

‘You met her at the end of France Street, didn’t you?’

‘No, I didn’t then. I met ’er on the stairs like I sed.’

‘I suggest that you did not go into the flat immediately. There was something you wanted to do. You remembered it after you had met Miss Dean and went out to get it.’

‘I didn’t want nothin’,’ replied Mrs. Cope. ‘An’ if I ’ad wanted anythink, I’d ’ave got it on the w’y. I don’t walk any further than I ’as to wif me corns stabbin’ me loike knives. I went straight up ter the flat when I’d seen Miss Dean an’ there I st’yed.’

‘You had other flats to visit.’

'That's right. After I've done for Miss Dean I goes on ter Mr. Smith.'

'What time do you leave Miss Dean's flat?'

'About tennish,' said Mrs. Cope. 'But that d'y I'd promised Miss Dean I'd st'y an' maike 'er sister a cup o' tea. You 'eard me s'y so to the other gentlemen, didn't yer?'

'I am now cross-examining you, Mrs. Cope. Kindly give me your attention.'

'Well, I am, aren't I?' inquired Mrs. Cope, not unreasonably.

'I suggest that you left Miss Dean's flat at the usual hour — about ten o'clock — and went to this Mr. Smith, returning about eleven to prepare breakfast for the respondent.'

Mrs. Cope looked at him blankly, and he was obliged to repeat his 'suggestion' in plainer language.

'Well, I didn't, then,' said Mrs. Cope. 'I didn't do no such thing. Mr. Smith's is at the other end of the street, an' I wosn't goin' trilin' off to the other end of France Street an' back agen — as a matter of fac', I never thought of it. Wot I did was this, if yer wants ter know, I finished at Miss Dean's an' it maide me a good hour laite, but it worked in all right, 'cos I did the sittin' room thorough, as well as the 'all wot I generally does the nex' d'y. So the nex' d'y I gives Mr. Smith the extra hour. See?'

Mr. Amber left that and passed on.

'While you were busy in the sitting room the respondent could have gone out of the bedroom into the hall — Mrs. Wisdon is the respondent,' he added anticipating Mrs. Cope's question.

'Not 'arf she couldn't,' replied Mrs. Cope. 'Miss Dean's flat is cozy, but it ain't big, an' the only w'y out of the bedroom is through the sittin' room — unless she 'ad wings an' flew out of the winder.'

'Do you mean to say there is no door out of the bedroom into the hall?'

'Well yes, there is a door, so there is. But it's blocked up wif Jeremiah standin' up against it — that's Miss Dean's grandfather's clock wot she brought wif'er from 'er old 'ome. You go an' look for yerself if yer don't believe me; nobody couldn't move that clock by themselves. It taikes up most of the 'all. I ain't big, but it taikes me all my time ter squeeze around it when I does the 'all. Besides, the door's locked an' always 'as bin ter my knowledge.'

'Regarding the bed. You informed the court that it had not been slept in — rather a rash statement wasn't it?'

'Wot's that?'

'Why did you think the bed had not been slept in?' inquired Mr. Amber impatiently. 'You informed the court that the bed had been rumpled about.'

'So it 'ad,' replied Mrs. Cope firmly. 'I knows wot I'm talkin' about when I talks about beds. If you'd 'ad as much to do wif beds as I've 'ad, you'd know soon enough when a bed 'ad bin slep' in.'

'A bed does not get rumpled unless it has been slept in.'

'If someone rumples it, it does. Someone 'ad wanted to maike it look like it 'ad bin slep' in, but they didn't do it right. If you wants ter maike a bed look like as if it 'ad bin slep' in, you get in, an' 'ump yerself about a bit — see?'

There was a good deal of laughter at this. How could they laugh? It disgusted me that they could laugh at such a moment. Mrs. Cope looked round, smiling at the success of her remark, and waited for the laughter to subside.

'It seems strange that you did not inform Miss Dean of this marvelous discovery,' said Mr. Amber sarcastically.

'Wot's that?'

'Why didn't you tell Miss Dean about your suspicions?'

'Oh that!' said Mrs. Cope. 'It wosn't no business of mine, I sees lots of funny things in my life an' I don't say nothin'. Yer never gets into no trouble for sayin' nothin' — that's flat.'

'When did you change your mind? Was it after you had seen the resp — Mrs. Wisdon — and she had admonished you for your impudence?'

'Not so much about imperence,' returned Mrs. Cope hotly. 'It wos her wot was imperent to me.'

'Kindly answer my question. Was it after you had seen Mrs. Wisdon that you decided to speak?'

'I didn't s'y nothin' ter nobody till I was arst,' said Mrs. Cope sullenly. 'An' when I was arst I sed wot I know'd, an' not a word more.'

Mr. Amber continued his cross-examination for some little time, trying to shake Mrs. Cope, but without success. I thought he had strengthened the value of her evidence rather than weakened it. When at last he sat down there was a little buzz in court and I saw the jury whispering to each other.

# 5

## *'She Asked Me Not to Disturb Her'*

I was so dumbfounded by Mrs. Cope's story that I could not speak to Kitty, could not look at her. I knew that Kitty would blame me for Mrs. Cope; it was my doing that Mrs. Cope had stayed and prepared breakfast for her and so found her out in her deception. For of course I realized now that Kitty had deceived me. It was impossible to doubt Mrs. Cope, she was trustworthy, she was completely and absolutely honest. She was one of those people who glory in honesty, who take a pride in their integrity. She would no more have gone into the witness-box and told lies than she would have flown. If Mrs. Cope said that Kitty had not spent the night in my flat, Kitty had not done so. I saw now that I had been used, that I had been deceived, made a dupe for Kitty's convenience. I saw now why Mr. Corrieston had not answered my questions, why Kitty had contradicted herself, and, even in her wildest moments, had been careful to conceal the facts of the case. She was guilty, that was why. Her assurances that Garth was mad and had 'made up the whole thing' were nothing but a pack of lies.

I was so angry at the way I had been duped that my terror fled. When I thought of how Kitty must have crept out of the flat while I was asleep, of how she must have looked at me lying there on the couch in the sitting room, and smiled to think of the success of her plan, and how easy it had been, my rage knew no bounds. I scarcely realized that the case for the petitioner was closed; I scarcely heard Mr. Amber's opening speech for the defense, nor Kitty's examination and cross-examination. What was the use of listening to it all? It was lies from beginning to end.

I was so angry that my terror fled, but only fled to return with redoubled force when I heard my name called and found myself getting up out of my seat and moving up to the witness-box. It was dreadful to stand there in front of the whole court and to know that I stood there to protect a lie. To know that although my evidence was true in every particular it was being used for an untrue cause. It was dreadful to stand there and answer Mr. Amber's questions — the questions that I had been told he would ask me — knowing what I knew, knowing that everybody in court was aware that I was either an accomplice or a dupe.

Mr. Amber began by asking the questions for which I had been prepared, but he went on to other questions which were infinitely more worrying. I suppose Mrs. Cope's evidence had altered his line of defense, the old line of defense had been swept away by Mrs. Cope. Even the fact that the milk (which I had left for Kitty's tea) had been finished was of no importance now, for Mrs. Cope had admitted to having drunk it herself. Mr. Amber left the subject of milk severely alone; he tried, instead, to get me to discredit Mrs. Cope, to say she was untruthful and dishonest. He wanted me to say I had missed things from the flat and had suspected Mrs. Cope — I couldn't do it. I was aware that my answers were not the answers that Mr. Amber wanted, and that they were unhelpful to Kitty's defense, but I could not make them otherwise.

At last, to my relief, Mr. Amber relinquished the subject of Mrs. Cope and passed on to other matters.

'Do you sleep very heavily, Miss Dean?' he inquired.

'No, I don't think so. Not unless I am very tired.'

'You were sleeping on the sofa that night?'

'Yes.'

'Was it as comfortable as a bed?'

'No.'

'It was not so comfortable as a bed. You would not sleep so well as usual, I imagine.'

'No, I don't suppose I should.'

'Is it likely that anyone — anyone at all — could have passed through the room without waking you?'

'It does not seem — likely,' I replied feebly. What was the good of asking me that? Kitty had passed through the room when I was asleep, she must have done so. We all knew that she had done so. The man was trying to make me lie.

He bent forward earnestly and said, 'Miss Dean, think for a moment. Can you remember hearing a sound from the bedroom the next morning?'

I knew the whole court was awaiting my answer with breathless interest.

'No,' I said faintly, 'I heard nothing.'

'You knew the respondent was asleep?'

'Yes, I went about the flat very quietly, I did not want to disturb her.'

'Did you open the bedroom door and look in to see whether she was all right? She had been indisposed the night before, if I remember rightly.'

'She had a headache.'

'Yes, so you looked in to see if she were better?'

'No.'

'Wasn't it rather strange not to look in before leaving the flat?'

'She asked me not to disturb her,' I replied.

I knew, the moment the words had left my lips, that it was the wrong thing to say. How dreadful it is that one can never recall words! There was a rustle in court. I looked toward Kitty and saw her eyes fixed upon me; they were full of scorn and hatred.

Mr. Amber cleared his throat and continued, 'Did the respondent visit your flat on the day upon which the Divorce Papers were served?'

'Yes. She called for me at Wentworth's and we went back to the flat together.'

'Was Mrs. Cope there?'

'Yes.'

'What took place?'

'My sister told me about the Divorce Papers — showed them to me.'

'Was Mrs. Cope present?'

'No, she had gone.'

'Why?'

'I told her I would make the tea — that she need not wait.'

'Was there any unpleasantness before she left?'

'Oh yes. At least Mrs. Wisdon asked me to send her away.'

'Can you remember the words she used?'

'Approximately. She said, 'Send that dreadful woman away; I can't think how you can bear her near you.''

'Did Mrs. Cope hear the words?'

'I'm afraid she did. I was sorry about it.'

'You were sorry about it. You knew that Mrs. Cope was easily offended, that she was a dangerous woman to offend.'

'I was sorry because I knew it would hurt her feelings.'

'Was Mrs. Cope angry?'

'Yes, I think she was.'

'What did she say?'

'She said, 'Oh, Mrs. Wisdon's tired is she, she's had a tiring day has she? Fancy that!' — or words to that effect.'

'She said it in a disagreeable way?'

'Yes.'

'Did you form the opinion that her feeling toward the respondent was amicable?'

'No.'

'You felt the respondent had made an enemy, rather a dangerous and unscrupulous enemy, perhaps?'

'I didn't think of that. I just felt sorry that Mrs. Cope's feelings were hurt.'

I saw by this time what Mr. Amber was driving at. He wanted to prove that Mrs. Cope was furious with Kitty; that she had given her evidence maliciously. It seemed to me a very frail straw to support his case, but I suppose it was the only straw left. I thought that it might be true up to a certain point. Mrs. Cope was not above getting her own back for the insult which had been offered her — probably she was glad of the opportunity — but she wouldn't have lied to get her own back, I was sure of that. I had known the woman for twelve years and she was a simple creature, simple and good-hearted; intensely loyal to her friends, implacable to her enemies. Kitty had made an enemy of Mrs. Cope by a few inconsiderate words and this was the result. It would have been just as easy for Kitty to have made a friend of Mrs. Cope, and, if she had done so, Mrs. Cope would have gone to the stake rather than given evidence against her. Those few words of Kitty's had lost her case, for it was lost entirely upon Mrs. Cope's evidence. The alibi which seemed to be the whole defense had been utterly destroyed; there was not a shred of it left.

Mr. Amber sat down, and Garth's counsel rose to cross-examine me. He did not trouble me much; he had won his case already, and he knew it — everybody in court knew it.

I did not go back to my seat after leaving the witness-box; I was too frightened of Kitty to go back. That look of hatred which I had caught was too clear in my mind. I leaned against the wall at the back of the court feeling sick and shaken. Suddenly I felt a hand on my arm and looked down into the red, cheerful face of Mrs. Cope.

'You come along wif me, Miss,' she said in a friendly manner. 'You *do* look green an' no mistaike. Come an' 'ave a nice cup o' tea wif me. They won't want us no more; it's all over but the shouting.'

I let her lead me away. What she said was quite true — it was all over but the shouting.

Mrs. Cope and I had tea together in the court restaurant. I was glad of the tea, and I was glad of Mrs. Cope's cheerful company. She made the whole affair seem unreal — *she* was real and human, the other was a bad dream. We talked about everyday matters, about the crying need for new linoleum for my hall, and whether the curtains in my sitting room could be made to last out another winter. When we had had our tea we went back to the courtroom, the three counsels had finished addressing the court and the Judge was summing up. He was very short.

' . . . the crux of the matter is this, do you or do you not believe in the honesty of the witnesses? If you believe them to be speaking the truth you have no option but to find the respondent guilty of adultery with the co-respondent, and the co-respondent guilty of adultery with the respondent. But if you believe the witnesses to be untrustworthy and moved by malice to give lying evidence you may discount their evidence or dismiss it entirely. I can trust you to give your best attention to the matter, weighing the evidence with care and impartiality. You may retire if you wish to do so.'

'There is no need for us to retire, my lord,' replied the foreman.

'You are agreed upon your verdict?'

'Yes, we are all agreed.'

'Do you find the respondent guilty of adultery with the co-respondent?'

'Yes.'

'Do you find the co-respondent guilty of adultery with the respondent?'

'Yes.'

I had known that Kitty's case was hopeless, but the bald words were a shock, nevertheless. I did not wait to hear the Judge; I blundered out of the place, found a taxi and went home.

# 6

## *Mr. Corrieston Explains*

I was ill, really ill, for several days. I lay in bed, burning and shivering by turns, and the pain in my head was appalling. Mrs. Cope came in twice a day and looked after me like a mother. She made me strange lumpy concoctions which she called milk puddings and stood over me while I tried to eat them.

''Ow's the pore 'ead?' she would ask, looking down at me with a commiserating expression upon her usually cheerful countenance. 'I remember the awful 'ead I 'ad two years ago when I 'ad the 'flu — that time I was off work an' my sister-in-lor came an' did for yer.'

'She very nearly did for me,' I replied weakly.

Mrs. Cope did not see my feeble joke. 'There's only a few spoons more,' she said, peering into the bowl, 'taike it all up now, an' ye'll feel better.'

We did not mention the divorce case at all. At first I felt too ill to speak of anything, and afterward it seemed unnecessary to go back and rake it up. I did not want to quarrel with Mrs. Cope; she was the only friend I had at this time, and she was a good friend to me. When I recovered a little, and was able to sit up in bed without the whole room going round like a whirligig, I began to look forward to Mrs. Cope's visits with something approaching eagerness. (It was so dull lying in bed, and I could not read for long without making my head ache.) I drew her out so that she should stay longer with me and Mrs. Cope was not loath to be drawn. She told me long tales — somewhat involved I found them — about the battles she had with the people on her stair, and especially about a certain Mrs. Ammet — or Hammet, I never knew which — who lived in the flat immediately below.

'She's a pore weak thing,' said Mrs. Cope scornfully. 'The kind wot taikes to 'er bed every time she 'as a pine an' leaves 'er 'usban' ter mind the baiby — *you* know.'

I nodded gravely.

'But fer all that she's a tongue like a asp,' continued Mrs. Cope, 'an' the other d'y when I wos comin' dahn the stairs we 'ad a bit of a argument so to speak. It's not the first we've 'ad by no means, an' it won't be the last. Wot bisniss is it of 'ers, I should like ter know, if Cope does taike a drop too much of a Friday night?'

'None at all,' I agreed.

'That's wot I s'y,' said Mrs. Cope. ''Er 'usban's T.T. an' a nasty ugly-tempered thing at that. Wot 'e don't spend on a friendly drop o' beer 'e spends on 'orses. Well, Mrs. Ammet ses — '

And with ghoulish glee Mrs. Cope embarked upon her complicated tale. Mrs. Ammet's tongue might be aspish, but it seemed to me that Mrs. Cope was more than a match for it. In the encounters reported to me, at least, Mrs. Cope always had the last word.

Mr. Wentworth was kind too. He came and saw me in bed, much to Mrs. Cope's excitement, and brought me grapes and a new book about the Antarctic to while away the time.

'Don't hurry back to work, Miss Dean,' he said as he rose to go. 'Take another week off. I miss you very much, but I can manage for another week, and you deserve a little holiday.'

I was glad of the week, it was lovely autumn weather, and, when I had recovered sufficiently I went and sat in Kensington Gardens and watched the children playing. I felt weak and silly, and the happiness of the children, as they ran about and shouted at each other, touched a spring in my heart. They were so gay and pretty in the sunshine, like a flock of bright birds flitting to and fro. I had missed all that in my life — all the joys of normal womanhood — I was a very lonely woman, on the way to a lonely old age.

I wrote to Kitty saying that I was sorry for what had occurred and asking her to come to see me if she was in town, but I had no reply. Kitty vanished out of my life. She was angry with me, I knew. She had wanted me to lie, and I would not lie — I could not. Even if I *had* lied and said that I had looked into the bedroom and seen her there before I left the flat, nobody would have believed me.

I went over the whole case — all that I could remember of it — as I sat in the gardens in the sunshine with the children playing round me. I thought that if I could only get the whole thing straight and understand it, I could dismiss it from my mind, and that was what I wanted above all things. It was so horrible, so sordid and shameful, it made me feel unclean to think about it; and yet I had to think about it, because I could not understand it. There were several things about the case that baffled me completely.

Strangely enough it was Mr. Corrieston who enabled me to see the case in its proper light. I was sitting on a seat in the gardens and I saw him walking past. He looked very dapper in his top hat and morning coat. He saw me sitting there and came over the grass toward me, raising his hat.

'May I sit down and talk to you for a few minutes, Miss Dean?' he inquired.

'If you want to,' I replied. It seemed strange that he should want to talk to me, considering that I had lost him his case. He had worked for victory with such amazing energy, and I had brought him defeat; but it was evident from his manner that he bore me no ill-will, and he did not look like a defeated man; he was cheerful and brisk as ever and very smart.

Mr. Corrieston smiled at me in a friendly manner and sat down beside me. 'Of course I want to,' he said. 'I should not have asked for permission to talk to you if I had not wanted it.'

'I thought you might be annoyed with me,' I replied, half smiling in return.

'It was not your fault, Miss Dean.'

'I know, but — '

'So I am not annoyed with you. I am not an unreasonable man.'

'Why did you advise my sister to defend?' I asked him. 'She had not a leg to stand on as far as I can see.'

'It was rather a strange case — but I was sure we could win, and Mr. Amber was quite confident.'

'But why?'

'For several reasons.' He ticked them off on his fat stubby fingers as he spoke. '*One* — Mrs. Wisdon is a very pretty woman and a very charming one. I was sure she would make a good witness, and she did. *Two* — Mr. Wisdon is hot-tempered and impatient. I was sure he would make a bad witness, and he did. *Three* — we thought the alibi was secure. Mrs. Wisdon had spent the night with her sister, therefore she could not have been at Maidenhead — these hotel proprietors and chambermaids can usually be discredited or bamboozled if the defense is at all convincing. *Four* — you have an honest face.'

'Then it all hung upon me?'

'It all hung upon you,' smiled Mr. Corrieston.

'But you said — '

'I said what I said for your good — and ours. I did not want you to think your evidence supremely important. You would have been even more nervous than you were.'

'And you think — but for Mrs. Cope — we would have won?'

'I think so. That woman upset the apple-cart — an interesting type, Miss Dean.'

'You don't seem at all upset at losing the case. I suppose you get used to it,' I said, not very tactfully I'm afraid.

He laughed heartily. 'I'm not so used to it as all that,' he said. 'To tell you the truth I don't often lose a case. If I had lost the case through carelessness, or for want of forethought, or through any mistake on my part I should have been very much upset. As it was, the case was perfectly handled.'

I disagreed with Mr. Corrieston, but I did not voice my opinion. I wanted to ask some more questions while he was in the mood to answer them.

'If you had trusted me, instead of bewildering me on purpose — ' I began.

'Ho! ho! So I bewildered you on purpose,' he said, laughing foxily. 'That was very reprehensible indeed.'

'It was very foolish,' I told him frankly.

'It was not foolish, Miss Dean. The first time I saw you I formed the opinion that you were too honest to be trusted — my judgment is rarely at fault. You would have made an excellent witness if you had been certain of your ground. If you had been sure that Mrs. Wisdon had slept in your bed — as you *were* until Mrs. Cope appeared on the scene — you would have convinced the jury quite easily and given Mrs. Wisdon the necessary alibi. That was all we wanted from you, but we wanted it badly. Everything would have gone well if it had not been for Mrs. Cope.'

'I could have warned you about Mrs. Cope,' I pointed out. 'If I hadn't been completely in the dark I *would* have warned you.'

'I didn't know that such a person as Mrs.

Cope existed,' said Mr. Corrieston. 'I didn't know that there was anything to be warned about. I could see no danger at all from keeping you in the dark — as you so aptly put it — and I could see the dangers of enlightening you quite clearly. I knew that you would be useless as a witness unless you could give your evidence with a perfectly clear conscience — and I was right.'

'I don't quite see — '

'You *were* useless,' he said smiling. 'Because you believed Mrs. Cope, you were worse than useless. But don't worry too much, the case was lost before you gave your evidence — irretrievably lost. It was lost when Mrs. Cope went into the box. She was the unexpected factor in the case.'

'I wonder how Garth's solicitor found her,' I said musingly.

'They made a fortunate hit. Law is like that, Miss Dean, there is a good deal of luck in the way the cards fall. I don't mind losing a rubber when the cards are against me and my conscience is clear.'

'And if you had won the case,' I asked him, 'won it knowing that you had won it by a lie?'

'Would my conscience still have been clear?' he said, laughing. 'That's what you meant, isn't it? Oh, Miss Dean, you have much too tender a conscience for this world! That is my living. If I can win a case for a client who is not altogether innocent of what he is accused I am all the more pleased. Some men refuse such cases when they can afford to do so, but I shall never do that. Such cases interest me intensely, there is more in them, and they require more careful handling. I love to pit my brain against another equally astute. To watch skillful counsel handling such a case is meat and drink to me. To listen as he makes a point, or skates gracefully over a thin patch of ice, to see him encouraging one witness or bamboozling another — it is a great game. The most fascinating game in the world.'

We sat in silence for a minute or two while I assimilated the information I had gained. Mr. Corrieston had surprised me. I found I did not dislike him now; in fact I quite liked him. He had opened his heart to me and shown me his real self. I saw his point of view, and, although it could never be mine, I found it less despicable than I had expected.

'I'm afraid your sister is taking this hard,' he said at last.

'I don't know — yes, I expect she is. I haven't seen her.'

He shook his head. 'She blames you — the most innocent and well-meaning of sisters — how like a charming lady!'

'Do you know where she is?' I inquired.

'I do. But I cannot tell you. She is not in London, I am glad to say. I found your sister slightly exhausting, Miss Dean. She is very charming, of course, but like many charming ladies she lacks balance, and she has too few reticences. She does not bear her burdens on her own back; she unloads them onto the nearest person with a sublime disregard of the said person's feelings. Just a *leetle* bit inconsiderate, don't you find?'

'So she was angry with you, too?' I said, and I couldn't help smiling.

'She was angry with me, too.'

'Will she marry Mr. Hamilton, now?'

'My dear lady!' exclaimed Mr. Corrieston with a return of the manner which I so detested. 'My *dear* lady, I do not know. If I knew I would tell you — that I do not know.'

'So that's that,' I said, laughing against my will.

'Yes,' he said. 'That's that — and I hope we part friends, Miss Dean. You do not bear me any grudge for keeping you in the dark I hope?'

'I still think it was foolish policy.'

'And I still think it was wise.'

We shook hands and he got up and walked away quickly.

# 7

## *The Cross-Roads*

I am now nearing the point where I want your advice, Clare. You will have been wondering why I have been so long in coming to the point, and why all this history — somewhat sordid in parts — should be necessary. I did not intend it to be so long when I started to write it. I thought a few pages would suffice to put the facts before you; but, as I wrote, I found that all that had happened in my life had a bearing on my choice of roads, and, to tell the truth, the task of writing it all down eased my mind and cleared my brain. Already I feel lightened, as if part of the burden of my loneliness and perplexity had fallen from my shoulders. I am doing what Mr. Corrieston deplored when he said of Kitty, 'She does not bear her burdens on her own back; she unloads them onto the nearest person.' You are my nearest person, Clare, so I am unloading my burdens onto you, but you will not *really* have to bear them upon your back, my dear, for you will never read this history.

When Mr. Corrieston had gone I went home slowly, thinking over all he had said. There was a big car standing outside the main door of my flat, and I wondered, as I passed up the stairs, whose car it could be. Big cars seldom find their way to France Street; the people in the flats below mine are all as poor and friendless as myself. As I reached the top floor, fumbling for my key, I saw that somebody was waiting for me on the landing — a tall, broad-shouldered man in a navy blue overcoat and a soft gray hat. He turned as I came up the last few steps and I saw that it was Garth.

'Garth!' I said in amazement.

'Yes, Garth,' he said, smiling rather sadly. 'Garth come to trouble you further with his unfortunate affairs. May I come in for a few minutes, Char?'

I opened the door and we went in. He had never been in my flat before and I wondered what he was thinking of it. It took him all his time to squeeze past Jeremiah into the sitting room. Even there he looked immense, towering over everything, filling the whole place with his presence.

'Won't you sit down?' I said.

He chose the old schoolroom chair which had come from the Parsonage.

'I feel quite at home in this chair,' he said, 'although it seems to have grown a good deal smaller since the last time I sat in it.'

I laughed nervously and began to make the tea.

'I suppose you are very angry with me, Char,' he suggested, after a few moments' silence.

'I don't know,' I said. 'I really don't know. I don't understand why you did it — it was so horrible — but you didn't come here to ask me that.'

'No, I didn't,' he admitted. 'I came to ask you — but you must let me do this in my own way, or it will be hopeless. I want to explain first of all why I had to do it, why I had to divorce Kitty.'

'I know you were within your rights,' I told him. 'She behaved disgracefully, but so did you.'

'What do you mean, Char?'

'You weren't kind to her,' I said. 'If you had been kind she wouldn't have wanted — other people. She was so young when you married her that I think you could have made something of her if you had tried. Couldn't you have tried, Garth? Couldn't you have helped her? You turned away from her — '

I stopped suddenly, for a lump had risen in my throat and I could not go on. I was still weak and foolish after my illness.

'Yes,' he said slowly. 'Yes, I turned away from her.'

There was silence for a few moments and a coal fell out of the fire which Mrs. Cope had lighted for me before she left. Garth leaned forward and put it back.

'I can't forgive you easily for that,' I told him in a voice that was blurred with tears. 'You are so much older than Kitty, so much wiser — and you had promised to love her and cherish her.'

'That's true, Char,' he said gravely. 'That's quite true, and I can't explain — anything. I'm sorry you feel it hard to forgive me because it makes it harder for me to ask you — what I have come to ask you.'

'What have you come to ask me?'

'A favor,' he said slowly. 'I'll tell you about it

soon — after we have had tea.'

I set the tea on the little table near the fire, Garth looked round the room and his eyes brightened. 'I wondered where the old schoolroom bureau had gone,' he said. 'It's friendly to see the old thing again. I always liked that nice fat bulge in front — what a job you must have had getting it through the door!'

'It was an awful job,' I told him.

'Did you know Kitty is going to marry George Hamilton?'

'No, I didn't know.'

'I'm glad. Hamilton loves her and I think they will be happy.'

'Then you did it for *her*,' I said eagerly. 'For her sake, so that she could be happy.'

'I did it for Clem's sake,' he said sternly. 'For Clem and nobody else at all. Kitty is not worth considering.' He moved uneasily in his chair. 'I could have divorced her before — there was a fellow called Bridges, and — well — one or two others, but they were all cads — none of them would have married her — and I didn't want to turn her loose. Kitty isn't the sort of woman who can fend for herself.'

I was aghast. I could not speak.

'Don't be so upset, Char,' said Garth, smiling sadly. 'Just think of us both as being caught in a trap from which there is no escape — except this horrible business of divorce.'

'It was so — so *dreadful*,' I said, shuddering at the recollection.

'I had to do it, Char. You must believe me when I tell you that. The whole atmosphere was so bad for Clem — it was ruining Clem. I'm not sure that it hasn't ruined her already. Clem is eleven now, and she is clever. I mean she sees things she shouldn't see, understands things she shouldn't understand. I'm sure we didn't understand the affairs of our elders when we were Clem's age. They would have passed over our heads. Children seem to be different nowadays; perhaps it is because they are so much with grown-up people. Grown-up people are interested in them, talk to them and bring them forward. When we were young we were just children — rather a nuisance to our elders, rather a bore. I felt that everything was all wrong for Clem and there was only one way out of the mess so I took it. I couldn't let Kitty divorce me because I had to have Clem; she is my daughter — she is all I have left out of the wreck. I had to have Clem, and anyhow I was sick of lies. If I had let Kitty divorce me I should have had to trump up a whole lot of evidence and lie myself blue in the face. I couldn't do it — besides I had to have Clem. You see that don't you, Char?'

'Yes,' I said.

'Well, that brings me to my reason for coming here. Will you come to Hinkleton and look after Clem while I'm away? Please do, Char. I've promised to go with Fraser on this expedition of his to Africa — or rather he has promised to take me — it's a great chance and I want to go, I must get away from everything — I *must*. I shall go mad if I don't get away, right away from everything. The expedition is going to penetrate into the heart of the desert — it will be marvelous, intensely interesting. I was out there four years ago — you read my book? Well, now I want to go farther, to penetrate right into the interior. Fraser is going on business, prospecting for an airplane route, and several well-known scientists are going for their own purposes. Fraser knows me and says he'll take me if I pay my way — it's a wonderful chance!' He got up and moved about the tiny room like a caged beast. 'Do think of it, Char,' he said. 'It would be a rest for you, wouldn't it? You look as if you needed a rest.'

'I couldn't afford to lose my job.'

'You are taking on another job,' he said quickly. 'It will be a business arrangement, of course. Don't think about the money part of it — trust me to see to that. Afterward, when I come back we can find you something else — Wentworth would take you back if you wanted that, or we could look about for something better. Don't think of that now.'

'I have to think of it.'

'No, you don't have to think of it. You shan't lose by doing me this service; surely you realize that I would not let you lose by it.'

'I see so many — difficulties,' I told him. He had swept me off my feet by his vehemence, and I was trying hard to find firm ground.

'What difficulties?'

'I am a hermit. I have not mixed with people for years.'

'You will find it quite easy to be a hermit at Hinkleton.'

'And another thing: I should find it very hard

to come back to this, after Hinkleton. Hinkleton would spoil me for the life I have to lead.'

He looked at me as if he understood, and then he walked over to the window and stood there, fiddling with the blind.

'I see that,' he said in a queer, strained voice. 'But I'm going on being selfish all the same. You see, I shall be away a year at least, perhaps longer, and I must have somebody I can trust at Hinkleton. Somebody to look after Clem. Nanny is there, of course, but she is getting old and she can't control things — she doesn't understand Clem. Clem is a difficult child to understand,' he sighed.

'How would Nanny like it?' I asked.

'It was Nanny's idea. She thought you would come for Clem's sake, because Clem is your god-child. She thought it would be good for you to have the rest.'

'I'll think about it,' I told him doubtfully.

'Do. You wouldn't find it dull, would you? There's hunting, you know. Clem loves it and you could hunt too.'

I did not answer that. I couldn't, without giving myself away completely. Dull! Dull to be at Hinkleton! No, Garth, it wouldn't be dull. It might be too painful, though, too painful to find myself temporary mistress of Hinkleton Manor.

He went away after a little and I said I would write and tell him when I had decided what to do.

* * *

So now you know, Clare. Now you know the whole story and can help me to choose my path. Am I to leave my hermit's cell and venture forth into the world, or am I to stay here and settle down comfortably into my old life? I love Hinkleton — but perhaps I love it too much, too much to go and live there for a year and then leave it. The last time I left Hinkleton it nearly killed me. It took me years to get used to my new life, years of misery, they were. But now the misery and the pain have passed, passed in long nights of tears, and I am resigned, almost contented with my lot. Am I to risk further misery and pain because Garth wants me to look after his child — Garth who took my heart and broke it, who left it dead and withered so that no other man could touch it, who took from me my womanhood, my wifehood, my motherhood — the best things in life. I owe nothing to Garth, he has ruined us both — Kitty and me.

Hinkleton will awaken memories that have slept for years. I shall see again the country lanes starred with flowers, the woods, the little stream, the wide green meadows. I shall live in a beautiful house surrounded by every luxury, with servants to wait upon me and anticipate my every need. All this I shall have if I accept Garth's offer, all this and more. Can I bear to have it for a little while and then come back to this?

If I decide to do this thing and face the pain, it will be for Clementina's sake. For the sake of a child I have not seen for six years. Garth said she was a difficult child; difficult to understand. He said that Nanny did not understand Clementina

— is it likely that I should do better? The prospect terrifies me. If I face it I shall face it because of the vows I made when I held Clementina in my arms eleven years ago. It seems strange that those promises, which seemed so empty at the time, should weigh so heavily in the balance now.

Oh, Clare, tell me what I must do! I have been content in my life here, in my life of books and dreams, and I could be content again. I am used to it now, used to the loneliness and the discomforts. I could settle down into the old groove peacefully — almost happily. What shall I do?

# 8

## *The Road Is Chosen*

I had written thus far. It had taken me many hours. I had written far into the night while the fire died down and the noises of London faded and grew dim. I had written thus far, and I put down my pen and wondered what you would say. Would you bid me go or stay? Would you choose for me the high road of adventure or the low road of safety? And then, quite suddenly, and naturally I heard your voice, Clare, and I saw your vivid face as you turned to look at me and held out your hand for the bunch of country flowers.

'Pain is worthwhile sometimes,' you said.

# Part Three

# *Clementina's Father*

# 1

## *Altered Circumstances*

Sixteen months have passed since I wrote the preceding pages, and much has happened. My life has completely changed in the interval, so much so that I sometimes think — like the old woman in the song — 'This is none of I.' And yet, though my circumstances have altered, the essential part of me is the same as ever. The same Charlotte, who lived in a poky flat and spent her days working in the dim library, now dwells in a mansion and orders things as she pleases. The same Charlotte, who sat up at night to turn her old winter coat, and dyed her shabby hat to make it do for a few months longer, can now have a complete new outfit whenever she needs it. But for all that she is the same woman, the same thoughts play havoc with her sleep, the same history lies behind her, and the same lean face — slightly browner and healthier looking I must admit — still looks at her from the mirror when she does her hair.

Sixteen months have passed, and, once more, I am taking up my pen. I intend to write an account of all that has happened since my arrival at Hinkleton Manor — the good things and the bad. I want to get my thoughts straightened out before I embark upon the task which lies before me. There are no cross-roads this time, my way is clearly marked. I can look ahead and see my way spread before me — a lonely way, but useful. A way marked out for my feet by the dead.

My reason for writing is different this time, it is not your advice that I am asking for, Clare, it is your companionship, your sympathy. I want to feel you here beside me in the long lonely winter evenings when the sun has gone down and I cannot work in the garden any longer; when I am tired of reading and the big empty library of the Manor is full of shadows — full of ghosts. So once more I am sitting down, pen in hand, at the old schoolroom bureau — which has been brought down to the library from my bedroom where it has been standing for the last sixteen months — and once more I look up and see you sitting by the fire with your bright eyes full of interest and understanding.

Clare, I was afraid I should lose you when I came here, but I have not lost you. You have come here too; I have felt you near me often and often, helping me over innumerable difficulties which beset my inexperience, giving me your advice, standing beside me, giving me confidence to go forward in my new life. You have come here too, you and I and Jeremiah and the bureau and the old chair and a few other odds and ends of furniture that I wanted to keep. Garth was kind about the old furniture, he did not sneer at the shabbiness which shows up so sadly among the polished perfection of Hinkleton Manor. He sent a van for my belongings, and when I arrived they were waiting for me — Jeremiah in the hall where Kitty had always wanted him, and the other things in the beautiful bedroom which had been prepared for me upstairs. It was nice to see them there (although, as I said before, their shabbiness was very apparent in their new luxurious setting); they made me feel more at home. And when things became too difficult, and my heart failed me, it was comforting to sit down in the old basket chair, whose knobby cushions had grown into my form, and to feel that it was my very own — an old friend, who had seen me through countless vicissitudes and countless crises.

The other things in the flat I sold. It seemed foolish to keep them and pay storage on them — they were not worth it. But I did not see them go unmoved. I felt somehow as if I were a traitor to them — they had grown old in my service, they were worn and pathetic. I knew every scratch upon the sideboard, every tear in the upholstery of the couch. And now I was selling them for a handful of silver — and a small handful at that. Where would they go, poor silent companions of my life? What hovel, what sordid lodging would give them house-room? Who would eat their meals off the table which had served me so faithfully for twelve long years?

I see you looking at me, Clare, with a whimsical expression in your eyes. 'How verbose the creature gets!' it seems to say. 'Has she brought me here to listen to a memorial upon her old furniture? Get on with the job, Charlotte.'

# 2

## *Arrival at Hinkleton*

It was wet and mild when I arrived at Hinkleton. The trees, touched with autumn color, dripped slowly. The gray light from the gray sky turned their wet leaves to silver and copper. Garth had sent a car to meet me at the station, and I stood in the rain while the porter and the chauffeur strapped my luggage onto the grid and disposed of my various bags and bundles in the car. I loved the rain, I loved the mild air with its smell of damp earth and dripping verdure, I loved the soft gray sky spread out like a canopy above my head. Even the station yard with its brown oily puddles pleased me — it was Hinkleton, and that was all that mattered.

I asked the chauffeur to stop at the church for a moment, and I went in and looked about me. Here everything was the same, dear and familiar. The old church did not change — generations might come and go but the old gray building did not alter. At first it seemed as if a thousand years had passed since I had stood within its portals, and then it seemed that I had been here but yesterday. Almost, as I gazed up the nave, I expected to see father come out of the vestry door and walk round the front of the pulpit and up the altar steps, pausing for a moment to bend his head reverently to his God. His spirit was very near me, his arms enfolded me. I kneeled down and hid my face. Prayer did not come easily to me for I always feel that prayer is a silent thing, an opening of the heart. To ask for earthly benefits, to reel out a list of requirements and expect them to be supplied is not prayer. It is putting God in the same category as an intelligent grocer. But that day in Hinkleton Church I felt that something was listening to the speaking of my heart. The spirit of my earthly father and the Spirit of my Heavenly Father blessed me in my new life. I was sure then that the road I had chosen was the right road, and I went on my way strengthened.

As I came out of the church I paused for a few moments at my parents' grave — it was more for my conscience' sake than from any emotional feeling about the small green plot of ground. They were not here (I had felt father's nearness in the church — here I could feel nothing). I saw that the grave was well cared for; the edges were tidy and the turf smooth and free from weeds. I wondered who had seen to this, for it had never crossed my mind to make any arrangements about it.

The chauffeur was waiting for me at the gate, so I could not linger. I got into the car and we drove on through the village.

Hinkleton village had changed very little; there was nothing to change it. No new houses had been built, so there was no need for any expansion in the shops. The shops had the same names over the doors, the same heterogeneous collection of goods in the windows. Hinkleton had not moved with the times. The ironmonger's window was full of nails, hammers, spades, etc. The sweetshop still contained bottles of highly colored boiled sweets. I wondered if Miss Canning was alive. She had been a true friend in my childhood, helping me with inexhaustible patience to decide how to spend my rare pennies to the best advantage. The butcher was standing at the door of his shop gazing out at the rain. His blue and white striped apron bulged over his portly stomach, his red double chin bulged over his collar — twelve years had done very little to Mr. Hetherington, save to increase the bulges. Behind him, as usual, hung the carcasses of sheep, waiting to be dismembered. They had that strange naked look which always disgusted me as a child.

The entrance gates of Hinkleton Manor are just beyond the village. We turned in through the narrow arch and sped up the drive. I remembered every turn. It was just here that I had fallen off my bicycle — *there* was the very holly bush which had received me in its inhospitable arms and left its signature upon my body for days. Garth had been trying to teach me to ride. He came and picked me out of the holly bush and his efforts not to laugh at my plight were nobility personified. And just here one caught a glimpse of the Hinkle meandering lazily through the park — there it was, a gray shining ribbon in the vivid green turf.

Garth came to the door as the car drove up, and behind him I could see a tall, slim child in a brown frock. I had no time then to look at her intelligently — she raised a cool cheek to be kissed and moved silently away — but afterward I was to study the face with anxious care, to learn its every feature. A smooth face, it was, pale, without being delicate, with a strange, shuttered look unnatural in a child of her age. She had a high, white forehead from which her brown hair swept back in a long shallow wave to be confined in two thick plaits which hung down her back. Her ears were small and well-formed, her cheekbones were rather high, her chin was determined, her mouth straight and red. It was the face of one who kept her emotions to herself. *She* did not lay the burden of her moods upon all and sundry, she went her own way, silent and withdrawn. If Kitty were an undisciplined woman she had not given birth to an undisciplined child. Clementina was not undisciplined, for she had herself well in hand, but she would tolerate no discipline but her own. All this I learned later, not then. It was a long time before I learned to understand her and accept her reticences.

Garth's trunks were in the hall, for he was starting the following morning. There were guns there too, and wooden packing-cases, nailed and roped; and long-shaped packages sewn up in sacking. He led the way into the library where tea was laid on a small table near the fire. Clementina followed us; she took a book and sat down on a small stool near the window while we talked over a few last arrangements and had our tea. It was easy to see how she heard and saw things that a child should not. She was so quiet that one forgot she was there.

'You can work in this room, Char,' Garth said. 'It gets the sun most of the day and is quiet and comfortable. Open the drawing room if you want it, of course.'

(My work was to consist of reading for Mr. Wentworth. He had been so devastated by my desertion that I had promised to read and send him criticisms of the latest travel books which he would dispatch to me weekly. And in return he had promised to keep my place open for me.)

'I should like to work here,' I replied. 'The drawing room is too grand for me.' To tell the truth I did not care for the drawing room at Hinkleton Manor, it was ornate and uncomfortable. I could not imagine myself sitting in its brocade chairs in solitary state, nor view with equanimity the prospect of seeing myself constantly, at full length, in the gilt mirrors with which its walls were adorned.

'It is a flamboyant room,' Garth agreed with a curl of his lips. 'Your sister had execrable taste.'

The words annoyed me. I felt my anger rise like a flood. I felt that Garth was deliberately insulting. There was no need for him to mention Kitty if he could not do so without a sneer. Heaven knows I held no brief for Kitty, but I felt bound to stand up for her against this incomprehensible man. He had ruined her, and broken her, he had cast her off like a worn garment, the least he could do was to let her memory rest in peace.

'You did not trouble to educate her taste,' I told Garth, with a flutter of fear at my heart.

Garth did not seem angry at my temerity. He glanced at the silent figure by the window and replied in a low voice, 'Kitty preferred to take her education from other hands.'

We left the subject there, and passed on to discuss other matters. The financial side of the business was already fixed. Garth had been generous — too generous, I thought. He had brushed aside my objections to his generosity with the remark that I should need new clothes. It was true, of course, and I had realized before that my wardrobe was insufficient for the temporary chatelaine of the Manor, but it did not please me that he had noticed my shabbiness. We are unreasonable beings.

'What about the servants?' I inquired.

'What about them?' echoed Garth. 'You will run the servants of course, and pay them. I've arranged for that at the bank. We went into that before.'

'I know. But supposing they are unsatisfactory?'

'Sack them,' he said. 'Sack the lot if you like and start fresh. I don't care. Sack all the maids, and Barling, the butler — he's a fat fool and drinks my port — and Naseby, the chauffeur, you may sack him, too; and all the gardeners — lazy devils. It would do them a world of good to be sacked. The only man you mustn't sack is Sim — the head groom. He's been with me for ten years and understands my ways. I'd be sorry if I came back and found that Sim had been included in your holocaust. The stables wouldn't be the same without Sim. So, unless you find him stealing the silver or dead drunk on the harness-room floor, don't sack Sim.'

'I don't want to sack anybody,' I replied with some heat. 'I hate the idea.'

'You'll soon get used to it, and you'll have a lovely time finding others.'

I suppose I looked somewhat dismayed at the prospect, for Garth laughed. 'Who did you suppose was going to do it?' he inquired.

'I've had no experience.'

'You'll learn,' he said. 'I'm glad I shan't be here to suffer from your mistakes.'

'I'm glad, too,' I replied with spirit. It was really unbearable that he should speak to me in that way when I had changed my whole life to look after his child. Surely he owed me civility if nothing else. I began to understand what Kitty had suffered at this man's hands.

'I suppose I shall manage,' I continued hotly. 'Other women do. But it seems strange to find oneself in a position of responsibility when one is totally ignorant of the rules. Like a man being put at the head of a business when his life has been spent on a farm, or being made colonel of a regiment without the smallest knowledge of military affairs.'

'It's true,' Garth said, looking at me in surprise.

'Of course it's true,' I replied. 'The whole thing is ridiculous. I shall do my best, of course, because I've taken on the job, but I'm not looking forward to it, I can assure you. I don't mind undertaking any job that I feel I can do, but this is a job I know nothing about and for which I am totally unfitted.'

'Nonsense,' Garth interrupted, but his manner was less rough than before. 'Don't talk rubbish, Char. It's a woman's job to run a house, and most women undertake it with complete confidence in their own ability. If you do make mistakes at first what does it matter? Kitty made a glorious hash of it, and never learned from experience to do better, but it was never *her* fault — dear me no — always somebody else's.'

I did not answer, it was no use. He was so bitter against Kitty that he could not refrain from speaking of her, and he could not speak of her calmly. We sat in silence for a little while and I was able to study his face more closely. How changed it was! It seemed to me the saddest face I had ever seen. There were deep lines of pain about the mouth, and the eyes were dark with trouble. It was the face of a man who was tired of life, totally disillusioned, sick in soul, the face of a man who did not care what happened to him. What was he thinking about, I wondered. The expedition ahead of him or the troubles that he could not leave behind? I was very vague about the expedition upon which he was embarking, it was to penetrate the interior of Africa — that I knew — and Garth had given me a paper with the names of the places he expected to visit and approximate dates so that I might communicate with him if I wanted to do so; but after the end of December there were no places, nor dates, and I supposed that the expedition would then be completely out of touch with civilization. Would it be dangerous, I wondered, and if dangerous why, and in what way? Did the danger (if danger there were) come from men or beasts, or from climate and fevers? I had read Garth's book on big game hunting when it came out, and enjoyed it. Garth was at his best writing about the vicissitudes of travel; he was a competent writer and had the knack of making small things interesting and amusing. I had liked his descriptions of the country and his account of the game to be found.

'What is your real objective?' I said to him at last.

He turned and looked at me, and I saw that I had brought him back from a long journey. He did not know what I meant.

'The object of your expedition,' I explained.

'Oh, that,' he said slowly. 'I expect to find the remnants of an ancient tribe. Perhaps it may be more truthful to say I *hope* to find them. I have not told anybody about this. For one thing nobody has asked me, and for another they would probably laugh at my credulity.'

'Why have you told me?'

'You asked, and it suddenly struck me that *somebody* ought to know, in case I never came back.' He looked across the room and added in a louder tone, 'Isn't it your bedtime, Clem?'

'Nanny will come for me,' she replied, without raising her head, which was bent over her book.

'You're too old for that now,' Garth said in a light, bantering voice. 'Too old to wait for Nanny to come and fetch you to bed — a great big girl of eleven!'

Clementina did not answer. The jibe —

friendly and provocative — ran off her like water off a duck's back. She turned over a page and continued to read.

'After dinner,' Garth whispered, and he reached for the poker to stir the fire. It struck me then that Garth's daughter was going to be a big responsibility — just how big I did not guess. Perhaps I had been wrong to undertake the responsibility. I knew so little about children. I had no ideas upon the subject — as so many childless women have. The only child I had ever known intimately was Kitty, and I could see already that whatever experience I had had with Kitty was not going to help me to understand her daughter. I must confess, Clare, that my heart sank. I felt that I should never find the clue to Clementina. The incident was small — she had not disobeyed her father, for he had not ordered her to go to bed, but her attitude was so strange, so unchildlike. I would have been less disturbed if she had shown temper, had resented his suggestion; it was the utter indifference of her attitude that frightened me.

We spoke of other matters until Nanny came for Clementina. I had expected trouble then, but there was none. Clementina rose at once, shut her book and came over to the fire to say good night to us. She waited quietly until Nanny was ready to go.

'Oh, Miss Char!' cried Nanny taking my hand. 'It *was* nice of you to come!'

I was touched at the welcome, the first real welcome I had had. 'It was nice of you to want me,' I replied. I saw that she had aged considerably since the last time I had seen her. There were flecks of gray among the smooth darkness of her hair. Her eyes had faded in color, and there was a blurring of the iris which one often sees in the old. She was thinner, and the red of her cheeks was not so smooth and healthy as of yore. I realized suddenly that the troubles of Garth and Kitty had laid their mark here also.

'You look as if you needed a good rest,' Nanny said. 'I'll see you get your breakfast in bed. Clemmie and me have ours in the nursery.'

'You're going to spoil me,' I told her.

'You want a little spoiling, Miss Char,' she replied smiling. 'You were always such a good child, so serious and conscientious.'

I laughed at that, and Garth laughed too. 'Oh, Nanny,' he said, 'you old fraud! You didn't think she was a good child at all.'

'I did indeed.'

'No, no. It was always Char who thought of the lovely, amusing, naughty things to do. You used to say you never had a peaceful moment when Char came to tea. You never knew what we would be up to next — it was always something different.'

'Never anything wicked,' Nanny said, laughing in spite of herself.

'Do you remember the day we dressed up as Red Indians, and Char took the feather out of your best bonnet?'

'She didn't do it a bit of harm!'

'You were awfully angry with me,' I reminded her, wiping my eyes. I had not laughed for so long that I felt quite hysterical.

'Oh well,' said Nanny, 'we're all older now, and we've been through a good deal, one way and another. I don't mind so much about feathers and such-like nowadays. There's more important things than feathers even if they are out of your best bonnet.'

Clementina stood and listened to the conversation — or perhaps she did not listen, it was hard to tell. She did not look sullen, or impatient, she was simply uninterested in our reminiscences. When we had finished talking she kissed us both lightly, and followed Nanny out of the room.

# 3

## *The Bracelet Men*

It was not until after dinner that Garth and I had any private conversation. I had left him to consume his port in peace, in the time-honored manner, but he soon followed me into the library and stood in front of the fire, leaning against the mantelpiece and looking down at the fire.

'I didn't want to say too much before Clem,' he said, and I had the feeling that he was choosing his words carefully. 'She's such a strange child. You never know whether she is listening or not. She picks up all sorts of information about things — you never can tell what is going on inside her head — and there's no doubt she knows — she knows all sorts of things she shouldn't know.'

'She's so quiet,' I said.

'Yes, it's unnatural, isn't it? I hope you will learn to understand her, Char.'

'I hope so,' I replied soberly.

He looked at me sharply. 'You don't seem to be sure about it.'

'I should be a fool if I were. I shall do my best, of course, because that is what I have come for, but — '

'Oh, well,' he said. 'Perhaps it is better to start by not being too sure. I don't know that I understand Clem myself if it comes to that. She is so different from what we were, when we were children. She is never naughty in an ordinary childish way. It wouldn't amuse Clem to take the feather out of Nanny's bonnet to dress up as a Red Indian.'

'No, I don't suppose it would.'

'You see that already,' Garth said eagerly. 'Sometimes I wish that Clem would do mischievous things — it would be more natural — but she never does. She is never wild and troublesome. If she is disobedient it is in a considered way.'

'What do you mean by that?' I asked him.

'I mean if you tell her to do something she doesn't want to do, she just doesn't do it. She neither flaunts her disobedience in your face, nor hides it. She simply goes her own way. It's very difficult to tackle. You'll find her quite amenable to discipline so long as your discipline does not inconvenience her or interfere with her affairs. If she wants a thing she asks for it, and if you refuse it to her you hear no more about it. If she can attain her object without your aid she simply attains it. She never tries to wheedle you — she has no charm, thank God!'

The last words were said with such a wealth of bitterness, such an intensity of feeling, that I was quite startled. I looked up at Garth; he was still standing on the hearthrug, gazing into the fire, and I saw that his face was drawn and haggard like the face of an old man. How he has suffered, I thought. I saw then, for the first time, that it was the mixture of strength and weakness in

Garth's nature which made him so vulnerable to suffering. A weaker man would have bowed his head before the storm; a stronger man could have ridden it out. Garth was so fashioned that the storm twisted him, tortured him beyond bearing, left him maimed, but still upright, still rebellious. Everything that followed confirmed me in my opinion; I had found some sort of clue to Garth, if not to his daughter.

After a little silence Garth continued, 'You can't drive Clem, you can't break her — she escapes from you into herself. She takes any punishment that you mete out to her without a word, simply accepts it. I'm telling you all this to help you. I want you to understand Clem, I want you to — to *find* her if you know what I mean. I love Clem dearly, she is all I have left out of the wreck, and I know she loves me, but to be quite honest I don't understand her. Perhaps it is difficult for a man to understand a girl-child. Sometimes when I think I have got her she slips through my fingers like a — like a ghost. But she has her good points: she is fearless, absolutely fearless, and I have never found deceit in her. I have searched for deceit in Clem, I have tried to trap her into a lie, but I have never succeeded.'

'Garth!' I exclaimed.

'It horrifies you,' he said, laughing unmirthfully, 'that I should lay traps for a child.'

'But why?'

'Can't you guess? I was looking for her mother in her, that's all. I wanted to find out how much of Kitty had found its way into Clem. So I laid traps for her — it doesn't sound very nice but I am not a very nice person, you see.'

'You used to be — nice,' I said with difficulty.

'Pshaw! That was long ago when I was young and ignorant. I thought the world was a marvelous place. I know better now, I know what hell life can be, and I know women. Women will always lie to gain their ends, they are made crooked.'

'Not all,' I exclaimed.

'Yes, all,' he replied. 'Thank God I shall be free from women for a year — you don't find women in the desert. For a whole year I shall live with men, reasonable beings who say what they mean and tell the truth. I'm sick of women, of their lies and subterfuges. Women clog the wheels of life — they take an unfair advantage of their reputed weakness. There is little weakness about a woman when she has a purpose to gain.'

'We are not all crooked, Garth,' I told him, in a low breathless voice — his violence frightened me. 'You have just said that Clementina is straight, that you searched for deceit in her and found none.'

'Clem is not a woman yet,' replied Garth. 'She will learn it all in time.'

I did not reply. His words had hurt me to the core. When had Garth found deceit in me, I wondered.

There was a long silence; he drifted into thought, his brow furrowed, his teeth gripping firmly the stem of his pipe. Presently he sighed like a person wakening from sleep and sat down in the big leather chair at the other side of the fire and stretched out his long legs. 'Africa has always fascinated me,' he said. 'That is why I went out there four years ago. The big game hunting was merely an excuse — it doesn't really amuse me to kill animals that have never harmed me — I wanted to meet Africa face to face. Of course I didn't because there wasn't time. I didn't know enough about it beforehand. I had engaged porters for a definite period, and I had not sufficient provisions. We were just approaching the really interesting part when I had to turn back. The porters were nervous, they thought I was cutting things too fine, they knew what it meant to be short of food — it meant death. But although I had not enough time to do what I wanted I saw enough to make me greedy for more. It is so wonderful to push off into the unknown, to leave civilization behind. You leave your troubles behind; they seem small in that immensity. A plain is more awe-inspiring than a mountain, because it seems limitless. The silence is healing, the stars — their brightness — they seem so much larger — oh, it is impossible to give you any idea of the unearthly beauty of it all. It is not really flat, you know. There are huge waves of sand. They stretch as far as you can see on every side — but it's no good. I can't *begin* to make you see it, Char. Just before we turned back a strange thing happened. One night I was sitting by the door of my tent — I was just going to turn in — when I heard a great jabbering of porters. I called the head boy and he told me that they had found the body of a man. It was half buried in the sand. I went over to have a look at it. The man had not been dead long. I was surprised at his appearance. He did not belong to any of the African races — at least none that I knew of. I am rather interested in physiology and I have studied the subject a bit so I knew enough to be fairly certain of my ground. After a brief examination I felt sure that the man belonged to some hitherto unknown tribe, it would take too long to tell you my reasons for this conclusion, suffice it to say he appeared to be higher in the social scale than the usual run of African. He differed from the known tribes in the measurements of his skull, and in the fine silky texture of his hair. His features were aquiline, his skin soft and pale brown. He wore bracelets of gold wrought with symbols and sights of which neither I nor any of the porters knew the meaning.'

'Did you bring the bracelets home?'

'I wanted to, but the porters made a terrific fuss when they saw what I meant to do. They are superstitious about robbing the dead. The head boy explained to me that the dead man's spirit would follow us and lead us astray and that we should all perish in the desert. I didn't care for that, of course, but the porters would not have stayed with me if I had taken the bracelets, and I didn't want to be left high and dry with no porters. That would have been the end of me, and not a pleasant end. I went back to my tent, meaning to try and get the bracelets later without being seen, I wanted them, not for their intrinsic worth, but for a proof that the man was real and not just a figment of my imagination. I knew that nobody would believe my story unless they saw the bracelets. The porters knew that I wanted the bracelets and they never gave me a chance to get them. In the morning the man had vanished, bracelets and all, vanished as mysteriously as he had come.'

'How exciting!' I exclaimed.

'You believe the story then,' he said, looking at me curiously. 'It's pretty far-fetched. Sometimes I hardly believe it myself.'

'You never found out any more,' I said.

'No, I could do nothing. Time was short and the stores were running low. We had to go back. But I made up my mind to return when I could manage it and try to find traces of the tribe to which the man belonged — it might be interesting. The man can't have fallen from the skies — there must be some explanation of his presence there.'

'How would you explain it?'

'I don't know,' he said thoughtfully. 'I should like to think that he belonged to an ancient civilized tribe, isolated in some fertile valley, but the real explanation is probably much less romantic. He might be some highborn Indian strayed from a caravan.'

'Oh no!' I cried. 'I'm sure you'll find the Bracelet Men.'

'Good lord! Why do you call them that?' he said quickly. 'That's what I call them when I think about them.'

I did not remind him that long ago we had been such close companions that our minds had constantly worked in unison — those days were dead. I could not speak of them. There were too many things about Garth that I did not understand; he was a man of mystery to me.

'Do you still keep a diary, Char?' he asked suddenly.

I said I did.

'So do I! The habit is rooted in me. I would as soon go to bed without brushing my teeth as omit to jot down the day's doings. It's funny how the diary habit persists. My last book was written entirely from my diary. I merely edited it, and added a few explanatory notes. I propose to do the same thing on this trip. I shall keep a full record of everything that happens and edit it on my return. I'm telling you this of set purpose, Char.' He laughed lightly and added, 'If I don't return you can write my book for me.'

'I hope there will be no question of that?'

'Do you?' he said, smiling wryly. 'I don't much care. Life isn't so damned wonderful.'

Garth filled his pipe again and puffed at it for a few moments in silence. The air was filled with a blue haze.

'Well, I think that's all,' he said at last. 'Perhaps you will excuse me, Char I've got some things to see to and I shall be off early in the morning. If there's anything you want ask Ponsonby — you've got his address.' He rose and held out his hand. 'Good-bye, Char. I'm sleeping tonight at the Parsonage. Rather funny, isn't it? Me at the Parsonage and you here.'

'At the Parsonage?' I exclaimed in amazement.

'Yes, at the Parsonage. Mr. Frale is old and deaf and a crashing bore, and the bed will probably be damp and stuffed with bricks but

I'm not taking any chances. I've been the butt of the County for years — every gossip-monger in the place makes free with my name. I prefer not to have it said that I inveigled you down to this house of ill fame and went to bed with you.'

'Oh, Garth, don't be so bitter!'

'House of ill fame is good,' he went on, with a sort of wild incoherence that was frightfully alarming. 'That motto in the hall — so appropriate don't you think — 'Valorous Men, Virtuous Women.' I thought at one time of tearing it down and putting a picture in its place — some biblical subject you know — but there were so many to choose from I couldn't make up my mind. I was deliberating whether to have David and Bathsheba, or Jezebel looking out of her window, when I suddenly saw the humor of it and decided to leave it as it was. It's the very thing to decorate a brothel, isn't it?'

'Don't torture yourself,' I said, or rather I tried to say it; he did not hear me or heed me.

'These things sound worse in plain language,' he continued with a wild laugh. 'I thought it was marvelous how they steered their way round all the nasty words in court; they referred to me as 'the petitioner' — it sounds much better than the cuckold, doesn't it? And respondent isn't really so offensive as whore — '

I felt as if I could not bear another word, it was cruel, cruel and disgusting. I think I hated Garth at that moment. I rose and made for the door without a word. He followed me and switched on the lights in the hall.

'Good night, Char,' he said when I was

halfway upstairs. I looked down over the banisters and saw him standing in the doorway of the library. He was smiling at me kindly, sadly. The harshness and bitterness had disappeared. 'Good night Char, and good-bye,' he said.

# 4

## *Brown Betty*

It was a long time before I could sleep, that night. Garth's outburst had upset me, had frightened me — he was obviously not normal. I wondered whether it was right for him to go to Africa when he was in such a state. And yet what could I do? I could not see myself suggesting to Garth that he should stay at home and see a doctor — what doctor could help him? It was his mind, not his body, that was diseased. I tossed and turned upon the comfortable bed, I went over the conversation word for word. Gradually the anger which had filled my heart waned, and was replaced by a deep pity. I saw that the pain of his wounds had maddened him so that he was no more responsible for his wild words than a trapped animal that snaps at a friendly hand. It was no use saying that Garth should have been able to rise above his troubles; none of us are perfect, and Garth was peculiarly vulnerable to the trouble which had befallen him on account of his family pride, his pride of race. He had been wounded in his most vulnerable part, and the wound was festering.

I remembered then what Garth had said about the peace of the desert, the healing silence. And how one's troubles seemed trivial in that immensity of space. Perhaps Africa would heal Garth's wounds. Perhaps he would leave his bitterness behind him and return, strong and well in mind and body, able once more to face life. The more I thought about it the more it seemed to me that it was the only chance for Garth — perhaps he, himself, knew this and was going to Africa in quest of his soul.

I slept after this, a light disturbed sleep full of vague dreams arid groundless alarms. The house awoke early. I heard the bustle of Garth's departure and then silence. It was better not to see him again before he went, much better. We had settled everything and there was nothing more to discuss. I had found last night that it was impossible for us to talk to each other like ordinary people, we had been too near each other for that, and now we were too far apart. We had been close friends, we had loved each other with passion, and then Garth had hated me — after all that how could we go back and be ordinary friends again? There was too much between us that could never be spoken of, never be explained. I realized very clearly that the less we saw of each other in the future the better it would be for us both.

When I had settled this in my mind I felt more peaceful. I was very tired, for there had been so much to arrange before leaving London, and the excitements and emotions of my arrival at Hinkleton had exhausted me. It was extraordinarily pleasant to lie in bed and have my breakfast brought to me on a tray. To glance through the papers at my leisure, and to know that I could stay in bed as long as I liked, and that when I chose to get up there was a bathroom — my very own bathroom — next door, complete with hot water, bath salts and towels hanging on hot rails awaiting my pleasure. Nobody can really appreciate luxury unless they have suffered long years of discomfort, I thought. I looked round the bright spacious room with its pretty chintz and polished furniture which was to be my home for at least a year. I should be ungrateful if I could not be happy here, ungrateful and foolish. I must make the most of my time, and look neither forward nor back. In the corner by the window stood the old schoolroom bureau which had come here to keep me company in my new life. Near the fireplace stood the old basket chair. They fitted into their new surroundings surprisingly well, in spite of their shabbiness; I hoped to fit into my new surroundings as easily.

Later on I got up and went downstairs. It struck me that Clementina might need a little companionship after her father's departure, and it was my duty to supply it. At first I could see no signs of the child; the house was full of soft sunshine. I went from room to room. It seemed strange that this house, which I had known and loved all my life, should now be mine to direct — even for a temporary period. I began to rearrange a bowl of flowers which stood on the hall table — big shaggy chrysanthemums from the hothouses — not so much because the flowers required attention, as because the mere fact that I was entitled to touch them gave me pleasure. I was still engaged upon my self-appointed task when the front door opened and Clementina came in. She looked as if she had been crying, and the sight of her small white face stirred my heart.

'Daddy's gone,' she said.

I slipped my hand through her arm and pressed it gently. 'I know,' I said. 'It was best for him to go. He will enjoy it. You and I must get to know each other, to love each other.'

She made no movement; it was like holding the arm of a wooden figure.

'I don't want to,' she said.

'You don't want to,' I echoed in surprise.

She drew her arm away and stood looking out through the open door. 'I don't want to love anybody,' she explained. 'Everybody that I love goes away. It's better not to love people.'

'Daddy will come back,' I told her, trying to speak lightly. My heart had sunk at her words, and it was difficult to hide my disappointment. How was I going to find the way to Clementina's heart if it were already closed to me? I realized that it was better not to pursue the subject, so I kept my feelings to myself. She stood and watched me while I finished the flowers.

'What are we going to do?' I said as I put the last shaggy head into its place and stepped back to admire the effect.

'Daddy said I was to take you down to the stables if you got up in time,' she replied. 'I've got some apples for the horses.'

We walked down to the stables together. Clementina was polite but distant. I found it difficult to make conversation with her; she made me feel shy and awkward. I asked her questions about her games and her lessons and she answered me. It was hard work, and I felt all the time that I was estranging the child still further. She would think me inquisitive and interfering with all my questions, but we could not walk along in grim silence and I had no other conversation to offer her.

The head groom came forward when he saw us approaching, and touched his cap respectfully.

'This is Sim, Aunt Charlotte,' said Clementina in her precise little voice.

I shook hands with Sim. He seemed a good type of man — quiet and capable. This was the one person on the estate whom I must not sack — I thought there was little chance that I should want to do so. I looked round the stables with interest and a strange pain. They were so familiar to me in the old happy days when I used to exercise Garth's pony for him. I saw that everything was beautifully kept, the yard clean, the taps burnished, the straw edging to the stalls crisp and golden. Sim led us across the yard and opened the door of a loose-box. He said nothing, but there was a queer mixture of eagerness and anxiety in his air. I looked in and saw a brown mare with the strong quarters and beautiful lines of a well-bred hunter. She looked round at me and moved uneasily. I went in and patted her. What a beautiful coat she had, soft as silk!

'She is a beauty, Sim,' I said. 'Is she Mr. Wisdon's hunter?'

'No, Miss,' replied Sim, smiling at me in a

friendly way. 'Mr. Wisdon bought 'er for you. She's a beautiful lady's mount. Plenty of spirit and no vice — pleasure to ride she is.'

'For me!' I exclaimed in amazement.

'Yes, Miss. Mr. Wisdon sold 'is own two hunters. They weren't suitable for a lady. Too big and heavy. Mr. Wisdon rides about twelve stone you see.'

'He bought — he bought this mare for me?'

'Yes, Miss, you will be huntin' with Miss Clem, won't you, Miss?'

Clementina put an apple into my hand and I gave it to the lovely creature. It was pure joy to feel her soft velvety nose in my hand, nuzzling at the fruit. The years fell away and I was a girl again, young and carefree, full of life and hope. It was all so much the same — the smells of the stable, the feel of the velvet nose — and yet everything had changed; I had changed, and Garth — Garth had changed most of all.

Sim came into the box and removed the cloths, he showed me the mare with pride, making her stand over and speaking to her with the strange mixture of affection and firmness which horses understand.

'Brown Betty, 'er name is,' he said. 'Mr. Wisdon kept the gray for me, and Miss Clem 'as 'er cob, Black Knight, so there we are, and we can 'ave two days a week easy.'

'Can I ride today?' I asked Sim.

'Why, of course, Miss,' he replied as pleased as Punch. 'Why not? Brown Betty's bin waiting for you. 'arf an hour in the afternoon — say three o'clock if that suits you.'

'Half an hour — is that all?' I exclaimed.

'Mr. Wisdon said you was to start easy,' said Sim gravely. 'He said you 'adn't ridden for some time, 'Don't you let Miss Dean start too sudden,' he says to me. 'She'll be keen as mustard,' he says, 'but I trust you to see she doesn't overdo it.' So you see, Miss, I got to be careful.'

I felt the tears pricking my eyes — what a strange creature Garth was! He seemed to me to be two different men, the one kind and thoughtful and incredibly generous. The other cynical, coarse, and unbelievably cruel.

'Three o'clock then,' I said to Sim (I could not trust myself to say any more), and I came out of the dim stable into the white glare of the yard.

# 5

## *'You're a Stranger, Aren't You?'*

The first few weeks of my new life were difficult. So difficult that if it had been possible I would have given up the struggle and returned to London. But there was no return for me. I had taken on the job, and, however difficult it was, I was bound to carry on with it until Garth's return. My chief difficulty was Clementina, she baffled me completely. I felt that I should never understand the child, that I should never win her confidence. She was always polite in a strange, unchildlike way but when I tried to approach her she withdrew, delicately but definitely into her shell. She took pains to make me understand that I was there on sufferance, that she bore with my vagaries because she had to. She showed me politely but firmly that I was quite unnecessary to her. I tried hard to interest her in games and pastimes which most children find absorbing, but without success. If I suggested a game, she played with me patiently, and, when it was over, returned to her book with visible relief. She read for hours without moving. I had never seen anybody so quiet, or so still. Sometimes I looked up from my own book and watched her as she read, it seemed unnatural for anybody to sit so still, doubly unnatural for a child. I began to wonder if she were ill or unhappy, perhaps she was lonely, perhaps she missed her parents. I decided that we must go about a little, the child must be amused. The flower-show was coming on — we would go to the flower-show together and see whether the grapes and the heavy-headed chrysanthemums which had been sent from the Manor had won the prizes they deserved. But Clementina refused to go to the flower-show, simply refused point-blank. I could not persuade her to go, and I had no intention of forcing her to go against her will. She was a strange child.

Every morning a young woman — Miss Milston by name — came from the village and gave Clementina her lessons. She appeared at the Manor on the stroke of nine, and left on the stroke of three. Clementina was not at all interested in her lessons; she bore them as she bore anything which had to be borne, without complaint. It seemed strange that Miss Milston could not make lessons interesting to a child who read with the intense concentration of Clementina. I had enjoyed my schooldays; Father had made lessons a pleasure, not a toil.

But Clementina was not my only difficulty by any means. The servants were slack and troublesome; they had been left to their own devices for so long that they resented any interference with their work. Any alterations which I wished to make in the daily regime were carried out with deliberate obtuseness. I began to think that I should really have to sack the lot, as Garth had cynically suggested. It was the last thing I wanted to do, but my present position was untenable. I was mistress of the house in name, but my authority was flouted, my orders made ridiculous.

One night after Clementina had gone to bed I went upstairs to the nursery and tackled Nanny on the subject. She was my one firm ally in the house; she had wanted me to come, it was to her interest that the house should run smoothly. She was sitting beside the nursery fire darning Clementina's stockings, with her skirts turned back over her knees and a small gray shawl over her shoulders. She looked at me over her spectacles as I came in and made room for me by the fire. I wasted no time in preliminaries but laid my difficulties before her and asked her advice. 'I suppose it is my inexperience,' I said rather sadly. 'I've never had to run a house before, and I seem to put my foot into it whenever I try to make things easier.'

'*You're* all right, Miss Char,' she said comfortingly. 'It's *them* that's wrong. Spoiled and lazy, that's what they are. They want somebody to take them in hand and chivvy them round. I'm glad you spoke because things aren't right and never will be till you show them who's master. One or two will have to go and the others will settle down. That's my advice.'

'Which of them?' I asked.

'Which do *you* think?' countered Nanny. 'You see, Miss Char, it's not a very nice job for me to say. But you tell me which you find troublesome and I'll tell you if I agree.'

It was like Nanny to split hairs of etiquette in

this way, and I could not help smiling. 'I shall keep cook,' I began.

'Then you'll never have no peace,' Nanny interrupted. 'Mrs. 'arcourt may be smarmy to your face, but her tongue's like an adder.'

She shut her lips tightly after this indictment and would say no more on the subject of Mrs. Harcourt's tongue.

'And what about Lizzie?' I inquired timidly. Lizzie was the head housemaid; she had been at the Manor for years but I did not like her. She was tall and thin and angular with shifty eyes and a plausible manner.

'Lizzie talks to Clem,' said Nanny. 'She ought to have gone long ago but she got round Mrs. Wisdon.'

'What does she talk to Clem about?'

'Things she hasn't no business to discuss,' Nanny replied mysteriously.

After an hour's talk I found that, if I wanted any peace and happiness at the Manor, I should have to dismiss four women. I was quite sick with fright at the prospect.

'Don't you worry, Miss Char,' Nanny said, smoothing out the darns in Clementina's stocking and admiring her handiwork. 'Don't you worry. It doesn't do no good worrying over things — just sail in.'

I took Nanny's advice and sailed in — it was less alarming than I had expected — and I spent several days in town engaging new maids.

These were my troubles. Perhaps you will think they were trivial, Clare, but, because of my inexperience, they worried me. My pleasures were in Hinkleton itself, in the country and the village. I looked up some of my old friends among the cottagers and found — for the most part — warm welcomes. It was for Father's sake that they welcomed me, they had all loved him, and the older people liked to talk of the old days and to compare them with modern conditions. Most of them were agreed that in spite of old age pensions and picture-houses the old days were best; they deplored the degeneracy of the young, and motor-bicycles, and silk stockings and short hair for village maidens. But to me the young seemed anything but degenerate. I thought them pleasant and frank. The freedom, which the older folk objected to, was not a bad thing, for it brought in its train a wider outlook on life, and courage and independence. I took a Hinkleton girl as under-housemaid, and found in her a treasure. She was stronger than a town girl and her round, rosy cheeks pleased me when I saw her working about the house.

Clementina and I rode every day and I regained my seat and my confidence. Sim was pleased with me and very soon suggested that we should attend a meet at Edgemoor Farm, which was about five miles from Hinkleton.

'I think we're all right now,' he said gravely, 'and it's always a good meet at Edgemoor.'

We rode over in the early morning; it was a glorious day, crisp and clear, with a pale yellow winter sun shining serenely in the pale blue sky. The wind was bracing, and a few white clouds raced each other before its breath. The horses seemed to know that something unusual was afoot, Black Knight sidled along like a crab, and even Brown Betty forgot her manners and shied at the brown leaves as they blew across the path.

The meet was at the farm itself, a long white straggling building on the edge of a hill with the moor sloping up from its encompassing fields to the skyline. When we arrived they were already moving off to draw a likely looking spinney beyond the farm buildings. We joined the crowd and followed slowly. The hounds were well ahead — a seething mass of white and black and brown bodies and waving sterns. Ahead, also, were the hunt servants in their neat uniforms. There was a good sprinkling of pink among the crowd, and the horses were beautiful.

We were nearing the spinney when a view halloo from one of the hunt servants announced the departure of a fox. I saw the red-brown body streak across a field to our left, and the next moment the pack burst from the spinney like a bombshell and streamed after him. Sim shouted that there was a gate lower down; we followed him, and the next moment we were galloping across a stubble field in a diagonal direction. This maneuver brought us into the first flight; the hounds were scarcely a hundred yards away. I saw a thick-set hedge coming to meet me and knew a moment of anxiety as I felt Brown Betty gather herself together for the jump . . . she went over like a bird, it was my first and last moment of anxiety that day. Away we went, Brown Betty pulling comfortably with excitement, her paces so easy that I scarcely knew she was galloping save for the pace and the whistle of the wind in my ears. Clementina was going well; she sat back in the saddle and rode with her hands down and her knees in. We sailed over a broad ditch and bore right, up the hill. The field had begun to string out now, for the pace was hot. A group of people who had guessed the line of the fox came cantering up a narrow lane and joined us. Hounds disappeared over a low wall; we followed. We were now on the open moor and the wind was keen. The hills rose gently upon our right; below, in the valley, lay the white farm-house and its scattered outbuildings. The moor was empty save for a few gorse bushes, and far away in front of us, a group of wind-riven trees. The fox was making for the sanctuary. I could see him well ahead of the pack, keeping his lead easily on the steep shoulder of the hill. Brown Betty needed no urging; she flew up the hill, Sim and Clementina were left behind. The short springy turf was delightful to ride on; I prayed that there were no rabbit holes. The pack was running silently, needing all their breath for the pace.

The group of trees for which the fox was making resolved itself into a small ravine with steep sides covered with brushwood. At the bottom a stream wandered among rocks. We pulled up here, and I, for one, was thankful for a few moments to breathe. The pace had been hot, and we had come all the way without a check. The hounds were clamoring wildly round the roots of an enormous oak tree which had been riven by lightning. It looked to me like a badger's earth which the fox had used as a temporary sanctuary. I watched the scene with interest. The hunt servants leaped down among the hounds and examined the holes. A woman on a raking chestnut pushed past me, swearing like a trooper. 'Why the hell can't they stop the earths?' she demanded of nobody in particular. She was lean, and limbed like a man; her face was lined and weather-beaten, her eyes were glittering with excitement.

The huntsman whipped the hounds off the earth with some difficulty. They started to draw the cover higher up the stream. I was fascinated by the clever houndwork. One old hound in particular, a tall old warrior with a scarred head and a torn ear, was working hard. His questing nose missed no sod of earth where the scent might lie. Suddenly he gave a deep, bell-like cry and raced up the bank among the trees, his stern waving triumphantly in the air. The other hounds followed, taking up the scent; and confirming the good news. They sped away down the hill. The field followed. Brown Betty was stirred by the general excitement; she threw up her head and whinnied. Away we went. A wall rose before us, there was a gate in it, but the gate was already blocked; it was no time for gates. Clementina flashed past with Sim at her elbow — they were over the wall and away — I wondered where they had been for I had lost sight of them after the first jump. It was marvelous the way the child rode; she had no fear in her makeup, that was evident.

I pulled out a little — for I did not like jumping in a bunch — and so lost ground.

Brown Betty took the wall in her stride. Hounds were already climbing the wall at the other side of the field. The woman on the raking chestnut passed me, Brown Betty shot forward and we ran neck and neck across the meadow. The fox was running upwind into a keen north wind, so cold that it cut my face like a lash of a whip.

'Follow me,' the woman cried. 'There's a duck-pond the other side of the wall.' I shouted, 'Thank you,' drew back a little and followed her lead. She bore to the right. As we passed I saw a man rising from the duck-pond like a draggled crow. My guide waved her hand toward the dreadful sight and I shouted, 'Thank you' again, more fervently than before.

I looked ahead and saw that hounds had checked, the ground was foiled with sheep. They scattered as we passed. The pace had been so hot that some of the horses were out of hand. 'Keep back,' shouted the master. I quieted Brown Betty as best I could and looked round for Sim and Clementina, but they were nowhere to be seen.

'That's a good-lookin' mare,' said the woman who had saved me from the duck-pond. 'She can go, too.'

We chatted amicably for a few minutes; she was eating sandwiches out of a battered old tin. Her strong white teeth went through the thick bread with enormous bites.

The hounds were still in confusion; it looked as if they had lost the scent for good. They spread out like a fan, working up the field toward a beech hedge on the other side. I drew to the shelter of a shepherd's hut, for the wind was like ice and I was not surprised when I saw white snowflakes falling lightly through the air like feathers. They increased rapidly and soon it was snowing fast. I turned up my collar and moved closer into the shelter of the hut.

The snow stopped as suddenly as it had begun, and the sun shone out on a world that looked as though it had been lightly powdered with sugar. The master had drawn the hounds off and was casting along the hedge. Suddenly there was a deep bay of triumph; the same battered old hound which had found before was onto the scent again. Away they went up the hill toward the ravine where the first fox had been lost and after them went the field. The powdering of snow was churned into slush by the passage of a hundred hoofs.

I had had almost enough for my first day, and I pulled out of the hunt, but Brown Betty was still keen; she bucked gently and sidled up the field pulling at her bit and champing impatiently.

'Sorry, old girl,' I said, patting her neck. 'It's bad luck on you, but it can't be helped.'

I rode slowly across the field toward a gate and found myself in a narrow muddy lane which led at right angles up the hill and down to the farm. A girl was standing in the lane; she was covered with mud from head to foot and looked somewhat dazed.

'I say, have you seen my horse?' she inquired anxiously. 'A bay with two white stockings — the brute fell with me and then bolted. I was stunned for the moment.'

'Are you hurt?'

'I don't think so — my head feels a bit queer.'

Just at that moment there was the snarling sound of a kill, it seemed to come from the direction of the ravine. The girl raised her head and listened.

'Blast that horse,' she said, 'I haven't missed a kill this season.'

I did not share her feelings. I had enjoyed the run immensely, but I had no wish to be in at the death. Fortunately I knew enough about the game to conceal such unworthy sentiments from my new acquaintance.

'Well, it's over,' she said. 'I suppose we had better make for the farm.'

We walked slowly down the hill together toward the farmhouse from which we had started. Fortunately it was quite near, for the hunt had gone full circle. We talked, as we went along, in a friendly manner. She admired my mount, and cursed her own.

'You're a stranger, aren't you?' she inquired. 'I know most of the regulars. I'm staying for the winter with my aunt, Lady Bournesworth — I suppose you know my uncle and aunt, they seem to know everybody.'

'Then I must be nobody,' I replied smiling. The girl amused me rather, she was so extremely naïve and her airs of a woman of the world were so transparent.

We had reached the farm by this time; the yard was cluttered with gleaming cars, some of them trying to turn under the direction of a farm boy who looked as if he knew more about farm-carts than motors.

'Talk of an angel,' said my companion suddenly. 'There's Aunt Anne in the Daimler, bless her heart! I'll introduce you, shall I? She always wants to know everybody.'

She hurried across the yard and poked her head into the window of a huge, old-fashioned Daimler which had backed precariously into a manure heap. I had no wish to be introduced to Lady Bournesworth, but I could hardly refuse the honor, so I waited for a little while to see what would happen. The field straggled into the yard; little groups of people on foot or on horseback drifted down the hill, talking excitedly. The yard became unpleasantly congested; grooms ran hither and thither ducking under horses' noses and avoiding their heels. I moved away from the vicinity of a meek-looking horse with a red ribbon on its tail.

'There you are, Miss!' said Sim's voice, at my elbow. 'I wondered where you 'ad got to — a beautiful kill, Miss.'

Clementina was just behind him; her shoulder was muddy, and her hat had vanished, but her eyes were bright with excitement. I saw that there was not much wrong with her and decided not to inquire about her muddy condition. I was beginning to know the child now — she hated a fuss.

'There's nothing to wait for, is there?' she said, drawing back from the crowd. 'We can go out the back way, can't we, Sim?'

Sim agreed that we could. I glanced over at the Daimler and saw that it was maneuvering out of the gate in the opposite direction — Lady

Bournesworth had evidently no desire to make my acquaintance. I was neither glad nor sorry. I followed Sim and Clementina down the back lane.

# 6

## *A Sentence Overheard*

'You went splendidly,' I said to Clementina, as we rode home together through the muddy lanes with Sim behind, walking his horse.

'You didn't do so badly yourself, Aunt Charlotte.'

I looked at Clementina and saw that she was smiling at me. I was absurdly elated at the child's praise. It was the first gleam of friendliness that I had seen. Something warned me not to notice the difference, not to force the small opening that had appeared in her armor. It was difficult to hide my pleasure and to maintain a detached air, for I had been trying to make friends with Clementina for weeks and had failed lamentably. Here at last was a faint sign of recognition — I must not misuse it.

'I used to ride a lot at one time,' I said quite casually. 'When your father was at school I always exercised his pony. And once or twice, when I could get hold of a mount, we hunted together. But of course I haven't ridden for a long time — years and years.'

'Why didn't you come and stay when Mummy was here?' she asked.

I was silent for a few moments wondering how to reply. I did not want to push her back into herself, but it was a difficult question to answer.

'Lizzie says you didn't like Mummy,' she added.

'That isn't true,' I said hastily, 'and Lizzie had no business to say so. It is not wise to discuss that kind of thing with servants, Clementina.'

'Well, I shan't be able to talk to Lizzie much longer — she told me you were sending her away.'

'Don't discuss things with any of them,' I said quite gently.

'I only do it when I can't find out things from other people,' she replied in an indifferent tone.

'Don't do it anymore. If you want to know anything, ask me. I will tell you.'

'Tell me that then,' she said quickly. 'Why didn't you come?'

'Because I love Hinkleton so much, Clementina. It was my home, you see. And I found it so hard to go back again to my poky little flat in London among all the smuts and the dirt and the noise. It made me discontented to come here.'

I saw that she understood. She didn't say anything for a few minutes and we trotted on in silence. The winter afternoon was closing in, but there was a queer ghostly light in the sky which shone upon the snow-sprinkled fields and hedges so that the land seemed brighter than the sky — it was almost as if what light there was emanated from the snow. I was meditating upon the strange effect, and had almost forgotten our conversation when Clementina spoke again.

'I thought you did not come because Mummy

had wronged you,' she said suddenly.

'Wronged me?'

'Yes, Daddy said she had wronged you, and I wondered what it meant. He said to Mummy one day, 'Of course you hate Charlotte. People always hate those they have wronged.'' She quoted the words carefully in her precise little voice.

'Mummy didn't wrong me,' I said, startled and dismayed. 'You can't have understood the words properly. When grown-up people talk to each other it is difficult for you to understand — you shouldn't listen.'

'I was there, and I couldn't help hearing. And I understood the words all right, although I didn't know what they meant. Of course I knew you didn't really mean it when you said I was to ask you anything I liked, and you would tell me.'

'I did mean it, Clementina,' I replied quickly. 'But I don't understand the words myself so I can't tell you what they mean. Can I?'

'Honor bright?' she asked.

'Honor bright,' I replied solemnly.

She dropped the subject without another word. She never pestered you with questions like some children do.

'I like being called Clementina,' she said.

'It is a pretty name,' I agreed.

'Nobody calls me by it except you. Daddy calls me Clem, so everybody else does.'

'Daddy would call you Clementina if he knew you liked it better,' I replied gravely. 'If you asked him.'

'It's not worthwhile,' she replied listlessly. 'I should know he was doing it because I had asked him to, and laughing at me in his mind all the time.'

There seemed to be no reply to that; at least I could find none. We relapsed into silence. My brain was busy with the words that Clementina had overheard. Hard, bitter words. No wonder that Garth and Kitty had drifted apart if that was the way they spoke to each other. I did not know what the words could mean if Clementina had really heard them aright, and the way she had quoted them had impressed me with their correctness. 'People always hate those they have wronged.' Did Kitty hate me? Had she wronged me? I could find no answer to the questions. Kitty had married Garth, but he was lost to me before that. He was lost to me when he came home from the war. Kitty had not taken him from me any more than any other woman who might have married him. I had always felt — perhaps not unreasonably — that Kitty was in the place which really belonged to me, but it was not Kitty's fault. If it was anybody's fault it was Garth's. He could scarcely accuse Kitty of wronging me on that account.

I tried to think of some other matter to which the words might have referred, but I could think of nothing. Father had left no money, so it could not have been anything of that kind. Of course Kitty had had the lion's share of the furniture, but that was only because I had no use for it, and I preferred her to take what she wanted rather than have it sold. There was no explanation to be found for the strange words.

I puzzled over the problem for days, and eventually gave it up.

# 7

## 'The Young Diana'

We hunted quite a lot that winter, Clementina and Sim and I. I tore her away from Miss Milston whenever there was a meet conveniently near Hinkleton. We had some splendid runs. The child went like a bird. I was proud of her in the hunting field for she rode well, and was so bold and fearless. Sometimes my heart rose into my throat at the sight of Clementina flying over a particularly nasty hedge on her black cob — it was a frightful responsibility for me. Supposing she came to grief, what should I do? Her father was somewhere in the wilds of Africa, lost to civilization, so the responsibility was all mine. But Clementina did not come to grief; she took one or two tosses, but she was always up again the next moment and anxious to pursue the chase. She never learned caution from her experiences.

'Miss Clem rides like the Squire,' said Sim one day. '*He* gives me the 'eebie-jeebies sometimes. They both ride as if they didn't care, and it's just the people that don't care that never takes any 'arm. That's my experience, Miss.'

This comforted me a little, because I knew it was true.

'Look at Lady Vera,' Sim continued (he was

busy bandaging the gray's off-fore, which was apt to fill a little after a long day). 'Lady Vera's ridden to 'ounds for more years than I'd like to say, and she's never come to no 'arm, not to speak of — a broken bone or two she may 'ave 'ad, but what's a broken bone, Miss?'

'Is Lady Vera very reckless?' I asked. It amused me to talk to Sim and watch his capable hands at work.

'Reckless!' Sim exclaimed. 'Why the Squire's *timid* compared to Lady Vera. You've seen 'er 'aven't you, Miss? A thin lady with a brownish face. She's bin huntin' a chestnut most of the winter.'

'Oh, that's Lady Vera, is it?' I said. 'Yes, I've spoken to her once or twice. She certainly seems a thruster.'

'Yes, that's her — she breeds horses, you know, Miss. We get quite a lot of our horses from Lady Vera. But what I wanted to say is don't you worry about Miss Clem. She'll be all right. Lady Vera doesn't come to no 'arm and Miss Clem won't neither.'

It was easy for Sim to say 'Don't worry,' but I found the advice difficult to take. I was watching Clementina one day. She was flying down a steep field toward a bank with a thick-set hedge on the top. I had decided that the hedge was impracticable and was casting about for a convenient gate, but nothing was impracticable to Clementina in the heat of the chase. The black cob was a marvelous jumper, and his mistress made good use of his skill. I saw Clementina gather the animal together with her competent hands, and the next moment they were over the obstacle and away.

I sighed with relief and found a gentleman at my elbow looking at me with whimsical sympathy.

'You find the young Diana something of a responsibility,' he suggested, raising his hat. He was a man of about fifty, a real hunting man, with a lean, red face and iron-gray hair. His eyes, set about with creases and shaded by rather bushy eyebrows, were friendly and humorous.

'She terrifies me,' I admitted. 'You see I am entirely responsible for her.'

'Wisdon is in Africa, isn't he? By the way, my name is Felstead and I know Wisdon quite well. You are Miss Dean, of course.'

We walked our horses down the field toward a gate. The hunt had swept on over a hill and left us behind. I was not sorry to draw out of the hunt, for it had been a long and tiring day. Brown Betty was tired too.

'I'm ridin' a green beast,' Mr. Felstead said. 'He's had enough for today and so have I. He's had me off twice, and I'm getting too old for that sort of thing. We may see something of the hunt if we bear left for Borland Corner. What do you say?'

I was quite pleased to accept Mr. Felstead's guidance; he was pleasant and kind and he knew Garth. Until now, nobody had spoken to me, except in the casual manner of hunting folk. I had exchanged civilities with various people over gates, and had chatted about the scent and the weather conditions, but this was different. This man knew who I was, knew Garth and asked about him — I found it unexpectedly pleasant. I had not missed friendly neighbors until now. I had been too busy trying to master the various intricacies of my new job. But it suddenly occurred to me, as I walked down the hill beside Mr. Felstead, that it was really rather peculiar how few friends Garth and Kitty seemed to have — in fact, as far as I knew, they had none. Nobody had called; nobody ever stopped Clementina in the village or spoke to her when we came out of church.

'May my wife call?' Mr. Felstead inquired, when I had answered his questions about Garth's whereabouts to the best of my ability. 'We are quite near neighbors, you know. Ten miles is nothing in these days. We live at Oldgarden. I have a girl just Clem's age.'

I said it would be nice.

'They used to see a good deal of each other, the girls,' he added, rather diffidently. 'In fact they were tremendous pals, but recently — the last year or so — er — my wife — '

He leaned over to open the gate, and I saw that his red face had grown quite scarlet with embarrassment, and suddenly I understood him — or thought that I understood him — perfectly. Mrs. Felstead had been unwilling to let her girl come to a house which was the subject of so much talk and gossip in the neighborhood. One could hardly blame her. The divorce case must have caused a considerable stir — it was foolish of me not to have realized this before — here was the explanation of our isolation at Hinkleton

Manor. How dreadful it must have been for Garth, how humbling to his pride to find himself ostracized by the County. (Humbling was the wrong word, he was embittered, not humbled by the experience.) No wonder he had left the place and gone to Africa — Garth's pride came into this again. Garth's pride of race which made him feel himself the equal of any man in England and the superior of most. I had heard no talk, of course, no gossip of any kind had reached my ears, but I was the last person who would be likely to hear anything — the whole County might still be discussing Garth and Kitty and their lamentable affairs for all I knew.

These disjointed thoughts flashed through my head as I watched Mr. Felstead open the gate, and in a few moments I made up my mind what to say.

'It would be kind if you would allow your little girl to come to tea with Clementina,' I told him frankly. 'She is a solitary child and needs the companionship of children of her own age.'

'I will speak to my wife about it,' he promised. 'She likes Clem — we all like Clem — and Violet will be delighted to see her again. My wife and daughter are away from home just now, but when they come back — '

There was a good deal left unsaid in the conversation, but I felt that we understood each other. I sensed Mr. Felstead's friendliness and was glad of it. Glad to feel that Clementina and I had one friend.

We had not gone far when we saw the hunt streaming across a field at right angles to our course and less than a quarter of a mile away. I looked at Mr. Felstead and smiled.

'Yes,' he said laughing, 'I'm an old hand at this game — Yoicks tally-ho.'

He clapped his knees to his green horse and cantered down the field — I followed him. We skirted a ploughed field, crossed a cart-road and emerged into the ruck of the hunt. Clementina was well in front, still going strong. Sim, on the lean gray, was close to her. We swept across a stubble field and over a low fence into a large square meadow. Before us was a small wood, hounds were already disappearing into it.

'We shall kill now, if the earths have been stopped,' said Mr. Felstead at my elbow.

Some of the hunt servants were skirting the wood and taking up positions to watch for the fox in case he should give the hounds the slip, but it was unnecessary. There was a burst of music followed by the unmistakable snarling of a kill.

'Do you want to see the end of Mr. Reynard?' inquired my companion. 'I'm afraid we're too late.'

I shook my head. 'It's the only bit I don't like,' I told him.

'Paula doesn't like it either,' he said, smiling. 'My wife, you know. She goes like the devil, but she looks the other way when the end comes. You're rather like Paula in some ways.'

We waited for a little at the edge of the wood, walking slowly up and down to cool off the horses. There was, perhaps, about a score of others like ourselves, who had chosen not to see the end. The women were eating biscuits, and the men regaling themselves from pocket flasks. The wind was very cold, and the sun was sinking behind the hills like a round red ball.

'Looks like frost,' somebody said.

Just at that moment a tall man on a bay mare approached me and raised his hat. He had a pleasant, open face, very brown and weather-beaten, and his eyes were intensely blue.

'You won't remember me,' he said, smiling. 'Geoff Howard is my name. My brother was up at Oxford with Garth Wisdon and we came down to Hinkleton for Garth's coming-of-age ball. It was just before the war.'

I shook hands with him and said, 'How stupid of me to forget!'

'My people have taken Fairways for two years,' he said and looked at me inquiringly.

'I am staying at Hinkleton Manor looking after my small niece — or rather trying to look after her,' I told him. 'Garth has gone to Africa with the Fraser expedition.'

He looked at me with a puzzled frown. 'Your niece? I thought — '

'Garth married my sister,' I explained.

'You are very like your sister,' he replied.

'Am I?' I inquired feebly. Nobody had ever told me such a thing before. He couldn't really think that I was like Kitty — we were totally different in every way — I felt that we were at cross purposes, but I didn't see how.

'No wonder you didn't remember me,' laughed Mr. Howard. 'It was your sister that I met at the dance of course. Wisdon was crazy about her that night. We were all crazy about her, but she had eyes for nobody else. We teased Wisdon like anything about her because he was such an innocent, wouldn't look at a girl, couldn't be bothered with girls, hadn't time for them, and then quite suddenly he was completely sunk. You know how it is with fellows like that — or perhaps you don't know.'

I saw now how we had got muddled, but it was impossible for me to explain the matter. The whole thing was too painful and intimate to expound to a strange man in the middle of a hunting field. We were surrounded by a chattering throng of people, and our horses were turning and backing every moment as new arrivals divided the crowd into fresh patterns. Could I say to the man, 'Garth jilted me and married my sister, and now he has divorced her?' I hadn't the moral courage to attempt it.

'Wisdon was as badly hit as any man I've seen,' continued Mr. Howard, laughing merrily. 'It served him right for saying he hadn't time for girls. I was jolly glad when I saw the marriage in the papers — after the war, wasn't it? — I've been in Canada ever since the war — just got home for a bit of a holiday. I told you my people have taken Fairways, didn't I?'

'Look out, you,' cried a gruff voice on the other side of Mr. Howard. 'Can't you manage your damned horse, sir? He's eating my boot.'

Mr. Howard pulled up his horse's head and raised his hat politely. 'I beg your pardon, sir. She must have mistaken your foot for a banana. She dotes on bananas. Queer taste, isn't it?'

The man grunted fiercely and turned away, leaving Mr. Howard free to resume his rather one-sided conversation with me. I had never met a man who talked so continuously as Mr. Howard without being boring or didactic. I found afterward that he had spent long months snowbound in Canada with nobody of his own stamp to converse with, and concluded that he was still busy making up for lost time.

The rest of the hunt was now emerging from the trees. Clementina rode up to me and displayed the brush. Her eyes were sparkling and her cheeks were flushed with excitement — I scarcely knew the child.

Mr. Felstead and Mr. Howard congratulated her warmly, and several other gentlemen followed suit.

'By Gad! You deserved it,' cried Mr. Howard. 'I saw you sailing over fences like a cavalryman. Your father will be proud of you when he hears about it. I'd no idea you were Garth Wisdon's daughter, thought you must be Diana at least. That's a damn good cob you've got. He's earned his feed today.'

Clementina looked up and smiled at him, then she stopped and patted Black Knight's shoulder, but she didn't speak.

The hunt was dispersing now, the luxurious ones dismounted and left their horses to be brought home by grooms while they themselves were whirled off in cars which had appeared in the road nearby as if by magic. Clementina and I walked slowly down the hill with Mr. Howard — our roads home lay in the same direction, for

Fairways was about three miles on the other side of Hinkleton Manor. I knew the place well, it was a charming old house flanked by Georgian pillars and covered with Virginia creeper. It was occupied, in the days when I had known it, by a couple of maiden ladies, the Misses Golding; they were rather terrifying to children, for they were large and stout and had very red faces — one of them had a beard. They used to ask us to tea sometimes, and we were obliged to go because they were important parishioners, but it was always an ordeal, and we breathed sighs of relief when we were safely out of the gates again and our feet set on our homeward way. The tea they provided was a poor meal — sandwiches filled with cucumber, and fancy biscuits, which were always very soft and stale, served on an enormous silver tray, and watery tea in an immense silver teapot. Mother hated going as much as we did, but she would never own to the fact; she had a very high conception of her duties as a parson's wife.

I came back from the past to hear Clementina talking to Mr. Howard in quite an animated manner. Her thin, light, childish voice was a strange vehicle for the mature conversation which she produced for Mr. Howard's benefit.

'He's by Black Boy out of Dark Lady,' she was saying. 'Daddy bought him for me as a two-year-old from Lady Vera. He's six now and I love him awfully.'

'I don't wonder!' commented Mr. Howard.

'Horses never let you down,' continued Clementina. 'I mean they never go back on you.

They aren't like people who pretend to be fond of you and turn their backs on you when troubles come. Horses love you because you're you.'

'That's quite true,' said Mr. Howard in some astonishment. 'But I should have thought you were too young to have found it out.'

'I'm not young,' Clementina told him in her childish voice. 'I'm a hundred years old, I think.'

He laughed at that, but not unkindly. 'Perhaps as you grow older you may lose some of that frightful burden of years,' he suggested.

We were now at the gates of the Manor, and I could do no other than ask him to come in and have tea. He jumped at the offer and we all turned in at the gate together and trotted up the avenue.

'I haven't been here since the dance,' he said, looking about him. 'It must be twenty years ago — or very nearly. It was my first grown-up dance; I suppose that's why I remember it so well. I was supposed to be going up to Oxford the following year, but of course I didn't.'

'Why didn't you?' inquired Clementina interestedly.

'Because a certain grandee got himself shot by a fanatic,' replied Mr. Howard smiling. I had never heard of the man before, but he stopped me going to Oxford just the same. His death set the world on fire; I don't suppose it would have done so if the world hadn't been ripe for a blaze.'

'Oh, the war,' said Clementina. 'I didn't know you were as old as that.'

Mr. Howard looked slightly taken aback by this frank statement, and then he smiled. 'That's a compliment, Clementina,' he said. 'I didn't recognize it as such at first sight, but it *is* a compliment, and a very nice one too.'

Tea was a cheerful, pleasant meal; we were all hungry and slightly tired after our long day; the buns and cakes disappeared like melting snow. Mr. Howard chaffed Clementina over her appetite, and she replied in good part. I had never seen the child so normal and childlike. When we had finished, and Mr. Howard had got his pipe going, he told us something of his life in Canada. He was an engineer and had been engaged upon an electric power scheme to supply electricity to a large and growing town. He told us some of his difficulties and disappointments and then launched out into an extremely funny but wholly incredible account of his adventures in the mountains with grizzly bears.

'Baron Munchausen,' I said at last, softly, under my breath.

He, looked at me and smiled wickedly. 'You believed quite a lot of it,' he said. 'I saw the moment when a wavering doubt of my veracity dawned upon your mind.'

'I am in the habit of believing my friends,' I told him severely.

'Rats!' he exclaimed, and rose stiffly out of his chair. 'Yes, I really must go. Mother will wonder where on earth I've got to. I said I would be home at five.'

Clementina and I saw him off at the door. He wouldn't let me call Sim to bring his mare round.

'I'll find her at the stables,' he said. '*Au revoir*,

you'll be out on Thursday, I suppose.'

'Unless it freezes,' I said, shivering a little as the cold wind swept round the corner of the house.

He waved to us, and disappeared in the darkness.

'A nice man,' I said to Clementina, 'I liked him, didn't you?' She didn't answer, and suddenly I saw that her eyes were full of tears. 'My darling girl, what is the matter?'

'Nothing,' she said roughly, pulling herself away from my arm which had gone round her shoulders. 'Nothing except — he won't come here again — not when he knows — not when he hears about — about us. He doesn't know — that's why he's friendly and nice.'

I held on to her arm. 'Clementina, a man like Mr. Howard wouldn't care. He has traveled, knocked about the world. He was friendly and kind because he liked us.'

'Because he didn't know,' she said, dragging her arm away. 'When he knows he'll be quite different — you'll see. You don't understand what it's like because you haven't seen it happen. He'll be polite — and — and in a hurry — he'll be in a hurry to get home — you'll see.'

She fled away, upstairs. I called to her twice, but she did not answer nor come back.

I went into the library and stood looking at the fire. It was difficult to know what to do with Clementina, what to say. I had not realized that Clementina knew so much. I wondered just how much she did know. It was dreadful to feel that she was suffering this misery alone, had been suffering it for months without saying a word. I remembered — looking back with newly found knowledge — that Clementina had always avoided meeting people when she could. 'We'll go down by the fields,' she would say, if there was an errand to do in the village. When we went to church she led me out by the side door, remarking, 'There's such a crowd at the front door, it's shorter this way.' When we hunted, Clementina took her own line; she avoided gates where she might find herself squeezed up against somebody she knew — gates were unnecessary to Clementina when she was mounted on Black Knight. I saw all this now, though I had not seen it at the time. Clementina took enormous pains to avoid everybody she knew. It was a dreadful position for a child, far worse for a child than for a grown-up person — I saw that clearly. She could not understand what had happened, nobody discussed things with her, nobody explained things to her. Any knowledge that she possessed was picked up through hearing conversations — or parts of conversations — which were not meant for her ears, or through the servants. She put the pieces together and brooded over them. What could she know about her parents' affairs? She knew that something shameful had happened; she knew that the house — once so proud and respected — was shunned by the County. She knew that her mother's name was never mentioned.

I sat down by the fire and thought about it for a long, long time, but I could see no way of helping the child. Save by guarding her as well as

I could and showing her that I understood and was her friend, I could do nothing for her. Perhaps you could have helped her, Clare — I wonder if you could. Would you have tackled the thing boldly, or would you have shirked the issue as I did?

# 8

## *Settling Down*

I had not been at Hinkleton long before I realized that Miss Milston — Clementina's governess — resented my advent. She had a great admiration for Kitty and thought that Kitty had been badly treated. She was too cautious to air these opinions openly; she was of the type which does and says nothing openly, but works in the dark to achieve its purpose. At first I thought that Miss Milston was stupid, that her rudeness and gaucherie arose from ignorance, but I soon saw that she was too subtle to give unintentional offense. She calculated to an inch how far she could go with impunity, and enraged me without giving me anything definite to which I could take exception. I never met anybody who could enrage me so easily as Miss Milston. However much I schooled myself beforehand to take no notice of the woman she always roused me to boiling point in a few minutes. She lunched with us every day and at last I came to dread the hour for lunch to be announced, solely on account of Miss Milston. She was really a greedy woman — sometimes I saw her licking her thin lips with her pointed red tongue when she saw an especially succulent dish appear upon the sideboard — but, after Mrs. Harcourt had left and been replaced by an eminently satisfactory substitute, she pretended to be very fastidious, wrinkling up her nose, and picking distastefully at the dishes which were set before her. She did it to annoy me, I know, and I am ashamed to say she succeeded in her amiable intention. All housekeepers know how vexing it is to have good food treated as if it were only fit for pigs, so all housekeepers will be able to sympathize with me in my troubles with Miss Milston.

'Clem can't eat liver, can you, dear?' she would remark very sweetly. 'Of course Auntie couldn't know that; she hasn't known you as long as I have,' and then, turning to me, 'Mrs. Harcourt did a little piece of fish for Clem when grown-up food was unsuitable.'

'Liver is very good for children,' I would reply, having discovered this important fact from a small book on the diet of children, which I had been studying with the purpose of remedying my ignorance on the subject. 'But not for Clem,' she would say, smiling sadly. 'I wouldn't eat it, dear, it is sure to disagree with you. Perhaps the new cook would make a poached egg for you instead.'

I was quite unable to cope with this sort of thing. If I showed any resentment, Miss Milston apologized in a hurt manner and assured me that she was only speaking 'for the child's good.' She was altogether too subtle for me and too careful.

Once I had realized the subtlety of the woman, I began to wonder what her object was in alienating me and making my life a burden. She was too clever to work without a purpose. I decided to observe Miss Milston carefully and try to get to the bottom of her antagonism. If I could not do this she would have to go; it was bad for Clementina to live in an atmosphere of petty strife. And then quite suddenly one day I saw through the woman, and saw her object. We were talking about London and Miss Milston had been telling us of her experiences as a teacher in a fashionable school. She turned to Clementina and said, 'It was so kind of Auntie to give up her appointment in London and come and stay with us, wasn't it? I'm afraid it must be very dull for her here, but it really wasn't necessary, was it, Clem? You and I could manage quite nicely by ourselves.'

Clementina didn't answer — she wasn't intended to answer. Miss Milston flowed on to other topics, but I had seen through her carefully concealed purpose at last. She wanted to make my position untenable, she wanted to get rid of me and rule the Manor herself. I almost laughed at her optimism — it was she who would have to leave the Manor, not I. I had been left in charge by Garth, and nothing short of dynamite would move me.

Clementina took no part in these verbal battles. I could not make out whether she liked Miss Milston or hated her — as I should have hated her if I had been a child — I did not even know whether she were on my side or against me. I could not believe she was as neutral as she seemed.

Another source of constant trouble with Miss Milston was Clementina's hunting; she made all sorts of objections when the meet happened to be on a lesson day. It was upsetting the child to take her away from her lessons, it tired her out, she never worked so well after a day's hunting. I was on firm ground here, for Garth had ordained hunting for his daughter, and, so far from upsetting Clementina, I saw that the excitement and the exercise were good for the child. Clementina on a horse was a different creature, more human and natural, easier to understand. So I overruled all Miss Milston's objections and informed her that Clementina's father wished her to hunt.

About a week later Clementina and I started off to a meet at Borland Corner. It was a splendid hunting day, rather mild and damp, with a gray sky and a slight breeze from the west. We were walking quietly down the drive when we met Miss Milston coming up from the village with her attaché case in one hand and her umbrella in the other. She signaled to us to stop and came running up to us, panting, and very red in the face.

'I told you that we were hunting today,' I said when she came within earshot. 'Had you forgotten?'

She took no notice of me, but addressed herself to Clementina. 'Come down at once,' she cried. 'Come down off that horse. You know very well what I told you yesterday. I told you you were not to go out hunting today, disobedient girl.'

Clementina looked at her and said nothing.

'Back you go to the house,' said Miss Milston.

'We have got to get those problems right this morning. Come along at once, Clem. No nonsense, please.'

Clementina did not move.

Miss Milston turned to me. 'Clem was very naughty yesterday, Miss Dean,' she said breathlessly, 'and I told her she was not to hunt.'

I was trying to make up my mind what to do. It was difficult, for I was entirely in the dark as to the nature of the child's offense. I knew, of course, that Miss Milston had chosen the punishment with a view to scoring off me, and this made me angry. There she stood in the middle of the drive, waving her umbrella at us and talking at us in her unpleasant high-pitched voice. She was as full of spite as a toad.

'I'm sorry this should have happened, Miss Milston,' I said, trying to speak calmly. 'I had no idea that Clementina had done anything wrong. Another time it will be better to inform me and allow me to choose her punishment. It is too late now for her to go back, our arrangements are made.'

'It is not too late,' screamed Miss Milston.

I was intensely conscious of the absurdity of the scene and of Sim's eyes watching us all. It was so undignified to brawl over the child, so bad for the child to be brawled over by two women in front of a groom.

'It *is* too late,' I replied. 'Our arrangements must stand. My niece is in my charge while — '

'You are undermining my authority,' she cried.

'I will speak to you tomorrow, we are late already,' I told her and signed to Clementina to proceed. We trotted off down the avenue leaving the wretched woman standing there on the path.

Clementina said nothing; her face wore the shuttered look that had become so familiar to me. I wondered, rather miserably, whether I had done right or wrong — that depended upon what Clementina was feeling about it. I felt I must know.

'Why didn't you tell me what Miss Milston had said?'

'I wanted to come,' she replied simply.

'You put me in a difficult position,' I pointed out.

The idea was evidently new to her. I saw her brows knit as she considered it. 'But it wasn't a fair punishment, you know. She had been waiting for something to happen so that she could prevent me from going out hunting with you. She had been waiting for days and days. It's not fair, is it, to have a punishment waiting ready for a person to do something wrong?'

I did not think it was.

'She knew I couldn't do the sums,' Clementina continued. 'And when I did them wrong, she said it was naughty, and I was to stay in today and do them. I didn't say I would.'

I saw Miss Milston the next morning and told her that she had better find another post. It was an extremely disagreeable interview. She told me that I had no authority to dismiss her; she had been with Clementina for three years. Mrs. Wisdon had engaged her. I pointed out, as tactfully as I could, that I was in charge now and that her salary was paid through me, which gave me the right to dismiss her if I thought fit.

'Clem has never been the same since you came,' she cried. 'You spoil her. You are ruining the child. You have upset the whole house.'

'That is quite enough, Miss Milston,' I said firmly. I paid her and sent her away.

The air was easier to breathe when Miss Milston had gone. I felt quite young and gay, and even Clementina seemed to cast off some of her hundred years. At lunch I inveigled her into playing a ridiculous game called 'Cross questions' which had been a great favorite with Garth and me when we were children. She picked it up very quickly and became quite human over it — I was absurdly pleased at my success.

I decided not to engage a new governess for the child; it was partly because I shirked the task, and partly because I hoped that by teaching Clementina myself I should come to know her better. We did lessons together every morning. I found Clementina an interesting child to teach — interesting but difficult; the subjects that she liked she tackled eagerly and with intelligence, the subjects that bored her she neglected entirely. Arithmetic came under the latter heading with Clementina; she was as ignorant of arithmetic as a normal child of seven. I could not determine whether her brain was incapable of assimilating the most simple rules of arithmetic or whether she simply didn't try — I never found out. I battled with her resolutely but with little success, and we both sighed with relief when the daily hour of arithmetic was over and we were free to consider other matters. She read books with amazing rapidity and an even more amazing catholicity of taste. Any book was grist to Clementina's mill, from boys' adventure stories and Hans Andersen to Dickens, Thackeray and Sir Walter Scott. I tackled her one day on the subject of *Little Dorrit* with which she was enthralled at the moment. I wanted to find out whether she really understood what she was reading.

'I like Tatticoram best,' she said.

'But, Clementina, she was so ungrateful.'

'She couldn't help it, Aunt Charlotte,' Clementina said eagerly. 'They wanted things from her. They wanted her to be grateful. You can't be grateful to people who are always expecting you to be grateful. They were always pawing her.' She shivered. 'I hate being pawed.'

'Dickens didn't mean us to like her.'

'He didn't understand her,' said the astonishing child.

'But, Clementina, he must have understood her to write about her.'

She was silent for a few moments and then she said: 'I know it seems funny, but I'm sure he didn't really understand her any more than the Meagles did. He had never been a little girl so he couldn't know just how little girls feel about things.'

After this conversation I began to feel that I understood Clementina better. She allowed me to understand her, and you helped me, Clare. I felt all the time you were helping me to understand the child. Perhaps you have girls of your own. I did not try to force the pace with

Clementina. I just went my own way. When she wanted to talk to me I was ready to talk, and when she shut herself away from me I turned to other things.

Mr. Howard continued to be friendly with us even after he had heard about the misfortunes of Clementina's parents. In fact, he was even more friendly with us than before. We met him constantly in the hunting field and he often rode over to the Manor for lunch or tea. He was always friendly and cheerful, and I liked him more and more.

One day he rode over from Fairways to have tea with us; Clementina had gone down to the stables, so I was alone in the library when he arrived.

'I'm glad you're alone,' he said. 'I wanted to talk to you.'

'What do you want to talk to me about?' I asked, smiling.

'About that wretched divorce; it makes me mad the way people go on. It's extraordinary to come back from the wilds and find people behaving like this.'

'Behaving like what?' I inquired.

'Refusing to have anything to do with Clementina,' he replied. 'It's not Clementina's fault if her parents made a mess of things. I thought the world had progressed a bit, but it's just as narrow as ever.'

'It's only a little bit of the world,' I told him, 'and you need not waste your pity on us. Clementina and I are quite happy in our own society — and yours.'

'Yes, it's their loss of course. That's what I said to — I mean — er — it makes me feel pretty sick all the same.'

I smiled at his slip; he had evidently been crossing swords with somebody over Clementina and me. It was nice to feel we had a champion, and such a vigorous one.

'Are they still talking about it?' I asked him.

'Well — er — a certain amount,' he replied, looking rather embarrassed at the question. 'It's not so much the actual divorce that they're mad about — lots of people get divorced nowadays. But the Wisdons resented any interference — they kept it all dark. Mrs. Wisdon was stuck up — so they say — and Wisdon snubbed one or two people who tried to poke their noses into his affairs. He was quite right, of course, but it alienated people. The Wisdons didn't want sympathy, they wouldn't tolerate busybodies — that, apparently, is their chief crime.'

I was interested. 'What are people saying — exactly?' I inquired.

'Oh, there are lots of tales,' he said. 'I don't believe the half of them — about what went on at Hinkleton Manor. They have to make up tales because they don't really know anything — that's what annoys them.'

'What kind of tales?'

'I'm not going to tell you. I couldn't, Miss Dean. Besides, they are all lies. You know the wild way people talk nowadays. They talk without thinking. I heard somebody say the other day that Wisdon should have let his wife divorce him, and quite a lot of people agreed.'

'You don't think so?'

'How could I? How could anyone who gave the subject a moment's thought? He would have had to surrender his daughter to a woman who was not fit to look after a child — I'm sorry, Miss Dean, I forgot for a moment she is your sister.'

'I asked for it,' I told him, 'and you haven't said anything as bad about her as I have thought.'

'And a trumped up divorce is a hateful thing to my mind,' he continued. 'Dishonest and degrading. Far worse than a straightforward, above-board case like the Wisdons'. But — would you believe it — they all agreed that Wisdon should have trumped up some evidence so that she could have divorced him — they would have forgiven him then — I think they're all mad. Don't let's talk about it anymore, Miss Dean.'

We didn't speak of it again; there was nothing to be gained by speaking of it. Clementina appeared from the stables and we had tea.

Mr. Howard was our only friend at this time. I heard no more of the Felsteads and concluded that Mrs. Felstead had decided not to allow her child to resume her friendship with Clementina. It was a pity, because I thought it would be good for Clementina to have a friend of her own age, but it could not be helped.

The winter passed, and with it hunting. Spring came to Hinkleton. I had not seen spring come to the country for thirteen years — spring in London is a sad travesty of the real thing. It came very suddenly that year. We had had weeks of cold wind, and then the rain came, and the sun, and a faint haze of green appeared on the face of the earth. It was so beautiful that I could hardly bear it. The small fat buds on the trees and hedges burst asunder, and the tiny leaves appeared and spread their frail green fingers to the sun. In the woods, patches of tender green shone like flames among the darkness of the conifers. The sun poured down, dappling the ground with tiny patches of light and shade. Primroses came, hiding in sheltered nooks, and the sweet woodland violets, and after these came bluebells like a carpet of sea-blue velvet beneath the trees. In the garden were lilacs with their sweet heavy scent, and laburnums, laden with golden rain. Azaleas bloomed in the borders like bushes of fire. The beauty of the spring filled me with happiness — I was glad now that I had chosen to leave my cell. Life in the city was not really life, it was only existence. I made up my mind that I would never go back to Wentworth's. I would rather take a job as a farm hand and spend my days in manual work, laboring in the fields, or tending the cows. It might be possible to get something of the sort, I thought. Perhaps when Garth came back he could find me a country job — I did not care what it was, so long as I could be out in the fields and watch the passing of the seasons and the coming of the flowers.

I walked in the woods finding treasures at every step, the sunlight, the leafy shadows, the flowers — I can't find words to tell you what they meant to me, Clare. I lay on the springy turf with the scent of the pines warm and sweet in my nostrils. I felt the soft moss under my cheek. I think I went mad, that spring, mad with the beauty of the woods.

# 9

## *'She Was Beautiful'*

One day in June, when I had been at Hinkleton Manor for about eight months I received a telegram from George Hamilton asking me to come at once to an address in Brighton: Kitty was ill and wanted to see me. The telegram had been forwarded from Wentworth's, and I realized that Kitty did not know that I had taken up my abode at the Manor. It seemed strange that Kitty should want me, but I could not refuse to go to her when she was ill. I showed the telegram to Nanny and told her I must catch the ten o'clock train.

'I suppose you *must* go, Miss Char,' she said. 'But come back as soon as you can. We won't tell Clemmie about it. It would only upset her.'

I had no time to arrange anything; I threw a few clothes into a suitcase and set off. All the way down to Brighton I thought of Kitty and wondered about her — how ill was she? Why did she want to see me, me of all people?

Kitty had dropped out of my mind so completely in the last few months that I had scarcely thought of her at all except in a vague way as the mother of Clementina. And now she had come back into my life like a thunderbolt out of a blue sky. She had a habit of doing that,

I mused. She had a habit of disappearing out of my life for months — or even years — and returning suddenly and unexpectedly with peremptory demands upon my time. What kind of Kitty should I find when I reached Brighton? Would she be the old carefree Kitty of her little girlhood, or the Kitty who had come to me in trouble and made me the receptacle of her moods, or would she be the hard woman with the hatred in her eyes who had looked at me across the crowded courtroom and frightened me so?

I was still frightened when I remembered that look of scorn and hatred; it came back to me very vividly, and a cold shiver ran up my spine. That look was the last I had had from Kitty; I had not seen her since.

I gazed out of the window at the flying fields and tried to calm myself and to reason with the strange fear which had seized upon me — was I afraid of Kitty? I thought about it for a little and decided that it was not Kitty of whom I was afraid; it was the hatred which had terrified me. And surely the hatred must have gone now or she would not have sent for me to come to her when she was ill. It was a comforting thought, and I held on to it and elaborated it. If Kitty had married Mr. Hamilton and was happy with him — as Garth had seemed to expect — she would bear me no grudge for the part I had played in the divorce. Happy people do not cherish grievances. It is only when people are miserable, when they feel that the world has treated them badly, that hatred finds a lodging in their hearts.

Soon I had convinced myself that Kitty was happy, and had sent for me to tell me so and to be friends with me. I was ready to meet her halfway, ready to wash out all the misunderstandings of the past few years.

The journey was a troublesome one, like all cross-country journeys; it involved innumerable changes, and long waits for dawdling trains. I became more and more tired and impatient as the day wore on, and wished at least a dozen times that I had made the journey by car.

I had wired to Mr. Hamilton to say that I would arrive at 5:10 and I more than half expected that he would be at the station to meet me. I tried to conjure up his face as I had seen it in court; a smooth round face, with a bewildered expression like that of a little boy who has been punished for something and does not understand why. (I had sympathized with the bewildered expression because I had felt bewildered too.) I had thought he looked kind and nice — not at all like a man who would steal another man's wife. I had wondered about him a little.

As the train drew into the station I scrutinized the faces upon the platform — the eagerly searching, anxious faces peculiar to those who have come to meet their friends and are afraid they may not recognize them before the doors are opened and the quiet platform becomes Bedlam let loose — but I could see nobody with the least resemblance to the man I remembered. I collected my suitcase and found a taxi with some difficulty. Brighton was glaring white in the afternoon sunshine; the brightness of it hurt my eyes, already tired with the long day's traveling.

The taxi stopped at a large square house standing well back in a formal garden. I looked up at it anxiously and saw that the blinds were drawn . . .

* * *

George Hamilton met me on the doorstep; he was pale and miserable — more like a little boy than ever — his eyes were rimmed with red.

'You're — you're too late,' he said thickly.

'Too late!'

He nodded. 'She died this morning.' I stared at him aghast. I had never thought of this — not once in all my imaginings had I visualized this ending to my journey.

'I came at once,' I stammered. 'I wasn't in London — your wire was forwarded.'

He made a helpless gesture with his hands.

'I can't believe,' I said stupidly. 'Kitty — she was so — so full of life.'

'I know,' he said, looking down at his hands and speaking in that thick, husky voice which is the aftermath of weeping. 'She was so full of life . . . it's difficult to believe, isn't it? You didn't see her when she was ill . . . and that makes it harder to believe. I wish you had been here.'

'I came at once,' I said again.

'You couldn't help it,' he replied drearily. 'These things just happen . . . she wanted you, that's why I wired, she wanted to tell you something.'

'What did she want to tell me?'

'I don't know, she said she wanted your forgiveness.'

'But I had forgiven her long ago.'

'I wish we had known,' he said, still in that dreary, expressionless voice. 'I wish we could have told her that you knew about it — whatever it was — and had forgiven her. She kept on saying over and over again, 'I must see Char — I must tell her about it — tell Char to come — I must see Char.' '

'I'm sorry.'

'I thought once she was going to give me a message for you,' he continued. 'She said, 'Tell Char it all happened so easily. It was such a little lie at first — such a little lie — and then it grew and grew.' And then she cried out that it had grown into a tree and we were all hanging on it, you and I and Wisdon and herself — she was delirious of course.'

'She must have been delirious,' I said. 'I had forgiven her for deceiving me over that night in the flat — I suppose it was that.'

'Perhaps,' he said. 'I don't know. I only know she wanted to see you, she kept on saying, 'I must see Char.' She was afraid to die. She was — afraid. It was dreadful,' he said, twisting his hands, 'dreadful, dreadful, dreadful.'

'I wish — I wish I could have been here sooner,' I said again. It seemed to me that I had said the same thing a dozen times; I could find nothing else to say to him, no comfort of any kind to give him.

'It was pneumonia,' he continued. 'First 'flu, you know, and then pneumonia. She wasn't so very ill at first, and then — two days ago — she suddenly got worse. I could see it in the doctor's face. I had specialists . . . they said they were afraid . . . they thought her heart . . . I did all I could, everything they suggested . . . '

'I'm sure you did,' I told him, as comfortingly as I could. 'Perhaps her heart wasn't very strong — our mother died very suddenly of heart trouble.'

He nodded miserably. 'It was when she — when she knew that she wasn't going to get better that she began to ask for you. She said over and over again, 'I can't die till I've seen Char.' She clung to my hand and said I wasn't to let her die — she was so afraid — so afraid.'

'I'm sorry.'

'She's happy now, isn't she?' he asked, looking at me with his pathetic brown eyes. 'She knows now that you've forgiven her and that everything's all right — you believe that, don't you, Miss Dean?'

I said I believed it.

We were still standing in the hall; he was too stricken to think of asking me to sit down. I leaned against the carved oak table, for my knees were knocking together and I felt that all the strength had flowed out of my body.

'I suppose — you'd like to — to see her,' he said at last.

He took me upstairs to see Kitty. It was a beautiful room, big and airy; Kitty was lying very peacefully in the bed. The room was full of flowers — great masses of roses and lilac — there were pink roses in the hands that were crossed so peacefully upon her breast.

'Isn't she beautiful?' he said softly.

She was beautiful. She looked very pure and holy, very young. Her face wore an expression of sweet austerity. It was very calm, very peaceful. I saw that the old Kitty had come back — the Kitty that I had known and loved long ago. And yet it was not quite the old Kitty, for this was a woman, not a girl, a woman who had sampled life, who had been tossed by its storms and had come at last into a haven of rest.

Memories of the past crowded into my mind — memories of the past — discarded fragments of days long fled. I was overwhelmed with grief — not so much for Kitty's broken life as for the mystery of Life itself. Kitty's life was but half run — a mere twisted fragment — how could I think that it was complete? Where could I find the purpose, the meaning of it all?

There had been none of this bewilderment in my mind when I had stood and looked down upon the still forms of my mother and my father — they had had their lives. Death is natural when it comes to the old, natural and even kindly. But this was different, this was a ruthless thing.

I realized that Mr. Hamilton was speaking. 'We had only been married for a few months,' he was saying. 'Just a few months, that's all, and I loved her more than ever. But I'm glad we were married because, you see, she belongs to me now. She doesn't belong to anybody else. She's my very own.'

He leaned over her and touched her hand

possessively, protectingly. It was almost as if he were afraid that I would claim her — God knows I had no thought of such a thing. His love for Kitty had given him the right to call her his.

'She was good,' he continued huskily. 'She really was good, Miss Dean. There was no badness in her. She just liked fun and amusement — she was so gay and pretty you see — and she needed love. We were very happy together. We suited each other. All I wanted was to see her happy, and when she was happy it made me happy too. She wasn't happy with — with Wisdon.' He raised his eyes and looked at me, almost sternly. 'He wasn't kind to her, Miss Dean, and she needed kindness so much.'

I nodded — I couldn't speak — it was true. Garth had not been kind to Kitty.

I stayed to dinner at Garton Lodge and went to a hotel for the night. Mr. Hamilton talked about Kitty all the time — I like to think that he found some relief in talking to me about her; he needed all the comfort he could get. He talked about her unselfishness, her goodness, her sunny nature, and the courage with which she had faced her ruined life. I listened to it all and I had to believe what he was saying — he believed it so implicitly himself — and yet, all the time at the back of my mind, I knew that Kitty had not been quite like that. I had seen another side of her, a side that George Hamilton had never seen. Perhaps the truth lay between our two visions — Kitty was neither all black nor all white but a mixture of the two, like the rest of humanity.

When the time came for me to go back to the

hotel he asked me to stay with him. He could easily put me in the spare room for the night, he said, looking at me with his pathetic brown eyes. But I could not stay. I was worn out. I had given him all the sympathy I could and I felt empty. I must have time for my own sorrow.

He walked back to the hotel with me and left me there. I stayed at Brighton until after the funeral and then went home.

# 10

## *Nanny's Story*

It was late at night when I arrived at the Manor. Nanny met me in the hall and we went into the library together. I had wired the news to her, but she was anxious to hear the details of Kitty's death. Nanny had ordered some Bengers for me, and I sat by the fire sipping it and telling her all that had happened.

'I'm glad she was happy,' Nanny said. 'Poor soul! She wasn't happy here. I'll be glad to think she had a happy time before she died. I liked that Mr. Hamilton — he was a wicked man, I suppose, but I liked him.'

'Did he come here often?' I asked her.

'Yes, quite a lot,' Nanny said. 'At first he came when Mr. Garth was here, and afterward he came when Mr. Garth was away. Mr. Garth used to go away a lot. There was one time he came for the weekend with his aunt (she was a nice lady), and something happened. I'll tell you about it, Miss Char. It doesn't matter telling you. Clemmie came and woke me up in the middle of the night. She'd been to the dentist the day before and her tooth was aching. Mrs. Wisdon had a bottle of aspirin, and the dentist said Clemmie was to have one if her tooth was bad. Clemmie said she'd been down to her mother's room to get the aspirin and her mother wasn't there. Well, I didn't think much about it, I thought perhaps Mrs. Wisdon had gone along to the bathroom or something. I got Clemmie back to bed and went down to get the aspirin myself. Mrs. Wisdon wasn't in her room and she wasn't in the bathroom neither. Well, I took the aspirin out of the cupboard and took it up to Clemmie and gave her one. 'Where can Mummy be?' she said to me, looking at me with her big eyes. 'Don't you worry, my lamb,' I said, 'Mummy couldn't sleep and she went downstairs to get a book.' It was a silly thing to say, because Mrs. Wisdon never was much of a reader, but it was the first thing that came into my head. I was upset and I couldn't think what to say. I didn't know where Mrs. Wisdon was, but I did have a kind of suspicion, and I wasn't going to have Clemmie worrying. Well, I could see Clemmie didn't believe that. She just looked at me, but she didn't say nothing. She's like that, Clemmie, if you tell her a thing, and she doesn't believe you, she just doesn't say another word, but you know well enough you haven't put her off with your story.

'Where was I? Oh yes, well I tucked Clemmie up, and then I thought I better see about Mrs. Wisdon. She might be ill or she might not. I went down again, and she wasn't anywhere about. I couldn't make up my mind what to do. I sat and waited a bit, and then I thought I'd go downstairs and see if she'd gone to sleep by the fire or something, but she wasn't there neither. It was four o'clock by the drawing room clock and bitterly cold. So then I came upstairs again to the first floor, and I heard voices on the landing. It was quite dark on the stair where I was, but Mrs. Wisdon's bedroom light was on and the door was open. I heard Mrs. Wisdon say, 'But, George, I know I left the light on. I always leave it on. I hate coming back to my room in the dark.' 'You can't have,' he says. 'If you left it on, it would have been on when we came back.' 'Unless somebody turned it off,' Mrs. Wisdon says. They talked a bit longer about the light in a worried sort of way, she saying she'd left it on and he saying she couldn't have. I couldn't remember whether it had been on or off when I came down, I'd been in such a state. Well, then they both came to the door and kissed each other and he went away. And Mrs. Wisdon she went back into her room and shut the door. I was all of a tremble, not knowing whether I ought to say anything or not. I went back to bed — it was no good saying anything *then*. I couldn't sleep a wink I was so upset.'

'Did you tell Garth about it?' I asked her.

'Not then, I didn't,' she replied. 'It was so awful, Miss Char. I couldn't make up my mind to tell him. I couldn't speak to a soul about it, and that made it worse. If I could have talked to somebody — but of course I couldn't. Well, it went on and on in my head and I began to think I was going mad with the worry of it. I couldn't sleep, and I kept forgetting things — it was more than I could bear. So at last I said to myself I'd go and tell him the whole thing — it seemed to me that things couldn't be worse than what they were. Mr. Garth was never at home and when he was he never spoke to nobody. I thought, 'Perhaps they'll have a row and it'll clear the air' — that's what I thought. So I wrote him a letter and said I wanted to see him — he wasn't at the Manor you see — and I got a letter back telling me to come to London to his flat that he'd taken. Well, I wrote out on a paper exactly what had happened and I went up to London for the day and saw him.

''Well, Nanny,' he said, 'what do you want — more wages I suppose. You're not worth it, you old fraud.' That was his joke, Miss Char, because he knew I'd have stayed on at the Manor for nothing. He'd wanted to raise my wages some time before, but I wouldn't have it. I was getting quite enough — you don't want much when you get to my age — and I knew Mr. Garth would give me a pension when I wasn't any more use, so what was the good of bothering? I was glad to see he could still make a bit of a joke — he looked *awful*, Miss Char, great black rings round his eyes as if he hadn't had a wink of sleep for weeks — but I couldn't joke — not if you'd paid me. My legs were trembling so I could hardly stand. He gave me some brandy and made me sit down, and I just took out the paper I'd written and gave it into his hand. I couldn't speak or anything. Well, he read the paper all through twice and then he got up and walked about. His face was awful.

'After a bit he began talking. He said, 'It's funny you coming today, Nanny. Why did you say nothing at the time and then suddenly make up your mind to tell me?' I told him what I told you, that I was worried to death, and things couldn't be worse. He laughed in a funny sort of way and said that's what *he'd* been thinking, and he had been to a lawyer about a divorce. That scared me, and I tried to persuade him it wasn't the right thing, but he talked me round. He said it was impossible to go on, and that I'd said myself things couldn't be worse, and what about Clemmie — he said — did I think this sort of thing was good for a child? I couldn't say it was. So then I said I supposed he could get a divorce with the paper I'd given him. He looked at me very quick and said, 'You'd have to appear in court, Nanny.' That frightened me. I thought perhaps if I just signed the paper with my name he could give it to the Judge or something. But he said no, they wouldn't do that, I'd have to stand up an' answer questions in court. It sounded awful, but I just set my teeth an' I said, 'I will if you want me to, Mr. Garth.' After all he was my baby, I would do anything for him and I didn't suppose the Judge would eat me.

'So then he walked about a bit more and stood looking out of the window, and then he said, 'No, I can't do it, we'll have to manage without.' 'I'll do it,' I said again. He turned round from the window and looked at me. 'And what about Clem?' he said. I saw what he meant of course. Clemmie was in it too, it was her that had gone down first and found her Mummy's room empty. 'I couldn't do that,' he said. 'Better to lose the case — no, the thing is impossible.' He meant he couldn't have Clemmie in court to tell the story against her own mother. So I thought a bit and then I said, 'We don't need to have Clemmie in it at all. I needn't say it was her that found the room empty. I needn't say anything about Clemmie at all. Just that I went down myself.' 'They would ask what wakened you,' he said. 'I might have had the toothache myself,' I said. 'You might have, but you didn't,' he said, and he smiled at me quite like his old self. 'How do you know I didn't have toothache?' I said. 'No, Nanny,' he said. 'It won't do. I won't have you telling lies for me.' 'It's only a little one,' I said. (And so it was. It didn't affect nobody whether Clemmie had been down first or not.) 'Not even a little one,' he said. 'There have been too many lies. The whole purpose of this horrible business is to clear up all the lies. I'll have nothing but the truth,' he said. 'I'm sick of lies. No, Nanny, it won't do. We'll have to do the best we can without you.'

'Well that's about all, except that he thanked me for coming to him and said a lot of nonsense about how I was his only friend in all the world. And he took me to a grand restaurant and we had lunch together — just him and me. I was glad I'd put on my best hat and coat, but even then there's not many gentlemen would have taken their old Nanny to lunch at a grand restaurant like that. And then he saw me into the Hinkleton train and I came home.'

'Poor Nanny!' I said. 'It was horrible for you.'

'Yes, it was,' she agreed. 'I was miserable; it made me quite ill not knowing what I ought to do or anything. I felt better when I'd told Mr.

Garth all about it. The worst was having it all on my mind and not knowing whether to say anything or not. I was glad I didn't have to go into court — I'd have done it if he'd wanted me to, but I wouldn't have liked it.'

We sat for a little longer, by the dying fire, talking about it. Nanny's story had justified Garth completely in my mind. For Clementina's sake he was bound to act. I had been a little dubious in my own mind about Garth's behavior. It had seemed to me rather mean to trap Kitty with detectives. I saw now that there had been plenty of evidence in his hands; evidence which would have given him his divorce without the slightest trouble, but he had refrained from using it and had chosen the harder way. He could not have dragged Clementina into the case — I saw that — but he might quite easily have accepted Nanny's offer and allowed her to tell the tale as she had suggested, without bringing Clementina into it at all. I don't know how it strikes you, Clare, but it seemed to me that Garth might have accepted Nanny's offer without any qualms of conscience; it seemed to me that Garth was ultra-fastidious to sacrifice such a valuable piece of evidence because the whole truth could not be revealed without bringing Clementina's name into the affair. Perhaps my conscience is too elastic, but that was what I felt. And I felt, also, an added respect for Garth, such as we all must feel for a man who sacrifices his own interests for a principle. We may think such a man foolish, but we are bound to respect him, we are bound to recognize his nobility and his strength. Truth at all costs, Garth had said. It was a noble aim.

There was just one more point I wanted to clear up, I felt I *must* know. It was a point which had worried me often and often.

'Nanny,' I said, 'do you think — was it — had it happened before — ever?'

'I'm afraid it had, Miss Char,' Nanny replied. 'That was what worried me so. I thought about it myself a lot, and I felt certain in my own mind it had happened before. You see when they came back and found the light turned off in Mrs. Wisdon's bedroom she said to him, 'I always leave it on. I hate coming back to my room in the dark.' That's what she said, Miss Char. You can't make nothing else of that but that it had happened before, even if the way they behaved hadn't showed as much.'

'Yes,' I said sadly. I was answered.

That was the first time Nanny and I discussed the matter and the last. It was all over now, Kitty was dead and Garth had disappeared into the wilds of Africa. The whole thing was over and done with, it was better not to talk of it, not even to think of it again.

We went upstairs to bed very quietly, for it was late, and the whole house seemed asleep.

'I suppose Clementina is asleep,' I whispered.

'Long ago,' Nanny assured me.

I decided to peep in at the child — I had missed her surprisingly during my three days' absence. I would not waken her, of course. I would just have a quiet peep at her and come away.

I saw when I opened the door that the room

was full of bright moonlight. The windows were wide open and the curtains pulled back. The moon streamed in and lay on the carpet in a pool of light. Clementina turned over in bed and held out her arms.

'Aunt Charlotte, you've come back,' she said eagerly. 'I heard the car ages ago.'

'My dear, I thought you were asleep. I've been talking to Nanny.'

I sat down on the bed and she put her arms round my neck, I felt her hot cheek against mine.

'I thought perhaps you weren't coming back,' she said.

I was too wise to say — would you have minded? She had shown me that she would have minded. Clementina could not give you love when you asked for it — I knew that now — she had given me love unasked and I was very happy. She lay back on the pillow and looked at me with bright, questioning eyes; she longed to know where I had been, but she was not going to ask.

'Do you want me to tell you where I have been?' I asked her.

'Yes.'

I told her. She lay and listened quietly while I told her about her mother's death.

# 11

## *'I'm Glad They Aren't Like the Other People'*

Clementina and I were out riding one day. There was a particularly beautiful ride through the woods and over the moor and we often went that way. We were cantering along on the springy turf when we saw a horseman approaching from the opposite direction.

'It's Mr. Felstead,' said Clementina, pulling up Black Knight. 'Let's turn and go the other way.'

'We can't, it's too late,' I said quickly. 'Besides Mr. Felstead was quite friendly.'

Mr. Felstead reined up and raised his hat. We exchanged the usual remarks about the weather, and then he said, 'I'm afraid you will think my wife very remiss. She fully intended to call upon you, Miss Dean, but she has been nowhere and seen nobody. We have had a very anxious time — I expect you have heard.'

We had heard nothing. Clementina and I were as isolated from our kind as if we had been living on a desert island.

'Our girl had a very serious accident last March,' he said. 'She fell downstairs and injured her spine. It was such a strange thing to happen to a child like Violet who has ridden since she could walk — and taken innumerable spills without turning a hair — to fall downstairs in her own house. At first we were afraid that the injury was permanent — they said she would never walk — it was dreadful — but now the specialist gives us hope that she may be cured in time.'

I told him I was very sorry indeed, and I *was* sorry. He was such a kind, friendly man, and he looked worn and sad, and years older.

'Thank you,' he said, 'I'm glad I met you. I wanted to explain why it was that my wife didn't call. She has been so anxious, so terribly anxious about Violet — you will understand.'

Clementina said nothing; she sat very still on Black Knight, looking straight ahead, with a queer, stony expression on her face.

'And what about Wisdon?' continued Mr. Felstead. 'No news yet?'

'No news,' I told him. 'But we don't expect to hear anything of him until October or November.'

'Let me know when you hear,' he said; 'I shall be interested. I should like to go trekking off into the wilds myself but here I am tied by the leg — the City three times a week — it's a dog's life.'

We talked a little more and then parted from him.

Clementina was very silent all the way home. It did not surprise me, for she often took these silent turns — even now — and I had found it was best to leave her alone. It was not until she was going up to bed I discovered what had been troubling her. I was reading one of Mr.

Wentworth's books and I kissed her a trifle absently — I was voyaging in Mexico at the time.

'Aunt Charlotte,' she said, 'are you — are you busy?'

'No, of course not.'

'Do you think I could send Violet something — a book perhaps?'

'Violet?' I said, still half dazed by my rapid journey from Mexico.

'Violet Felstead.'

'Oh, yes. Yes. I think it would be nice to send her a book. We'll get one and send it to her. What kind of books does she like?'

She hesitated, looking out of the window. 'She didn't like any kind of books much, but perhaps she will like them now. It would be dreadful to be ill and not like books.'

'Yes,' I encouraged.

'We were friends,' she said slowly and thoughtfully. 'We were friends before. And then Mummy and Mrs. Felstead quarreled. So we couldn't be friends anymore. Mummy wouldn't let me go to Oldgarden when they asked me, and she wouldn't let me have Violet. So of course they left off asking me, you see.'

'Yes, I see.'

'And I thought they were like all the other people and didn't want to have anything to do with me — but it was because Violet was ill. I didn't know she was ill.'

'That was the reason,' I agreed.

'I'm glad,' Clementina said. 'I don't mean I'm glad Violet's ill, but I'm glad they aren't like the other people. You see, I liked them all so much

— all of them. You would like Violet, Aunt Charlotte, and Violet's Mummy — she's so nice and full of fun. Poor Violet — how ill do you think she is, Aunt Charlotte?'

'I think she has been very ill, but she is getting better now, Mr. Felstead said so.'

'Is she in bed all the time?'

'I'm afraid so. I'm afraid she will have to be in bed for months.'

'Poor Violet,' said Clementina thoughtfully. 'I would hate to be in bed all the time, but Violet will hate it even more.'

We sent a book to Violet Felstead and Clementina got a letter from her friend thanking her and asking her over to Oldgarden to tea.

That summer was a happy time. Clementina and I did lessons together in the morning, and in the afternoon we rode or went for picnics. Sometimes we took the car and went down to the sea, thirty miles away, and bathed or paddled. Clementina and I became friends; she opened the door of her citadel and let me in. I saw that it was the life she had been leading which had made her so strange, so silent and withdrawn. The secrets in the house had weighed her down, the tension between her parents, the loss of her one friend, had all conspired to make her what she was. And Miss Milston had not helped matters. There was nobody near her to whom she could talk openly, nobody who understood her, nobody who really wanted her or valued her for herself. It was no wonder that the child had been difficult, no wonder that she had been strange. The resumption of her friendship with Violet Felstead was a great joy to Clementina; she went over to Oldgarden once a week to lunch or tea. Mrs. Felstead called upon me, but I was out, and she was out when I returned her call so I had not met her yet. I was anxious to meet the mother of Clementina's friend, but she was still very much tied with her sick child. She went nowhere and saw nobody. Clementina told me that she scarcely ever left Violet for a moment.

'Violet gets restless when she's not there,' said Clementina. 'I think it's rather bad for Mrs. Felstead, but of course Violet has been awfully ill. They're all so happy, now that Violet is going to get better. It must be nice to have people as fond of you as that.'

'I would be very happy if you had been ill and were going to get better,' I told her, smiling.

She blushed and looked down. 'You always seem to know what I'm thinking,' she said.

# 12

## *Bad News*

The summer passed, and in September came a message from Garth's solicitor asking me to expect him to lunch. Clementina and I had been out cubbing since six o'clock; we got back about eleven and found the message waiting for us. Clementina picked it up and read it with a little frown.

'What do you think he wants, Aunt Charlotte?'

I was desperately afraid that he might have bad news of Garth for us, but I hid my feelings and replied casually, 'Business, I expect. You know that Daddy left the management of the estate in Mr. Ponsonby's hands.'

'Yes, I know,' she said doubtfully, 'but he has never been down here before — not since Daddy went away, I mean.'

'All the more reason why he should come now,' I replied. 'You had better hurry up and have your bath, my child. You are going over to lunch at Oldgarden, aren't you?'

'Perhaps I had better not go.'

'Nonsense, I'll deal with Mr. Ponsonby.'

I wanted her to go. I felt it would be better to have her out of the way. It might be business, of course (I tried to think that that was all it was), but somehow or other I was sure that he was bringing bad news of Garth.

I hustled Clementina out of the house before Mr. Ponsonby's arrival. The car was to take her to Oldgarden and pick up Mr. Ponsonby at the station on the way back.

Mr. Ponsonby arrived before I was ready. I found him standing in front of the fire in the library warming himself and drinking sherry. I remembered that I had seen him in court, sitting next to Garth — a thin, dapper man, rather above medium height, with gray wavy hair and a single eyeglass.

'Ah, Miss Dean,' he said, putting down his glass and shaking hands with me in a rather perfunctory manner, 'You will wonder why I have come down to see you like this, without adequate notice. I am the bearer of sad news.'

'Garth?' I said breathlessly. 'Not Garth! Oh, it can't be — it can't be Garth.'

I sat down in the nearest chair, and Mr. Ponsonby poured out a glass of sherry and made me drink it.

'Is he — is he dead!' I asked in a dazed way.

'I'm afraid so.'

'Garth — dead?' I said incredulously. 'Oh, it can't be true! I can't believe it — there must be some mistake.'

'I'm sorry,' Mr. Ponsonby said, 'I'm afraid that I should have — should have prepared you for the news . . . I didn't know — ' He stopped suddenly.

'You didn't know I would mind,' I said in a choking voice.

The room swayed around me and grew dark;

Mr. Ponsonby's voice seemed to come from a long way off . . . I clung to the table . . . it was the only solid thing in the universe. I thought — so this is what fainting is like . . .

* * *

The first thing I saw when I opened my eyes was Nanny's face; she was holding a glass to my lips and whispering to me to drink some. Barling was standing near with a tray in his hands.

'Has he — gone?' I asked.

'Who? Mr. Ponsonby? Yes, my dear, he's having his lunch. What a fright you gave us!'

Her arm was underneath my head as I lay on the sofa. I looked up into her face. I was remembering now, remembering . . . Garth was dead . . . Garth. He would never come back . . . I should never see him again. It was all over. He was dead. Kitty was dead . . . I had seen her lying in bed with flowers in her hands, but I should never see Garth . . .

'You'd better drink some more brandy, Miss Char,' Nanny said.

'No, I'm all right,' I told her. 'Just leave me, Nanny. I shall be all right soon.'

She stood up and looked at me. Her poor old face was quivering.

'I never thought of this,' she said tremulously. 'He was so strong, Mr. Garth was. Oh, why did we let him go?'

I hid my face in the cushion and let the tears come — slow, bitter tears. Garth had gone, all that part of my life which had been bound up with him — all the best part of my life — had gone with him. I had loved him so; I had suffered so much through him and with him. I had agonized over the change in him. All this had bound me to him in some strange, mysterious way. Living in his house, and looking after his child had brought him nearer to me than he had ever been before. I thought of him as the old Garth. (That other Garth, the cynical, cruel Garth, was not really Garth at all. A sort of madness had taken possession of him, a madness begotten of his pain and shame.) It seemed so dreadful that I should never see him again to put things right between us; I should never know now what had gone wrong. If I could have him back — even for five minutes — I would fling myself at his feet and ask him why he had changed to me, why he took pleasure in hurting me. But the dead can never come back — not even for five minutes, so that the living may abase themselves.

After a little while I sat up and tried to control my tears. Although I had wept for him I knew that I had not really accepted the fact that Garth was dead, nor visualized the frightful gap that his death would leave in my life. That would come later. For the moment I must try to gain some measure of composure so that I could speak to Mr. Ponsonby and learn the details of the tragedy. I must know what had happened to Garth — how he had died. Mr. Ponsonby could tell me. I got up and rang the bell, I felt better now — strangely empty and light-headed, but quite calm.

Mr. Ponsonby came in looking rather frightened and remorseful. 'I cannot tell you how sorry I am to have broken the news so — so badly,' he began.

'Don't let's talk about it,' I said. 'I'm sorry I was silly — I've never fainted before and I don't know why I did it.'

'I should have prepared you.'

'You see I have known him so long — I can't remember a time when he wasn't there. So it's difficult to — to realize.'

'I know,' he said, 'I know.'

'If you would just tell me the details — and then — go away,' I said, not very politely, I'm afraid.

Fortunately he seemed to understand — he was really very kind — he took a slip of paper out of his pocket-book and handed it to me.

'This is all I know,' he said. 'It is a wire from Mr. Fraser — the leader of the expedition of which Mr. Wisdon was a member — we shall hear further details of the accident when the letter arrives.'

I took the slip of paper and read the message: '*Grieved to inform you Garth Wisdon lost his life letter follows am forwarding effects, Fraser.*'

'Could there be any — any mistake?' I asked him as I handed it back.

'I'm afraid not,' replied Mr. Ponsonby, looking down at the fire. 'It would not be kind for me to encourage you to hope. Mr. Fraser would not have wired unless — Mr. Fraser is a most trustworthy, capable man. He would not have been chosen for such a post if he had been otherwise. It is really kinder to tell you this now.'

'Yes,' I said, and then, 'You will let me know when you get the letter.'

'Of course. I shall come down later and bring the letter for you to see. There will be various matters to discuss — I have Mr. Wisdon's will, he revised it before he sailed.'

Mr. Ponsonby paused and looked at me expectantly.

'Then he must have known,' I said, 'known that he might not come back. I wondered if it was — dangerous.'

'No, no, Miss Dean. The will had to be revised after the divorce. Circumstances had altered — it was a mere formality. Perhaps Mr. Wisdon consulted you about his will?'

It was a question, couched in significant tones. I looked at the man in amazement. 'Consulted me!' I echoed.

'Why not? It would have been quite natural — at any rate you will be interested to hear it?'

I did not answer. How could he expect me to take an interest in Garth's will? I could scarcely believe yet that Garth was dead.

'It is a very simple document,' continued Mr. Ponsonby. 'We shall have no trouble over it.'

I let him talk, my thoughts were elsewhere. I was bowed down by the sudden realization of the awful task before me — the task of breaking the news of her father's death to Clementina.

# 13

## *Simple Documents*

It is an astonishing thing how one goes on from grief, passes through the sharpness of it and leaves it behind. Clementina and I passed through our grief together. We comforted each other and so comforted ourselves. The misery passed, but the sense of loss remained, the sense of emptiness, the sense of exposure. I felt as if the winds were blowing through the house; it was not so safe and comfortable as it had been in Garth's lifetime. The world rocked upon its foundations, the house sat heavily upon my shoulders. It was the more strange because I had no idea that I depended upon Garth in any way. He had been gone nearly a year, and for most of that time I could not even write to him — I suppose that I had been depending upon the prospect of his return without being conscious of the fact.

Clementina and I ate and drank, we went to bed at night and got up in the morning, we rode and studied and walked. Everything went on exactly the same and yet everything seemed different. The sun shone just the same as before, and the same view lay before our eyes when we looked out of the window. Nothing had happened at all, and yet everything had happened.

The only visible sign of Garth's death was in Clementina's wardrobe. We went up to town in the car and bought her a gray frock with white collar and cuffs, and a gray winter coat and hat. Clementina wanted it. She had not been able to mourn visibly for her mother, but there was nothing to prevent her from mourning for her father. She could be proud of him, and she was proud.

Mr. Ponsonby came to Hinkleton about a month later, with Mr. Fraser's letter and Garth's will. Clementina had lunch upstairs with Nanny, but after lunch she came down to the library, as we had arranged, to hear Mr. Ponsonby read the letter. He eyed her doubtfully as she came in, she looked very childish in the gray frock, with her hair drawn back from her delicate forehead and hanging down over her shoulders in two plaits; she looked very young and pathetic.

'Do you intend Miss Clementina to hear the letter?' he asked. 'It is rather painful — wouldn't it be better — '

'I think she has a right to hear it if she wishes to,' I replied.

Clementina looked at me gratefully. 'Please, Mr. Ponsonby,' she said in her light childish voice, 'I want to know all about Daddy.'

I could see Mr. Ponsonby did not approve of the arrangement; he probably thought me a peculiar guardian for the child, but. I felt sure that I was doing the right thing. Clementina had suffered so much misery from being kept in ignorance of her parents' affairs that I had made up my mind she should be kept in ignorance no longer. She should know all there was to know — all that I knew, and, what was more important still, she should know that there was no more to know. Knowledge is less hard to bear than ignorance if you possess an imagination like Clementina's.

Mr. Ponsonby opened the letter and cleared his throat. 'This was written in the desert,' he said, 'and sent to the nearest town with the same runner who dispatched the wire. Mr. Fraser has given us a very clear account of the whole affair.

' 'The expedition has been moderately successful from my point of view. I have done what I set out to do and have mapped out sites for depots for an airline within the radius apportioned to me. Observations of a scientific nature have been made by the various experts who accompanied the expedition. Garth Wisdon joined us as an independent member, that is to say he paid his way, but was to all intents and purposes a member of the company. I suspect that he had an objective in joining us, but he was reticent about it. I was glad to accept him on his own terms, as he was an acquisition to any company; brave and cool in the face of danger, resourceful in trouble, and bearing with fortitude the discomforts and inconveniences of our daily life. He made copious notes during our journey, and embodied them in a diary. The diary was to form the foundation of a book. I am forwarding the diary with the rest of his effects and would suggest that it should be edited by some accredited person and published. It will, of course, be some months before Wisdon's effects reach England.' '

Mr. Ponsonby stopped for a moment and looked at me. 'The diary of the expedition is yours, Miss Dean. It is especially mentioned in the will.'

'I shall edit the diary,' I said huskily. 'He asked me to do so if — if — '

Mr. Ponsonby nodded. 'I am glad,' he said. 'It would be a pity if Mr. Wisdon's diary were not to be published. His writings are worthwhile. I am glad we are to have the book. Let me urge you to do it soon — as soon as the diary arrives.'

He took up the letter again and continued.

' 'We had penetrated to the limit of our supplies. That is to say we had used half the quantity of provisions carried. I pointed this out to my companions and we agreed that it was time to return; Wisdon followed me to my tent and asked whether it would be possible for us to remain another week in the neighborhood. By reducing rations slightly it would have been possible to do so, but I did not feel justified in taking the risk. As it was, I had not allowed any margin for unexpected delays on our return journey. Wisdon was disappointed at my decision — I could see that — but he realized that I did not feel I could agree to his request, and accepted my decision without argument — he was under my orders as leader of the expedition and his sense of discipline was high. I told him that we would stay in camp two days longer and then start homeward. He thanked me and went away.

' 'That night we were disturbed by lions. They came down quite near our camp and roared continuously. I was surprised, because we had seen no lions for some time; it is on the fringe of the desert that lions are found, not in the interior. It struck me that there must be an oasis fairly near (though our guides had no knowledge of one) as lions do not stray very far from water. In the morning it was discovered that one of the native porters had been carried off by the lions — this surprised me still more, for the real desert lion is not a man-eater. Wisdon asked my permission to go out after the lions. I agreed, but advised him to take his servant and one of the native hunters with him. I anticipated no danger, for Wisdon was a very fine shot and the native hunter knew his job. 'Don't stay out after dark,' I said as he was going out of the tent. He looked back at me and laughed. 'Don't worry, I can look after myself, you old granny!' he said, and with that he dropped the tent flap and disappeared — I never saw him again. We were busy all day repacking the stores for our return journey. As the day wore on I became anxious. I sent out two search parties in the direction which I knew Wisdon had gone. Night fell and still there was no sign of him or his companions. We searched all night without success. The following day there was a bad sandstorm, the tents were nearly buried and two of the camels perished, suffocated to death before we could go to their assistance. Nobody could have lived through the storm without shelter. We realized that if Wisdon had not been carried off by the lions he must certainly have perished in the storm. We searched the surrounding country thoroughly for nearly a week without finding a trace of him. We could not delay our return any longer without undue risk to the remainder of the expedition and indeed it would have been no use to delay longer. A sandstorm buries everything; it changes the whole face of the desert. It was a very sad and dejected party that struck camp and turned its footsteps homeward. We all liked Wisdon; he was a brave man and a splendid comrade.

''The expedition as a whole wishes to offer its sympathy to Mr. Wisdon's family.''

Mr. Ponsonby laid the letter on the table and looked up. Neither Clementina nor I offered any comment. Indeed, there was nothing to say. Garth's death was too dreadful to contemplate.

'I shall, of course, see Mr. Fraser on his return,' said Mr. Ponsonby. 'But it is doubtful whether he can tell us any more.'

I thought it doubtful too. The account was short, but it was extraordinarily clear. It was obviously written by a man who was accustomed to condense much matter into few words.

When we had recovered a little from the effects of Mr. Fraser's letter Mr. Ponsonby produced the will.

'I'm sorry to worry you any further today,' he said gravely. 'But I want to set things in motion, and I can do very little until the will is read. Mr. Wisdon was a man who detested euphemisms, and he laid very strict injunctions upon me to make the document short and simple. I try to please my clients in these matters when possible, so the will is couched in simple language.'

He started to read it.

To me the will seemed neither short nor simple. It took me all my time to follow it, and I wondered vaguely what a complicated will could be like if this were a simple one. I managed to discover, among the rigmarole, that Garth had left the bulk of his property in trust for Clementina, the trust to expire when she reached the age of thirty or married a man approved by her guardians, who consisted of Mr. Ponsonby and myself. If Clementina married a man of whom we did not approve the money was to continue in trust until her death, and then be divided among her children. Hinkleton Manor was Clementina's, of course. The estate was to be managed by a suitable man appointed by Clementina's guardians. I was to remain at the Manor in full charge of everything 'until such time as my daughter, Clementina Mary Wisdon, marries, or becomes independent or until such time as the aforesaid Charlotte Mary Dean shall marry. An annuity of eight hundred pounds per annum shall be paid out of the estate quarterly to the said Charlotte Mary Dean to continue to her death, irrespective of whether she shall marry or not. This annuity is in recognition of her kindness in resigning her appointment in London at my request and taking up her residence in Hinkleton Manor to look after my daughter in my absence. Also to the aforesaid Charlotte Mary Dean I bequeath my diaries to be dealt with according to her discretion, the monies accruing from the publication of any book or books based on the said diaries to be the entire property of Charlotte Mary Dean to compensate her for the work of editing which will be necessary. Also to the said Charlotte Mary Dean I bequeath the mare known as Brown Betty — by Autumn Leaf out of Queen Bess — and the gold half-hunter watch which was presented to me by the Reverend Mr. Charles Dean — father of the aforesaid Charlotte Mary Dean — when I went to Eton.'

We listened to it all in silence. I don't know how much of it Clementina understood; she sat very still looking out of the window at the rain which fell in slanting needles against the window. I realized with amazement and gratitude that Garth had made me independent financially. Eight hundred pounds a year was riches to me. I need never worry about money again — it was a strange thought. I was to stay on at Hinkleton with Clementina; there would be no need for me to go back to London to work. Even if — in the dim future — Clementina were to many I should still have enough money to live in the country. To live quietly by myself in a tiny house with a garden of my very own.

The will ended with directions for a generous pension to be paid to Nanny, and with legacies to the tenants and the servants. Garth had forgotten nobody.

Mr. Ponsonby stayed the night at the Manor. There was a great deal to arrange. Legal documents to be signed and witnessed and various other matters to be decided. Mr. Ponsonby thought that the estate required a bailiff to manage it; there were four large farms on the property quite apart from the home farm which supplied the Manor. He asked me if I would agree to the appointment of a bailiff — I agreed. It was strange to feel that I had the power to appoint a man to manage Garth's property.

'That is settled then,' Mr. Ponsonby said. 'You will leave the appointment to me I suppose. I wish to speak to you about another matter, Miss Dean. About the wages and housekeeping money which has been paid into the bank monthly for you to draw upon. I find a large surplus — may I ask if there are any outstanding bills?'

'I pay them all weekly,' I replied — it seemed funny that he should be worrying about a surplus.

'How do you account for the surplus?' he inquired.

I could not help laughing. 'I can account for it quite easily. I dismissed the cook who was wasteful and extravagant and engaged an economical woman at less wages. I am running the house with two housemaids instead of three, and I dismissed Clementina's governess and have been teaching her myself.'

He smiled in quite a friendly manner. 'Admirable, Miss Dean,' he said. 'The laugh is on me. I have been worrying for months because I thought you must be running up bills.'

After this point had been cleared up he became more human and helpful. He listened carefully to several suggestions which I made, and explained various things which I had not understood.

'I'm afraid I'm very ignorant,' I told him.

'You do not possess the knowledge, Miss Dean,' he replied with the meticulous precision of his kind, 'but that is what I am here to supply. If you will excuse my saying so I am surprised at your perspicacity. I did not anticipate such an easy task. I thought — '

'You thought I was a fool,' I said rather sadly. 'Well, I'm not surprised at that.'

'You are too quick to put words into my mouth,' he objected. 'I was not going to say such a thing.'

'But you thought it, and I don't blame you, Mr. Ponsonby. You heard me give evidence in the divorce case — I was made to look pretty foolish, wasn't I?'

'Oh *that!*'

'Yes. I was a dupe, Mr. Ponsonby,' I told him. I felt it was necessary that he should know the true facts of the matter. If I was to work with this man he should know that I was honest — a fool rather than a knave.

'They misled you?' he inquired.

'My sister and her solicitor kept me completely in the dark.'

'I remember. Yes. I wondered at the time. To be quite honest with you, Miss Dean — as you are being quite honest with me — I thought that you had been coached by Mr. Corrieston. But Mr. Wisdon would not have it. Mr. Wisdon was sure that you were telling the truth as you knew it. The case was a curious one; it worried me very much at the tune. I felt that my client was not being entirely frank with me, and Mr. Corrieston is a clever lawyer.'

'He bamboozled me on purpose. It was easy because my brain was not working properly at the time. The whole thing had come as a great shock to me, and I was overworked. I see now, looking back, that I was very near a breakdown of some sort.'

'I thought you looked dazed.'

'I was dazed. I had a dreadful pain in my head and the whole thing was like a nightmare.'

'It was good of you to tell me,' he said. 'I am glad you have done so. It makes it easier to work with you. I confess I was aghast when Mr. Wisdon nominated you as co-trustee. I protested, but he was not to be moved from his purpose. Mr. Wisdon had a very high opinion of you, Miss Dean. I see now that he was justified.'

# 14

## *'I Shall Never Be Like Other Girls'*

There was a great deal in the papers about 'The Fraser Expedition' during the next few weeks. Their adventures caught the imagination of the public. There were photographs of the desert, photographs of the camp, photographs of the sites of the proposed airplane depots, and photographs of the explorers themselves. People were talking about the expedition and discussing the practicability of the scheme (so Mr. Howard informed us) and wherever the subject was discussed the name of Garth Wisdon was mentioned with respect. He was the hero of the hour. There were a dozen theories as to how he met his death — we shall never know the truth — but everybody seemed to agree he had met it nobly, like the brave Englishman that he was.

Clementina and I devoured all the accounts in the papers with interest and pride. Her admiration for her father was profound. It was the first thing that brought her real comfort in her sorrow. I, too, was comforted by my pride in Garth. I realized that this was the kind of death Garth would have chosen. He would have chosen to die alone, far from civilization; he would have chosen to die on his feet with his gun in his hand. I remembered that he had said to me, 'It does not amuse me to kill animals that have never harmed me.' It did not appeal to him to hunt a defenseless animal, but this lion that he had gone out to kill was neither harmless nor defenseless. It had carried off one of the porters already and might do so again now that its taste for human blood had been whetted. This lion was an enemy worthy of his steel, and he had gone out to meet it gaily with a laugh and a joke on his lips.

Garth's end was in the Wisdon tradition, the great Wisdons of the past had died for their country, fighting for her honor or exploring for her welfare. They had died face to face with their enemies just as Garth — the last of the line — had done. There were pictures of Wisdons hanging on the walls in the library and the dining room and in the hall. Men with stern faces and determined mouths, men with smiling mouths and straight-gazing keen eyes, they all looked down from the walls upon Clementina and me as we sat at dinner or moved about the house. For some reason I was more conscious of them after Garth's death, and Clementina must have felt the same.

'It's a pity I wasn't a boy,' she said one day, looking up at the ancestor who had died at the taking of Quebec.

'You are a Wisdon,' I told her, answering her thought. 'Whether you are a boy or a girl you have their blood in your veins just the same. It is a fine heritage and you can well be proud of it. Perhaps someday you will have a son.'

'If I ever have a son I shall call him Wisdon,'

she said. 'But it's a pity, all the same.'

I realized that if I were going to write Garth's book I should not have time to give Clementina her lessons — it would be impossible to do both these things adequately. And this brought me face to face with a problem — should I engage a governess for Clementina, or should I send her to school? I thought it over carefully, and the more I thought about it the more sure I became that Clementina ought to go to school. She required the companionship of other girls, and the discipline of school life. I had brought her out of her shell (she was much more like a normal child than she had been) but I saw quite clearly that she had idiosyncrasies which I could never eradicate, and which never would be eradicated unless she had girls of her own age to tease her and chaff her and chivvy her about. I did not come to the decision to send Clementina to school without a struggle. She would hate it at first, and I would hate it all the time — we were friends now. I would miss her, the house would be too dreary for words without Clementina — but the child's welfare was the important thing. I wanted her to be a whole woman, not a crank.

Mr. Ponsonby agreed with me, and we found a girls' school about twenty miles from Hinkleton which was run by a woman with a positively alarming array of letters after her name. I went over and saw Miss Scales and found her a sensible, cultured woman — I liked her at once and I liked the school. It was comfortable but by no means luxurious, and I thought it would suit our purpose admirably. We arranged for Clementina to go there after the Christmas holidays.

Clementina was anything but pleased at my arrangements for her welfare. She retired into her shell, not sulking, but simply withdrawing the essential part of her soul from contact with the world. I left her alone, it was the only way I could deal with these moods of hers; but I reflected that school would deal with them less gently and that this would be all to the good. After a few days of silent contemplation Clementina came to me and broached the subject herself.

'Aunt Charlotte, why must I go to school?'

'It's good for people.'

'But I shall miss the hunting.'

'Your father missed the hunting when he went to school.'

'He was a boy.'

'You said it was a pity you were not a boy.'

'That's not the point,' she said, and of course it wasn't. 'Boys have got to go to school, but girls needn't. If you won't have time to teach me why can't I have a governess?'

'You could, of course,' I said. It was no use to be anything but frank with Clementina, and, after all, a reasonable being deserves the truth. 'You *could* stay at home and have a governess, but I do want you to go to school. I was never at school myself and it is a drawback. I did not think so at the time for I loved my lessons with my father, but I found it a drawback afterward. I found I knew less of the world than other women. Lessons are not everything. You learn about other girls at school, and you learn to get on with people and to rub shoulders with people you don't like without minding, or at least without showing that you mind. I don't want you to be like other girls under your skin, but I want you to be more like other girls on the surface. It will be so much easier for you afterward — life will be easier.'

'I shall never be like other girls.'

'Perhaps not, but you will learn to appear like them.'

'I shall hate it.'

'So shall I. But we shall both know we are doing the right thing,' I replied firmly.

# 15

## *The Rock Garden*

Clementina and I spent Christmas together quietly but happily. She was resigned to her fate. We both felt the approaching separation and the feeling that we had so little time to be together brought us closer. We had some good hunting, for the weather remained open and the skies were soft and gray. Violet Felstead and her mother had gone abroad to escape the damp and cold of the English winter; they had left Mr. Felstead behind and he was very lonely all by himself in the big, empty house. He came over to Hinkleton quite often, either to lunch or tea. We saw a good deal of Mr. Howard too; he and Clementina had become tremendous friends.

Mr. Ponsonby came down once or twice on business connected with the estate. I had found some rough plans of a rock garden in one of the drawers of Garth's writing table and I was anxious to put the project in hand. I thought it would be nice to carry out Garth's ideas; it would be a sort of memorial — far more individual and personal to Garth than the brass tablet in the church which bore his name. Mr. Ponsonby agreed to the expenditure, and agreed also to dismiss the head gardener — an argumentative man, who resented my interference — so that I could have a free hand. The site of the rock garden was the hill behind the house where the path leading to the station and the Parsonage climbed up through a wood of conifers. It was a sheltered spot, an ideal position for a garden which would be at its best in spring.

From the veranda, a broad green lawn sloped gently to the bottom of the hill, so that when the rock garden was made, it would be in full view when we sat in the veranda having our tea. The broad green lawn, the rock garden, and, above that, the dark trees. I could visualize it very clearly in my mind's eye and I was sure it would add greatly to the beauty of the Manor. Garth's plans showed a path of uneven steps made of huge slabs of the local gray stone winding up the hill and disappearing into the woods. On either side of the path were natural rocks and boulders, and smaller stones which would give the necessary background for alpine plants and heaths. The whole thing was on an ambitious scale and would take months to complete.

The gardener engaged in place of Fulton was a Scotsman called Walker; he was a man after my own heart, with all the virtues of his race and few of the vices. He rapidly became one of my chief amusements, and a firm ally. We did not always see eye to eye, but we respected each other's vision, and he was always willing to defer to me and to carry out my ideas even when they were at variance with his own.

'Och well,' Walker would say when he had tried to persuade me and failed, 'he who pays the piper calls the tune,' and so turn away with admirable philosophy to put my 'daft-like ideas' into practice.

The rock garden appealed to the engineer in Walker which lies dormant in every Scot. We studied books together and combined half a dozen ideas with our own and Garth's and the amenities of our site. But before we started on the rock garden itself I turned my attention to its approach. The broad green lawn, which sloped so admirably toward my rock garden, was disfigured by round beds in which bedding out plants — calceolarias, geraniums, and antirrhinums — succeeded one another in formal array. I had some trouble with Walker before he agreed to eliminate these atrocities and turf the beds, but when it was done even Walker admitted that it was a vast improvement. The lawn looked twice as big, and the untroubled sweep of green carried the eyes up to the entrance of the rock garden — in our vivid imaginations already a blaze of color — and the dark trees which rose behind.

In the rock garden itself the rough stones formed an uneven path winding up to the hill into the woods. Among the natural rocks flanking the path, we planted heaths which were specified to flower at different seasons of the year — and dianthus in the crevices to reach out over the stones, and large clumps of anemones and primroses and small alpine plants. Higher up, at the entrance of the wood, we planted rhododendrons, and, in the wood itself, bluebells and foxgloves.

But this is anticipating. There was a

tremendous lot of work to be done before the thing took shape, and I spent many long hours in the rock garden having the stones arranged as I wanted them and discussing the mixture of colors with Walker and his satellites. At Christmas it was merely a fairy vision in our minds. I had ordered the stones for the path and they had come: big, uneven, rough-hewn stones, gray and jagged. They lay in a confused heap waiting to be sorted out and placed in position. At present they were an eyesore, and my heart sank when I looked at them — would they ever be as I wanted them to be?

One mild windy morning soon after the new year I was busy among my heap of stones. They were so heavy that it took four men to lift them and we had had to engage extra labor for the job. One of the largest stones had just been placed and the men were resting after their Herculean task when I heard a shout, and looked up to see Mr. Howard approaching. I left the scene of action and walked slowly across the lawn to meet him. I felt dirty and untidy. The warm gusty wind had loosened my hair; it blew in little tendrils across my mouth. Far above us, the clouds were blowing in white streaks across the blue sky.

Mr. Howard waved to me as he approached. 'What d'you think you're doing?' he said when he was still some yards away.

'I think I am making a rock garden,' I replied with a smile. Mr. Howard amused me; he was always so alive and vivid, so full of excitement and eagerness about everything. He always seemed to me much younger than his years, much younger than myself although in reality there was only about a year between us. I suppose it was his life which had kept him young; he had lived his life in the wilds untouched by the frets and boredoms of civilization.

'I don't mean that,' he said. 'You can make a dozen rock gardens if you like — it doesn't affect me. I mean what are you doing with Clementina?'

'Clementina is down at the stables; she always goes down at teatime to take Black Knight an apple.'

'I know. I've seen her. She says you're sending her to school.'

'Yes.'

'You must be mad!' he cried. 'You must be crazy! Do you realize the risk?'

'The girls are well taken care of, I can assure you. Hill House is an excellent school.'

'I daresay it is. One of those high class establishments for the daughters of gentlemen, I suppose.'

'You're very old-fashioned in your ideas,' I told him, trying not to laugh. 'Hill House is not a seminary. Nowadays the daughters of gentlemen rub shoulders with the daughters of sausage-makers quite happily — it prepares them for modern life.'

'It may be an excellent school for ordinary girls, but Clementina — the idea of sending Clementina to *any* school!'

'Why not?'

'Why not?' he echoed with disgust. 'The

woman asks me why not. Do you realize that Clementina will become like other girls?'

'That's what I'm hoping,' I replied inaccurately. It was rather fun to tease him; he was getting more and more furious at my obtuseness.

'My God!' he exclaimed piously. 'You're hoping that, are you? You're trying to turn Clementina into a simpering, giggling schoolgirl.'

I had to laugh. I couldn't help it. The idea of a simpering, giggling Clementina was so absurd.

'It's no joke,' he said furiously.

'I can't help laughing,' I told him. 'You're so funny when you're angry, and Clementina will never learn to simper if she stays at Hill House for twenty years.'

'How old is she?'

'Thirteen.'

He did some rapid calculations. 'I'm old enough to be her father,' he said sadly.

'Yes. What a nice idea that is!'

'Nice!' he cried. 'It's absolutely hellish, that's what it is: Look here, Charlotte, I've come here to talk to you this afternoon. I've been offered a job in Australia; it's a dam. I meant to take a long holiday, but I've changed my mind. I shall go away for four years — it's a four years' job — I shall accept the job and build their damned dam for them. I shan't hang about here and watch you turn Clementina into a modern young lady with plucked eyebrows and painted lips.'

'Very wise of you,' I agreed.

'Wise! I don't know whether it's wise or not. Probably not. Most likely I shall come back and find her married to some lounge lizard of a creature with oiled hair.'

'I think it unlikely at seventeen.'

'Curse you, Charlotte!' he cried. 'Can't you be decent to me? Don't you see that I'm half-crazy with all this?'

I burst out laughing in his face. 'Not if you curse me. You can call me Charlotte if you like, but you ought to know better at your mature age than to curse a lady, especially if you want something out of her.'

'Be serious, for God's sake,' he adjured me. 'It's serious. I'm serious. Clementina is the most serious thing in my life. I suppose you think I'm a fool to go on like this about a child, but Clementina isn't a child; she's a person, and she's absolutely perfect as she is — and you go and send her off to a boarding-school so that she can be made like other girls.'

'Don't worry,' I said, taking compassion on him. 'Clementina will be all right. She must learn to mix with her kind, but it won't change her — not inwardly. The real Clementina is too strong a personality, too formed in character to be changed by a few years at school.'

'That's true,' he said more quietly and thoughtfully. 'She's a strong character, but the risk is frightful — simply frightful.'

'Go and build your dam and leave Clementina to me.'

'I suppose I must. I've no option really. I'd chuck the dam if it would be any use, but it wouldn't, would it?'

'None,' I replied firmly. 'None whatever. For heaven's sake go and build your dam.'

'I shall come back.'

'Come back when the child is grown up. I shan't stand in your way if Clementina loves you.'

He scraped about on the ground with his toe. 'Thank you, Charlotte — you couldn't say fairer. I must just take my chance I suppose — I'm old enough to be her father — damnable, isn't it?'

He went away sadly.

# 16

## *Waiting and Looking Back*

I took Clementina to Hill House and left her there. I was all alone now in the big empty Manor, waiting for Garth's diary to arrive, so that I could start the book. I was used to being alone, but I was not used to idleness. I had always had as much to do as I could accomplish; ever since I was a small child my days had been full. In my parents' house I had helped old Martha to make beds and puddings, and when father grew older, a considerable amount of parish work had fallen quite naturally upon my shoulders. In London I had my job and small household tasks as well, and latterly Clementina had filled my days and occupied my mind. This was the first time in my life that I found myself a lady of leisure.

The Manor was now running on oiled wheels, it required little or no supervision — my housekeeping took me about an hour in the morning, and for the remainder of the day I was absolutely free. I spent as much time as possible in the rock garden, and I rode, of course, but the weather was too cold and wet to spend many hours out of doors, and the evenings were long and empty. It was then that the idea came to me that I should write the third part of my life story for you, Clare. To beguile the long winter evenings and to bring you here to keep me company and listen to my tale. I had the old schoolroom bureau brought down to the library — Garth's desk was too big and shiny, it took my mind off my work — and settled down to write the story of Clementina's father.

It is strange how the figure of Garth has dominated my life. He dominates this third part of my story — I see that quite clearly — even though he only appears in it at the very beginning. Garth is still here: death has not obliterated him; the house and garden are redolent of his personality. Perhaps it is because he loved his home so dearly that his spirit returns to watch over it and see that all's well; I don't know. But I do know that he is here. When I come into the library I have a feeling that Garth has just left the room, I can almost smell the sharp tang of smoke from his pipe, and the strange, peaty perfume of his Harris tweeds. When I work in the garden he is with me in spirit guiding my choice so that the rock garden which he planned shall be as he imagined it.

The thread of my life has been tangled with Garth's, and, even now, when he is dead, I cannot escape from him. Even now I am waiting for Garth, waiting for his diary to come, so that I may write his book — the task that he entrusted to me. Everything is prepared, and I am waiting impatiently to begin. How much of the real Garth shall I find in the diary, how much editing will the diary require?

Once before, long years ago, I waited for

Garth to come. It was spring then, and the flowers put on their brightest colors to welcome him home; it is winter now, and the branches are bare — that is how it should be. I hope that the diary will not disappoint me, as Garth did, long ago. He would not be welcomed then; he had turned from me; his face had changed. That dreadful change in Garth's face still haunts me. I looked for love and found hatred; I found lines of cynicism where gentleness and kindness had been — it still haunts me. I shall never know, now, what changed him. I want to put the old Garth in the book that I am going to write — if the diary will let me — want to wash out the memory of that bitter, ruthless man who came home from the war, who looked upon the world through distorted lenses and would believe good of nobody. He tortured himself as well as others; he twisted his life out of shape. Why did he do this, why? Oh, Clare, I wish I could find the answer to that question! Even if it were a terrible answer — some dark secret that preyed upon his mind and changed his nature — I could face it better than the uncertainty; better than the possibilities conjured up in my imagination. The scales swing this way and that. One part of me argues that Garth would do nothing shameful, he was so straight, so clean; he detested lies and deceit with every fiber of his being. And then another part of me replies: 'What was it that changed him then? It must have been something terrible to change a man like that. Men have temptations that we can never know.' So the scales swing this way and that, and I shall never know the answer to the question. The third part of my story is finished, and still the diary has not come. I shall read over all that I have written and put the papers together — with the first and second parts of my story — in the bottom drawer of the old bureau.

# Part Four

# *Charlotte's Dream*

# 1

## *Clare*

The fourth and last part of this history is written solely for my own satisfaction. I feel that the thing is incomplete. Problems are set and left unsolved. There are half a dozen loose tags and ends to be drawn together and finished off. I can now elucidate the problems and collect the scattered threads, and that is what I have set out to do.

The first three parts of my story have lain for two years in the bottom drawer of the bureau waiting until I could find the time and the opportunity and the inclination to write the fourth part. The fourth part is not written for you, Clare, but only for myself — there is no need for me to write to you anymore.

I shall start this part from the moment when I left off writing the third part, from the very moment when I had finished writing and collected the loose sheets of paper to put away in the drawer. It was nearly time for tea, and I went upstairs to tidy my hair and wash my hands. I was still busy with my hair when the front doorbell rang, and, a few moments later, Barling came to say that Mrs. Felstead had called and was waiting in the library.

As I went downstairs I wondered what Mrs.

Felstead would be like. We had so nearly met on several occasions. She had called on me, and I had called on her. I had been asked to Oldgarden and had been unable to go; it had almost seemed as if we were fated not to meet. It was natural that I should want to meet Mrs. Felstead; Clementina spoke of her with affection — she had been very kind to Clementina, she seemed to understand the child. I knew that only a very understanding sort of woman could possibly understand Clementina, therefore Mrs. Felstead must be an understanding sort of woman. I felt quite excited — would I find somebody congenial waiting for me in the library, a potential friend . . .

* * *

I found Clare. She was standing at the window gazing out at the darkening garden, and she turned toward me when she heard me come in. I saw at once that it was Clare. She was older than I had remembered her, and her face was thinner and sadder — she had been through a lot of trouble in the last year.

I stood there, gazing at her stupidly; I could not make up my mind whether she were a real woman of flesh and blood or a figment of my imagination.

'Oh, Miss Dean!' she began, and then she laughed and added, 'Why, we have met before — do you remember?'

'Of course, I remember you,' I said slowly — she was real then. My imaginary Clare never called me Miss Dean, never asked me if I remembered her —

My first instinct was fear; fear lest I should be disappointed. Clare had been with me so long, and meant so much to me — would this woman take from me the Clare of my dreams?

'I have often thought about you,' she was saying, in that curiously deep voice which I remembered so well. 'I have often cursed myself for being such a fool as not to ask your name. Perhaps you think it rather silly.'

'I wanted to ask yours,' I told her.

'Good,' she said, laughing at me with her eyes. 'You felt it too — that we should understand each other I mean — then we needn't begin at the beginning. We are old friends.'

'Old friends,' I agreed.

I knew I was being stupid and gauche. I was leaving the whole thing to her, I was not even meeting her halfway. But I could not help it; I was dazed with the unexpectedness of our meeting — I was bewildered because my dream had become flesh. If I had started to say anything *then* I would have, gone on and said too much. The woman would think me mad if I said one quarter of what I felt. I knew that. I must say nothing until my brain recovered and could choose my words calmly — I must not expose my dream.

I busied myself over the tea-things, inquiring about milk and sugar — my hand trembled foolishly. It seemed so extraordinary to be having tea with Clare, and the next moment it seemed quite natural. How often had we had tea together? Never. A thousand times. The two answers were both right and both wrong — my head whirled.

Clare was talking about Clementina now.

'I have always been interested in that child,' she was saying. 'I don't know much about these complexes that people discuss nowadays, but if ever anybody had a complex Clem had. She was — she was *frustrated* by life, if you know what I mean. Always on guard before the portals of her soul — or nearly always. One caught a glimpse of the real Clem now and then, and the real Clem was worthwhile — always. What a difference there is in the child!'

'A difference?' I could do nothing but stupidly echo her words.

'Since you came,' Clare said, biting into a buttered crumpet with obvious enjoyment. 'Clem is much more human now. She lets herself enjoy things . . . her guard is down . . . she does not hold herself apart. I see a great difference in the child.'

'I'm glad.'

'Yes, it was worth doing. I was very fond of Clem, even when she was so difficult, and I liked having her at Oldgarden. She and Violet are as different as can be. Clem so quiet and thoughtful and Violet as harum-scarum as they make 'em — at least she was, poor lamb. She hasn't much opportunity to be harum-scarum now — but she will be again — we shall have her tearing about again — someday.'

'I'm glad,' I said again.

'Yes, it's wonderful,' she said. 'Sir Maxton Grant has almost promised — the few months that I had her away in the South of France improved her enormously.'

'You have had a terribly anxious time.'

'It has been — almost unbearable,' she said in a difficult voice. 'But somehow one just — bears it. They told us at first that she would never walk again.'

I could say nothing, my heart was too full; I put my hand out and she took it.

'You understand,' she said in a surprised voice. 'So few people understand, but I can feel that you do.'

'I do,' I said.

'It is strange how few people understand,' she said. 'People say it was good of me to give up everything to be with Violet — good of me! That annoys me, makes me furious. Silly to be furious, of course, because the poor things can't help not understanding, can they? I would have given up anything, *everything* to have been able to ease Violet's pain. I would have given my own body to bear it for her gladly, eagerly. There is nothing wonderful or self-sacrificing about *that*; it would have been easier for me. When you see the child you love suffering . . . ' She was silent for a moment and then she added in a lighter tone, 'So there was nothing 'good' in my giving up hunting to be with Violet because she wanted me near her all the time, because she felt a little easier when I was there and the pain was harder to bear when I was away. It was just pure selfishness . . . I don't know why on earth I am talking like this. I don't, as a rule.'

'Because you know I want to hear.'

'I believe you really do.'

'I do,' I said earnestly. 'I'm stupid at saying things, but you have been so often in my thoughts all these years. I don't want the usual tea-table talk from you. It would be almost — almost an insult.'

'The first time we met we talked of real things,' she agreed thoughtfully.

'I know. We said so much . . . I seemed to know you . . . seemed to know exactly what you were like. It is difficult for you to understand because you have people to love and to care for, but I had nobody.'

I stopped suddenly, afraid that I had said too much. I had known that if I started to talk to her I would say too much.

Clare was stirring her tea, she did not look up. 'I knew you were lonely,' she said in a low voice. 'Your face haunted me. Not unpleasantly, but I could see you when I shut my eyes. I thought *there's* a woman who could see my jokes, and I've let her go!'

I laughed at that, she was so funny in her annoyance, and it relieved the tension.

'That was *not* a joke,' she said in mock disapproval. 'So you have no business to laugh. It is very sad when people don't see your jokes — and lots of people can't, for the life of them, see mine. My jokes are either very subtle or very poor — I can't think which it can be.' She handed me her cup for more tea and continued, 'You were very kind to Bob when I was away. It was good of you. He's a lonely person without his family.'

'We loved having him,' I said. 'It was kind of him to come.'

She laughed. 'Tea-table talk — we can't escape it.'

'Not on my side,' I told her quickly.

'I was only teasing you, Miss Dean,' she replied smiling. 'No, I simply can't call you 'Miss Dean.' '

'Charlotte would be much nicer.'

'Charlotte — a lovely, old-fashioned name! I'm Paula. Is this too rapid for you?'

'We have known each other a long time,' I told her. I tried to call her Paula, but I couldn't. It took me a little while to get used to her as Paula, she had always been Clare to me. Long afterward she told me that I had called her Clare that first day — it must have slipped out when I was not looking — and that she had wondered why I called her Clare. She had thought, perhaps, that it was the name of a friend, and that I had called her Clare by mistake; she told me that she had always liked the name.

'How does Clementina like school?' she asked.

'Not much, I'm afraid. She's too much of an individualist. I think you were right to send her.'

'I hope so. I felt it was right. Clementina hated the idea.'

'It will do her good to mix with other girls. (Isn't it funny how different children are? Violet would love to go to school.) Don't worry about her not liking it at first. Things we dislike are often very good for us — horrid that it should be so.'

'Horrid,' I agreed. 'But fortunately Clementina does not seem to hate it as much as she thought she would. Her letters are fairly happy. It is I who am to be pitied.'

'You feel at a loose end? But you will be busy when the diary comes. Bob told me about Mr. Wisdon's diary — that you are going to write the book.'

We talked about the book until Barling came and cleared away the tea-things, and then, somehow or other, the conversation veered back to the girls.

'They are so good for each other, those two,' she said. 'They seem to bring out the best in each other — you know how some people do that?'

I nodded.

'You will let Clem come over *often* in the holidays, won't you? It is not all selfishness for Violet; she is as good for Clem as Clem is for her. I'm sure of that.'

'As often as you like. I want Clementina to have a real friend of her own age — I want it as much as you do.'

Paula Felstead hesitated for a few moments and then she said, 'I was sorry when — when Mrs. Wisdon stopped Clem coming to Oldgarden — it was really my fault, in a way. Do you mind if we talk about the whole thing quite frankly? I didn't mean to, *yet*; but then I didn't know what old friends we were.'

'No, of course, I don't mind. I would rather,' I told her quickly.

'I knew Mrs. Wisdon fairly well,' she said slowly, choosing her words. 'She was not the sort of person you could ever know *very* well, but I saw quite a lot of her. The children were great friends, and were constantly together — either here or at Oldgarden. Then a certain amount of talk started in the neighborhood and it came to my ears — I mean talk about Mrs. Wisdon. This all happened long before there was anything — anything definite . . . I'm telling this very badly, I'm afraid.'

'It's all right, I understand.'

'Well, I was worried. It was horrid talk and I was sure everything was all right. I was rather sorry for her being left alone so much when her husband was away. Anybody would get talked about under the circumstances — I made up my mind to speak to Mrs. Wisdon. (It was foolish of me, of course, but I like people to be straight with me and I resolved to be straight with her.) I came over and saw her and warned her about it. I told her that people were talking about her and Mr. Hamilton — there was nothing in it, of course, I said, but *there* it was, and she knew how people talked. I thought, myself, quite honestly, that there was nothing in it; I thought it was just carelessness on her part. She is a pleasure-loving woman. She didn't hunt — what else was there for her to do but entertain her friends?'

'Kitty was angry?'

'Very angry indeed. She told me to mind my own business. The County could say what it liked. It could go to the devil for all she cared — she raved on and I came away. I was sorry I had offended her, of course, but the thing I minded most was the children's friendship being spoiled. I swallowed a certain amount of pride and wrote to her quite pleasantly, saying that I was sorry, and asking her to allow the children to continue to meet. She never answered.'

'Kitty was — was like that,' I said difficultly. 'She never considered other people's feelings. Only her own, always.'

'You talk as if she were dead!'

'She is dead,' I said.

I told her about Kitty's death, and she listened silently, and sympathetically.

'You must have felt very sad about all that happened,' she said. 'There must have been so many happy things shared by you both, long ago, when you were children together. That is such a sad thing — to lose the child you played with when you were a child.'

'I had lost that child before.'

'That is sadder still. Death is not the saddest way to lose somebody you love.'

Before she left I took her into the conservatory to see the camellias. They were very fine — perfect waxen blooms, growing back to back among their dark green shiny foliage.

'How beautiful!' she said. 'They remind me of a Victorian beauty dressed for a ball.'

'There is something old-fashioned about camellias,' I agreed.

I cut some for her and she smiled as I gave them to her. Somehow I knew that she was thinking of our first meeting, and the country flowers.

'These are much more beautiful,' she said.

'I like country flowers best,' I replied.

'So you really do remember?'

'Every word. I've often wondered about the woman who lived in a basement.'

'She doesn't live in a basement now,' Paula Felstead said. 'We put her into our lodge at Oldgarden with her three children — she's a widow. It was rather pathetic to see her joy at returning to the country. She could talk of nothing but the greenness of everything — she almost went mad.'

I could understand that very easily. It was the living green of the country that had amazed me when I returned.

'She must have been grateful,' I suggested.

'Far too grateful,' Paula said, smiling a little. 'I couldn't go near the lodge for months — gratitude is such an uncomfortable thing — don't you think so, Charlotte? It takes God to receive gratitude graciously.'

After she had gone I thought about her, and all she had said. I realized that a new pleasure had come into my life, the pleasure of having a real friend. I had always longed for a woman friend of my own age, and now I had one. A real one at last. We saw each other often after that first day, and had many talks, and, gradually she superseded the shadowy Clare who had been with me so long. The two merged into one, and I could never really separate them in my mind.

# 2

## *Garth's Diary: 'The Desert Wind'*

Garth's luggage arrived. The men carried it up to his room and put it down softly. The cases, the trunks — all the paraphernalia which had been arranged in the hall the day that I came to Hinkleton Manor — had returned, without their master, quite safely. Only he had failed to return.

Naseby, who had superintended the operations, lingered after the other men had gone.

'I never thought when I carried it down — ' he said huskily.

'None of us thought,' I told him.

'Perhaps you'd like me to undo the straps, Miss.'

'Please, Naseby.'

He knelt and loosed the straps rather clumsily; his big hands were not so steady as usual. Then he got up and stood for a moment, looking at the pile and fingering his cap.

'He was a good master,' said Naseby. 'Stern at times, and he wouldn't stand no nonsense, but you didn't mind that because you knew he'd be fair — that's what counts, every time.'

He went away.

I stood for a few minutes looking at the things — the battered trunks, the cases, the packages done up in sacking. Garth's camp-bed, his rubber bath, his tent, everything except the cases which had contained his guns — the guns had vanished with their owner; they were buried in the desert, beneath the sand.

All these things, and especially the camp-bed and the rubber bath, were so much a part of Garth's daily life that they brought him very near, they made him very real. I could scarcely believe that Garth himself had gone, it seemed incredible. The luggage lying there in his room seemed to promise his return. I felt that the door would open and Garth would walk in. It was foolishness, of course, because I knew, beyond any doubt, that Garth was dead.

I looked at the trunks and wondered which of them contained the diary. It seemed wrong to open them — what right had I to open Garth's trunks? But that was a foolish idea, I *must* open the trunks; I had been waiting for them to arrive; I had been waiting for months.

I began to unpack. Nanny came down and helped me. She hung his suits in the wardrobe and smoothed out his ties and folded them away in the drawers of his dressing chest. The soiled linen she put aside for the laundry. It was almost as if she were expecting him to come home . . .

'Oh, Miss Char!' she said suddenly, and I saw that the tears were running down her face unchecked. 'Oh, Miss Char, how often I've unpacked for him! I know where he likes all his things kept, you see. He liked things just so, and he used to say nobody did his unpacking as well as me. I'd been with him always, since he was a tiny baby, so I ought to have known how he liked things. I never thought he'd be the first to go — so strong he was, so full of life, and me an old woman! Oh dear! Oh dear!'

I couldn't say anything to comfort her, I needed comfort myself. My own cheeks were wet.

'Look at these socks, Miss Char! All holes. I don't suppose he had anybody with him to mend them for him. I always mended his socks — such awful holes he always made — look, Miss Char, this one's got no heel left.'

'You take them and mend them,' I suggested.

'Yes, I must mend them,' Nanny said. She stopped suddenly and looked at me with a sock over her hand, 'You're not going to give his things away, are you?'

'Not yet,' I said quickly. 'We needn't do anything yet.' I could not bear the thought of giving away Garth's clothes — they were all that was left of Garth — all that was left. A white riding glove was lying on the floor, I took it up and slipped it onto my hand, and the glove was so shaped that it was Garth's hand I saw — no, I couldn't give away his clothes.

'Not yet,' Nanny agreed, with a sigh of relief. 'I couldn't bear to think of anybody wearing them.'

I had found what I was looking for, now, a pile of fat shiny copy-books in the bottom of the trunk. The books were the same as those I always used, the same as those father had given us, so long ago. I left Nanny to finish unpacking, it was her due. She could unpack Garth's things for the last time, and mend his torn clothes and put them all away tidily in the drawers. It was the last personal service she could perform for Garth. She, who had spent the best years of her life in his service, had the right to do this. It was quite useless, of course, because he was far beyond our ken, he did not require earthly service anymore; but, sometimes, it is comforting to do useless things for those we love. I understood that. I understood Nanny. My last duty to Garth was different; I collected the books containing the diary and went downstairs.

The mere fact that the diary was written in the same kind of books that I always used for my diary brought Garth closer. It was a bond between us — a secret bond. I turned over the pages with interest and excitement. I saw very soon that the diary required very little editing — I saw that Garth had written with a view to publication. Here and there a piece of the real Garth peeped through; here and there a few lines seemed too intimate for the public eye. There was good stuff here. I saw that, and rejoiced. This book would not be the least of Garth's works. There were wonderful descriptions of the country couched in language so vivid that the scenery seemed to spread itself before my eyes. There were descriptions of the game encountered, interspersed with racy anecdotes about the porters and the native hunters. One native hunter, especially, had excited Garth's interest. 'He's a thorough gentleman,' Garth had written. 'Intrepid to the point of lunacy — a man after my own heart.' It was this man — so we heard later from Mr. Fraser — that had gone with Garth to track the lions.

The whole diary was colored with Garth's personality; the turn of a phrase brought him back to me vividly. I could hear him speaking as I read. Was it my imagination that the *tone* of the whole narrative changed gradually but perceptibly as the days went by — that the cynicism disappeared, and was replaced by a healthier, more natural spirit? I turned backward and forward eagerly. No, it was not, it could not be imagination. The desert was healing him. The peace of the desert had sunk into his soul. I had hoped for this to happen, and, after I had heard that he was dead, I had longed to believe that it had happened. His last laughing words to Mr. Fraser had seemed to show a happier, saner Garth — I had pinned my faith to these joking words and tried to believe that I was justified in doing so. It was still too early to be certain; I should have to study the diary carefully, to read and reread every page a dozen times before I could be sure of my ground, but I saw that there was room for hope, and my heart lightened. I wanted, so *terribly*, to believe that Garth had died a whole man.

I spent the evening poring over the books. Quite apart from my own special interest in the narrative — my interest in its author — it was an enthralling tale. Travel books were my specialty and this was a good specimen of its kind. I came across an interesting description of a tribe of Bedouins, their dirt and squalor and their fierce, wild faces. A thumbnail sketch of a hooded face with a hooked nose was appended, and beneath it were the words 'Drawn for me by Stewart. I wish I could draw. This sketch would lend itself well as a design for the jacket of my book. The man allowed me to measure his head and take other particulars. (This was difficult to achieve on account of their weird superstitions, but they understand money here as well as in other more civilized parts of the world — I made the man rich, and he allowed me to measure his head. It does not take much to make a Bedouin rich.) I was anxious to secure the measurements to compare with those of the Bracelet Man. They are totally different, just as I hoped and expected. The Bracelet Man is in no way related to Bedouin.'

The following day there was another entry about the Bedouin. 'The Bedouin returned and requested me through our Arab interpreter to give him back the magic which I had taken out of his head. He had brought back most of the money I had given him — all except some he had lost in gambling the night before — I told the interpreter to ask why he wanted it back. 'His head feels funny,' replied the man gravely, 'He thinks he will die soon if he does not have the magic back.' I gave him the paper upon which I had written the measurements and took the money from him — he was a fine, strong, wild creature, I did not want his death upon my hands. He pressed the paper to his forehead and went on his way rejoicing.'

I came upon a passage which read strangely in view of what happened later. The expedition was on the fringe of the desert. 'This place is infested with lions,' Garth had written. 'The lion is not a noble animal — none of the cat tribe is noble — nobility does not slink upon its belly, does not spring in the dark, does not eat carrion. The lions have not harmed us and I have no desire to harm *them.*' I put down the book and turned to the last, the unfinished one. Garth had made a scribbled entry before he set forth on that last expedition, the expedition which was to cost him his life. 'Lions roaring all night,' he had written, 'and one of the porters has just come to my tent to tell me that his brother has been carried off. There is a trail of blood on the sand. These porters have their feelings, like other people — the poor creature was weeping. I promised him that I would go after the lion, and his eyes gleamed with pleasure at the news. I have no hope of finding the poor wretch alive, but revenge is sweet, and, if I bag the lion, the victim's brother shall have the skin.' I turned back and read the entry of the previous night. 'We are to turn back. Fraser is right, of course, he cannot take unnecessary risks, but it is a sore blow to me. It looks as if the Bracelet Man had fallen from the skies — I have seen no signs of his tribe. The desert is so vast, it has convinced me of the hopelessness of my quest. And yet, in spite of my failure, I do not feel downhearted, I feel strengthened, healed, rejuvenated. I shall return to life with courage. The desert sun has burned the poison out of my brain; the desert wind has blown away the evil humors. I was mad, I think, possessed by some evil djin. The people here believe in such things and such beliefs are infectious. Tonight, in spite of my disappointment — and it is not a light one — I feel free and clean. I can even forgive Kitty. My God, I had never thought to write such words! There may yet be beauty in life for me, if it is not too late.'

* * *

Day followed day and I scarcely noticed how they passed. I was enthralled by the task of editing Garth's book. I went with him step by step upon his journey, I shared his vigils, shared his discomforts, shared his keen enjoyment of the beauties which had encompassed him. I grew to know his companions through Garth's eyes: the silent, able Fraser, who always seemed to know what to do in every emergency, a king among men; the light-hearted Stewart, who wielded a pencil so ably and had a joke — not always printable — for every occasion; the garrulous Clinton who wanted everyone to share his enthusiasm for his geological specimens — they were all alive and vivid — Garth had limned them in a few words.

I used the blue pencil as little as possible; it was easier than I had expected. I scored out only what was intimate or trivial, and, here and there, where I thought it necessary, I elaborated a little or altered the wording to read smoother. The trivialities which I eliminated were mostly in the first part of the expedition — Garth had written, 'A letter from Char today. (This is the last I shall get before we plunge into the unknown.) She is pleased with Brown Betty — ridiculously pleased. Could I do less than provide a decent mount for Char? She says very little about Clem — merely that the child is well — what does that mean I wonder. Does it mean that things are going smoothly, or that she does not want to worry me with her troubles? I should like to be able to peep in at the Manor and see how they are getting on.'

I was glad he had not been able to peep in at the Manor *then*, he would have seen little to reassure him. Those first few months at Hinkleton were like a nightmare to me when I looked back at them. My struggle to understand Clementina and find the way to her heart; my troubles with the maids, my sordid quarrels with the odious Miss Milston — these were not the things I liked to remember, I should not like Garth to know of these things. But later, when all the difficulties had been solved and the tangles straightened out, I should have liked Garth to peep in, and I should have liked him to see the rock garden, which was shaping so satisfactorily, just as he had planned it.

# 3

## *The Steeplechase*

Geoff Howard rang up to tell me he was sailing for Australia at the end of the month and to offer to come to lunch at Hinkleton and say good-bye. I told him he could come to lunch if he liked, but I hated good-byes.

'It's your own fault,' he said. '*You* are sending me to Australia and nobody else. I shall come and weep upon your shoulder.'

'Forewarned is forearmed,' I replied.

'What d'you mean?'

'Just that I shall wear my mackintosh,' I told him.

Geoff arrived early. I was working in the garden and I showed him a hand covered with earth.

'What's a little mud between friends?' he asked, shaking it warmly.

'I see you are determined to keep on the right side of the dragon,' I replied.

'It's my only hope. I suppose I can write to you, if I can't write to Clementina?'

'Yes, you can write to me.'

'Generous woman!' he exclaimed.

We walked up to the house together, sparring a little in our usual manner. I felt quite a different person when I was with Geoff. He brought out a certain quality in me which I had never known I possessed. His light-hearted impudence provoked a light-hearted return. I was young and gay in his company and full of repartee.

'We're going to the hunt point-to-point this afternoon,' he said. 'Did you know?'

'Who are you going with?'

'With you, of course.'

'No, Geoff.'

'Yes, Charlotte.'

'I'm far too busy. I write in the afternoons.'

'Not today you don't. I'm determined to take you, so just make up your mind to it and accept the invitation gracefully. You're working too hard at that book — it will be as dull as ditchwater — you know what all work and no play made of Jack.'

'Seriously, Geoff, I'm not coming,' I said. 'It isn't only the book, it's partly because I don't want to meet people. Yes, I know. I meet them out hunting, but that's different; I feel safer on a horse, and people don't snub you in the field, they're too busy.'

'You won't get snubbed,' he replied. 'I'll take care of you. We needn't go into the enclosure if you'd rather not. We can go up onto the hill and see the whole thing. It's a lovely day. You *must* come, Charlotte. I want to go and I've nobody to go with — I want to back Red Star for the Ladies' Cup, it's a snip.'

'I don't know about that, with Sweet Molly running.'

'Good, you'll come.'

'I never said so.'

'Of course you did. You said you wanted to back Sweet Molly for the Ladies' Cup.'

'Oh, Geoff!' I said.

'Be a sport, Charlotte! You won't see me again for four years — you won't be bothered with me all that time. You'll be sorry when you think of me toiling and moiling in Australia among a lot of woolly headed blacks living in a tin shanty and eating dampers — or whatever they're called — and drinking tea. Australians live on dampers and tea, I know that from the war.'

He persuaded me to go — I could hardly refuse, for he was a wheedling man — and after lunch I found myself in his two-seater Fiat on my way to the race meeting which I had determined to avoid at all costs.

We left the car in a field near some buses and walked up onto the hill. It was a real March day — a cold wind blew from the east but the sun was hot and golden. A few white cotton-woolly clouds moved across the pale blue heavens with the dignity of galleons, and their pale gray shadows followed them slowly over the sunlit land. The country was very beautiful — the meadowland a radiant green, and the plough a dusty brown. The hills rolled softly to the horizon, broken by the uneven line of woods, black woods touched by a faint haze of green. Spring was coming, coming slowly but sweetly despite the cold dry winds of March; they could stay her progress but could not stop it, for there was warmth in the sun, and the earth was turning her face toward its beams.

Two partridges rose from our feet with frightened cries and swirled away with a flutter of brown wings across the field.

'God, how I love this country!' Geoff said. 'I used to think about it when I was in Canada with a kind of pain. And now I'm pushing off again to the ends of the earth — life *is* hell!'

We reached the top of the hill and looked down. Below us in the shallow valley was an orderly line of cars, winking and glittering in the bright sunlight, and beyond them, straggling up the farther slope was a scattered line of tents. The enclosures and the surrounding fields were black with people. They swarmed like ants and, like ants, seemed to be hurrying busily in all directions. Groups formed and divided and reformed endlessly, aimlessly; it was a curious sight. The noise of the crowd and the raucous voices of the bookies shouting the odds for the first race drifted up to our ears.

'We'll watch the first race from here, shall we,' said Geoff, 'and then I'll go down and put my shirt on Red Star. It is funny how few people come up here. You can see the whole course — or very nearly.'

There were half a dozen people on the hill besides ourselves — a couple of bus drivers, a farmer with a rubicund countenance, two tweed-clad women, and a horsy-looking man in a bowler hat with field glasses glued to his eyes.

'Yes, it is queer,' I agreed. 'They start from the tents I suppose. Where is the first jump?'

Geoff tried to explain the course, which was mapped out in the usual way with white and red flags, but he was a little hazy about it, and the horsy-looking man came to the rescue. He pointed out the water-jump and explained that they had to make a circle of the hill upon which we were standing and go over the shoulder of a neighboring hill behind a clump of trees. He seemed to know all about it and to be quite glad to share his knowledge with the bus drivers and ourselves. I seemed to remember the man's face and concluded that I must have seen him out hunting. 'The water-jump is the worst of the lot,' he told us, 'and that tall fence comin' off the plough is a bit nasty, but there's nothin' in it really. It's a stayer you want for this course.'

It was true, I saw that. The jumps were not so serious as I had expected, and I half regretted that I had not entered Brown Betty for the lightweights. Sim had tried to persuade me to do so, and to get somebody to ride her, but I was so afraid of something happening to her, and I disliked the idea of a stranger riding her. If Sim could have ridden her I would have consented at once, but she was not up to Sim's weight for a grueling race like this, so I had dismissed the idea from my mind.

'They're off!' exclaimed Geoff.

They streamed across the meadow — a dozen little toy horses with toy men on their backs, gay in pink or workmanlike in black. They took the first jump in a bunch — it was a low wall — and turned toward us across the plough. The dry earth rolled away from beneath their hooves like smoke. Another jump — a hedge this time — and they were breasting the hill. A pink coat on a bright chestnut was leading, and, two lengths behind, came a group of five. The rest had strung out, they were already outpaced. They approached quite near us, so that we could hear the thud of hooves on the dry turf and see the strained faces of the riders as they leaned forward a little to ease the horses up the hill. They rose easily over a turfed wall and fled away toward the woods, where a hunt servant in a pink coat stood like a colored statue against the deep blue of the sky.

'That first feller is going well,' Geoff remarked.

'Gay Day,' said the horsy-looking man. 'He has the race in his pocket.'

'It certainly looks like it,' agreed Geoff.

They were approaching the water-jump now. Gay Day had increased his lead and was going easily. I thought the race was safe to him and was already regretting, in the time-honored manner of race-goers, that I had not backed the horse. He was obviously in a different class from his rivals.

'By gad!' exclaimed the horsy man.

Gay Day had refused the water-jump — he had swerved to the left, nearly unseating his rider, and the others had swept past. We watched with some excitement. Gay Day's rider was by no means beaten yet; he tugged at his horse's mouth and forced him over the stream. Away he went up the hill after the others. He was still fresh and had plenty of stamina — I felt he might do it yet. They swung round the corner of the wood and disappeared for a few moments. When next they came into view, Gay Day was making up on them with every stride. They took a fence in fine style and went down the hill toward the enclosure at a rattling pace. Gay Day had almost caught them. As they swung into the straight piece of meadow that led to the winning post, he came into the bunch and forged through it. The sound of shouting increased.

I was tense with excitement. He was a splendid horse, and I wanted him to win. I felt he would do it. I was sure he would do it. There was only the black in front of him now, and he was overtaking the black with every stride. His nose was creeping along the black's side as they raced for the post but the black made a spurt and held him. It was too late for Gay Day; he was beaten by a neck.

'As foine a race as ever I did see,' exclaimed the farmer.

'And as fine a horse,' added Geoff.

'He is, sir,' said the horsy man, shutting his field glasses with a snap. 'Gay Day is a fine horse. I've ridden him all the winter so I should know his points. The devil only knows why he refused the water. I've never known him refuse anythin'.'

'A hunter doesn't understand racing,' Geoff said. 'Give a hunter hounds to follow and he'll take you over the moon.'

'You're right, sir,' replied the other eagerly. 'By Jove, you're right — it's what I've always said. Huntin' for hunters and racin' for racers. I didn't want to race Gay Day, but my boy persuaded me. He wanted to ride him, so there you are.'

He put his field glasses into their case, and set

off down the hill with the rolling gait of a riding man. I looked at my race-card and found — somewhat to my surprise — that Gay Day's owner was Lord Bournesworth.

'Did you know it was Lord Bournesworth?' I asked Geoff.

'No, and I don't much care. He was a decent little cuss. Come on, Charlotte, are you coming to back Sweet Molly or shall I do it for you?'

'I'll come,' I said. 'We needn't go near the members' enclosure.'

We followed Lord Bournesworth down the hill, crossed the brook and skirted a bit of plough. As we approached the enclosures, the noise of the shouting increased; it became a roar. Geoff pushed through the crowd which surrounded the bookies' stands.

'Take a good look at them, Charlotte,' he said. 'They're a dying race. The Tote's killing them off slowly but surely. In another four years, when I come back from Australia to marry Clementina, the last bookie will be exhibited in a glass case. You'll probably have to pay sixpence to look at him and another sixpence to hear him shout.'

'I'd rather pay sixpence not to hear him shout,' I replied breathlessly. The bookies looked anything but dying to my inexperienced eyes. Their faces were red and shiny, their voices were deafening. One of them was standing on a couple of packing-cases signaling wildly to a friend in the members' enclosure.

'I always choose the fattest, they can't run so fast,' Geoff explained, pushing his way toward an enormous man with a walrus mustache to lay his bet. I followed him and put a pound on Sweet Molly at eight to one. She belonged to Mr. Felstead and although she was not much of a jumper she had plenty of stamina and I knew she could stay the course. Geoff only got three to one for Red Star, he was the favorite.

As I was turning away, I felt a touch on my arm and found a small, fat woman in gray tweeds standing beside me.

'Miss Dean isn't it?' she inquired. 'I am Lady Bournesworth.'

'Oh yes,' I said, slightly dazed with surprise.

'Yes,' she said perkily — she was rather like a fat, perky little bird. 'I used to know your father, Miss Dean, a very fine man. The parish has never been the same since he died. Mr. Frale is too much of a recluse. Very clever, of course, but not human. The human touch is missing. I should like to call.'

I was not altogether pleased at these sudden overtures. For one thing I could not understand them, and for another, Hinkleton Manor had been shunned by the County for so long that I had grown used to the solitude of my life. My work and the garden were enough for me. I did not want to be invaded. Last, but not least, I was angry with the neighborhood for ostracizing Garth and his daughter, angry and sore. I had resolved that they could go their own way and Clementina and I would go ours — we could do without them very easily. And now, all of a sudden, for no reason that I could see, we were to be received into the fold — I did not want to be received. But, before I had answered Lady

Bournesworth ungraciously, I had changed my mind — what sort of a guardian was I to dream of refusing to be friendly with Clementina's neighbors? I had grieved because she had no young people to play about with, and here was the opportunity to supply the want. I must pocket my pride — Garth's pride it was, really — and meet the advances as amiably as I could.

Lady Bournesworth had been watching my face — she was no fool.

'I hope you will allow me to call,' she said graciously. 'I should have done it long ago, but I am the world's worst caller. We want your niece to come over to Bourne in the summer for tennis. There are so few young people about. My grandchildren come to me for the holidays and — '

'Don't call,' I said. 'Come and have tea instead — perhaps one day next week?'

'Yes, that would be delightful . . . so good of you . . . Wednesday? No, Wednesday is the Unionist Meeting. We shall have to rope you in to some of our activities, Miss Dean — Thursday would suit me admirably.'

She called to Lord Bournesworth, who was backing a horse, and introduced him to me.

'Diddles, this is Miss Dean,' she said.

'We've met before,' he said, smiling. 'Miss Dean knows the best place to see the racin' from. And she knows a good horse when she sees him.'

Several other people who had seen me talking to the Bournesworths came up and introduced themselves, or were introduced. It was quite a social triumph, but, unfortunately, I did not enjoy it. My head buzzed with their names, and I wondered vaguely what it was all about. I saw that if I accepted the various invitations to tea or bridge or to 'see the garden' which were being showered upon me, I should soon find myself involved in a social round for which I had neither the desire nor the aptitude. I struggled wildly as I felt the toils closing round me, assuring everybody that I couldn't play bridge and that I was very busy editing my brother-in-law's book.

'Are you rahlly?' inquired a sallow youth with an eyeglass whose name I had not caught. 'Most int'resting job, what? I read his last book but it was too clever for me, what?'

'I've seen you out huntin', haven't I?' inquired a tall angular woman with a brown face and bright eyes — she was the woman who rode the chestnut, and I remembered that Sim had told me she was Lady Vera Hill.

'Yes,' I said. 'You saved me from a duck-pond.'

There was a general laugh.

'You're lucky, Miss Dean,' said a thin man with a weather-beaten face. 'Next time you follow Lady Vera she'll lead you into a bank with a thorn hedge on the top.'

Lady Vera took no notice of him. 'Why didn't you enter that brown mare?' she demanded. 'I noticed her at once. Fine action she has — and good hocks. I like good hocks.'

'You've pretty fair hocks yourself, Vera,' said the thin man, smiling with bared teeth.

'They're not too hairy,' she admitted gravely. 'But you're interrupting, Harry. I'm talkin' to Miss Dean about her mare. You didn't think of enterin' her for the lightweights, Miss Dean?'

'I did think of it,' I said, 'or rather my groom thought of it — but I hate anybody else riding her.'

Lady Vera looked at me with friendly eyes. 'I know,' she said. 'It's hell to see a stranger ridin' a horse you're fond of. I lent a man a mare once to ride in a 'chase and he pushed her to death. She came in first and fell down dead. I nearly killed the feller . . . nicest mare I ever bred. Come and see the stables one day, Miss Dean. I've got somethin' might int'rest you . . . geldin' just about your weight . . . '

I was hemmed in on every side. Geoff had disappeared and left me to my fate. It was not until the horn sounded for the lineup of the runners in the Ladies' Cup that I found an excuse to escape. I took to my heels and fled from them down the course toward the first jump.

'Good God!' exclaimed Geoff, appearing somewhat breathlessly at my side. 'You should go in for a race yourself, Charlotte. You'd beat every horse in the country with your long legs.'

'Where were you?' I asked indignantly. 'You said you would look after me if I came to the races with you.'

'I was watching,' he replied giggling feebly. 'It was as good as a play. Hallo, here they come!'

They came down the course bunched together and were over the jump and away in a moment. Red Star was leading, but Sweet Molly was lying nicely and going easily. I felt a thrill as they passed, for, quite apart from the money I had staked upon Sweet Molly, she was a friend, and I wanted her to win for that reason. I knew, too, that Paula was going to back the mare, and the Felsteads were not too well off these days. Violet's illness had cost them a small fortune.

We watched the horses sweep up the hill and disappear.

'You can't see so well from here,' Geoff remarked sadly.

'I came here to escape. You know that,' I told him. 'Why didn't you rescue me from those awful people? I hate people.'

'I told you they wouldn't snub you.'

'I only want to be left in peace.'

'They can't do that. It's snubs or kisses with that bunch. I guessed it would be kisses today.'

'How did you guess? I was never more surprised in my life.'

He looked a little uncomfortable. 'Well, Mother's tune changed a bit,' he said, 'and she's a good weather glass.'

'But *why?*' I demanded. 'For heaven's sake tell me why. I've done nothing to change their tune or send their barometer up.'

'Wisdon's a hero now,' replied Geoff lightly. 'And you're his sister-in-law. It's odd how far that goes with some people. Personally, I like people for themselves — I mean if you were the sister-in-law of a sweep — by the way I've got an invitation for you to tea at Fairways.'

'I've had enough invitations today,' I told him ungraciously.

'That's right. I hoped you'd say that. I told Mother she would have to call if she wanted to know you.'

'Geoff!'

'Well, I did. I'm just about as fed up as you are with the way people have behaved, only neither of us is going to show it.'

He broke off to watch the race (we had seen nothing of it until now). The horses were leaping the last fence and coming up the straight. Sweet Molly was lying second to a blue roan. Red Star was fourth.

'What the devil!' cried Geoff, gluing his glasses to his eyes. 'My God, Red Star's all out! Not an extra ounce left in him. What possessed me to put a pony on the C 3 brute?'

'I told you Sweet Molly would win.'

'How like a woman — besides she's not winning, it's that blinking roan. I hate roans! Unnatural sort of beasts.'

There was a burst of cheering as the horses passed the post, but we were too far away to see which of the first two had won.

'It's that roan,' Geoff declared. 'The devil is in all roans, they ought to be shot when they're foaled.'

I gave him my ticket and told him to go and make sure which had won, and collect my winnings if any. (I had only backed Sweet Molly to win, and not for a place.)

'Come on,' he said. 'We'll put something on the Farmers' Race. That old chap on the hill said 'Danny Boy.''

'I'm not going near the enclosures,' I replied firmly. 'And your money will be safer in your pocket.'

'All right, I'll meet you on the hill. I don't know why you object to be petted — you remind me of a bull-terrier bitch I had in Canada. She hated anybody to touch her.'

'Yes, I'm exactly like that.'

He went off smiling (quite undaunted by the loss of his money, which I knew he could ill afford), with his hat on the back of his head and his hands in his pockets.

I thought, as I watched him, how much I liked him. He would make a good husband for Clementina if she cared for him in that way. Personally I hoped she would. He was the sort of man who would suit Clementina, frank and cheerful and full of nonsense, with a sound core of understanding and tenderness. They were utterly unlike in every way, but they fitted in to each other wonderfully.

I sighed a little, and thought of Garth, and made my way slowly up the hill.

# 4

## *'The Good Companion'*

Paula Felstead came to tea with me the day after the race. She came to tell me all about it and how Sweet Molly had won the Ladies' Cup by half a head, and she was much surprised when I told her that I had been there and seen it with my own eyes and was eight pounds richer for the outing. Her surprise was natural, for she had tried her best to persuade me to go and I had refused.

'Well, I'm glad you went,' she said. 'Even though it *is* slightly galling to find you prefer Geoff's company to mine.'

'But I don't. I would much rather have gone with you. The man wheedled me into going — I simply couldn't refuse.'

'He must be a champion wheedler,' said Paula. 'I thought you were adamant.'

'I was,' I declared. 'I didn't want to go. I only went with him because I was sorry for him — I felt I had been rather brutal.'

Paula looked at me and raised her eyebrows. 'So you turned him down?' she said.

I nodded. 'What else could I do? Clementina's only thirteen . . . I told the man he could come back in four years and we would see.'

'Char!' she exclaimed. 'What on earth made you do that?'

'What else could I do?' I inquired, somewhat puzzled by her dismay. 'Do you mean I should have sent him away altogether? I hadn't the heart to do that, and I really hadn't the right to do it, had I? If he is still of the same mind in four years — '

'But why four years?' she cried. 'Why send the man away at all?'

'I didn't want him hanging about here looking miserable.'

Paula gazed at me in amazement. 'My dear Char, I'm an interfering person, I know, but I can't let you make this dreadful mistake without a word. Geoff may never come back at all, have you realized that?'

'Of course I realized it. But what could I do? Clementina is only thirteen.'

'Clem can look after herself. There is no need to sacrifice yourself for Clem. If you care for Geoff — '

'Good heavens, what are you talking about, Paula?' I cried incoherently. 'It's Clementina, not me at all — how could you have thought it was me? It's Clementina.'

'Clem?' she said incredulously. 'D'you mean he's in love with Clem?'

'Yes, but he didn't put it quite like that. He is very fond of her, he thinks she is perfect.'

'Goodness!' said Paula. 'How I should hate any man to be thinking of Violet in that way! But, of course, Violet isn't Clem. Violet is still a child, and Clem has never been a child; she has missed her childhood, poor lamb. I daresay an older man would suit Clem as a husband. She requires a lot of understanding.'

'That's what I thought — and I like Geoff,' I said.

'He's sound,' she agreed. 'And not a bit dull (as sound people so often are), in fact he amuses me immensely. I'm very sorry about the whole thing. I thought it was you the man was after. He would have made you an excellent husband and there is plenty of time for Clem.'

'Whereas he was my last hope,' I added smiling.

'Don't be silly, you know what I mean perfectly well. The man's a fool.'

'You said just now he was sound.'

'In some ways,' she returned unblushingly. 'Sound in some ways, but a fool to think of Clem when you are anywhere about.'

'I shall never marry,' I told her firmly. 'So don't try to match-make for me, Paula. You see there was only one man . . . one man I ever cared for . . . and something went wrong . . . he's dead now.'

She looked up at me with clear, bright eyes. 'I'm sorry,' she said. 'I didn't mean to be interfering, Char. I say things before I think.'

'But I like you to be interested. I never find you interfering,' I said quickly. 'You're such a help to me with everything, with Clementina. I know nothing about children, you see, and — '

'Shucks!' said Paula smiling. 'You have worked miracles with Clem. You understand her to the bone, and you know it, and are proud of it. Don't play the modest spinster aunt to me.'

'But you *will* go on being — being interested?'

'Oh, yes, I shall go on interfering,' laughed Paula. 'I can interfere in any way I like except that I must not try to find you a husband — is that it?'

'That's it,' I said with a sigh of relief.

I was glad we had discussed the matter frankly, and that the misunderstanding had been cleared up. It was a horrible misunderstanding, but quite natural under the circumstances. I saw, now, how the neighborhood had construed Geoff's constant attendance at the Manor — Paula was probably by no means the only person in the County who had read a wrong meaning into Geoff's friendship for Clementina and myself and his fierce championships of our cause — everybody would say that he had proposed to me and I had refused him, that was obvious.

'Paula,' I said at last, 'for God's sake tell everybody that there's no truth in the story. I don't want it to be even *hinted* that there was anything between Geoff and me. These tales have a way of spreading and cropping up years later. If Geoff comes back and wants to marry Clementina — '

'Yes,' she said thoughtfully, 'I see what you mean. You don't want any malicious gossip about yourself and Clem's future husband. It would be — nasty. I'll do what I can to quash it. The worst of it is we can't tell them the truth — it will have to be all strictly platonic, and so few people believe in platonic friendship I don't, myself, for that matter.'

'You must make them believe in it,' I told her earnestly.

She rose to go. 'I always stay hours longer than

I mean to,' she said as she seized her hat, which she had removed for comfort, and crammed it carelessly onto her head. 'By the way, that reminds me, when are you coming with me to choose a new hat? I promised myself a new hat if Sweet Molly won.'

We arranged a day. Paula was less tied now that Violet was so much better, and, although I was working hard at the book, I did not grudge the loss of a day when it meant shopping with Paula. It was good for both of us to shake a leg loose now and then, she from nursing and domestic cares, and I from my book. After an outing with Paula I came back to my work with renewed vigor and a clearer judgment; she was an invigorating companion, she struck sparks from my mind. Her moods were as swift as an April day — from grave to gay, and from gay to grave — and they were as infectious as measles.

My dominant mood was one of sadness for Garth's untimely end; but no one is forever occupied with sorrow, and there is a kind of gaiety that goes hand in hand with sorrow. Sorrow stands aside for a while to make room for mirth, and then steps forward to take her victim in a stronger grip. It was like that with me. My heart was sad for the loss of my old-time friend, and the future looked empty and lonely when I dared to look at it at all, but there were times when I was possessed with a strange, almost hysterical gaiety, and this happened quite often when I was with Paula, and sometimes when I was with Geoff.

The day we had fixed for our trip to London

was damp and mild. Paula arrived to fetch me in the car, which she drove herself with verve and a neat judgment. The London traffic never bothered Paula, and policemen were as wax in her hands.

'Do you mind, Char?' she asked. 'Bob wanted me to take Banks, but I feel silly today, and Banks is so proper.'

'I always feel quite safe with you,' I assured her.

'Misguided woman!' she giggled.

She was sparkling with merriment and high spirits that day, and I soon learned the cause. Sir Maxton Grant had seen Violet and had been full of cheer. 'He's never been like that before,' Paula said as she turned out of the gates of the Manor into the main road. 'I've always thought him a melancholy individual — kind but melancholy. He's got a long face and red hair — a typical Scot — but yesterday he was quite lively and skittish . . . He says Violet will make a complete recovery . . . she is to have a quiet pony . . . Oh, Charlotte!'

She was quite mad that day — full of the most idiotic nonsense — and she infected me. We giggled like a pair of schoolgirls at the slightest provocation. At the hat shop she pretended to persuade me to buy a straw saucer which the assistant perched jauntily over my left eyebrow.

'Quite perfect,' she said gravely.

I looked in the mirror and burst out laughing in the assistant's face. My long-shaped brown face beneath the straw saucer was irresistibly comic.

'Paula,' I gasped, 'I'm like a horse . . . those

horses with little straw hats . . . It only wants two holes and two ears sticking through . . .'

The assistant snatched the hat off my head and replaced it with a brown mushroom straw. I thought it was quite nice, but Paula would have none of it.

'Never buy a hat that you think is quite nice,' she said, dragging me away. 'A hat should be a tonic, not a head covering.'

'Aren't you going to buy one?' I asked, following her breathlessly out of the millinery department.

'No, I'm not. It wouldn't be safe,' she replied firmly. 'If I were to buy a hat in this mood I should buy a mad hat and I could only wear it when I felt mad. I don't feel mad often enough to make it worthwhile. You want tumblers, don't you?'

I said I did, and after some trouble we found the china and glass department.

'I want a drinking trough for the dogs,' said Paula. Oldgarden swarmed with dogs of all sizes.

A fat, stolid young man came forward to serve us. 'A drinking trough for a dog. Yes, Moddam. Would you prefer a plain trough or one with 'dog' written on it?'

Paula looked at him gravely. 'It doesn't really matter,' she replied. 'My dogs can't read and my husband never drinks water.'

The young man looked at her disapprovingly; he was a very serious young man. We were so weak with repressed laughter that we staggered out of the department with our purchases unmade.

'I'm sorry, Char,' Paula said, wiping her eyes. 'It is disgraceful of me to behave like this. I don't suppose you will ever come shopping with me again.'

'Shopping!' I echoed. 'Do you call this shopping? We haven't bought anything yet and I can't possibly go back to either of those departments.'

'I'm mad today,' said Paula remorsefully, 'quite mad. If you want to shop seriously we had better separate. I can't promise to be good because I know I couldn't be.'

'It's after one now and I'm starving,' I replied. 'Laughing always makes me hungry. Did you ask me to lunch at your club, I wonder?'

'Dare we go to the club?' asked Paula. 'Supposing I do something mad there, they might turn us out.'

It did seem a risk under the circumstances; we decided to lunch at a quiet restaurant where nobody would know us.

'They might think I was drunk or something,' Paula said, 'and Bob would hate it so. I *am* drunk really, Char. Drunk with happiness, not wine. Supposing I get taken up for being drunk with happiness in charge of a car, what will the fine be?'

'Look out,' I told her. 'We were nearly into that bus.'

'My dear, what a fuss you are! There was at least an inch to spare.'

'I like rather a bigger margin.'

'A miss is as good as a mile,' Paula said. 'Don't worry, Char, it's my day out today, nothing horrid can happen. Do you ever have days like that when nothing can go wrong? And then there are the days when nothing can go right,' Paula continued. 'When your hair won't lie down properly, and your stockings develop ladders at the worst possible moment, or your suspender breaks, and buttons fly off your gloves. When you say the wrong things to the wrong people, and spill coffee on your favorite frock, and break your reading glasses, and your cook asks for a raise — you know the kind of thing I mean,' said Paula, swerving to avoid a fat woman, who had darted off an island in the middle of the road without looking. 'You know the kind of thing I mean. I always think on these occasions that my guardian angel is having a holiday.'

'He's on duty today, anyhow,' I told her curling up my toes as we swept down a one way street and swung to the right.

'Yes,' said Paula calmly. 'That's exactly my point. I'm leaving it all to him. What about that little restaurant over there for lunch? It looks rather nice.'

We lunched at the little restaurant cheaply but amply. It was one of those little 'arty' places that spring up all over London and endure for a while before they disappear as mysteriously as they came. The food was clean and good and the service adequate. Paula fell into conversation with the proprietor — who had appeared from the back premises to inquire whether we were satisfied — and elicited various interesting details about the restaurant business, and its peculiar intricacies. Wherever Paula went she made friends and gathered information — she was interested in everything and everybody, and her interest drew people toward her and opened their hearts. Her manner was always natural and sincere, and it rarely failed to evoke a natural and sincere response — she was never patronizing, never gushing, never subservient, she was always herself.

We dallied at the restaurant long after our simple meal was ended, drinking coffee and smoking cigarettes while the proprietor bared his soul. He told us that his wife was an invalid and that he had borrowed money to start the restaurant so that she should have a home of her own. He told us that he rose at four every morning to buy his food at the markets, and that he superintended the cooking himself because he could not afford to engage a first class chef. He told us that his son had gone to Paris to study continental cooking and that he hoped to take him into partnership when he was sufficiently trained. Paula leaned forward over the little table and drank in every word. She was not pretending to be interested in the man's story, she *was* interested. She promised to recommend the restaurant to her friends, and to arrange for the man's invalid wife to have a fortnight at a convalescent home near the sea.

'I won't forget,' she said as she rose and reached for her coat — and she didn't forget. The restaurant proprietor had made a friend, and so had Paula. We were escorted to the car with royal honors.

Paula drove me to Mr. Ponsonby's office and left me there. She had an appointment with her hairdresser and we decided to meet at five and drive home together.

I had to wait for a few minutes in the dingy office, for Mr. Ponsonby was engaged. It was a dull, dreary room, furnished with heavy mahogany furniture of the Victorian period. The walls were lined with shelves upon which stood black tin boxes painted with white names. Bereft of Paula my mood changed to one of black despondency. Garth was gone, the future was drab. I had probably at least thirty years of life before me, thirty years of loneliness and frustration. There was nothing for me to look forward to except loneliness; there was nothing for me to look back upon except loneliness. I had lost the hardly gained content which I had won during my years at Wentworth's; I was no longer resigned to a hermit's lot — I wanted more now. I wanted all the things that other women had — a husband, children, a full and useful life. Hinkleton had awakened my dormant desires. Paula had shown me how full and useful a normal woman's life could be.

I was deep in the slough of despond when Mr. Ponsonby appeared. He was full of apologies for keeping me waiting and inquired eagerly after the progress of the book. I pulled myself together and replied that I was getting on with it, and found it very interesting work.

'Good!' he said rubbing his hands. 'That is excellent news. I have spoken to a publisher — Mr. Falks, of Messrs. Falks and Lamb — they handled Mr. Wisdon's other books and are very anxious to have this one also. They suggest that the new book should be prefaced by a biography of Mr. Wisdon — the man and his work — I said I would speak to you about it.'

'You mean me to write it?' I asked doubtfully.

'Who else? You knew him so well. It need not be long nor detailed, just a simple biography comprising his childhood, his life at Oxford, his war career and a short criticism of his books.'

'It sounds rather ambitious — I have never done anything of that kind,' I told him.

'Please try, Miss Dean. Mr. Falks was exceedingly anxious for something of the sort to be attempted. He pointed out that Mr. Wisdon's writings have not received the notice they merited. Mr. Wisdon was feeling his way toward the expression of his individualism. If he had lived he would have been a great writer — so Mr. Falks says, and I believe in his judgment in such matters; he has had wide experience, very wide experience.'

I had been considering the matter while he spoke and had begun to think I might do it. I saw vaguely how it might be done. The biography took nebulous shape before my eyes.

'I will think it over,' I told him cautiously.

'Don't put it off too long,' said Mr. Ponsonby. 'Mr. Falks is anxious to have the book as soon as possible. We don't want to hurry you, that would be a fatal mistake, but Mr. Wisdon is in the public eye. The book should come out if possible before the public has forgotten him.'

'Their memories are short,' I said. 'You are asking me to hurry and yet not to hurry.'

He laughed. 'You are always condensing me,

or putting words into my mouth, Miss Dean. I must remember my P's and Q's when you are about.'

There were several other matters to settle, business connected with the estate. Mr. Ponsonby had engaged a bailiff and he was to take up his duties almost immediately. All sorts of papers required my signature and it was getting on for five when I left the office.

Paula was waiting for me. 'You look dazed,' she said.

'I feel dazed,' I replied. 'Legal papers are dazing to an ordinary woman like myself. And I've been let in for something rather — rather big.'

I told her about the biography — all that Mr. Ponsonby had said and Mr. Falks as reported by Mr. Ponsonby.

'You must do it,' she told me earnestly. 'I feel you could do it well, and it would be worth doing. We need biographies of men like Mr. Wisdon. Men who stand for the old ideals of truth and justice. Make it the biography of an Englishman — he was that before everything. He was the product of generations of Englishmen — his feet were planted deep in English soil. I always used to feel that there was something strong and deep about Mr. Wisdon — there was weakness too, but that weakness was merely the offshoot of his strength. He hated anything shoddy or mean; he hated deceit. These things found his weak point, his Achilles heel. He was truth and generosity personified, but he veiled his virtues with cynicism.'

'I think you had better write the biography,' I

told her with gentle sarcasm.

Her mood changed swiftly from deep earnestness to raillery. 'I could do it beautifully,' she agreed, 'if I had time. D'you know, Char, I once heard a woman say that to Mr. Walpole. It was at a dull dinner, a dreadfully dull dinner. 'I admire your books *so* much,' she told him gushingly, 'I could write *too* if only I had *time*. I've *always* wanted to write, you know, but I have such a *busy* life that I scarcely have time to write my letters. I have five dogs, you see, and *really* I never have a *moment* to myself.' 'The dogs are more fortunate than we,' he replied gravely. I thought it was a lovely answer.'

'It was, but how does it affect me?'

'I was only illustrating my meaning. If I hadn't five dogs I could write the biography for you, Char. But let's be serious.'

'I thought we were serious.'

'No, but we will be. Are you just going to do it out of your head or have you any data to help you? However well you know a person, it must be difficult to write a biography without anything to go on. There must be spaces in his life that you know nothing about.'

I had not thought of that, but now I saw that what Paula said was true. I had imagined that I knew Garth well, and yet for twelve years I had scarcely set eyes on him.

'Perhaps there are old letters, or something,' Paula suggested. 'He was away from home so much, he must have written to his wife when he was away, or to Clem.'

'There are diaries,' I told her, 'he always kept a

diary, he told me so himself.'

'Splendid.'

'But I can't pry into his diaries, Paula.'

'That's nonsense!' she said firmly. 'Of course you must read them.'

'I couldn't.'

'What will you do with them then?' she asked.

It was a reasonable question, but I had no answer for it. What should I do with Garth's diaries? They must be somewhere in the Manor — Nanny would probably know where.

'You would never burn them,' Paula continued. 'You might burn something valuable. The man was a born writer, he had greatness, he had wonderful ideas. He had not reached his zenith, of course, his two books are merely a promise of better things to come — it is sad to think that the promise can never be fulfilled. You must read the diaries, Char, and put extracts into the biography.'

I saw that what she said was true. If the biography were to be more than a mere outline of Garth's life, and an incomplete outline at that, I must read the diaries. I shrank from the task. It would be painful to pry into Garth's life. The diary of the expedition had been written with a view to publication, it had been left to me to do with it as I thought best. The earlier diaries were quite a different matter; they were the private expressions of Garth's soul. Could I violate that privacy?

'You *must*, Char dear,' said Paula answering my thoughts. 'Think it over quietly and you will see that you can't do otherwise.'

# 5

## *Bluebeard's Chamber*

I could not work that evening, the thought of the old diaries haunted me, came between me and the page that I was trying to write. I found myself sitting idle, staring in front of me with unseeing eyes. I had not thought about the old diaries before, but now that my attention had been directed to them they drew me in a strange fashion. Had Garth meant me to have the old diaries as well as the diary of the expedition? 'Also to the aforesaid Charlotte Mary Dean I bequeath my diaries' — did that mean all his diaries or merely the diary upon which the book was to be based? I tried to look at it calmly and without prejudice, and it really seemed to mean all his diaries. He could so easily have worded it more explicitly if he had intended it to mean the diary of the expedition only. In law the diaries were mine — that was clear — but what was Garth's intention?

If I read the diaries I should be able to make a real biography of Garth. I could put extracts from the diaries into the biography to show the trend of his thoughts; to show how he grew from childhood to manhood; to show his aim and the clean shining light of his ambition, and how he moved toward it from the childish games of make-believe-travel to the reality of exploration. I wanted to do this, I wanted to write Garth's story from the inside. It was a fascinating prospect.

I had ascertained from Nanny that the old diaries were in a chest in the front attic. She had given me the key of the chest — the key of Bluebeard's Chamber. The key lay on the bureau beside me, a small shiny key with a strange ward.

I could not sleep that night. The moonlight, strong and white, poured through the open window and lay upon the floor of my room in a bright swathe. The owls hooted mournfully as they wheeled round the old house. I heard a mouse scraping industriously in the wainscot. I tossed and turned upon my bed, I lay and stared at the ceiling — should I read the diaries or not? Did Garth mean me to have them? Should I burn them?

The moon sank behind the trees and left me in darkness.

* * *

I was busy all the morning in the rock garden, but after lunch I took the key and went upstairs. The attic was full of lumber; mirrors and chairs and pictures which had been discarded by various generations of Wisdons stood about, dirty and forlorn, or leaned disconsolately against the walls. The sun streamed in through a small round window showing up the thick fine dust that lay over everything and floated suspended in the air. It seemed to me, as I looked about me, that there was valuable stuff here. Someday I would go over it all carefully and pick out what was good. I would refurnish the drawing room, discarding Kitty's modern trash, and transform it into the beautiful room it was intended to be. That old spinet should have an honored place, and so should the Chippendale table with the beautiful inlaid front. I visualized the drawing room (denuded of its gilt mirrors and purple carpet) papered with cream, and with a few Persian rugs on its polished floor. It should be a restful room; I would give it back its soul.

The big, carved wooden chest stood beneath the round window just as Nanny had described. The key turned easily in the lock, I flung the lid back and there were the diaries — piles of them, with the dates written upon little labels gummed onto their shiny covers — Garth's diaries!

I took some of them out and looked at them without opening them — it was extraordinary how strong the feeling was that held me back from opening those diaries. The Unwritten Law of childhood warred with my reason. The Unwritten Law that our diaries were sacred, not to be pried into by alien eyes. This was one thing that held me back, but there was another feeling, equally strong — it was fear. I was afraid of what I might find in the diaries. I might find something dreadful, something that would force me to take Garth from his pedestal of Valiance and Virtue.

There was something in Garth's life which had changed him in a few months from a gentle-natured boy into a cynical, disillusioned man. I had told myself that the war had done it, but I did not really believe it was the war. I believed that there was something else, something more personal than the war, and I feared to know what it was. The diaries would tell me Garth's secret — I was sure of that. They would resurrect the past which had been buried for so long; they would open old wounds; they might change the whole tenor of my thoughts toward their author. Could I bear it?

I sat down and argued with myself. There were two courses open to me, I must either read the diaries or burn them. It was balking my fence to keep them where they were, unread. If anything were to happen to me they would fall into other hands — Clementina's most likely — they would be read by other eyes than mine, less interested, less understanding. I must either read them or burn them . . . and I couldn't burn them. They were Garth, the essence of him, all that remained of his personality . . . I couldn't burn them.

I picked up a book at random and began to read. I read a bit here and a bit there, passing over weeks or years, dipping into Garth's past — and my own past too. Sometimes the tears rained down my cheeks so that I had to stop and wipe them away before I could see the words. I forgot, very soon, the purpose of my reading — to gather material for the biography — that could wait. I could do that afterward (go back and gather up the threads of Garth's life, sifting, weighing, putting in a passage that showed his development, leaving out another because it was too intimate, too poignant, too passionate. Garth would have hated his soul laid bare to the public eye; he was fastidious, he hated to show his feelings, he hated sentiment. I should have to apply the touchstone of Garth's fastidious mind to all I wrote. There was much that was beautiful here, much that I could gather for my book, but that was for afterward; today I was concerned only with Garth and myself, with our relationship to each other; with the part I had played in his life, and the part he had played in mine.

# 6

## *Garth's Diary: 'Old, Unhappy, Far-Off Things'*

*January 1st, 1919. Lines of Communication.*

Very busy today. There is more work than ever for the 'A' branch and we are all stale and longing to get home. I saw Carruthers and Staines and pointed out the mistakes in the returns. They were pretty fed up and I don't wonder . . . had only one hour in the middle of the day for my ride. I must have that or my brain goes absolutely dead. (I am never in bed before midnight and it is more often 2 a.m.) I took my favorite route to the top of the hill. The place reminds me of the hill at home, the hill that Char and I christened Prospect Hill because of the glorious view. It was there I kissed her, my darling girl. How I long to get back to her out of all this muddle and worry. My brain is so tired. I have vowed not to go to Char till the muddle is clear and I am free. Then we shall be happy together with no troubles to mar the perfection of our love. Hinkleton and Char — that is all I want — to stay quietly at home and watch the seasons pass. Later on we shall travel together, for she loves traveling as I do. I remember saying to her once long ago, 'What a pity you are not a man, Char, we could go off together and explore the world,' or words to that effect. It seems curious now that I should ever have wished for such a thing — for Char to be a man. And yet it is beautiful that the foundations of our love were laid in such a perfect friendship. She has had a dreary time of it, my poor Char, but I will make it up to her. She shall be happy all her life if I can accomplish it — dear Char, wonderful Char, the woman I love, the only woman in the world for me, the woman I want for the mother of my son.

I think a lot about my son, these days. The war has made me think. We must build a sure peace so that our sons may live. I think a lot about the Wisdons. I am only a link in the chain of Wisdons stretching far back into England's history and, please God, as far forward. I am only a link in the chain, but I am the only link for this generation, and I am glad the war has spared me to carry on. Wisdons have helped to hold England against her enemies in the past — there will be no more enemies. (This war is to end war for all time; we must believe that or lose our sanity.) But although there be no more enemies England will still need faithful sons and daughters — Wisdons, Valiant Men and Virtuous Women, to build up her prosperity, to guard her ideals, to serve her in peace if not in war. Char's son and mine — a true Wisdon, he must be, staunch as steel and tempered to sword strength. He will love the old house as I love it, every stone in its gray, weathered walls. He will guard the traditions of our race — my son and Char's, another link in the Wisdon chain.

I think a lot about the beautiful old house, I see it more clearly during this compulsory exile than I did when I was living in it and was part of its life. Exile seems to sharpen the inner eye for the beauties of home. (The greatest poems of our land have been written by exiled sons.) I have only to shut my eyes to see Hinkleton Manor set like a gray gem in the green country of home — the wide, sloping lawns, the woods with their delicate green leaves in spring or their fine tracery of black branches in winter. I can sense the inner peace of the house that flows through me like a cool stream as I cross the threshold — there is peace and safety here, there is something strong and enduring, something which speaks to me from the past, from the people who have lived here, loved it as I love it, and died for its traditions. I am theirs and they are mine, bone of my bone, flesh of my flesh, their blood flows through my veins. I am a link in the chain, I, too, will pass on, but part of me will go on down the years in Wisdon bodies. I shall pass on the warm living traditions to my son.

These things are needed today more than ever, these links with the past. Old houses with England in their bones. The war has torn up many roots, torn down age-old beautiful ideas. This passion of destruction which has fallen upon the world is a dangerous thing — so it seems to me — it is a madness that cannot be cured all in a minute with treaties written on a piece of paper and signed by diplomats. England's soul must be kept safe till she needs it again and the devil let loose by the war is chained up.

What a lot of nonsense I have written tonight! I have got it off my chest now and perhaps I shall sleep the better for it.

* * *

*January 4th. Lines of Communication. France.*

Christmas Leave! I have not dared to think of it, and here it is, only ten days late. I must have one peep of Hinkleton, and see Char — just one peep, that's all. I dare not have more or I should feel it impossible to return here and carry on. I must finish this job first — it can't be long now. Staines is grumbling, he says three days' leave is not worth having, but he is preparing to take it 'toute même.' How strange to think that I shall be in London tomorrow night! The Eltons have asked me to stay with them, and I have decided to do that. I shall not sleep at Hinkleton until I am free to stay there and soak myself in its peace. I shall run down to Hinkleton the day after tomorrow and surprise father, and Char. Then back here to finish the job. I hope the job won't take too long to finish for the strain is telling upon me now. Sometimes my brain goes dead, and sometimes it is too active. I can't sleep properly.

* * *

*January 5th. London.*

I have no heart to write tonight, and yet I must write, for I can't sleep. Char is lost to me. Char is lost to me. I can't believe the words are true. They have no meaning. They are like the ravings of a madman. Kitty is staying here with the Eltons — we are a big party — the child is 'almost grown up now' — her own words. At dinner there were veiled allusions to Char and her refusal to come and spend a few days in London while I was here on leave. There was some laughter about 'the superior attraction at Hinkleton.' I could not understand what it all meant. After dinner I got hold of Kitty — the others were playing billiards — and asked her what it meant. She was loath to tell me at first, but I got it out of her. Char is engaged to a man called Senture, an archaeologist as far as I can make out. He has been staying at the Hinkleton Arms all winter and they are together every day. She is helping him with a book about Hinkleton Church — they spend hours in the church — and they go for expeditions together all over the country. One day they went to Canterbury and did not get home till after midnight. Kitty was very sweet to me, I think she knew that her news had knocked me out badly, though I tried to hide my feelings as best I could. I asked her if Char were very much in love with the man (I had to know). She looked down and twisted her little hands and replied in a low voice, 'She can talk of nothing else.' I asked her if Char knew that I was to be at the Eltons' when she refused their invitation. Kitty looked away and said nothing. 'She knew, Kitty?' I asked again. 'Oh, Garth, I hate hurting you,' she said. 'Don't worry,' I told her, 'there are other women in the world.' So there are but there is only one woman for me. There has never been anyone except Char, never will be. I shall marry, of course, because Hinkleton must have an heir, but my heart is dead. My heart feels numb and cold. 'You don't really mind, then?' Kitty was saying. I laughed at that, or tried to laugh; it was a sorry exhibition I'm afraid. 'Why should I mind?' I inquired. 'It's nothing to me.' Nobody should see my pain. I would not give them the satisfaction of knowing that my heart was broken. Gerald Elton came up and wanted to know what the joke was. I was too upset to turn the question aside, but Kitty came to the rescue with some nonsense or other. She is a kind little soul. It was a strange feeling to laugh and talk and feel all the time that my heart was broken. Now I have come up to bed and am writing my diary. I am so tired, so dreadfully tired, yet I know I shall not sleep. It is a nightmare to me to think of any man touching Char, holding her hand, kissing her. Oh God, how can I bear that thought! To think that Char could be unfaithful, to think that she could let some other man steal her from me (for she was mine, I know that. She was all mine that night I kissed her on the top of Prospect Hill).

I shall not go to Hinkleton tomorrow — what is the use? I could not bear to see Char, nor the man she loves. The man that Char has chosen. I must have time to recover from the blow before I can face that. It seems to me that I shall never be able to bear it — and why should I? Why should I have to bear it? I shall stay in France until she has married and left Hinkleton; I shall never see

Char again. Kitty has asked me to go with her to a concert tomorrow — it is kind of the child to try to comfort me.

* * *

*January 6th. London.*

Why did I come on leave? It has been a ghastly day. Thank God I am going back to France tomorrow. The work will take my mind off my troubles. Oh, Char, how could you! Didn't you know what I meant when I said I was coming back to you? You said 'Come back safely' — didn't that mean you would wait for me until my work was done? Faithless Char, you knew it all; you knew you were mine and I was yours. Staines is right: there is not a woman in the world worth a tear, not one.

* * *

*January 8th. Lines of Communication. France.*

Back in the midst of work again with arrears to make up. No time to think, save at night when I tumble into bed, worn out. Then my mind flies off and I can't stop it — Oh, God, this is hell! Why can't I sleep? My dreams have fallen into ruins. If we had not been so near each other I would not have minded so much; if we had not understood each other so well I would not have felt so bitter. I pinned my faith to Char. She was my friend before she was my beloved. I thought I knew her through and through. I thought I could depend upon her though all else failed.

⋆ ⋆ ⋆

*May 2nd. Hinkleton Manor.*

Home, what a mockery the word is! I have been here for a week now but have found no peace. I suppose Hinkleton is the same, and it is I who has changed! Tonight I dined at the Parsonage. The poor old man is very feeble; it is tragic to see him. He is a travesty of himself. Char is still here, she is not married yet. I could hardly bear to look at her. She tried to speak to me as if we were friends — how can we be friends? She has given her love to another man and I do not want her friendship. What good is her friendship to me when I love her with all my being? Yes, in spite of everything, I still love Char. That is the dreadful part of it: I have tried to tear her out of my heart, and I can't do it — I can't. She wore the yellow dress, she flaunted it before my eyes — how could she be so cruel, so heartless? It is strange that those we love have the power to hurt us so desperately. I would not let her see that I cared, even when she belittled the dress and said it was old-fashioned and she had put it on for a joke. She shall not have the satisfaction of knowing how deeply her faithlessness has wounded me. Kitty warned me not to speak of Mr. Senture before Mr. Dean; he does not like the idea of Char getting married and leaving him. It is strange how selfish people get when they grow old. Mr. Dean was the most unselfish man alive, and the most clear-headed. This poor old man is not Mr. Dean at all. There are other subjects besides Char's marriage which are taboo when he is present. To speak of the war sends him into a frenzy — Char warned me of that.

I had no intention of mentioning Senture but Char brought up his name at dinner and boasted of the fact that she had spent hours with him in the church helping him with his book, and had gone to Canterbury with him to spend the day. She offered to show me the leper window which he has discovered, but I told her the idea of a leper window disgusted me — so it does. Char has changed utterly.

* * *

*June 2nd, 1919. Hinkleton Manor.*

I have been at home for a month but I am still restless and unhappy. Father spoke to me last night. We had a long serious talk. Now that the war is over and I am free he wants me to take the management of the property into my own hands (there are three farms on the estate so I should find plenty to do) and he wants me to marry and settle down. The traditions of the Wisdon family are important to him. For nearly three hundred years the property has been handed down from father to son in an unbroken sequence and he wants to see the line assured. The desire of his heart is to hold a grandson in his arms before he dies. He spoke of Charlotte and seemed surprised when I told him she was engaged to be married to another man. Then he sighed and said, 'There are other women, Garth.'

I did not answer. There are no other women for me.

All the same I can see the advantages . . .

* * *

*June 20th, 1919. Hinkleton Manor.*

So much has happened since I wrote the above entry in my diary that it seems more like two months than two weeks. I must write down the whole story: it began with domestic troubles — the troubles which afflict a house like Hinkleton Manor which has no mistress (two men living alone are at the mercy of their staff). Father has been ill and depressed. He spoke to me again of his desire for a grandson to inherit our family traditions and the estate.

I had been for a long walk over the hills and returned home tired and dispirited . . . and I found Kitty Dean in the flower room.

Kitty turned to me and smiled a little shyly. She said, 'Oh Garth, the roses were withered so I threw them away and cut fresh ones. I can't bear to see withered flowers in this lovely old house — and you have nobody to do them for you.'

It was then that I saw the answer to all our problems and asked Kitty to be my wife. 'Oh Garth, do you mean it?' she asked. I told her I meant it and took her in my arms and kissed her. She was kind and sweet. She had been like a little sister. I had seen her grow from a tiresome child into a charming girl — so she was no stranger. I knew that father would be delighted to welcome Kitty as a daughter. He had always been fond of her.

We are all very happy tonight.

* * *

*July 16th, 1919. Hinkleton Manor.*

Kitty and I are to be married tomorrow (there seemed little sense in a long engagement) but already I have begun to wonder if we are suited to each other. Kitty is sweet and pretty but there is no depth in her; she will never be a real companion, a friend to share my thoughts. It is strange that sisters can be so dissimilar. They have the same blood in their veins, the same heredity, the same upbringing. Did I hope subconsciously that beneath her skin Kitty would resemble Char? They are utterly different. Char has depth and serenity and strength of character; Kitty lives upon the surface of life, she lives for the hour. But it is too late now to indulge in vain regrets. I have determined to be a good husband to Kitty. I must be patient and gentle; I must remember how young she is and give her time to mature. If she is unable to share my interests I must do my best to share hers. Somehow or other we must find common ground and make a success of our life together.

This would be easier if it were not for her friends (her friends can never be mine). The

Eltons think me a dull dog. Perhaps I am! I cannot laugh at their jokes. Their jokes are often unkind or in bad taste. Their talk is wild and reckless, they dress extravagantly. They amuse Kitty but their influence is bad for her. I can only hope that once we are married she will settle down and be content to play her part as chatelaine of Hinkleton Manor.

* * *

*January 12th, 1920. Hinkleton Manor.*

Kitty is to have a child! It is almost too good to be true! Our son is to be called Charles Dean after his two grandfathers. God grant that he will resemble them in strength of character and integrity. I ask nothing better. Kitty is weak and shallow (I see that more clearly every day) but I am not blind to my own faults. I, too, am weak for I have allowed myself to brood over my troubles. Char's faithlessness broke something inside me — some vital spring. I was war-weary, of course, but that is a coward's excuse. I should have stood up to the blow and borne it like the attack of an enemy. Now, however, I shall have something to live for — I shall live for my children and seek fulfillment in their lives.

We have lost another tree: one of the old chestnuts — planted in the reign of Mary Tudor — came down last night in the storm. It always saddens me when we lose a tree. I am planting trees now for my children and my children's children. They will be green and growing long after I am dust.

* * *

*January 14th. Hinkleton.*

Father is overjoyed at Kitty's news. He and Kitty get on very well together. He has always liked Kitty. Father has the old-fashioned way of treating a pretty woman like a pretty toy — something brittle and valuable, something to look at and admire. He does not want friendship from women, so Kitty satisfies him. He is charmed by her playfulness.

I saw Banks about the tree and told him to get it sawn up, then I walked down to the village. Mr. Frale was coming out of the church when I passed and I stopped to speak to him. He is a poor substitute for Mr. Dean. He told me that Mr. Senture has returned to Hinkleton — he had some long story about the man's book on Hinkleton Church. I didn't listen. I hope I shall not see the man while he is here.

# 7

## *Garth's Diary: 'Battles Long Ago'*

*January 16th. The King's Head,*
*Upper Pemblebury.*

I could not write last night. My whole life fell to pieces. In a few moments of quiet conversation I saw an abyss open before my feet. Nothing happened and yet everything happened. I have lost everything that made life possible — all comfort in the present, all hope for the future.

This is raving. I must write sense. I must write the whole thing down in black and white and decide what to do. How am I to go on with life when it means nothing, when there is no use in anything anymore? How am I to believe in anybody when I have been sold, tricked, deceived? I left the Manor last night, after dinner — no, this is not the way to start. I must go back to the beginning and follow every step, and watch how my world tottered and crashed about my ears; how the awful suspicion that I had been tricked was born, and grew into a certainty.

I must be strong now. I need all my strength to bear this. I must be calm. Writing calms me.

How did it begin? It began that afternoon, the afternoon of the fifteenth — yesterday? (Good God, it feels a hundred years ago.) Father told us at teatime that he had invited Mr. Senture to dinner. 'He's an interesting man,' father said. Kitty's face changed at the news. (I put it down to anxiety on my behalf. She knew it would be awkward for me to meet the man.) 'I wish you hadn't asked him,' Kitty said petulantly, 'I don't feel like meeting strangers just now . . . ' Father was all concern; he reviled himself for his thoughtlessness and suggested that Kitty should dine upstairs. 'Oh, I must just bear it, I suppose,' Kitty said. 'He won't stay late, I hope.' 'You must go to bed when you feel tired, my dear,' father told her. 'Mr. Senture won't mind. He is coming to speak to me about the church — he wants some further information for his book. Don't trouble about the man, my dear. Just go off to bed.'

There was more talk on the subject; Kitty fretful, and father apologetic. She wanted father to put off Mr. Senture's visit, but father did not feel he could do that. 'The man will have told them at the Hinkleton Arms,' said father reasonably. 'I really think it would be very inconvenient for him. Why not have dinner in your room?'

I let them argue and said nothing. I wondered if I should make an excuse to absent myself, but I decided that I would not run away. I would stay and see the man who had usurped my place, the man whom Char loved. Kitty came to me and suggested that I should go up to town. 'You don't want to meet the man,' she said. I wavered, and then something inside me decided the matter. 'I think I do want to meet him,' I told her. She put her cheek against mine. 'Let's go up to town together, just you and me. It's ages since we had a jaunt together.' 'No, you're tired,' I told her. 'You must take care of yourself, my dear, go to bed early and have a good sleep.' She did all she could to persuade me to go, but the more she persuaded me, the more I determined to remain and meet the man.

He came early. I found him talking to father in the library. He rose and bowed to me . . . a funny little old man . . . as old as father . . . rather frail . . . with little white whiskers and a fringe of white crinkly hair round his bald crown . . . rather a pathetic little man.

'Mr. Senture?' I asked incredulously.

He bowed again.

The suspicion was born then. It was a puny child. There was some mistake, of course, this was not Char's Mr. Senture, the man with whom she had gone to Canterbury, the man who had spent hours with her alone, the man who had lured her away from me. This must be the father of Char's man.

Kitty appeared, and we went in to dinner. Mr. Senture talked a great deal, he never ceased talking. Perhaps it was as well, for the rest of us were silent that night. Father never talked much; I was occupied with my thoughts; Kitty was — what was Kitty feeling? I would have given a lot to know what Kitty was feeling. She was silent and pale, her eyes avoided mine . . .

Mr. Senture talked about the church, and then he talked about his wife. He told us that she was delicate, had been delicate for years. He told us her symptoms, which specialists she had seen, and all that they had said and done. His voice trembled as he described the sufferings of his wife, and his poor old hands trembled so that he spilled his wine upon the table.

'You have a son?' I asked him.

No, he had no son, no children. His wife had always been delicate . . . the risk was too great . . .

'Perhaps you have a nephew?'

Yes, Mr. Senture had a nephew — his sister's boy. The lad was out in China . . . had been out there for years . . . was expected home almost immediately.

'Your book,' I said. 'You are bringing out a book, I hear.'

Ah, that got him! His eyes glistened, he was only too ready to talk of his book, he talked about it interminably. I saw at last that unless I mentioned Char's name it would not be mentioned. I felt I must get to the bottom of the mystery. I was very near the bottom of it already, but I must clear it up completely. There had been enough mistakes, enough misunderstandings through lack of plain speech.

'I believe Miss Dean helped you with your book,' I said.

'Miss Dean?' he asked in a bewildered voice — I had pulled him up in the middle of his story about the leper window, and it took him a moment to adjust his mind to my question. 'Oh yes, the parson's daughter. She was most kind, most helpful. I am glad you spoke of her, for it has reminded me that I must send her a copy of my book when it is published — I must really. Her patience was inexhaustible.' He took a notebook out of his pocket and continued, 'Please excuse me if I make a note of it. My memory is deplorable, and Miss Dean was really so very kind. I must write it down at once or I shall forget, and Miss Dean will think me ungrateful — *a copy of book to Miss Dean, The Parsonage, Hinkleton* — there, I shall not forget her now.'

'She is not at the Parsonage now,' I said.

'Indeed,' he said. 'She has left, has she? Of course, how stupid I am! Her father died and Mr. Frale is here in his place. I met Mr. Frale yesterday morning in the church so I ought to have realized that Miss Dean had left. Perhaps you could oblige me with her address.'

I gave it to him calmly. My world was shaking, but I could feel nothing yet. I was perfectly calm, my hand was steady as I filled up Mr. Senture's glass, my pulse beat normally. I have seen men mortally wounded carry on with what they were doing for a few seconds before realizing what had happened to them, before they fell down on the ground and died. It was like that with me. I glanced at Kitty and I saw that her face had gone quite gray . . . she had pushed her plate aside with the food upon it untouched . . . her hands were gripping the arms of her chair.

'Kitty!' said father's voice anxiously. 'Kitty, you are feeling — unwell.'

'I feel — queer,' Kitty said and tried to rise from her chair.

'Garth!' cried father in alarm.

I rose and took her arm and helped her out of the room. She leaned upon me heavily. I took her across the hall and into the library. She sank into a chair. Father brought her some brandy and then went back to his guest; we were alone.

'So that is the man Char is going to marry!' I said quietly.

'Garth, don't look at me like that . . . you frighten me . . . Garth, for God's sake . . . I thought she was. I swear I thought so. I didn't know he was married . . . it was all true what I told you about Canterbury, and the hours they spent together in the church . . . How was I to know . . . ? You said you didn't mind . . . '

Her voice died away, she lay there in the chair, whimpering.

'You liar,' I said.

I went upstairs and changed out of my dinner clothes into a tweed suit. I put a few odds and ends in my pocket — my comb, my toothbrush, my diary — and I walked out of the house. (I couldn't stay in the house any longer, I had betrayed the house. I couldn't stay near *her*, she had betrayed me.) I went out at the big gates and up the hill and away. It didn't matter where I went; I didn't know where I was going; my one idea was to get away as far as I could, to walk and walk until I could walk no longer.

The night was fine, but very dark. The cool air blew against my cheeks and temples but it could not cool them. I was burning all over with an inward fire. I walked and walked. I passed through country I knew, and found myself in a strange land. The moon came up over the hills, pure and cold, turning the whole world into black and white like a dry point etching. I felt no fatigue. I walked on. Sometimes I found myself on country roads, and a belated car passed me with a glare of light and fled away to be swallowed up in the darkness. Sometimes I took a field path, and passed through farms and set the dogs barking. It clouded over about 3 a.m. and there was a flurry of snow. It melted as it fell. I sheltered from it in a shed and then went on my way. There were hills above me. I took a path leading upward and found myself on a moor. The low walls of a sheep-fold threw black shadows on the tussocky grass. All at once I was tired and cold, the fever had left me. I sat down under a low wall out of the cool stream of wind. I had been here before, hunting, and I knew that there was a little village in the hollow with a small inn. I had had tea there after the hunt. It was too early to approach the inn yet, scarcely five o'clock, but I could go no farther. My body was tired, but my brain was active, more active now that I had stopped walking.

My thoughts were very bitter, Kitty had tricked me. I was married to a cheat. This was the woman I had taken into my house, whom I had chosen out of all the women in the world to be the mother of my son. A woman who could stoop to lie, and lie smiling, who had kissed me with a lie upon her lips. A woman who could live a lie, and only faltered when she was found out — this woman was to be the mother of my son. I flung myself upon my face. My rage against Kitty almost choked me, everything went black. I felt I could go to her and tear my child out of her body, she was not worthy to bear my child.

At six o'clock I went down to the village through the fields. My feet left black marks on the rimy ground. The inn was open and a girl with her hair in curl-papers was shaking rugs at the door. She looked at me with amazement. I suppose I looked wild, my whole appearance must have been disordered and dirty. I told her I had walked a long way, had been walking all night, and I wanted a room to rest in, and some breakfast later.

'You be the second gentleman lost on the moor this winter,' she said in a relieved voice.

I let it go at that. I had been lost. She was quite kind. She took me upstairs and showed me into a pleasant, clean room. She brought me hot water to wash in. I felt better after I had washed, calmer and saner. I climbed onto the big four-poster bed and slept.

I have spent all day at the inn. The food is clean and plain. I have the whole place to myself for nobody comes here in winter, it is too bleak. I went down to the bridge where a little stream flows beneath a gray stone arch and watched it for a long while. The monotony of the flowing water soothed me, its turbulence, and the splash and hurry of its course. I stayed there until some men came, and then I moved away, I could not speak to anybody yet, not even strangers. My thoughts were still colored by my anger, sometimes it rose like a red flood until it almost burst my brain, and sometimes it sank into a sort of misery, a sort of gnawing pain. I walked up the hill through the bare woods.

Until now I had not thought of Char. I had

pushed the thought of Char away from me. I had pushed all softness away from me. I had given rein to my anger. I had raged against Kitty for tricking me and against myself for my foolishness in allowing myself to be tricked. But now, in the woods, the thought of Char came to me and would not be denied. We had roamed the woods of Hinkleton together so often, in summer and in winter, accepting each season as it came and enjoying its beauty. These woods were very like the woods round Hinkleton; there was the same mixture of trees, the same damp yellow undergrowth. The pale winter afternoon sunshine filtered through the bare branches of the trees.

I sat down on a log and rested my head in my hands — God, how my head ached! Char, what have I done to you, I thought. What had I done to her? I had failed Char, not Char me. If I had had faith in Char I would have gone to her and asked her if the story was true — if I had had a grain of faith! Instead of giving her a chance to defend herself I had believed at once that she was false. I had condemned her unheard. I had listened to a lying tale and believed it. I went over the whole affair painfully step by step. I remembered how she had tried to be friends with me when I returned from France, how she had gone out of her way to be friends with me. I remembered how I had repulsed her friendly advances — I would not be friends with her, it was all or nothing, and she had chosen another man. I would not be friends with Char. I had trampled on her feelings. I had hurt her deliberately — I knew exactly how to hurt her, for I knew her so well — I had crushed her, laughed at her, scorned her. Mad, crazy creature that I was! How she must hate me, how she must despise me!

I wanted her so much now — that was the next phase. I wanted her desperately. I started up thinking that I would go to her, go to her now and tell her everything. I would go on my knees to Char and ask her forgiveness — and then what? No, I must not do that. I must think it out first. I must see where that path would take me before I set my feet upon it. Where would that path take me?

I stayed in the woods until it was dark. Sometimes I sat on the log, and sometimes I strode about, crashing through the undergrowth like a madman. When it grew dark I came down to the inn. I shall stay here for a little, it is quiet here, and nobody speaks to me.

* * *

*January 16th. The King's Head,*
*Upper Pemblebury.*

I spent the day in much the same manner as yesterday, wandering about the village and the woods. I feel as if I had been here for a long time. The people here think me mad. I am sure of it by the way they stare at me and turn away their heads when they see that I am looking at them. Perhaps they are right, perhaps I am mad, how can I tell?

It would be easy to die up there in the woods.

It would be easy. The landlord has a gun; it stands behind the door in the little parlor where they give me my meals. It would be so easy to take the gun and go up into the woods — but I can't do it. I can't take the coward's way out of the mess. I am weak and incredibly foolish and easily tricked, but still I am a Wisdon. I can't get out of the mess that way; it seems to me that there is no way out of the mess. The more I think about it the more hopeless it seems. I am trapped, just as surely and hopelessly trapped as the rabbit I saw in the woods this morning. It was caught by the upper part of its foreleg, poor creature; its leg was bleeding and broken where it had tried to tear itself out of the cruel, steel-toothed trap; its eyes were scared, scared and puzzled; it tried to wriggle out of my hands. I took it out of the trap and killed it — one sharp blow on the back of its neck and its troubles were finished — one moment it was frightened and struggling, and the next it was at peace — fortunate rabbit!

It was then that the idea came to me, how easy to end life! I put the idea aside; I trampled it out of my mind, not that way for me, not the coward's way. What way then? What other way is there out of the mess? What way can I take that will not ruin us all — Char, father, Kitty and myself? — I can see no way.

* * *

*January 17th. The King's Head,*
*Upper Pemblebury.*

I am calmer today. The rage has passed; the froth of my anger is gone, only the bitter dregs are left. I am cold and calm. I can think of Kitty without the choking feeling in my throat. She is not worth my anger. She is a despicable creature. There is only one thing to do, I see that clearly now. I can't get out of the trap, so I must stay in it. I must go back to Hinkleton and live my life there as if nothing has happened. I must walk about and speak to people. I must pretend that everything is exactly the same. I owe it to father to behave as if nothing is wrong. To father and to myself, and to the Wisdons. I must speak to Kitty when people are there — there must be no scandal, no food for malicious gossip. I must school myself to see Kitty sitting at the end of the table, and in the chair opposite father at the fire. I need do no more than that, I need not touch her. This is the task I have set myself, a hard task; but I feel, now, that I can do it. A strange power, a strange calmness possesses me. My heart is very cold; it is like a lump of ice in my breast.

As for Char, I must leave her alone. It is all I can do for Char. I must leave her to make her own life, not involve her in the shipwreck of mine. I must keep out of her way and let her continue to think me despicable, crazy, faithless. It is too dangerous to have any explanations with her, much too dangerous. She must continue to hate me. Strangely enough this is the hardest part of the task I have set myself. I have battled with myself for hours over this business. If I could clear myself with Char I could shoulder the rest of the burden with ease, but I must not clear myself with Char. I long for Char's sympathy, I long to go to her and make a clean breast of the whole thing, to lay my head upon her shoulder.

Too dangerous! I love her too much to risk meeting her in friendship. I have harmed her enough already. I must leave her alone. I must never be friendly with her in case she should forgive me and the way be opened — the way be opened to I know not what. This is the hardest of all — to bear Char's hatred, Char's scorn. To know that she will go through life despising me while I shall love her in secret until I die.

* * *

*January 18th. The King's Head,*
*Upper Pemblebury.*

My last day here. I have spent it arming myself.

* * *

*January 19th. Hinkleton Manor.*

I left Pemblebury in the morning and walked home. I got a lift in a baker's van part of the way. I found the house in a turmoil, Kitty ill, and father beside himself with anxiety on my behalf. I explained very little; there was little I could explain. Father was too pleased to see me safe and sound to bother about explanations. I believe he thinks I lost my memory. I am sorry for the anxiety I caused him, it is the last time I shall cause him any anxiety. I have made up my mind to that. To Kitty I explained nothing, there was no need. From now on we are strangers. Kitty understands me, and, at last, I understand her. We start level for the first time.

I saw Sim and told him I would hunt on Thursday. Lady Vera has sent over the hunter for me to try. A nice-looking beast but I am doubtful if he is up to my weight. Sim thinks he is. The Tudor tree is being sawn up for fuel.

* * *

*May 16th. Hinkleton Manor.*

Kitty gave birth to a daughter this morning. There is great excitement in the house over the event. Doctor Gray told me that both were doing well, and added that there was plenty of time for an heir. He evidently thinks my lack of enthusiasm is due to the child's sex. I am glad the child is not a son, sons are said to take after their mothers. I am glad I am the last Wisdon, the line is enfeebled. I am a dead husk; there is no life left in me, no feeling for anything or anybody. Even Char has become shadowy to me, a pathetic ghost.

* * *

*July 3rd. Hinkleton Manor.*

Char arrived in time for dinner. The child is to be christened tomorrow. It was, I suppose, the obvious thing to invite Char to be the god-mother (she is our only female relation) but the whole thing seems a farce to me — a tragic farce. I have been dreading Char's visit for days; to see Char again knowing what I know; to see her and to have to take her hand, coldly; to see her and speak to her as if she were nothing to me — this is the task I have set myself. No wonder I have been dreading her visit.

Char arrived. She looks tired and unhappy and very shabby. The shabbiness hurts me as much as the unhappiness; it is my fault that she is shabby. I would so willingly give her all I possess, and I may not give her anything, not even a new dress. I have fought it out with myself and I know I must not. I am afraid she is having a hard time, a weary time — London in this weather, and Wentworth's and, perhaps, not enough food! I don't know how I am going to bear it. She was very quiet, she hardly spoke. I saw that Kitty was telling Char her troubles, complaining about me, most likely, and the servants, and the drought. Rather amusing, really, that Kitty should lay her troubles on Char's shoulders. These things amuse me nowadays; they amuse some queer contrary devil that has taken up his abode in my empty heart.

I forced myself to be gay and talkative. I saw Char looking at me wonderingly and my heart went out to her so that I could scarcely bear the pain. I knew what she was feeling when she looked at me like that; I knew she thought me changed from the boy she knew so well. I was suffering so acutely that it was easy to be cruel.

Biting words rose to my lips and I uttered them. I saw her wilt under my sarcasm. There will be more pain tomorrow, more suffering. My heart that I thought was dead has recovered sufficiently to suffer.

* * *

*July 4th, 1920. Hinkleton Manor.*

The child's christening today — what a farce the whole thing is! Char felt the same as I did. Her voice faltered as she made the promises for my child. She knew she would not be able to fulfill them, and she hates lies as I do. I went away into the woods when it was over and wrestled with my devil, and armed myself afresh. I find pleasure in cynicism, the habit is growing. Let it grow, it is a fine protection against the world . . .

# 8

## *Charlotte's Tears*

I read until the light grew too dim to see anymore, and then I sat on, beside the little window, with the books piled round me. The light lingered for a while among the trees; the tops of them were still bright when there was nothing but darkness and shadow on the ground. Then the light faded swiftly, and only the sky was faintly gray.

Nanny came up and found me sitting there.

'Miss Char!' she said, coming over and touching me in the darkness. 'I've been looking for you everywhere, and then I remembered about the diaries. Miss Char, are you ill? You are all wet, my dear!'

'Tears, Nanny. Just tears.'

'Oh, Miss Char! There have been too many tears in this house — it's a sorrowful house — too much pain and tears — all the time I have been here . . . a lifetime . . . no happiness . . . all tears. I hoped so much that you would come here — long ago — and make us all happy. That night of the birthday dance I was sure you would come. And then the war came and everything went wrong, and I thought — when he comes back from the war he will bring her home. Oh, Miss Char, what was it that happened? I've often wondered . . . often and often. We would have been happier if it had been you, my dear. You understood him . . . it was always you . . . never Miss Kitty . . . you could have made him happy.'

'I know, I know!'

'What was it, Miss Char?'

'It wasn't . . . my fault, Nanny. I didn't know what it was . . . that changed him . . . never until now. I know now. It was all a ghastly mistake.'

'A mistake?'

'You remember Mr. Senture, Nanny?'

'Not the old gentleman, you don't mean him?'

'Yes. Garth thought — was told that I was going to marry him.'

'He couldn't have thought it. Mr. Senture was old — as old as Mr. Wisdon — and married too. How could he have thought it?'

'He never saw Mr. Senture. He was told about it, told about how often I was with Mr. Senture, and about our expedition to Canterbury.'

'I can't believe it,' Nanny said.

'It is difficult to believe,' I agreed. I could hardly believe it myself. It was incredible to me that Garth could have thought I would ever look twice at another man.

'Who told him?' said Nanny at last.

I hesitated a moment, and then I said, 'Kitty told him.' It was no use to hide anything from Nanny. She was too deeply interested in us all, and I wanted a confidante so badly.

I heard her draw in her breath. 'I see it all now,' she said. 'I see it all as plain as plain — him going off by himself that night when Mr. Senture came to dinner. Yes, I'll tell you about it, Miss

Char. It all started from that night — the quarrels and the bitterness. They were happy enough till that night, the two of them, and then Mr. Wisdon (old Mr. Wisdon, I mean) asked Mr. Senture to dinner and Mrs. Wisdon was angry with him for asking him. Mr. Senture had come back for a few days to draw something else in the church for his book. Well, old Mr. Wisdon wouldn't put him off, not for all Mrs. Wisdon's wheedling (though he usually did give in to her), and Mr. Senture came. Mrs. Wisdon was taken ill in the middle of it, and I got her to bed. Then we found Mr. Garth had gone — just disappeared, without saying a word to nobody. He stayed away nearly a week, and we were all scared to death about him. (He wasn't the sort of gentleman who did things like that; he was always so considerate, so thoughtful and kind.) Nobody said much, we just looked at each other's faces and looked away. It was awful. It seemed like a year. None of us knew where he was, but Mrs. Wisdon suspected something — I was sure of it. I thought at the time they'd quarreled, and I was angry with Mr. Garth for going off like that, and her in the condition she was in. And then one night he just walked in, as if he had been out for a walk in the park, and nothing was said — nothing that I heard. I meant to speak to him, but when I saw his face I couldn't get up the courage — it wasn't Mr. Garth's face at all, it was so hard and bitter, so lined. He looked as if he had been ill for weeks. I never saw such a change in a person. He moved his things out of her bedroom and they were never moved back. It nearly broke my heart to see it all going wrong and not be able to do anything.'

'Oh, Nanny!'

'It all went wrong after that — worse and worse. He never went near her, never gave her a kind word. I was sorry for her, she was a young, pretty thing and she loved a good time. It was a dreadful house! Oh, Miss Char, it was a dreadful house! The maids felt it too. They wouldn't stay, they said they couldn't settle; they said it was haunted. It was the secret between those two that haunted the house — no ghost, just hatred.'

'Not hatred,' I whispered.

'Yes, hatred. You could feel it in the room when they were there together — a black cloud. He went away a lot. I was glad when he went away — I loved Mr. Garth like my own son, but I was glad when he went away.'

She paused for a few moments, and then she went on again in a low hurried tone, 'And then she began to be friendly with other gentlemen — it was very wrong, of course — there were others before Mr. Hamilton. Oh, it was wrong, I knew that, but how could you blame her? She was young and pretty — such a pretty thing — and she loved company, and she loved to be gay.'

I clung to her hard old hand in the darkness. I couldn't speak. I felt broken, utterly exhausted.

'Come to bed, Miss Char,' Nanny said. 'It's all over long ago. They're both dead — God rest them — and they're not suffering anymore. Come to bed, my dear.'

I let her put me to bed, and fuss over me with hot-water bottles and eau de Cologne. She brought me some soup for my dinner and made me take it, and she came and sat by my fire with her knitting until I went to sleep. It was very comforting to be fussed over by Nanny. She was a well of tenderness.

# 9

## *The County Calls*

The next morning was sunny and bright; I got up as usual and went into the garden. I felt strangely shaky. I felt as if I had been ill and was just recovering. I felt as if my whole life had been riven by an earthquake. The foundations of my being were disturbed. I had built up my life upon the assumption that Garth had ceased to care for me, that his heart had changed. I knew now that he had loved me always, that he had never changed. He was all mine, had always been mine. I could think of him as mine without shame. He had never been Kitty's at all; she had stolen him from me by a trick.

I understood, now, the satisfaction that George Hamilton had derived from the fact that Kitty belonged to him. When he had said, 'I'm glad we were married, she belongs to me,' I had thought it strange, I had not really understood; but now I understood what he had meant. Garth was dead, too, but he belonged to me. We had been tricked out of our life together but he was mine in death.

I walked slowly round the garden; my legs felt weak, and the sunshine hurt my eyes, but there was a strange happiness in my heart. I scarcely understood why I should be happy, nothing had changed. My future was still a lonely road — can one have happiness without hope? It appeared that one could. I had had so little in life to make me happy — perhaps this was the explanation.

I knew it was useless to try to write, useless to work at Garth's book until my mind had adjusted itself to the new ideas. The book must wait. There was so much to think of. I had to go back down the years and look at every incident in the new light which Garth's diary shed upon it. That night when I had worn the yellow frock and Garth had been so heartless — how differently I saw it now! He had been suffering as much as I; he had been tortured. The weekend that I had spent at the Manor for Clementina's christening wore a completely different complexion, seen from Garth's point of view. He had been cruel, not because he had ceased to care for me, but because he cared too much. How easy it was to forgive, now that I knew the truth.

I walked down to the rock garden and sat on a sun-warmed stone. It was Sunday, so I had the garden to myself. The birds sang in the woods and a golden light filtered through the budding trees. What would have happened, I wondered, if Garth had come to me, all those long years ago, and told me the whole story, had bared his heart to me as he had so wanted to do, had laid his head upon my shoulder. Oh God, how I wished he had! I could have borne to lose him if I had known of his love; I would have asked nothing more than to be allowed to love him in secret all the days of my life. This would have been enough for me, I thought; I would have asked no more, not even to see him sometimes. I realized, vaguely, however, that this would not have been enough for Garth; he could not have been content with this pale shadow of love. He must have known that; he must have known himself and seen that it could never content him. He had written so often of the danger — 'dangerous to be friendly with Char.' The danger must have been very clear to his mind. How differently we were made, Garth and I, for he must have all or nothing, while I would have been content with the touch of his hand. I did not see, then, as I see now, that it was the difference between a woman and a man.

At first I felt very bitter against Kitty. I told myself that she had always wanted Hinkleton Manor and the position and luxury that would be the portion of Garth's wife. It was not Garth she wanted, just to be Lady of the Manor. She had made up the whole story with the intention of gaining her end by any means in her power — this was a dreadful thought. I could not bear to think it. I went back over what had happened very carefully. I thought of Kitty's message to me as she lay dying, the message she had left with George Hamilton. 'Tell her it was such a little lie,' she had said, 'such a little lie to start with and then it grew and grew,' and she had gone on to say that it had grown into a tree and we were all hanging on it. Poor Mr. Hamilton had thought her delirious, and it had certainly seemed so to me at the time, but now I understood the words, and saw that Kitty had not uttered them in delirium. The lie had grown into a tree and we were all hanging on it, Garth and Kitty and George Hamilton and I. It was a gruesome thought, horribly gruesome, but that was how Kitty saw it, and, now that I knew the facts, I saw that the simile was true. We had all been ruined by Kitty's lie — we had all been hanged on the tree she had planted.

'It was such a little lie at first' — what had she meant by that? What could she have meant! I began to see, as I thought about it and cast my mind back, how the thing might have started. The talk was loose at the Eltons'; it was mischievous talk, the kind of talk that I could never achieve if I tried. It was always full of laughing allusions and sly innuendoes. How easy it might have been for Kitty to hint that I was occupying myself very pleasantly at Hinkleton! It would only have needed a hint, a few joking words, a knowing look and the lie was told. Kitty always took color from the people she was with. At the Eltons' she outdid the Eltons at their own game. I visualized it all quite clearly. It was possible that Kitty half believed in the story herself. She knew very little about Mr. Senture. I remembered that she had only seen him once, in the half darkness of the church. She could not have known he was married. Once it had started, the lie would grow, and it would be difficult to stop it growing. It would grow and grow until it became a tree. It was less difficult to excuse her for the other lie — for saying, or at any rate allowing Garth to think that I had known he was to be there when I refused the Eltons' invitation — perhaps she really thought I knew that Garth was coming, perhaps she thought Mrs. Elton had told me in her letter.

This reasoning was far-fetched, but it comforted me strangely. I was glad to find an excuse for Kitty; it is a terrible thing to be angry with the dead. I could forgive her now, and I wanted to forgive her, I had said long ago that I forgave her (before I had known what it was I had to forgive), and I wanted to hold myself to that. I wanted to sweep all the bitterness away and go forward feeling free and clean. It was easier to forgive Kitty when I remembered that she had ruined her own life too. She had been punished enough, I thought (remembering what her life with Garth had been); even Nanny had pitied her, and condoned her sin, Nanny, who loved Garth like her own son, and was the soul of propriety.

The days passed. March went out like a lamb and April came. My strength returned. I had put Garth's book aside in the meantime and I decided to leave it where it was. Clementina was coming home for the holidays in a few days' time, and I could do no work while she was here. The book must wait until the holidays were over and I could settle down to it with an easy mind. It was better to wait than to spoil the book by forcing myself to work at it when I felt so restless and distraught. The book was too good to spoil. I knew it was good. I knew that I had found something I could do, something that would fill the empty years of the future, and fill them pleasantly. When Garth's book was finished I would write a book of my own, a book about the country, for country people who had to live in towns. I would make a bunch of country flowers for women who lived in basements. But, just at the moment, I could write nothing worthwhile, nothing that had any life in it, any verve. And I could not read either. The thoughts and emotions stirred up by the revelations in Garth's diary came between me and the printed page. I read pages, and found that I had made no sense of them, had not the slightest idea what they contained — it was hopeless.

The only thing which was any use to me at this time was the garden. Fortunately the weather was good so I was able to spend long hours digging and hoeing and planting among my rocks. The work was good for me, it turned my mind outward, and the fatigue and the fresh air helped me to sleep.

Lady Bournesworth came to tea as she had promised and admired my bulbs. The daffodils were nearly over now, and the tulips were opening. I had planted groups of them in my rock garden to cover the bare patches, and the effect was very fine. Lady Bournesworth's visit was followed by a stream of callers. The County had forgiven Garth because he was dead, and because he had died spectacularly. I found it difficult to be agreeable to my unwanted guests. They wasted my time and exhausted me with small talk — I was not used to small talk and tea-table conversation and I was too old a dog to learn new tricks. I walked them solemnly round the garden and listened to the same comments, and answered the same questions — or forbore to answer. These people had nothing to give me, and I had nothing to give them; their thoughts moved in a different orbit, they had different values, different pleasures, different cares from me. When the subject of gardens failed they discussed their servants and their clothes — what a waste of time it was, what a waste of energy!

Barling was the only person who enjoyed my visitors — after the long eclipse of the Manor it had once more taken its rightful place in the County. He ushered in the callers with pomp and circumstance, and delved in the plate chest for the largest and most ornate silver tea-service that he could find. My stock went up with leaps and bounds — he had always been respectful, but now he was positively obsequious — I saw the humor of it all but I was too annoyed and bewildered to be amused.

At last, after three days of County calls, I decided that I had had enough. If I had to go round the garden again and listen to another set of people saying the same things I should scream from sheer boredom. I told Barling to say I was 'not at home,' and, donning my oldest clothes, went down to the rock garden to do some planting. A case of small alpine plants had arrived and I wanted to get them in before Clementina came home. I wanted to give Clementina all my time and attention during the holidays. I was looking forward to the holidays eagerly, and had planned all sorts of jaunts and pleasures to fill the time.

I thought of many things as I sorted out the plants, and dug, and planted, and watered. What a much more useful and enjoyable afternoon I was spending than trailing round the place with chattering strangers! The sun shone warmly upon my back, and the perspiration trickled down my nose. I was muddy and dirty, but quite happy and busy and useful.

I stood up and stretched my back — a long back is a disability to a gardener — and suddenly I saw a woman approaching; it was Lady Vera. She waved to me cheerily.

'It's not the man's fault,' she called out, when she was still some distance away. 'He said 'not at home' quite nicely, but I wanted to see you, so I took a snoop round on my own. What are you doin' here, Miss Dean?'

'Trying to make a rock garden,' I told her, not very amiably I'm afraid.

'I like it,' she said. 'Those rough stones are jolly. They look natural. As if they'd grown there. Most people's rock gardens look as if they'd ordered a car-load of stones from the nearest builder's yard and dumped them down.'

'Yes.'

'I like the way you've made that path curvin' round and disappearing among the trees. Never could stand gardenin' myself, but I like seein' good results. Must have taken some doin' getting' those stones into place!'

'Yes, they are frightfully heavy,' I told her. The woman was so altogether unconscious of my ill-humor that I could not continue to be angry with her for invading my solitude. Besides there was something very likeable about her — perhaps it was her naturalness — she had no airs, and you felt she really meant what she said. If she had disliked the effect of my rock garden she would have expressed her views just as frankly. I was convinced of that, and it made her praise worth having. My other visitors had admired everything that they saw — it was no wonder that they had to coin new expressions of admiration and ecstasy, they had used up all the old ones in the first ten minutes.

'Everybody's talkin' about you,' said Lady Vera suddenly and surprisingly.

'How dull for them!'

'It's a change from clothes and servants. Don't get bitter about them — they're not worth it.'

'I don't think I'm bitter,' I said frankly, 'only bored.'

Lady Vera laughed; I liked her laugh, it was a deep, chuckling sound of real enjoyment.

'You'll do,' she said. 'And now to business. I don't pay afternoon calls for pleasure — what about that geldin'? Anythin' doin'? Come over to Pollen Lodge and see him — or I'll send him over for you to try, if you like. Just suit you. I'll let you have him cheap.'

'I don't really want another — '

'Nobody does,' she interrupted. 'This depression's gettin' on my nerves — not that I have any to speak of. Been breedin' horses for twenty years, and sellin's never been so stiff.' She sat down on a rock and lit a cigarette with the flick of a nickel lighter. 'Brown Betty doin' you well?' she inquired, the smoke pouring from her mouth as she spoke.

'She's perfect.'

'Where d'you get her?'

'My brother-in-law bought her for me.'

'You couldn't swindle Garth,' she said. 'Garth knew a good horse when he saw it. D'you mind talkin' about him?'

'No, why should I?'

'I wondered. Lady B. says you're writin' a book about him.'

She was looking over toward the house and her eyes were dreamy. Her hair (she had taken off her beret and thrown it carelessly on the ground) was dark brown, liberally sprinkled with gray. It was closely cropped about her well-shaped head. Her tweeds were shabby but well cut — probably by a man's tailor — they had that indefinable look of belonging to her, and to her alone. Her hands were long and thin — the fingers stained with nicotine. Her feet matched her hands; they were long and thin and encased in well-cut dark-brown brogues. She had crossed one thin long leg over the other and was swinging the crossed foot idly to and fro.

'Yes,' I said, 'I am writing a book about Garth — a biography — I find it — difficult.'

'Why? You knew him well, didn't you?'

'Almost too well,' I said slowly. 'He's too near for me to see him properly. You know what I mean — when you are close up to a wood you can't see it. You can only see the individual trees.'

'Yes,' she said, 'I've never done anythin' of that kind — writin', I mean — but I see the point. You want to stand back from a horse to see its paces.' She sat and thought for a few moments and then she said, 'I liked Garth. He was a good sort. I could have talked to Garth, but he never gave anyone the chance of gettin' near him. He was a strange man, Miss Dean, a secret man.'

I did not answer that. I knew that Garth was a secret man, nobody knew better than I the load of secret trouble that he had carried for so many years.

'I'll tell you somethin' about Garth,' she said suddenly. 'It's so typical of him, of the strangeness and secrecy of him. But you mustn't put me in the book.' She dropped the butt of her cigarette and extinguished it with her heel like a man. Then she looked up at me and smiled. 'You mustn't put me in the book, Miss Dean. I've got my reputation to think of — the reputation of bein' as tough as leather and as hard as nails. 'It's no use tryin' to get the better of Lady Vera,' people say, so they *don't*. If they thought I was soft — I'll tell you this, though, in strict confidence, I'm not as tough as I'd have them believe. Life's a bit of a battle at times.' She broke off and said, 'Look at that blackbird lookin' for worms where you've been diggin' — I like blackbirds, they're so cocky and independent, so full of spunk. Where was I?'

'You're not so tough as you would have them believe,' I prompted her.

She threw back her head and laughed. 'That's right,' she said. 'But you keep that to yourself, young woman, or you'll find I'm tougher than you thought. Well, one day I was huntin' a mare that I'd sold to a man from Leicestershire. I'd only sold her that morning and I was a fool not to go straight home, but when I'm huntin' I get crazy, and I wanted to see the finish. We were crossin' a road, and I let her down, and broke her knees. My God, I was sick! It broke me all up when I saw her knees. I was sailin' pretty near the wind at the moment — things looked as black as hell for I'd banked on the mare to pay my rent and fodder bill. When I saw her knees I just burst out at the nearest person — burst out about all my troubles (it was yellow, but I couldn't help it, I was half-crazy). I'd have burst out at anybody, it was just chance that the nearest person happened to be Garth. 'What were you gettin' for the mare?' Garth wanted to know, when I'd finished makin' a fool of myself. 'Two hundred,' I told him, 'and I'll be lucky if I get sixty now.' 'I've always liked that mare. I'll give you three hundred for her,' he said, just casually like that.

'I thought at first he was jokin' and I told him I wasn't in the mood for it. 'Don't be a fool,' he said, 'I'll give you three hundred for the brute. When I say a thing I mean it,' and he did mean it. He sent a groom over next day with a check and a box and orders to bring the mare over. I told him I wouldn't take it, and he told me to go to hell. He got a vet down from town and they mended her up — you'd scarcely have known she'd been let down. That was Garth all over. People said he was hard-hearted and cynical — well, he wasn't full of soft sawder, I've heard him say pretty brutal things myself. You had to be down and out before you saw what he was like inside.'

I recognized Garth in the story; it was like him to do a generous thing, and to do it roughly, ungraciously. He hated gratitude, he hated softness and sentimentality. He tried, all the time, to be hard and cynical, but sometimes he couldn't manage it, and the true kindness and generosity of his nature showed through.

Lady Vera and I walked down to the stables together and fed the horses with apples. Sim was very respectful to my companion; he asked her advice about the gray's off-fore which was still causing trouble. She felt it with her thin, capable hands and discoursed gravely about the respective merits of cold compresses and hot fomentations. When she left I found, somewhat to my surprise, that I had promised to take Clementina over to Pollen Lodge in the holidays.

# 10

## *Prospect Hill*

Clementina arrived the following afternoon. She was obviously very pleased to be home again. She hugged me tightly, and she hugged Nanny (who was delighted at the unwonted embrace) and then she ran off to the stables to hug Black Knight. We had tea together in the library, and I told her all my news — the County had called in force and the stable cat had had kittens.

'What a ghastly bore!' Clementina said, licking her fingers which were covered with butter, and helping herself to another muffin. 'I don't mean the kittens, of course, I've seen them already. They're sweet aren't they? Especially the one with the white feet. Can I have it for my own, Aunt Charlotte?'

'Yes, of course,' I said — the kittens were all hers, but I didn't point that out to her, it was wiser not to.

'What's happened to Naseby?' she inquired. 'I *was* surprised when I saw a new man arrive at Hill House with the car. Is Naseby having his holidays or something?'

'He's having 'flu,' I told her. 'He's better, but don't go near the garage, like a dear. We don't want the holidays spoiled.'

'No fear!' exclaimed my niece.

I nearly laughed. It was natural, of course, that she should pick up the expressions of her contemporaries and use them, but the slang sounded very strange upon Clementina's lips, and I was glad Geoff Howard had sailed for Australia. He would have seen it as the beginning of the ruin which school was going to wreak upon his perfect child.

'How's Violet?' asked Clementina. 'I'm longing to see Violet and tell her all about school.'

'You are to spend tomorrow with her,' I said. 'They said you were to go over as early as possible and stay until bedtime. Violet is much better, she can ride now.'

'Right you are! I'd really rather have stayed at home tomorrow with you. There's such lots of things I want to do — but we've got lots of days, haven't we?'

'Thirty, isn't it?'

'Yes, thirty. Pity there's no hunting, Aunt Charlotte. By the by, Sim suggested putting up some jumps in the lower park. I said I'd ask you if we could.'

'I think it would be a splendid idea.'

'We may then? How lovely! Oh, it *is* lovely to be home!'

'But you quite like school?' I asked, rather anxiously.

'I don't mind it. It's rather fun in a way. You know I was awfully frightened of the girls at first — just scared stiff — but they're quite decent really, and Old Scales is a lamb.'

I laughed. 'Is that how you talk of your headmistress?'

'Unless she's present,' answered Clementina smiling. 'Then we say, 'Yes, Miss Scales; No, Miss Scales; Oh Miss Scales,' like good little girls should. She takes us for arithmetic.'

'Poor woman!' I exclaimed feelingly.

'She thinks I'm half-witted,' Clementina admitted. 'But the other mistresses assure her I'm sane. It's very funny.'

We talked a lot that evening; there seemed so much to tell each other. Clementina stayed up to dinner for a treat. She was a delightful companion, and I was sorry when Nanny came for her at nine o'clock.

'I suppose you're too big to be bathed now,' Nanny said.

'You can come and watch me,' said Clementina kindly. 'I'm nearly as tall as you are now, but not so fat.'

'You've plenty of time for that,' said Nanny dryly.

Clementina put her arm round Nanny's neck and they went off together laughing.

I was pleased with the success of my experiment, pleased and relieved. It had been a risk to send the child to school; she was so different from other children, so mature for her age, but I saw that I had been right to take the risk. Clementina had not altered fundamentally, she was still the same thoughtful, serious person at heart, but she *had* altered superficially, and altered for the better. She was more human, more considerate for others, less moody and self-conscious. She was able to take a joke directed against herself and laugh it off, and, what was best of all, she appreciated her home far more, and the kindness and consideration of her friends. When I looked back and thought of what Clementina was like when I first came to Hinkleton — the prickly, self-conscious child, full of weird complexes and inhibitions — and compared her with the Clementina who had spent the evening with me and just gone upstairs to bed, I could hardly believe that it was the same being. I wished Garth could have been here to see the change. It seemed very sad that he would never see the new Clementina; she was a daughter that any man could be proud of.

* * *

Clementina went over to Oldgarden next morning. She had decided to ride over, in case Violet wanted to ride in the afternoon.

'It will be so lovely if she does,' Clementina said as Sim held out his hand and she sprang, as lightly as a fairy, on to Black Knight's back. 'It will be just like old times. D'you think there's *really* any chance of it, Aunt Charlotte?'

'Every chance,' I told her. 'Violet rides every day. Of course she doesn't go far.'

Barling came out onto the steps, where I was seeing Clementina off, and said I was wanted on the telephone. I waved to Clementina as she cantered off down the drive and followed Barling into the house.

'Who is it, Barling?'

'Mr. Ponsonby, Miss.'

I took up the receiver casually; it would be

about the new bailiff I supposed. I had written to Mr. Ponsonby telling him that I did not like the man — nobody liked the man — he was too hard and businesslike to fill Garth's shoes; he had no sympathy, no tact. He could not differentiate between a shirking tenant and one who had had really bad luck. I had told Mr. Ponsonby that the man would have to be replaced.

'Hallo!' I said.

'Miss Dean?' inquired Mr. Ponsonby's voice.

'Yes, Mr. Ponsonby.'

'I have good news, Miss Dean.'

'Good news?'

'Yes, can you guess what it is?'

'Have you found another bailiff?'

'My good news is from abroad.'

'What *do* you mean?'

'I have just heard some good news from abroad — from Africa.'

'You can't mean — ?'

'I have reason to believe Mr. Wisdon is not dead.'

'Garth — alive!'

'It is incredible, isn't it?'

'How did you hear? Where is he?'

'A gentleman has just called this morning at my office. He has news of Mr. Wisdon.'

'News that Garth is alive?'

'Yes. This gentleman was traveling. He was in Africa — '

'Did he see Garth?'

'Yes, he saw him.'

'Oh, heavens — he saw Garth, alive and well?'

'Alive and well. Mr. Wisdon was captured by a nomadic tribe. He suffered a considerable amount of hardship, but eventually escaped — it is a long story, a very long and exciting story.'

'Is he well? Is he coming home?'

'Yes, he is coming home as soon as certain formalities have been accomplished. There are certain formalities when a man's death has been presumed and his will executed.'

'I know, never mind that. When is he coming? You're quite sure it was really Garth — there's no mistake?'

'I am quite sure. This gentleman has given me ample proof that his story is true.'

'I can't believe it.'

'It is difficult to believe.'

'Don't you think we had better wait — I couldn't bear it if we believed it and then found there was some mistake?'

'There is no mistake, Miss Dean. I would not have told you unless I was convinced that there could be no mistake.'

'Could I — could I see the gentleman myself?' I asked.

'I think you should do so,' replied Mr. Ponsonby. 'He could answer your questions far better than I can.'

'When can I see him? Shall I come up to town?'

'Wait a moment and I will ask him.'

Mr. Ponsonby went away for a few minutes and then returned. 'He will come down to Hinkleton and see you, Miss Dean. Today if that would suit you.'

'Yes — oh, yes, please tell him to come.'

'Shall I tell him to take the train which arrives at Hinkleton station at 12:30 — the train I usually come by?'

'Yes, I will send the car to the station. Please thank him very, very much.'

I put down the receiver and sat staring at it stupidly. The news I had just heard had stunned me, I could not take it in. It was too good, too wonderful to be true. Garth was alive, Garth was coming home. It couldn't be true — Garth was dead, his clothes had been sent home, his body was buried in the desert. And yet it must be true, for Mr. Ponsonby would never have accepted the news and handed it on without being certain of his ground. Garth was alive. In a few hours I should be talking to a man who had seen him quite recently, a man who knew all that had happened to Garth and could tell me what he had looked like, and whether he was well. Could tell me the details of his escape!

I tried to remember whether Mr. Ponsonby had said Garth was well. Yes, he had said 'alive and well.' Garth was alive and well. Garth was coming home. What did this mean to me? I could not tell. I could not realize that it was true, far less what it meant to me. I pressed my fingers over my eyes and said aloud, 'Garth is alive,' but the words were meaningless. I could not believe that Garth was coming home nor visualize his arrival.

Garth was coming back to Hinkleton Manor. The door would open and he would walk in, and immediately he would be at home, with all his own things round him; the atmosphere of the house that he loved so dearly would meet him on the threshold and enfold him in its peace. But I — what should I feel when Garth walked in? What would it be like to meet Garth? Why did my heart tremble at the thought of it? Was it because I had learned his secret from his diaries, had read the outpourings of his heart — wild words which he had imagined that nobody but himself would ever see? Was it because I knew his secret and was free, at last, to tell him mine — that I had never ceased to love him, that there had never been another man in my life, that even when he had scorned and rejected me my disobedient heart had remained faithful to its love? Could I tell him that? Could I look him in the face and tell him that I loved him? My face burned at the thought.

The mountain and the wood were between us no longer; all the barriers were swept aside. I had claimed the dead Garth for my own in the secrecy of my thoughts — he was mine in death I had said and had rejoiced to say it — but now he was alive, and on his way home, and I was not sure — how could I be sure — that he still loved me. It was all so long ago; he might have changed; it was years since we had been on terms that were even *friendly*: our last interview had been stormy and troubled; Garth had been cruel to me in that interview, brutal.

I shrank, too, from the man in Garth. I had had nothing to do with men in my life — in my inner life. Garth's maleness frightened me. I was shy of Garth. My heart trembled at the thought of Garth loving me, and trembled again at the thought that he might have ceased to love me. How could I meet Garth? I was dazed and dizzy with the turmoil of emotions which besieged me.

After a little I rose and pulled myself together. It was no use to sit here and think about it. Garth could not possibly be home for some time — days, perhaps weeks would elapse before I should see him — I should have time enough to look into my heart and set my house in order before Garth came. Meantime there was much to be done. I must put my feelings aside; I must thrust my personal emotions out of my mind. There was much to be done and I was wasting precious time.

First of all I must tell Nanny what I had learned, and the servants, and send a message down to Naseby, who was still in bed, and I must prepare for my visitor — the man who had actually seen Garth and was coming to tell me about it — Barling must open wine for the bringer of good tidings, and I must on no account forget to send the car to the station for him. I hesitated over Clementina and decided not to ring up Oldgarden — I would wait until later, until I knew more about it and could give her all the details — I think I was still just a little doubtful as to whether the news could possibly be true.

I carried out the program I had made in a kind of dream. Nanny was tearful with joy. Unlike me, she accepted the news at once and believed it. The mere fact of telling her made the news more real to me and, paradoxically, less alarming.

Nanny's point of view was so matter of fact. She was not concerned with Garth's mind; she was merely rejoiced over the news that his body was safe and sound. She followed me about the house like a dog, but, unlike a dog, she was full of questions, questions that I could not answer.

'Where did the gentleman meet Mr. Garth?' she inquired.

'I don't know, Nanny, I never asked.'

'How long ago should you think it was, Miss Char?'

'I've no idea.'

'What is the gentleman's name — did he know Mr. Garth before? How did he know it really *was* Mr. Garth?'

'I don't know, Nanny.'

'Perhaps it was another gentleman pretending to be Mr. Garth.'

'Mr. Ponsonby said he had ample proofs,' I told her.

I wished, now, that I had thought of asking Mr. Ponsonby more. At the time I had been overcome by the astonishing news that Garth was alive. Nothing else seemed to matter in the least. But now my brain was busy with the subject, and I could not understand why I had been such a fool.

'Will the gentleman take sherry or a cocktail, Miss?' asked Barling.

'I don't know,' I said.

'You see, Miss, if he's a youngish gentleman he'll probably like a cocktail, and if he's an oldish gentleman he'll prefer sherry.'

'I don't know anything about him, Barling,' I

said with some exasperation. 'Did you tell Naseby — I mean Barker — to take the car to the station?'

'Why, yes, Miss. Half an hour ago. About the sherry, Miss — '

'Never mind the sherry. Have both ready,' I said, rushing upstairs to change my frock.

Nanny pursued me and hindered me with her excitement. It was after twelve when I was ready. 'I wonder what Mr. Garth has been doing all this time without his clothes,' she said. 'You didn't think to ask?'

'No, I didn't.'

'Was it in Africa the gentleman met Mr. Garth?'

'I suppose so. We shall soon know all about it.'

'You'll tell me, Miss Char.'

'Of course, Nanny — is that the car?'

It was the car. I fled downstairs and arrived, breathless at the front door. Barker got out and came up the steps.

'Oh, Barker, did you miss the gentleman? Hasn't he come?' I asked. I couldn't bear the thought that there should be any hitch.

'Yes, Miss,' replied Barker, ''e's come all right. 'E's walking over the 'ill through the woods. Said 'e would rather walk. Said the train was stuffy and 'e wanted some air.'

'Oh, Barker, does he know the way?'

'I told 'im, Miss,' Barker said.

I could not rest quietly in the house; I was strung up to concert pitch by this time and bursting with the hundred and one questions I wanted to ask. I decided to walk over the hill and meet my guest; it would show him how much I appreciated his kindness in coming to Hinkleton.

I ran out through the garden and climbed the hill. My rock garden was really beautiful now. The warm sun had encouraged the primroses and the polyanthi; they made a brave show. It was a lovely spring day. The trees were budding and the birds were singing. There were wild violets among the long tufty grass.

As I drew near the top of the hill I saw a man standing on the pile of boulders which had been such a favorite haunt of our childhood — Garth's and mine. He was standing very still admiring the view. He had taken off his hat and his smooth black hair shone with the rainbow colors of a raven's wing in the golden sunshine. What broad shoulders he had, and what long legs! His figure resembled Garth's, but this man was thinner than Garth, tougher looking. His clothes were rather shabby, and they did not fit him well, they looked as if they had been bought off the peg.

The man turned as I came out of the shelter of the trees and looked down at me — it was Garth.

'Garth!' I cried. 'Oh, Garth, it isn't really you? Oh, Garth!'

He sprang down off the rocks and I ran forward and flung myself into his arms. I felt them tighten around me, tighten around me so that it hurt . . .

'Char!' he said in a queer, husky voice. 'What a lovely welcome!'

'I know everything, Garth,' I told him, clinging

to him, and sobbing a little from sheer happiness. 'I know everything . . . all about the terrible mistake . . . I loved you all the time . . . only you . . . always.'

'And I you,' he said, kissing my hair.

'I know . . . I know!'

'Char, my dearest girl, my own darling, it isn't too late now, is it! It isn't too late to go back to the beginning and start again. We can put everything right, Char, say it isn't too late.'

'It may be too late for me to give you a son,' I told him, half laughing and half crying.

'Good God, what does that matter!' said Garth.

* * *

But it wasn't too late for that, either.

*Other titles published by Ulverscroft:*

**LISTENING VALLEY**

**D. E. Stevenson**

In Scotland on the eve of World War Two, Tonia and her sister Lou grow up as thick as thieves in a world apart from their detached parents and other children. But when Lou runs off to get married at eighteen, Toni is left alone, unsure of who she is and wants to be. She accepts an offer of marriage from a kind but older man, and is soon in London amid bombings and rationing, her life filled with purpose as never before. However, when tragedy strikes, Tonia must return to Scotland and attempt to refashion her life once more . . .

## WINTER AND ROUGH WEATHER

**D. E. Stevenson**

Newlyweds Rhoda and James arrive at their new home, Boscath Farm House near the Scottish village of Mureth. James must adjust to the responsibility of running a sheep farm — and Rhoda, an accomplished artist used to the bright lights and bustle of London, to life in an isolated rural area where the winters are harsh and unforgiving. Encouraged by James, Rhoda continues to paint, in addition to taking a young boy under her wing and nurturing his artistic talent. But one of her portraits will stir up the embers of a long-buried secret, with unexpected consequences for the community . . .